The Montgomery Ink Box Set

CARRIE ANN RYAN

Author Highlights

Praise for Carrie Ann Ryan....

"Carrie Ann Ryan knows how to pull your heartstrings and make your pulse pound! Her wonderful Redwood Pack series will draw you in and keep you reading long into the night. I can't wait to see what comes next with the new generation, the Talons. Keep them coming, Carrie Ann!" – Lara Adrian, New York Times bestselling author of CRAVE THE NIGHT

"Carrie Ann Ryan never fails to draw readers in with passion, raw sensuality, and characters that pop off the page. Any book by Carrie Ann is an absolute treat." – New York Times Bestselling Author J. Kenner

"With snarky humor, sizzling love scenes, and brilliant, imaginative worldbuilding, The Dante's Circle series reads as if Carrie Ann Ryan peeked at my personal wish list!" – NYT Bestselling Author, Larissa Ione

"Carrie Ann Ryan writes sexy shifters in a world full of passionate happily-ever-afters." – *New York Times* Bestselling Author Vivian Arend

"Carrie Ann's books are sexy with characters you can't help but love from page one. They are heat and heart blended to perfection." *New York Times* Bestselling Author Jayne Rylon

Carrie Ann Ryan's books are wickedly funny and deliciously hot, with plenty of twists to keep you guessing. They'll keep you up all night!" USA Today Bestselling Author Cari Quinn

"Once again, Carrie Ann Ryan knocks the Dante's Circle series out of the park. The queen of hot, sexy, enthralling paranormal romance, Carrie Ann is an author not to miss!" *New York Times* bestselling Author Marie Harte

Praise for the Redwood Pack Series...

"You will not be disappointed in the Redwood Pack." *Books-n-Kisses*

"I was so completely immersed in this story that I felt what the characters felt. BLOWN AWAY." *Delphina's Book Reviews*.

"I love all the wolves in the Redwood Pack and eagerly anticipate all the brothers' stories." *The Book Vixen*

"Shifter romances are a dime a dozen, but good ones aren't as plentiful as one would think. This is one of the goods one." *Book Binge*

"With the hints of things to come for the Redwoods, I can't wait to read the next book!" *Scorching Book Reviews*

"Ryan outdid herself on this book." *The Romance Reviews*

Praise for the Dante's Circle Series...

"This author better write the next books quickly or I will Occupy Her Lawn until she releases more! Pure romance enjoyment here. Now go put this on your TBR pile—shoo!" *The Book Vixen*

"I, for one, will definitely be following the series to see what happens to the seven." *Cocktails & Books*

"The world of Dante's Circle series is enthralling and with each book gets deeper and deeper as does Carrie Ann's writing." Literal Addiction

Praise for the Montgomery Ink Series...

"Shea and Shep are so cute together and really offset each other in a brilliant way. " *Literal Addiction*

"This was a very quick and spicy read. I really enjoyed reading about Sassy, Rafe & Ian. I really hope there will be more of these three in the future." *Books n Kisses*

Praise for the Holiday, Montana Series...

"Charmed Spirits was a solid first book in this new series and I'm looking forward to seeing where it goes." *RR@H Novel Thoughts & Book Thoughts*

"If you're looking for a light book full of magic, love and hot little scenes on various objects, then this book is for you! You'll soon find that tables are no longer for eating meals of the food variety ... Bon appétit!" *Under the Covers*

"The book was well written and had the perfect setting the steamy bits where really really hot and the story one of sweet romance. Well done Carrie" *Bitten by Love Review*

CONTENTS

Ink Inspired

The Beginning to The Montgomery Ink Series

Ink Inspired

Shepard Montgomery loves the feel of a needle in his hands, the ink that he lays on another, and the thrill he gets when his art is finished, appreciated, and loved. At least that's the way it used to be. Now he's struggling to figure out why he's a tattoo artist at all as he wades through the college frat boys and tourists who just want a thrill, not a permanent reminder of their trip. Once he sees the Ice Princess walk through Midnight Ink's doors though, he knows he might just have found the inspiration he needs.

Shea Little has spent her life listening to her family's desires. She went to the best schools, participated in the most proper of social events, and almost married the man her family wanted for her. When she ran from that and found a job she actually likes, she thought she'd rebelled enough. Now though, she wants one more thing—only Shepard stands in the way. She'll not only have to let him learn more about her in order to get inked, but find out what it means to be truly free.

CHAPTER ONE

"**C**an you make her boobs bigger?"

Shepard Montgomery raised a brow but didn't say anything. Honestly, there really wasn't anything he *could* say at the moment without laughing.

Or knocking the dude out cold.

"No, really. I want her boobs, like, enormous. Way bigger than Justin's."

Shep blinked.

"Justin's?" he drawled, his voice gruff. Seriously, this kid was going to kill him.

The client snorted. "Oh, you know what I mean. Justin. My friend? The chick he has inked on his back has big boobs. I want mine bigger."

Shep closed his eyes, trying to think of a delicate way to put the fact that, no, he did not want to ink this virgin with a big-breasted woman just because the dude wanted to show up his bro. Oh, and the other dude was totally a bro in every sense of the word. These two noobs had to be the most ignorant college pricks to ever walk in this shop demanding Shep ink them with whatever shit they wanted. Sure, he hadn't inked Justin, but still...they didn't even care that they would have to live the rest of their lives with shit ink—not that Shep gave shit ink—because they were fucking idiots.

He should just tell this prick to fuck himself, but this was his job. He probably shouldn't be so honest.

No, wait, he didn't actually care what this dude thought of him.

It wasn't as if he was *trying* to be the best customer service rep in the biz.

Oh no, he didn't give a fuck.

"No, kid, I'm not inking you with a big-breasted woman just because you want to show up your bro."

The kid's eyes widened then narrowed in that annoying rich-kid-on-daddy's-dime sort of way.

"Hey, I pay for it. You do it, bro. I don't see the fucking problem. I just want a chick with big tits on my back. Bigger tits than Justin's bitch."

Shep slowly put down the pen he'd been about to take notes with and scooted his stool back. His six-five frame didn't make it comfortable, but he didn't give a shit at the moment.

"Okay, *bro*, this is how it's gonna go. You ain't getting a tat here. Not now. Maybe not ever. You think money gives you the right to come into the best shop in New Orleans and boss us around like you fucking own the place?"

"It's your *job*," the little prick spat.

"No. It's my job to ink art on canvas. That canvas just happens to be skin. Today, though? No fucking way. Not on you. You're welcome to come back when you got a fucking clue what you want to ink on yourself, but fuck right now, dude. You want some strange woman's face, some generic shit on your back? It's not even a sexy old-school pinup. No. That's not how it's done. You want bigger tits on the woman because you want to one-up your bro? Dude, if you ain't got the bigger dick, that ink ain't gonna help."

The kid blinked, the slow crawl of crimson staining his cheeks either from anger or embarrassment—probably a mix of both—making him look even younger than nineteen.

"You should get a tat that means something to you, or at least isn't a fucking joke. You don't come in here waving your dick and ordering me around."

"Hey!"

"Oh, and another thing. You ever, *ever*, fucking call a woman—*any* woman—a bitch again, I'll knock that little smirk right off your fucking face. Get out of my chair. You're done."

"Fuck you! I'll go get my tat from a place that actually treats their customers like they're supposed to. Not from some washed-out, has-been artist who doesn't know shit."

The kid stomped out, every eye on the place following him.

Shep closed his eyes and prayed for peace.

Fuck.

He was thirty-eight years old, and this was what his life had come to.

Douchebag college boys who wanted big boobs.

Great.

"Smooth, dude. Why don't you just kick the puppy next time? Make it easier," Sassy, Midnight Ink's receptionist and all-around crazy person, sing-songed as she walked past him.

"Shut up, Sass, please. I'm not in the mood."

"You never are anymore, baby. That's the problem. Though, honestly, I have no idea why you said yes to that little prick for a consultation in the first place. You could tell from just looking at him he'd be a B-back."

A B-back was a dude who said they'd be right back after they went to the ATM or gave some other lame excuse, saying they'd 'be back' only they'd chicken out and never come back.

Yeah, the kid looked like he'd be one, though if he'd wanted to impress his friends enough, maybe not.

"Sass, really? I'm not in the mood," he grumbled as he cleaned his station. He hadn't had a client yet that morning, but he wanted no trace of that *bro* near his place.

"You should have let Caliph take it," Sass said, an annoyingly bright grin on her face.

Midnight Ink, their shop right on Canal Street, had several artists who worked in shifts. They didn't have to come in every day, only if they wanted to get paid. Since everyone working there needed money to pay for shit, they all came in. Most worked on walk-ins around their scheduled clients, but a few took on only clients they'd hand-picked off the waiting lists. Those guys also only did ink with certain elements because they were the *shit* at it.

Shep did a bit of everything, so, even though his shading was fucking awesome, he didn't specialize too much. His best friend, Caliph, was the same way.

Shep would have given his left nut to see his brick house of a best friend take on that college kid.

"What's this I hear about me taking on a bro?" Caliph asked, stomping through the room to his station.

Shep was big.

Caliph was bigger.

And scarier.

"Had a perfect kid for you," Shep yelled across the shop, causing a few of the customers to turn toward him. "Wanted big tits like his bro."

Caliph snorted, then flipped him off. "Fuck off, Shep."

Ah, a decade of friendship never lost its shine.

Shep shook his head then gave Sassy and Caliph a chin nod to say he was going out for a coffee. Sassy might make some of the best brew right in their shop, but he didn't want to sit there too long. He needed space.

Again.

He needed to think, and the muggy air of New Orleans always did it for him. Sure, it wasn't the crisp, clean air of the Rocky Mountains where he'd grown up, but he liked it. His family—who all still lived up near Denver—thought he was fucking nuts for moving down to New Orleans to set up shop, or at least find a shop he could fit into, but he loved it.

Well, at least he used to.

Fuck, he needed to get his head out of his ass and figure out what was wrong with his mood. He was thirty-eight, not some young kid, but sure as hell not on his way out. Maybe he needed a change.

He just had no idea what kind of change.

Shep turned the corner to make his way to the coffee shop then cursed as a little bit of a thing ran straight into him.

He sucked in a breath as she looked up at him—way up at him.

Damn, her eyes were something else. A pale, pale blue that looked almost like crystals in water on a sunny day.

Those had to be fucking contacts because no way were those eyes real.

"I'm so sorry, sir. I wasn't watching where I was going. Excuse me." The little blonde thing walked around him after she mumbled her apologies heading the other direction.

Shep blinked.

Well, hell. That was weird. He hadn't even had a chance to say anything—something like "fucking sexy eyes" or anything along those lines that could have made her want join him for coffee.

Shep shook his head. Fuck, he needed that coffee. In the long scheme of things, what he didn't need was a wide-eyed woman who probably thought he looked like some ex-con with his full sleeves and the scar on his brow, not to mention the other piercings and tats hidden from view.

No, he didn't need that shit.

What he did need? Well, that was the problem.

He didn't know.

He ordered a coffee from the girl at the counter, who fluttered her lashes at him. Shep held back a groan—and not the good kind. This kid had to be in her early twenties, if that. There was no way Shep would cross that boundary, even if she was hot as hell, which she was.

He walked to one of the tables outside the café and sat down with his cup, not ready to go back to work yet. Fuck, if he was thinking some twenty-something was hot, maybe he just needed to get laid. That might be the answer to all his problems, though even a long night of against-the-wall sex might not be enough to get him out of his funk. The fact that he'd blown up at a silly kid just now told him something was far from good.

He needed to figure out what the hell was going on with him, find his path, find his inspiration.

And fast.

Shep took a deep breath of humid New Orleans air then a sip of his coffee. Damn, he loved the coffee down here. Nothing bitter or over-brewed about it. Sure, when he went up north to Denver to visit his folks he didn't mind the little cafés, but to Shep, nothing was better than New Orleans coffee.

Since they were in the Deep South, it didn't really feel as though they'd just hit the start of January. The holidays seemed like something in the distant past, and the New Year's parties—something New Orleans did fucking right every time—were a fading memory.

What wasn't a memory was his resolution.

Nope. The fact that he'd told himself *this* year would be different wasn't lost on him. He'd resolved to find his inspiration and actually do art that meant something to both him and the client rather than just walk-in after walk-in.

Shep ran a hand over his five-day-old beard and sighed.

When the fuck had he turned into some emo teen?

His phone buzzed in his pocket, and he pulled it out of his jeans. When he saw his cousin Austin's name on the screen, he smiled. If anyone could get him out of his funk, it was Austin.

"Hey, what's up?"

"Nothing," Austin said, his voice even deeper than Shep's. "Just got done with a whole back piece that took six sittings. Now I'm trying to get my head out of phoenix feathers and into dragon scales."

"Did you take a pic?"

"Sure as fuck did." Austin laughed. "I'll text it to you in a bit. Fine piece of work if I do say so myself. I was bored and didn't feel like walking anywhere to grab a bite. Figured I'd call and see how you're doing. We didn't get to talk much when you were up for Christmas."

Almost the entire Montgomery clan lived up in the Denver area. Shep was one of the few who had ventured out. Though he and Austin were the closest and the same age, when Shep had gone up for the holidays, he didn't have that much time for his favorite cousin. Oh no. Between Austin's seven siblings, Shep's three siblings, the other Montgomery cousins, plus all the aunts, uncles, and parents, the holidays were a bitch, giving him no time to breathe.

"Yeah, it sucked that we couldn't get together much when I was up there. You should come down here for a visit. Come see the color and culture. Put it in your ink."

Austin and his sister Maya owned Montgomery Ink, a shop in Denver and were hella good at what they did. The three of them frequently went around the country to see what inspiration they could find and what they could translate into their work.

Maybe he needed to do that again and find that *thing* he was looking for.

Whatever the hell that *thing* was.

"Maybe," Austin hedged, causing Shep to frown. "We'll see."

"What's up, man?"

"Nothing. Just getting old."

Shep snorted. "Tell me about it. We're the same age, remember? What's going on?"

Austin sighed. "Fuck it. I'll come down there. Leave Maya alone with the shop for a bit. God knows she likes to be by herself with the place most days."

Shep smiled at Austin's description of Maya. Fuck knew Austin was right.

"I'm here when you come down. You know I have the guest room you can bunk in. We're not kids anymore where you have to find a futon or couch."

"Thank God for that. Thanks, man."

Shep smiled. "You're welcome. I think we're just hitting the age where we're too old to figure out what the hell we want but know we need to find it someway."

"Maybe, Shep. Maybe."

They said their goodbyes, and Shep ended the call, feeling a bit better that his cousin was coming down soon. They'd finalize plans later since Austin would have to talk to Maya before traveling. There was no way they'd cross that woman and her sharp tongue.

Shep finished his coffee and headed back to Midnight Ink. He needed to get some work done. He might not have an appointment that day—something rare for him, thankfully— but there were bound to be walk-ins.

As soon as he stepped inside, he spotted her.

That sexy fairy who'd walked into him on the street.

Her blonde hair was even lighter than he'd thought considering they'd been out in the sunlight before. No, that hadn't been the sun making her look gorgeous.

That was all her.

She wore a light gray pencil skirt with a light pink top and gray jacket. Her heels were demure, but fuck, they made her legs look sexy

She looked like someone's assistant or an accountant.

Totally out of place in a tattoo shop, at least in most shops.

Midnight Ink didn't discriminate. They knew some people had to hide their ink because of work so they made sure it looked hella good underneath their clothes.

This woman though?

Totally out of place.

And lost.

Shep smiled.

He could totally help her with that.

Sassy stood by the woman, her brow raised. "Honey, you sure you want this one? I know you were looking at something else a minute ago."

The woman turned and bit her lip, forcing Shep to hold back a groan.

Holy fuck. He was acting like some teenager with a hard-on, rather than a not-so-young man with a hard-on.

Sassy spotted him and waved him over. "Here's Shep, honey. He'll be the one to ink you since he has time and you said it didn't matter who did it. Shep, this is Shea. She's all yours." Sassy raised that brow again and Shep smiled.

Oh, yes. He wanted to get his hands on this woman in every way possible.

Ink would be just the first step.

The woman turned toward him, and Shep bit back a curse.

Fuck.

That wasn't just indecision in her eyes. That was pure fear mixed with something else. Something like determination.

The kind of determination that led to inked regrets.

Sassy walked away, leaving Shep and Shea alone in the corner, a stack of albums between them.

"So, uh, Shep," she started, her voice just as smooth and sexy as it had been outside. "Sorry again for walking into you earlier."

"Like I said, it's no problem."

"So, uh, I guess you'll be giving me my tattoo? I think I want this little daisy. Or maybe this butterfly. Can you do that?"

Shep looked down her body, her out-of-place clothes, the fear sliding right off her, and her weight shifting from foot to foot. He raised his gaze and met her eyes.

"No."

CHAPTER TWO

"N o?" Shea Little squeaked.

"No," the very sexy tattoo artist, Shep, repeated. He folded his arms—his *very* sexy, tattooed, muscled arms—over his chest, and she blinked. A lock of dark hair fell over his eyes, making him look even more dangerous—and even a little dashing.

Oh great, now she made him sound like a romantic rake. Not the man telling her no.

"But...why? Just no?" She couldn't understand what he was saying. She'd come in to Midnight Ink after talking herself in and out of doing this for two straight weeks, and the first artist she'd spoken to said no?

That made absolutely no sense to her.

Shep raised a brow. "Tell me why you want a tattoo." His forearms flexed, and she pulled herself away from the tantalizing sight.

"Why?" she croaked, annoyed with herself for sounding like an idiot.

She normally didn't have an issue speaking intelligently, but apparently standing in front of a way-too-attractive man, along with her frayed nerves for even *thinking* about getting a tattoo, was too much for her.

"Yes, why. Why do you want a tattoo? You stick out like a sore thumb, babe. Not that that's an issue usually, but right here, right now? You should tell me why you want it. Is this just a sudden urge to show off your bad-girl side? Or do you have more ink under those prim and proper clothes of yours? I'm guessing not, considering you look like you're freaked the fuck out by just being here."

"I'm not freaked out," she lied.

Oh, she was definitely freaked out.

This...this *man*, though, didn't have to be so rude and call her out on it. She'd already spent all morning pacing her apartment trying to figure out how to gain the courage to even come into the shop. Now this man wanted to know why she wanted a tattoo when even she didn't even know the answer.

Plus, she was pretty sure he'd just insulted her looks—or at least what she was wearing.

Sure, she knew her normal attire didn't fit in with what the clientele of this establishment usually wore, but he didn't have to point it out.

God, he was infuriating, and she hadn't even spoken with him using complete sentences. Not logical ones anyway.

Shea forced her gaze from his strong build and the tattoos that covered his arms and peeked out over his collar, and looked around at the shop. She was pretty sure every set of eyes was focused on them. Some looked intrigued, some bored, others openly gaped at the spectacle of she and Shep arguing.

Well, *him* arguing.

She hadn't exactly stood up for herself yet, something she knew she needed to do one way or another. It was about time she did so. After all, the whole idea of getting a tattoo was to prove to herself she could be assertive.

There.

That was it.

That was what she'd tell this Shep with the dreamy blue eyes, not that he deserved an explanation since he was acting like a butt.

"Shea?" Shep asked, and she froze at the sound of her name coming from his lips.

Oh, yes, she liked that a lot.

Way too much, in fact, considering she didn't know him, and from what she'd seen, she wasn't sure she even *wanted* to know him. He was an egotistical asshole for sure and not someone she *needed* to get to know.

She'd just have to ask that receptionist with the pretty pink streak in her hair. Sassy. Yes, that was her name. Sassy seemed as though she'd be able to help her.

"What?" she snapped, the anger lying under the surface finally threatening to break free.

Something flashed in his eyes, and he grinned.

Darn it, the man looked hot when he did that.

And he had a dimple.

Great.

"Why do you want a tattoo, Shea?" he asked softly.

His tone got under her skin this time. Or at least it did in a whole new way. He seemed as though he genuinely wanted to know, rather than asking just to be a prick about it.

At least that's what she hoped she got from his voice.

Knowing her luck, she was totally wrong and he was actually a jerk.

"Why do you need to know?" she asked, almost unable to get the words out. She was losing her nerve, and she knew it. She shouldn't have come. She pulled her purse tighter to her body and lifted her chin. She'd just have to leave the shop.

There wouldn't be a second chance for her. She'd been an idiot for even considering coming here and doing something so radical for her.

Her mother and ex were right. She was a stiff, cold mannequin.

Totally not appropriate for a man like Shep.

She swallowed.

Jesus. Why was she even thinking about this man? This was about a *tattoo*, and she wasn't getting one. Shep had nothing to do with any of it.

Nothing.

"Sorry to have bothered you and taken your time." She pulled her purse closer to her and walked quickly toward the door, her high heels clicking on the smooth wood floor. It took all she had to hold back the tears and keep her body from shaking.

She knew her face had to be red, but she ignored it.

This had been a stupid, stupid idea.

A large, warm hand gripped her elbow as she reached the sidewalk, and she tried to pull away.

"Wait, Shea, don't go."

"Unhand me," she spat through clenched teeth. "Don't touch me."

Please don't touch me.

He didn't let go but pulled her toward him so they were facing each other. Sweat dripped down her silk-covered back, and she tilted her head so she could look at his bearded face as the cloying New Orleans heat surrounded them.

Shea could hear the hustle and bustle of tourists and locals, either working or sightseeing. She could hear children laughing, couples talking, a lone man humming, another yelling on his phone. Yet all of that became background noise and paled in comparison to those pretty blue eyes rimmed in dark lashes and against striking cheekbones beneath a few days' worth of beard.

Shep finally pulled back but was close enough to her that she couldn't move away and run like she wanted to. Damn it. She hated not being in control, not having all the answers and everything in its place. Yes, this also didn't fit with her current circumstances, and it annoyed her to no end.

She shouldn't have come.

"I didn't mean to hurt you or grab you like that," Shep said, concern in his tone. "I just wanted to stop you from running out of the place because I was acting like an asshole."

If that was an apology, she still wasn't sure what she should think.

"I already said I was sorry for taking up your time. Thank you for coming out here and trying to make yourself feel better, but I think I should go. I'm clearly in the wrong place." God, even when she was trying to be bitchy, she needed to make people feel better. Hell, those southern roots never died.

"You won't find a better place for ink, Shea."

She raised her chin. "That may be, but I'm not in need of *ink* anymore. I made a mistake. Goodbye, Shep."

She turned, but he caught her elbow again. "Jesus, Shea, you put up that ice princess mask quickly, but hell, I saw the fear in your eyes when I walked up to you. Plus I saw it when we bumped into each other on the street before I even knew you were coming to Midnight for a tattoo. Tell me what's going on in that mind of yours."

He reached up and tucked a lock of hair behind her ear, and she froze. The gesture was so intimate, so close, that she wasn't sure what to do. She didn't even know this man, and he was touching her, making her want to know about his own ink.

There had to be something wrong with her.

"I...I...why are you doing that?"

"Doing what?" he asked, his voice low.

Jesus, his voice was sexy. It had a low, throaty sound that rumbled against her skin, forcing her to hold back a shiver. She thought only sexy guys on TV or in the movies had voices like that.

"Why are you touching me? I told you not to touch me." Her voice had risen at the end of that, her fear of something...new coming out.

"I'm an artist, Shea, not a mind reader."

She blinked. "What?"

"I'm an artist. I fucking love what I do." He stopped and shook his head, this time a little doubt entering his eyes that confused her. "Well, I've always loved what I do. I've been in a little rough patch lately, like I need to find my muse or whatever."

Shea snorted. "Seriously? Does that line work on anyone? No. Don't even bother answering. I've already told you I was sorry for taking your time, and now you're taking mine. Just let me leave, and I will be on my way. Soon I won't even be a memory for you, and you can use that muse line on some unsuspecting coed."

Shep threw his head back and laughed. It had to be wrong that she loved the way his throat worked as he did so.

Yeah, she totally had issues.

"Honey, I'm way too fucking old to be looking at some coed, and that wasn't a line, the thing about the muse. I've been in a funk, and that has nothing to do with getting laid or even working on your ink. And I do, by the way, want to work your ink. When I saw you on the street a little while ago I was intrigued. That doesn't happen often. Not anymore. So, yeah, I want to see what tattoo you want and why. I want to get to know you."

That threw her. Get to know her? Just what exactly was he saying? And now he wanted to ink her? This Shep was making her head spin in more ways than one.

"You're going to have to take this one step at a time for me, Shep," she finally said after she took a deep breath to gather her thoughts. "One minute you're acting like a brute, telling me I can't have a tattoo and I stick out like a sore thumb. You say you aren't hitting on me, but you're intrigued and want to work on my *ink,* as you put it."

Shep smiled, a flash of white against his beard. "Sounds about right."

"You make no sense. I'm just going to go." She was done. She had been an idiot to even think about coming down to Midnight. Though this hadn't been an impulsive decision— not by far—she still felt out of her depths. That feeling wasn't something she enjoyed, and giving up at this point seemed like the best option.

"Don't go, Shea."

She hated how much she loved the sound of her name on his lips.

"Why should I stay?"

"Because you came here for a reason. I don't know what it is yet, considering I'm still waiting for that answer to my first question. You should also stay because, despite the clothes you're wearing, the ice you've shielded yourself with, and the fear in your eyes, you still had the balls to walk through those doors. Now, don't get me wrong, we're not that scary in there. Okay, maybe Caliph is, but other than that, we're good. We wouldn't hurt you, and we're not the scary deviants you might think we are from watching movies or some shit."

Shea had no idea who Caliph was, but she knew the people in that building weren't too scary. She didn't judge people on their appearances like so many others did, like so many judged her.

"I need to go," she whispered, scared now for a whole other reason.

"Tell me why you want a tattoo."

She huffed out a breath and looked into his eyes. "I want one because...because it's not me. Or at least not the me everyone else thinks I am. I'm tired, Shep. So, so tired of being...this." She pointed down at herself and sighed.

He cupped her face, and she gasped, unprepared for his heated touch. "That's all I wanted to hear, Shea. Now, what do you want?"

You.

She blinked. Well, that stray thought was just freaking crazy. She didn't even know him.

"I don't know," she answered honestly. "I want something that's me. I just don't know what or who that is."

Shep pulled away slightly, and she felt the loss of his touch down to her bones. "Okay then. I'll help you. Whatever you want, it should be something that's just for you, a design that makes doing something different worth it." He grinned. "Plus, in order to find out what will work for you, I get the opportunity to know you better. A definite plus for me."

He wanted to get to know her? Her? The ice princess in pale clothes who liked to blend into the woodwork if she could?

"Do you always get so personal with your clients?" she asked, a strange line of jealousy threading its way through her. She didn't want to be just another woman he *got to know* before he inked her and left.

Well, hell, now she sounded crazy.

He brushed her cheek with the tip of his finger, and she held back a shudder. "I've never done it like this before," he said softly. "I'm marking someone's skin forever. It's always personal. It doesn't matter if I don't know everything about them or what makes them tick. I do know what that tattoo means to them—at least a semblance of it. I can't just sit back and watch you make a decision you might regret."

"You don't know me well enough to know I'll regret it."

No one did.

"I want to know you enough."

She'd come to Midnight Ink for a reason, and now Shep was going to help her. No matter that she thought she was crazy and everyone who knew her would think the same, there was only one answer.

"Yes. Okay. Let's do that."

Shep grinned and leaned forward. Shea's chin raised on its own accord, but he didn't kiss her. She felt oddly bereft that he didn't even try, but she didn't say anything. He brushed her cheek once more and smiled softly.

He reached around to his back pocket and pulled out a card. "Here you go. Take this and I'll get yours."

She nodded and pulled a card out of her purse. He looked down and smiled. "Accountant. Totally knew it."

Great. She even *looked* boring.

"Hey now. I like prim and proper. I'll call you in a bit, and we can talk about what we're going to do and how I'm going to help you find the perfect ink."

"Okay," she whispered, not feeling at all like the cold woman she usually was. Shep seemed to heat her up from the inside out, and she wasn't sure how she felt about that.

With one last look, he walked back into Midnight, leaving her on the street, dazed. She shook her head, made her way back to her car, then back to her house, his card still clutched in her palm. She never took days off, but she'd taken this one off to get it done and now the day was ruined, wasted.

She had no idea what she was doing.

Shea walked into her home and took a look around. The prim house, the prim decorations, the prim...everything. None of it showcased who she was.

No, it told her who her mother was and what her mother wanted for her when Shea bought the house. Shea had long ago given up the fight when it came to what her mother wanted.

Well, other than leaving Richard, her ex-fiancé. Her mother had screamed and threatened to disown her for making what she considered the mistake of a lifetime.

Shea never could live up to her mother's dreams.

She took off her shoes and walked to the couch, sinking into its cushions. Everything around her was so cold, uninviting, but the cushions on the couch were soft enough that she could at least get somewhat comfortable.

The card in her hand called to her, and she looked down at it. What the heck was she doing? She had gone into Midnight Ink because her New Year's resolution was to do something for herself, something so out of character that she just might be able to find the person she wanted to be.

She'd always loved ink. She loved the way people looked with it. She thought the swirls, dark colors, and shading were freaking sexy. She'd always been too chicken to do anything about it before. Now, though, she wanted it.

She just didn't have a clue about what design she wanted. Shep was going to help with that though.

Shep.

His dark hair and light eyes called to her, even if she had no idea why. He was going to help her find herself. Okay, that sounded lame, even though it was true.

Everything could go up in flames if she made the wrong choice, but it didn't matter.

It was all or nothing.

Her cell rang, and she frowned. God, she hoped it wasn't Richard or her mother. They never stopped bugging her with their own opinions on how she should run her life.

She didn't recognize the number on the screen, so she answered as coolly as possible.

"Yes?"

"Shea? It's Shep."

Her pulse beat in her ears, and she swallowed hard.

"Yes, this is Shea."

"I'm glad you didn't give me a fake card. That's why I asked for that rather than you putting your number in my phone. Harder to fake that on the fly."

"Oh. I guess."

Great. She needed to learn to use complete sentences, or he was going to think she was a complete idiot.

"What do you say I take you out for a night on the town tomorrow night after my shift?"

"Why? For what?"

He gave a deep chuckle, and it shot straight between her legs. Dear Lord, even the man's laugh was sexy.

"I told you I want to get to know you to help you. And fuck, just to get to know *you*. I'm thinking we can pick up a quick dinner then spend the rest of the night exploring to see what you like. What do you say?"

He wanted to do something without a firm schedule she could check over and over again? She wasn't a hundred percent sure of that; this wasn't normal for her. She didn't *want* it to be normal.

"Okay. That sounds fine."

"Good. I'll meet you in front of the shop at seven tomorrow. That way you'll feel more comfortable than me coming to your house and freaking you out."

She relaxed and smiled, even though he couldn't see it. She didn't know how he knew she was worried about him knowing where she lived, but she liked it.

"Okay."

"Okay then. See you tomorrow, Shea."

"Tomorrow, Shep."

He hung up, and she stared at the phone, not sure what had just happened. She'd spent too much of her life on the sidelines, and this man and his ideas could help her.

Those striking blue eyes, the scratchy voice, and his sexy tattoos just might be worth upsetting her whole world order.

CHAPTER THREE

S hep changed needles, finished with the overall outline and ready for shading. He rolled his shoulders and took a look at his work.

Not bad.

Okay, it was better than that. Way fucking better, but he knew it was a process, and he was never happy with his work until the finished project. Each layer of outlining, shading, and color added to the overall look. He knew what he wanted and how that blended with what the client wanted. Eventually, once he added the final layers, the tat would look fucking amazing. Now, though, it was only a half-finished piece.

"How's it looking?" the man on the bench asked, careful not to turn around.

Shep was in the middle of putting a kick-ass phoenix on the man's back with its wings wrapping around the side. He'd finished the outline in their last session and was going over certain spots today to make sure they were perfect. Then he'd be doing some of the initial shading before he added color. He usually waited to do the shading, but he wanted to make sure it didn't look too dark since the vibrant orange and reds really needed to pop in the finished piece.

"It's gonna fucking rock," Shep answered and began the shading. The buzzing sound of the needle shot straight through him as it always did. He loved shading the best because the needle moved at a slower pace, and for most people, it felt hella good.

From the way his client moaned, Shep wasn't wrong.

He worked for another two hours, his mind on his hands and his ink. While some people might daydream while working, his job was a little different. One wrong movement and he'd fuck up someone's skin.

Not cool.

Even as he tried to keep focus, though, his thoughts went to the woman with pale, pale blue eyes...like crystals in water on a sunny day and a pixie face.

Shea.

Jesus, he liked that smooth-as-silk yet hard-as-ice woman, and he didn't even know her past a few words and touches.

There had to be something wrong with him. He'd never been drawn to a woman like her at all.

Shep moved back and shook his head while cleaning off the leftover ink, plasma, and blood from where he was working. He seriously needed to get his mind off Shea and their date tonight. She might not call it a date, but he would. He wanted her, and he wasn't going to lie to himself about it. He was way too damned old for that.

He rolled his shoulders and got back to work. This phoenix was going to fucking rock. He'd known it when he'd first done the sketches over a month ago, but it wasn't until now that he really thought it could be something big.

There was another spark running along his skin, getting him excited about what he was doing for the first time in way too long.

It had to be Shea. She was the only thing different in his life, even though she really wasn't a huge part of it.

At least not yet.

He was going to change that.

He grinned and started on some of the color for the wings, getting into each stroke of the needle.

After another hour and a half, he pulled back, sweat marking his brow and his back straining. Too many hours bent over a table would do that to a man.

He snorted, thinking about what Caliph or Austin would say to him if he'd said that aloud.

Yeah, not sharing that thought.

He cleaned up the guy's back then put ointment on the area. "Okay, you're all done for this session. I think one more should do it."

The guy got up and smiled. "You're a god with the needle, Shep. It didn't hurt a bit."

Shep grinned. "Even if it did, you'd like it."

He threw his head back and laughed. "True. So when can we do our last session?"

Shep went through the aftercare instructions. This guy was a regular, but it never hurt to go over them again. The last thing Shep wanted was a shitty healing and cleanup job to ruin his art. They scheduled the session for three weeks from then when they both had time, and Shep went back to clean up his space.

He'd really gotten into the piece, and it had taken a full hour longer than he'd intended. It was already quarter 'til seven. He wouldn't have time to head home and grab a quick shower.

Shit.

He hadn't wanted to look like a sweaty loser for his date, but she'd have to take what she got. After all, he was just Shep. He'd have to be good enough.

He went to the employee restroom and stripped off his shirt, then pulled another on. He would still wear his worn-in jeans and boots, but at least he had a black button-down to wear. It was just getting to that time of year when it was muggy at night too, so he didn't bother with his leather jacket. He ran his hand through his hair and called it a day.

He didn't look like some *GQ* model with the tats, nipple piercings—and more—but he did all right for himself. From the way Shea's gaze raked his body the day before, he had a feeling what he had did it for her. What she had sure as fuck did it for him.

"Looking good," Sassy said as she walked to the back to get her purse. "Though you might have wanted to shower before your big date with the ice princess."

He scowled. "Don't call her that. And how the hell do you know I have a date tonight with her?"

"Sassy knows all."

Shep rolled his eyes. "You were lurking around the corner when I called her yesterday, weren't you?"

She just raised her brow. "I have no idea what you are talking about. Sassy doesn't lurk."

"Stop talking about yourself in third person. You're creeping me out."

She just shook her head and laughed. "Spray yourself down with some cologne but not that frat-boy crap with the shitty commercials."

"I don't even own the frat-boy crap, Sass."

"Then we won't have a problem. Good luck with your main squeeze tonight, sugar. You're gonna need it."

"What the fuck do you mean by that? You saying I'm not good enough for her?"

She held her palms out. "That's not what I'm saying at all. I'm just saying that woman had a shield around her so tight that even I couldn't see through, and you know I'm good as fuck when it comes to that. You'll have to break through that ice if you want to know who she is. And what the fuck is with you saying you're not good enough? You've never been one to lack self-esteem, Shep. What's going on?"

Shep shook his head. "Never mind. I'm just antsy."

Sassy smiled and twirled the long strip of pink hair between her fingers. "I see. So this one's special. Good to know."

Shep narrowed his eyes. "Back off, Sassy."

"Don't worry, sugar. I'm sure everything will work out." With that, she sauntered out of the room, hips swaying.

Jesus, that woman was a nut job sometimes.

Shea would be outside within the next five minutes, and he didn't want her to wait. Remembering the way she'd looked like a frightened rabbit the last time he'd seen her, he wasn't about to leave it up to fate that she'd actually stay.

His phone buzzed against his leg, and he cursed. It better not be Shea calling to cancel.

Without looking at the screen, he answered. "You better be outside and not ready to cancel on me, babe."

"Having to threaten your dates now? What the hell is going on in New Orleans that a Montgomery is losing their street cred?"

Shep cursed at Austin's words. "Jesus. I thought you were someone else."

"Clearly. What's wrong? Having trouble in the sack?"

"I'm not talking about sex with you, Austin, just because you aren't getting any. I don't have time to discuss it right now."

"Ouch. Cruel words for a man who thinks his date is about to dump him."

"Shut it. I've got to go since Shea is probably outside waiting for me and I'm here talking with you."

"Shea, is it? Pretty name."

"Austin," Shep growled.

"Hey, don't jump on me. Go on your date if she shows. Hope she does because I'm not in the mood to deal with your emo bullshit if she doesn't. I called to tell you I booked a flight to come down there in three days. That cool?"

Shep sighed. He knew Austin needed to come down and clear his head for whatever reason, and Shep wanted to help. Even though they got on each other's nerves, they were family.

"Yeah, man. It's cool."

"Good. And, Shep? For what it's worth, I hope she shows. Just the way you said her name made me think she's something."

He hung up, leaving Shep staring at his phone. Jesus. Did he have a sign around his neck saying that Shea was different? He hadn't even really told himself that, and yet everyone seemed to know.

He just hoped he didn't scare her off.

Shep made his way through the front door and froze.

Holy fuck.

Shea was even sexier than he remembered, and he remembered every detail about her from the day before.

She wore a white dress with one of those cuts that went right across the shoulders but still showed some skin and made her look hella tantalizing. She had on a light pink cardigan that covered most of her arms and pearls.

Fucking *pearls*.

Not too big, but Jesus, she was classy.

Her dress was tight at her waist and hips and flared out at her knees. Her legs looked fucking delicious in high-heeled pink pumps with skinny little heels.

She'd put her hair in a bun at the nape of her neck so he could see all the contours of her face. Though she wasn't all bones and angles, her cheekbones were sharp and made those hypnotic eyes pop.

Right now, though, those eyes were full of fear...and excitement.

He could work with the latter.

And he'd have to get rid of the former.

She stared up at him, a small, strained smile on her face, and he took a deep breath, forcing himself back so he wouldn't jump on her like a frat boy in public.

"Shea, you made it."

She blinked up at him, her gaze moving from his chest to his face.

Nice.

"I told you I'd be here. I don't back away from my engagements." She blushed. "Except for when I'm cornered and not wanted. Then I leave. I mean..."

He took two steps toward her and cupped her face. "Breathe, Shea. I know I freaked you out yesterday. Let's go have fun, shall we? Let loose a bit?"

She snorted. "I'm not one to let loose."

Oh, he'd figured that, though the fact she'd come into Midnight Ink in the first place told him she was beyond ready to do just that. She might wear the clothes of an ice princess, but he had a feeling she was hot as hell underneath them.

It was his goal to find out.

And not just for heat.

Oh no.

He wanted more.

"You'll have fun tonight. I promise." He moved to pull her closer, wrapping his arm around her shoulders. She stiffened for a moment then relaxed a bit against him.

Progress.

"I have no idea why I'm doing this, but the heck with it. I'm doing it." She looked up at him from beneath her lashes. "So, what exactly is it I'm doing?"

He grinned down at her and kissed her nose, unable to stop himself. She jerked back slightly, a blush rising in her cheeks, but she didn't call him out on it.

"We're going to Frenchman Street."

"The street? Not a specific place?"

"You've been down there before?"

She nodded. "A couple of times. It's very...colorful."

"Tactful, baby. It's not the main tourist destination and doesn't have the most famous places and foodie type things, but it has great fucking music in the bars and even right on the streets. It's just about getting to the time where people will be doing pub crawls and enjoying themselves. We'll blend in and find out if you like it." He looked down at her dress and pumps. "Well, we'll try to blend it. You'll look like a tourist, but I'll take care of you."

She stopped, her face blushing. "Oh crap. I'm sorry. I didn't know where we were going, so I just put this on. I can go back and change. Shep, darn it, I don't know what I'm doing."

He turned her in his arms and crushed his lips to hers. She sucked in a breath, her lips parting. His tongue bushed against hers, and he lost himself, inhaling her scent, tasting it, savoring it.

He pulled back, out of breath. "Calm down, baby. It's okay. Dress the way you want to dress. I won't judge. Just don't hide yourself. Got it?"

"You...you kissed me."

"Fuck yeah. It was perfect."

She touched her swollen lips with her fingertips, her gaze dazed. "Oh...my." She blinked. "Next time give me an idea of where we're going, and I'll dress better, okay? I hate standing out. I just put on something cute for the night. I wasn't thinking."

He nodded, loving the fact she'd said next time because, fuck yeah, there'd be a next time. "You pulled off cute and then some, Shea. I'll warn you what we're doing next time, though. You'll always stand out to me though, baby. Got that?"

She tilted her head. "I'm not sure that I do." She held up her hand. "Don't explain it. Everything is going a little too fast for me right now, so let it go. I'll dress differently next time, and we'll be okay."

He smiled, nodding. "You going to be okay in those fuck-me pumps?"

She looked down at her feet then looked up at him, her gaze wide. "Fuck-me pumps?" she blurted. "These aren't black, and I could have added another inch and been fine. Oh no, Shep. These totally aren't fuck-me pumps."

Shep had to swallow hard at the thought of her in taller heels.

In nothing but those heels.

Holy. Fuck.

"Okay then, babe. You told me. Let me know if your feet hurt though. I'll take care of you."

She smiled and his heart lurched. Fuck, he was in trouble.

"I'll be fine, Shep. I love heels. But thank you for thinking of me."

They made their way to Frenchman Street, not talking much on their way. Sure, he wanted to get to know her, but right then, the sweet silence felt good on them. It was as if they'd known each other for a hell of a lot longer than a few hours.

Yep. He was totally in trouble.

"What are you in the mood to eat?" he asked.

"I thought you had all the plans worked out," she teased, and he smiled. She was losing that ice shield, and he was loving it.

"You should know that, beyond ink and this night, my plans in life are more of a vague guideline."

Shea stopped suddenly, and he stopped with her.

"What is it?"

"I need plans, Shep. I like plans. I like schedules and calendars and color-coded things. They make me happy. When things are organized just so, the world is a better place. You should know that."

"You're a touch OCD, aren't you?"

"For me, when it comes to schedules it's more CDO." At his blank look, she smiled. "It's OCD, but the letters are in the right order. As they should be." Her lips twitched, and he threw his head back and laughed.

His calm, collected Shea was shitting with him.

Oh yes, tonight was gonna go fucking perfect—not matter what happened from here on out.

"Okay, so next time, I'll let you know where I want to take you, and then you can plan your outfit and what exactly we do for the night. How about that?"

She leaned into him, her eyes dancing, the joy there free and uninhibited. "That sounds perfect."

He smiled and took her lips again, unable to help himself. She sank against him, her body going lax. He slid his hand down the back of her dress to her ass and squeezed. Oh yeah, a perfect handful. His tongue tangled with hers and she opened wider, moaning.

"What's happening, Shep?" she asked once they pulled away from each other.

"I have no clue, Shea, but I can't wait to find out."

CHAPTER FOUR

"**S**hea, baby, arch your hips up. Let me see that pussy of yours."

Shea did as she was told, her moans breaking through her lips, her body writhing.

"Fuck, Shea, I can't wait to fill that pretty pussy of yours and feel you on my cock as you come around me."

Shea gasped at his words, wanting to come but unable to.

The phone rang, and she opened her eyes.

Well, crap.

She was tangled in her sheets, her nightie up around her waist and her panties at her ankles.

Shep was nowhere to be seen.

Well, he wouldn't be here, would he?

No. After an amazing night of listening to jazz music, eating sandwiches while standing in the street, and going from bar to bar, drinking, kissing, and laughing, he'd taken her home and kissed her goodnight on her doorstep.

They knew he wanted to come in.

They knew she would let him.

And they knew it wasn't the right time.

Her dreams, however, had other ideas.

Her body ached from lack of release, and it took all that she had not to pick up her phone and dial Shep so he could come help her.

Oh crap. That totally didn't sound like the Shea she knew. On the other hand, it was totally the Shea she wanted to be.

Her phone rang again, and she cursed, turning over on her stomach to reach for it on her nightstand, pulling up her panties at the same time.

It was six thirty, and she'd been out until almost two.

There was no way the person on the line would be the one she wanted it to be, so it was either her mother or Richard.

Not answering either one would just annoy them and they would eventually annoy her.

She looked at the display, cursed just like Shep would have, and answered, her voice icy.

"Mother."

"Sleeping after six am? I don't understand why you act this way. It's as if you've forgotten all of your training. I spent years on you and now look at you. Worthless. You could have married well at a young age and to Richard. He comes from a good family. Now look what you've done. You're nothing but an accountant who sleeps in like a whore."

Shea closed her eyes. Why had she answered her phone? She could have put it on silent and slept in just a bit more with the Shep of her dreams.

"Mother."

"Yes. I'm your mother, for all the good it has done. I gave you good breeding, a roof over your head, and a future so bright and filled with promise that I should have won awards for it. And yet what do you do? You leave all of that to work with numbers and become some tramp who lives alone and sleeps in with god knows who."

Her mother's fantasies of her life were much more enjoyable than the reality.

Just saying.

"Mother. Good morning to you too." Honestly, there really wasn't anything else to say when her mother started one of her tirades.

"It would have been a good morning if you'd been the daughter I wanted you to be. Not the daughter you are."

Ouch.

No, she hadn't said anything different than what she'd been saying for years, but still...

Ouch.

"Is there a reason you called this morning?" It was Sunday, after all. Since it was normally a day of rest, Mrs. Reginald Little the Third should at least be preparing to cut down other women at tea while not actually looking as though she was doing the cutting, *not* bothering her only daughter.

Her mother gave a long, drawn-out sigh. Seriously, the woman had that down to an art form.

"You're expected at brunch this morning. Richard will be there, and you can apologize. Hopefully, he will be gracious enough to take you back. I've worked all I can at this point to make up for your failures. Don't disappoint me by being yourself."

Shea ran a hand through her hair, the pang at her mother's familiar words like a sharp lance across her chest

"I can't go today, Mother." *Or any day.* "I have plans." Her plans with Shep weren't until later in the day, but her mother didn't need to know that.

"Plans? You?" Her mother laughed, and Shea winced. "Honey, you don't need to lie to me. I know you have no plans. Who would want to be with you? Now get dressed and wear something I've picked out for you. It won't do you any good to look like a whore in front of Richard. Look demure but make sure your breasts are high. He likes breasts. Once he gets a good look at what you have—which isn't that much, honestly—you can use those whore wiles of yours to get him to put that ring on your finger."

There wasn't enough freaking coffee in the world to deal with this.

Seriously?

She had to be both a whore and demure to keep a man she didn't want?

Jesus, did her mother even listen to herself?

"On that note, Mother, I'm hanging up now."

"Don't you be an ungrateful brat. I've done *everything* for you, and this is how you repay me? I will see you at brunch, or there will be hell to pay."

Shea hung up as her mother continued her tirade—something she wouldn't have done even two days ago.

It seemed laughing at night on the street with a man who held her close had helped her more than she thought. Just the idea of having a plan for that night—even if it was her job to make the plan more concrete—was worth any amount of yelling her mother would do later.

Although she would have liked to sleep in, she couldn't now. Not with the oily feeling sweeping over her at that early morning phone call.

She'd just have to get up and begin her day.

Shea showered, ate breakfast, and then planned their date for that night at the Preservation Hall. When Shep told her where they were going, she'd blinked. It wasn't a real date-like place, but he wanted to take her anyway. He said they'd do dinner and...other things afterward.

She blushed when she thought about what those other things could be.

Shea might not be the whore her mother thought she was, but she was ready to see what happened with Shep. She couldn't help herself.

By the time late afternoon rolled around, she was dressed and ready to go. Shep would be there any minute to pick her up. Unlike the previous night when they'd arrived separately, she was fine with him knowing where she lived. Considering he'd dropped her off at her doorstep the night before, it was a little late to be worried about that.

Also, unlike the previous night, she wasn't dressed like an assistant or someone going to a high-end cocktail party.

Nope.

She'd had to search in the back of her closet for her outfit and luckily had enough on her "never-going-to-happen" rack, that she could be comfortable. She wore skinny jeans, a cute blouse, and those black fuck-me pumps she'd told Shep about.

She usually wore those with a dress, but she wanted to be a little daring today.

Hopefully he'd like it.

Damn it! She had to stop doubting herself. It had taken only one phone call from her overbearing shrew of a mother for her to revert back to the adolescent she'd been.

She was not that person anymore.

She just had to remember that.

A knock on the door pulled her out of her thoughts, and her hand went to her neck, her pulse fluttering.

He was here.

Okay, Shea, you can do this.

She smoothed out her top, her heart speeding the entire time. When she opened the door, she sucked in a breath—her usual reaction to seeing him.

He wore another dark button-up shirt that clung to him in all the right places.

He was beautiful.

Freaking beautiful.

"I knew you'd look fucking amazing in jeans, and I was not wrong. Not by a long shot."

Shep's words slid over her, and she sighed.

Yes. Sighed like a schoolgirl, and she didn't care.

She ran her hands down her jeans, still not sure she was wearing the right thing—even with Shep's obvious approval.

Jesus, she needed to get control over her insecurities. She wasn't sitting in her mother's living room being yelled at for spilling punch on her dress or for not wearing the latest fashions. Tonight she could not have cared less.

A hand palmed her cheek and forced her to gaze at Shep's face. He frowned, his brows lowering.

"What's wrong, baby? Too crass for you?"

She blinked, confused. "Oh, no. I don't mind what you said." She blushed. "I *liked* what you said."

He let out a breath then brushed her cheekbone with his thumb. She sucked in her lips, loving the feel of his touch a little too much.

"Then tell me what's going on in that head of yours. You were a million miles away, and it didn't look like you were in a good place. What's wrong, baby?"

"Nothing," she lied. She always lied when it came to her mother and her *issues*. She didn't want to put a damper on their date any more than she already had. He didn't need to know that her mom was a psychopath who beat her daughter down with words every chance she got.

Her mother didn't know Shea had a storm brewing beneath the calm exterior.

She wanted to be different, but was too afraid to be that way. She'd shut her true self away for so long she didn't know how to get back out.

Shep tilted her face up then brushed her lip with his thumb. "You don't have to lie to me, Shea. We're supposed to be getting to know each other, remember?"

"For my tattoo. You don't need to know everything, Shep."

"Baby, you know it's more than the tattoo. It's been more than the tattoo since you ran into me on the street and I couldn't breathe when I stared into those gorgeous eyes of yours. Yes, I will give you the best tattoo in the world. You're already so beautiful that anything I put on your skin will only enhance the art. But that's not all. I also want to find out what makes you tick, to know you. Last night we didn't talk about tattoos or designs. We talked about who we are. What we want. I don't want to go back. I'm here now because I want to know you, and I *know* you want to know more about me. Don't pull away now, Shea. Talk to me."

This man.

Damn it.

He took all she had and gave so much more back.

How the hell did he do that?

Leaning on him would take too much from her, but, hell, she wanted to do it.

"I'm sorry."

He shook his head in a quick jerk. "No. You don't get to be sorry, Shea. You're not doing anything wrong. Don't you understand? I want to know you. Every part of you. I can't do that if you close up and hide behind your apologies."

"Shep..."

"Talk to me, precious. What was on your mind that took you so far away? Why are you hiding from me? I know we haven't known each other long, but can't you feel it? That connection that means more than just a passing glance?"

She closed her eyes. "Yes. I feel it."

"Look at me, Shea."

She did, his piercing blue eyes taking her in.

"Tell me what happened."

"My mother is a bitch."

He blinked, and she held back a snort.

"That was a little blunt," she said.

"Uh, yeah. I'm not disagreeing with you on the bitch part, though, if she's making you feel like you looked just then." He moved, tugging her to her couch. "Tell me about it."

She loved the way he looked in her house, his tattoos and devil-may-care looks against her prim and proper decorating. He could totally dirty it up but in the best way possible.

She sank into the cushions like she had before, but this time, Shep pulled her even closer. The heat from his body scorched her, and she took it all in.

Oh yes, she wanted this.

Wanted him.

She just had to figure out a way to say it.

"Well, like I said, my mother is a bitch. No matter what I did as a kid, and even as an adult, it has never been good enough for her. I was born to be a debutante, to be the personification of the Little name, to use our money and influence to gain even more money and influence. From a young age, I've known that I was to be a pawn in my family's political and power games. I was born to marry well—to whomever they chose—and to be the best wife I could be. I wasn't taught to cook, but how to order servants around. I wasn't taught to clean, but to live in a pristine house taken care of by other people."

She took a deep breath, the resentment that she'd always tried to hide filling her.

Shep brushed a lock of hair from her face, and she leaned into his touch, needing him more than she dared admit.

"I'm not that person, Shep. At least, I've tried not to be that person. This house? I paid for it on my own. It's small, too small for my mother, who tells me that repeatedly. It's only two bedrooms, but fits me wonderfully. The things you see in it? They're all my mother. I couldn't stop her from decorating it so it would at least look 'decent' for her. I tried, but she found a way in and decorated when I was away for work."

"Jesus. She wouldn't even let you have a little bit of yourself in it?"

"Who am I, Shep? You're trying to figure it out for ink...and because you want to," she added as he narrowed his eyes. "I don't even know who I am. I'm trying to figure it out though. I *want* to figure it out."

Her chest constricted then lessened as she said the words she'd been afraid to.

"I want to grow beyond the person my mother has deemed me to be and failed at being for her. I...I just don't know how to do that. And, no, I didn't tell you all she's said to me, even what she said this morning, but I'm ready to move on. I have to."

Shep moved on the couch so he faced her. "Damn, baby. I want to know what your mother said to you to make you hide like that, but I'll wait. Now, as for finding yourself? God, woman, you're already shining through. I can't wait for you to find out who you are because I'm seeing her right now and liking it."

"Really?" She smiled, liking that he was so passionate about his words.

"Really, baby."

She moved then, cupping his face with her hands. "I don't want to go out tonight," she blurted out.

A look of hurt crossed his face before he smoldered, his eyes darkening, a slow smile crawling over his face. "Oh really?"

"Really."

He traced a finger along her cheek, and she shuddered. "What do you want to do tonight, baby?"

She traced her hand along his beard, loving the way his scruff brushed her skin. It made her wonder what it would feel like on other parts of her body.

She felt herself blush, and Shep chuckled, a rough sound that shot straight to her pussy.

"I take it by that blush you have an idea of what you want to do tonight. Let me guess. Does it involve me licking every inch of your body, sucking on those nipples and that sweet pussy of yours, then filling you with my cock?"

She swallowed hard. "That sounds like a plan," she croaked out.

"Do you know what you want first?"

Would asking for all of it be too much? Too brazen?

"Anything. Just tell me what to do."

By the way he groaned, she knew she'd said the right thing.

"Fuck yeah. Just do what I tell you and you'll come hard, baby. You'll love every minute of it."

She squirmed in her seat. "I already do."

"Hell yeah, you do."

Shep took her lips, his tongue sliding along the crease then tangling with her own. She moaned into his mouth, wanting, no, *needing,* more. He nibbled and licked along her lips then kissed down her jaw to bury his face in her neck. She arched toward him, wanting him to bite, suck...do *something.*

His hands found her breasts through her top, and she pressed her body closer.

"You like it?"

She just moaned, unable to speak.

"I'm going to fuck these pretty breasts of yours, Shea. Maybe not tonight, but soon. They're more than a handful, perfect for my cock. I can't wait to see my dick sliding between them as you hold them together. Maybe I'll even fuck your mouth at the same time so your plump lips will lick and suck the crown of my dick as I fuck your breasts."

Jesus, the man was good at dirty talk.

She was about to come just by listening to him.

He stood up, bringing her with him. "Let's get these clothes off so I can see you. All of you."

She swallowed hard. She wasn't ashamed of her body, though she knew she wasn't the skinniest of girls. Her breasts were still perky, but not as high as they'd been when she was younger. Once she'd reached thirty, her body had curved and started to settle. She could only fight gravity for so long without losing a few battles.

Shep put a finger under her chin and forced her gaze to his. "Eyes on me, Shea. Stop with the doubt. You're fucking sexy, and I want to see you naked. Got it? You're beautiful, so stop thinking that you're not."

She smiled then reached for the bottom of her blouse. Shep's hands covered hers.

"No, let me."

He slowly tugged her shirt over her head then threw it behind him. "Jesus, Shea. How many layers are you wearing?"

She smiled at the annoyance in his tone. Apparently he wanted her naked quickly. Well, so did she.

"Just this cami and a bra. Then my jeans and panties. Oh, and my boots and socks."

Shep just shook his head then lowered his head to capture her lips. "I don't mind, baby. It just makes the anticipation that much sweeter."

Shea huffed out a breath. "Any more anticipation and I'll combust."

"Oh, honey, just you wait."

She gulped. "That's what I'm afraid of."

He divested her of her cami then knelt before her. He shucked off her boots quicker than she would have thought possible, tugged off her socks, and then slid her jeans down her legs, leaving her in her matching bra and panties.

He stayed kneeling in front of her, his gaze openly hungry. "Gotta say, Shea, love the fucking pink bows on black lace."

She blushed and lowered her head. She loved wearing sexy things under her clothes, and now that she'd seen that hungry look on Shep's face, she'd be sure to *always* wear something sexy for him.

At least underneath her clothes.

His calloused fingers slid up her body as he stood, bringing her closer. "God, Shea, you're beautiful."

He took her lips before she could answer, leaving her breathless.

His fingers made quick work of her bra, and he tossed it over his shoulder. Her breasts fell, heavy, her nipples already hard little peaks.

He brushed his thumb over one peak, plucked it, then did the same to the other. She arched, wanting more.

"Look at these nipples of yours, baby. Like berries, suckable, ready for my tongue." He bent down, captured one in his mouth, and sucked.

Her pussy clenched, and she moaned.

Hell, he felt so good.

His tongue flicked her nipple, and then he bit down gently. The shocking sting went straight to her core, and she rubbed her legs together, needing release.

He pulled back and gripped her hips. "No you don't. You don't get to make yourself come. That's my job. My treat."

"Shep."

He had to be kidding.

She needed to come.

Now.

"Nope. Go sit on the couch and spread your legs, baby."

She sucked in a breath at the order, but did as she was told. The quicker she did it, the faster Shep would let her come. It didn't make sense to dawdle.

She sank into the cushions, blushed, and spread her legs so he could see how drenched her panties were. There would be no hiding from him now.

"Jesus. You're so fucking wet I can see it with your panties on. You want this as much as I do."

"I want it more," she said, leaving herself vulnerable.

"Oh, honey, I don't think it's a competition. We'll tie in this." He sank to his knees, fully clothed, and pressed his face to her pussy, inhaling.

"Shep!" She tried to close her legs and move away, but he pressed her thighs with his large hands, keeping her open.

"Nah-uh, baby. You smell so fucking sweet. I can't wait to taste you."

He twisted his fingers in the sides of her panties and tugged them down her legs. He tossed those over his shoulder too.

The man was really working on making a mess of her house in short order.

All thoughts of a clean house and her clothes fled her mind when Shep lowered his head and took one long swipe along her clit.

Her butt rose off the couch, pressing her heat closer to his face. He pushed her back down then went to work, licking, sucking, and nibbling. He licked around her clit then moved the hood back to suck hard.

Her body shook, her legs going numb as she came with that one lick.

Her arms tingled, and her pussy clenched, wanting more.

Jesus, the man was good.

"Fuck, Shea, you came so hard, so quick. I knew you'd be responsive, but hell. I'm going to make you do it again. And again. Got me?"

"Whatever you say," she rasped out, too much in her pleasure zone to care.

He went back to what he was doing before and licked along the seam of her lower lips before moving his hand so his fingers found her wet, aching center.

He pumped his finger within her pussy then added two more as he sucked her clit. Her body, already high from her previous orgasm, shook then tightened as she rose again. He fucked her with his fingers and moaned against her. His beard scraped against the soft skin of her inner thighs, and she came, the sensation too much for her to hold back.

She'd never come like that during sex.

Let alone more than once.

And she hadn't even seen him naked yet.

Go, Shep!

No. Go, *Shea*!

He moved back and kissed up her body until he found her mouth. Her limbs heavy, she used all her strength to tangle her fingers in his hair. She could taste herself on his lips, and it made her even hotter.

"That was amazing," she whispered.

"You haven't seen anything yet." Shep pulled back and stripped.

Her eyes greedily took his body in. He was broad, built, tan, muscular...perfect. His tats covered his arms, thighs, and chest. They were fucking hot. He also had a little tat on his hipbone she knew she'd have to lick later.

Her gaze caught the metal adorning him, and she blinked. "You're pierced."

Shep chuckled and ran a hand over the barbells in his nipples. "Yeah, and I can't wait to have your tongue on them."

Her gaze lowered, and she swallowed hard.

"It's a dydoe piercing," Shep explained. He had two barbells on the top of his cock near the tip. They weren't that large in respect to his cock, but damn, it had to have to hurt.

"Didn't they hurt?"

"Hell yeah, but it's worth it. You'll see. The piercings will hit that one spot in that sweet pussy of yours, and you'll never want to leave my cock."

She bit her lip and squirmed on the couch. "What about if I...." She blushed. Jesus. She'd just had the man's mouth on her pussy, yet she couldn't say the words.

"Later, when I fuck that mouth of yours and have that little tongue run up and down my cock, you'll see. You don't have a tongue ring, so it won't be a problem if you give me head while I have the piercings in."

She blinked up at him. "So if I were to get a tongue ring?" Not that she'd ever thought about it, but she knew from others that tongue rings meant amazing blow jobs—there, she at least thought the word—for men. And if what she was thinking was right, Shep's piercings were for her, not for him. It would only be right to return the favor.

She squirmed again.

"Fuck, baby. If you do that, then I'll take them out when you want to go down on me. Right now though? Now I want to fuck you hard because I'm about to blow. You get me?"

Oh, she totally got him.

He pulled her up to her feet, steadied her, and then sat down on the couch. She watched as he rolled a condom down his length.

"Where did you get that?"

"It was in my jeans pocket, baby. If you hadn't been paying so much attention to my cock—not that I mind—you would have seen. Now hop on. Ride me."

She smiled and did as she was told, straddling his thighs. His cock brushed her pussy, and she gasped.

"Holy shit, Shea. You're so fucking wet." Shep met her gaze, and she sucked in a breath, waiting.

She placed both hands behind his head on the couch, bracing herself. Shep's hands palmed her ass, squeezing, teasing.

Slowly, their gazes never wavering, she slid down his cock, the wide girth stretching her, but since she'd just come twice, she was slick and ready for him.

She rocked her hips slightly as she sank onto him, and he sucked in a breath. Yes, he liked that. Finally, she was fully seated, and she had to sit for a moment, trying to get used to the feel of him deep within her.

"This is heaven, Shea. Pure, fucking heaven."

She agreed, but she couldn't speak. Not right then. Finally, when she could breathe, she rocked again then slid up his cock.

"Jesus," he breathed.

She went slowly up then slammed back down, loving the way both of them gasped at the same time.

"Do that again."

"Of course," she whispered.

She repeated the action, over and over. Shep kept one hand on her ass, balancing her, while the other hand roamed, palming her breast then moving down to slide over her clit. She never let her gaze leave Shep's though. While she would have loved to throw her head back, close her eyes, and ride him like a cowgirl, right then, all she wanted to do was have this moment with him.

Have him know what he did to her.

From the look on his face, he knew.

She quickened the pace, feeling her inner walls tighten, her breasts grow heavy, and that tingle racing up her spine.

"Come now, Shea. I'm gonna go with you."

Needing no other motivation, she came hard, her pace never slowing. She felt Shep come inside the condom buried within her even as he shouted her name.

Their gazes locked and never broke.

"Let's do that again," Shea breathed.

Shep rocked his hips, and she moaned. "Give me two minutes, and I'll go fuck you on your bed. You've come three times, so I'll do all the work."

"Sounds like a plan," she said into his neck.

"Damn straight."

And he totally did most of the work when he fucked her on her bed a few minutes later. She helped though.

Some.

CHAPTER FIVE

Shep groaned, images of the previous week's activities filling his mind. He leaned against the shower stall, needing to breathe. Jesus, he'd spent the past week working or by Shea's side.

Or inside Shea.

Yeah, he liked that part too.

He needed to stop thinking about the way she made those little moans and how her body flushed all over as she wiggled on his cock. He needed to get to the café to meet Austin, and going there with a fucking hard-on wouldn't be the best thing.

But *fuck*.

The image of Shea on her knees, his cock tapping against her lips, and her fingers in her pussy as she fucked herself filled his mind.

He gripped his cock, using the soap he'd just used on his body to slide up and down the length. He squeezed hard then fucked his hand harder. He closed his eyes, imagined his hand was Shea's warm little mouth, that each squeeze was her hollowing her cheeks, sucking him hard, that each movement of his thumb on the crown was her tongue darting out, licking and tasting him.

Shea gave fucking great head, and she knew it now. Those losers she'd dated before didn't know the gem they'd had. Oh yeah, they knew she was hot because there was no denying that, but the fact that she laughed and gave great head made him want more.

Oh yeah, she was perfect for him.

He pumped his hips, fucking his fist while imagining Shea's pretty lips around his cock, her fingers finding that plump flesh between her legs.

He came hard, throwing his head back against the shower wall, his seed spilling to the floor as the water washed it down the drain.

Holy fuck.

Now he was rubbing one off in the shower like some damn high school kid even though he was regularly getting laid.

Shea would be the death of him, but what a way to go.

He finished washing up, his cock still semi-hard, but that seemed to be the norm when he was thinking about Shea, around Shea, or just breathing.

After he pulled on some clothes, he made his way to the café where Austin would be waiting. His cousin had shown up two days before, but instead of staying with him, he decided to stay with another of their friends.

Apparently Austin wanted to give Shep some time with Shea.

He'd take it.

Austin was sitting underneath one of the covered tables on the patio, sipping his coffee, a grin on his face that couldn't hide the weariness. Something was going on with his cousin, and Shep didn't know what to do about it or even if he *should* do something about it. Hopefully, staying in New Orleans at least for a couple weeks to chill would help with whatever the heck was going on.

"It's about time you showed up," Austin said then took another sip of his coffee. Shep sat down next to his cousin, tired as all hell since he hadn't had enough sleep. "Your coffee by the way? Fucking amazing. I mean Denver is all about clean air and health. I love the brews, the microbrews, the views, everything. I wouldn't change it for anything. But down here? Coffee is pure decadence. Pure indulgence."

The waitress came over, and Shep held up two fingers. Shea was joining them soon, and the waitress knew what Shep liked. The little redhead smiled prettily, her eyes an open invitation, but he just smiled and shook his head.

She walked away, still smiling, but not as brightly.

"She tried that flutter and smile with me as well," Austin said as he lay back in his chair, the tattoo on his shoulders peeking around the collar of his shirt.

"And you didn't take her up on it? You're losing your touch."

Austin raised a brow. "You didn't either. And it's too early in the day for that shit. Plus, she's like what, twenty? Technically, she could be our kid."

Shep groaned. "Jesus. Why the fuck did you say that? Now I feel really old. And I didn't take her up on that because I'm with Shea. There's no way I'd skip out on her for anything, let alone that."

He shut his mouth as the waitress set down the two drinks, her eyes still inviting.

"Thanks," Shep said, his voice gruff. If she didn't take the hint, then he'd say it, but she should be able to read signals if she was going to flirt like this in public.

"I'm here if you need me. For *anything*."

She fluttered her eyelashes and sauntered off.

"Jesus. I am officially too old for this shit."

Austin gave a rusty chuckle. "Good to know you want to stay faithful to Shea. Not saying you've ever cheated—I don't do that shit either. But it's still good to know where this is heading."

"Why don't you just ask me what you're fishing for?" Seriously, the Montgomerys were always up in all the family's business. It didn't matter that Shep was far away. He was still family.

Austin took another sip. "Things serious between you and Shea? You're not getting any younger, you know."

"We're the same age, so stop bringing up the old man crap. And as for me and Shea?" He sat back and thought about it. He'd had a couple of serious relationships before, but nothing that'd made him want to rush to the altar or picture the woman round with his child. Shea though? She was different. "Yeah, it's serious."

"Good to know, man. Good to know." Austin's gaze brightened as he looked over Shep's shoulder. "And here she is. Hey, Shea. Good to see you again."

They'd met when Austin had first come to New Orleans. He'd taken one look at her and announced he was staying at another friend's rather than Shep's.

Good man.

Shep turned and sucked in a breath.

Yeah, he was falling for that sexy blonde woman in the red dress.

Fast.

If he looked carefully enough, he might just find that he'd already fallen for her, but he knew both he and Shea weren't ready for that.

Yet.

The ruby red dress hugged her curves but went up to her neck in that same old-fashioned style she loved. She kept her flashes of skin just for him. The dress brushed the top of her knees, and this time she wore red flats rather than heels.

He'd told her they were going to need to walk today for their date, so she'd dressed just for him.

Yep, he totally was falling for her.

He stood and went to her, unable to wait any longer. He cupped her face and tilted it up to him. Her lips were barely open, and he took it as an invitation and captured her mouth.

Damn, he loved her taste.

He pulled back breathless and looked down at that sexy, flushed face. "Hey."

She grinned. "Hey."

"Hey to you both," Austin called from behind them. "Now sit down and stop making out on the street. Your coffee is getting cold, and I want to order beignets. I'll eat them all you know."

Shep turned, wrapped an arm around Shea's shoulders, and walked them toward Austin. "You eat all those and you'll lose your girlish figure."

Austin ran a hand over his flat stomach and grinned. "It'd totally be worth it."

Shea laughed, the sound filling his soul. God, the woman needed to laugh more, and he knew she was starting to do so. The ice was breaking, and the wild fire was burning.

His Shea was more than what her mother wanted her to be—much, much more.

"You got me coffee?" she asked.

He kissed her temple then relaxed back into his chair. "Yeah. It's the chicory that you love."

She grinned and took a sip, the little moan escaping from her mouth going right to his cock.

Out of the corner of his eye, he saw Austin grin, but he ignored the bastard. That little moan was just for Shep.

"So, where are we going this morning?" she asked after they ate their beignets.

"Well, I need to go into work for a bit like I said, and you said you were going to come with," Shep answered.

She smiled brightly but her eyes held a trace of nervousness. "I want to see how you work. You know, get ready for my own tattoo."

"It's good that you get used to the feel before you do something like that," Austin added. "Plus Shep is fucking phenomenal at his ink, so you're in good hands. If I didn't think so, I'd take care of you myself."

Shep frowned at his cousin. He had a feeling Austin was talking about more than ink when it came to Shea, but he didn't want to harp on it in front of her. That would be something he beat his cousin for later.

"I trust him completely," Shea said, and Shep sucked in a breath.

Fuck yes.

Finally.

"So, where are you taking me after you work?"

Shep grinned. "The St. Louis Cemetery."

Austin barked out a laugh while Shea's eyes widened.

"A cemetery? That's your idea of a date?"

Shep shrugged then stole a kiss. "You'll love it. I promise."

"I don't really like being scared, Shep."

He tugged her close. "Baby, it's not an amusement park where they try to scare you on certain rides. Here there's real history. We'll go for a bit. Take a look around. See something we wouldn't normally see. Then go home."

"Where Shep will be sure to keep you warm if you get too cold," Austin butted in dryly.

"Shut it, Austin," Shep bit out.

Shea grinned up at him. "Oh really? And just how will you keep me warm?"

He leaned down and bit her bottom lip. "Minx. Don't make me tell you in detail in front of Austin. We have to head to Midnight Ink, and I'm not gonna want to ink with a hard-on."

Shea snorted. "That would be awkward."

"Uh, yeah, considering I'm inking a sixty-year old woman today with her grandkids' names." Actually he was working their names into an intricate piece with lilies of the valley and lavender. He was revved up for it—something he hadn't been in a while.

Shea's eyes widened then she threw her head back and laughed. "Oh poor baby."

"Shut it, woman." He kissed her hard then stood. "I'll make you pay for laughing."

Her eyes darkened, and she licked her lips. "I'm sure you will."

Fuck. It was going to be a long day.

****

Shep closed the door behind them then pushed Shea against it. He wrapped her hair around his fist, pulled her head to the side, and buried his face in her neck.

She wiggled against him and laughed. "So, you said something about warming me up?" she said, panting.

He pulled back and rocked his erection against her. "Oh yeah. Were you scared when we walked amongst the dead tonight?"

She tried to move closer, but he pressed her to the door. "Let me touch you."

"Answer me, Shea."

"Of course, but you were there, so it wasn't that bad. Just hold me now, and I'll be okay."

He grunted, pressing his hips flat against hers. "I'll hold you, Shea. Don't forget that. I'm not letting go."

"Deal."

He smiled then lowered himself to the floor.

"What are you doing?"

"I'm going to eat you out with your leg wrapped around my shoulder. Then I'm going to fuck you against the door. Okay?"

"Oh. Okay," she rasped out, and Shep chuckled.

He knew Shea loved his head between her legs, his mouth on her pussy. She'd come hard when he'd done it the last time, so he was gonna do it every chance he had.

Even if that meant his cock might explode.

He helped her take off her shoes and tossed them behind him. If they had been heels, he would have made her wear them when he fucked her since that was hot as hell. That would just have to wait for another time.

He stripped her panties off and smiled. He loved the little triangle of pale blonde hair above her pussy. He just loved her pussy, actually.

All of it.

He spread her legs, wrapped one around his shoulder so she could have the other to support herself, then got to business. He licked around her clit, ran his hands up her thighs, and spread her lower lips so he could see that pink, glistening pussy.

Oh, yes.

He fucked her with his tongue then his fingers then his tongue again, her sweet taste coating his tongue. He heard her panting above him, so he kept his pace the same, not letting her come until he was finished.

Not that he'd ever get tired of eating her out.

He sucked on her clit while his fingers found that little bundle of nerves and pressed down. She came apart, her pussy tightening around his fingers like a vise.

He pulled away while she was still coming, pulled his cock out of his jeans, slid on a condom, then pistoned into her heat before she could gasp.

"Fuck, Shea, you're so tight."

"Oh, God. I love it. Please fuck me."

"That's my dirty girl."

He pumped his hips as she wrapped her legs around him. He gripped her ass, keeping her against the door. He buried his face in her neck as she tugged on his hair, hard.

Her hips met his stroke for stroke, so hard that the sounds of their fucking echoed in the room. He didn't care.

He wanted her.

Now.

She let out a little gasp then tightened around him, coming. He slammed into her once more and came right behind her, his seed filling the condom.

He couldn't wait until he could go bare with her.

They stood like that for a few minutes, his cock still hard as if he hadn't just come. He wasn't a young man anymore, but, fuck, he knew he could go again if Shea wanted to.

Finally he pulled out and let her feet hit the floor. He left her for a second, ran to the kitchen to get rid of the condom, and came back into the room.

Her gaze met his then lowered to his cock.

"Go sit on the couch," she ordered, and he raised a brow.

"Shea..."

"Go sit on the couch," she repeated.

"You saying you want to suck me?" He'd totally be game for that.

"I totally give great head. Just saying." He laughed, loving the way she was starting to speak her mind and get dirty about it, a far cry from the Shea he'd first met.

He took off the rest of his clothes then stripped Shea's dress off. She gave a little yip, and he laughed before taking off her bra.

"I thought I was going to do you," she said, trying to sound firm.

"If you're going to suck me, I want to make sure those tits are free so I can play with them at the same time. Sound good?"

He watched her nipples tighten. "Sit. Couch. Now."

He strolled to the couch, his cock bobbing. Yep, heaven. Pure heaven.

As soon as he sat, Shea was there, kneeling between his thighs, a hungry expression on her face. He didn't have a chance to speak before she'd gripped his length and started stroking. He was still wet from coming so she could slide easily along his cock.

She smiled at him, her eyes inviting, then licked the slit at the stop of his cock. He sucked in a breath then watched—and *felt*—as she licked around the bar bells at the tip of his dick. She sucked along the length of him, rubbing him down where her mouth wasn't. Her mouth trailed to his balls and his ass left the couch, the pleasure increasing as she sucked one ball into her mouth, rolled it around, and then did the same to the other one.

"Fuck, you were right. You're totally amazing at giving head."

She pulled away and licked her lips. "And I haven't even sucked you down yet."

He swallowed hard, put his hand at the base of his cock to hold himself still, and lifted his chin. "I'm here, baby."

She grinned then took the crown of his cock into her mouth. She sucked down, and he about lost it. Jesus, she felt good.

She bobbed her head, each time taking more of him. What she couldn't swallow, her hands held and squeezed.

Unable to hold himself back, he wrapped her hair around his fist and pulled. She let him go with a pop and frowned.

"I was busy."

"I'm going to fuck your mouth, Shea. You okay with that?" He didn't want to hurt her.

Her eyes widened, and she nodded. He lowered her head to his dick, and she swallowed the tip then let her jaw relax.

He tightened the grip on her hair, keeping her in place, then pumped his hips, slowly at first. The sight of his dick sliding in and out of her mouth had to be one of the hottest things he'd ever seen.

She kept her mouth wide so she didn't hurt herself on his piercings. If he wanted to go harder in the future, he'd have to take them out.

He fucked her mouth slowly, keeping a tight hold on her hair.

"Touch yourself, Shea. Make yourself come."

She nodded, his dick still in her mouth, and then slid her hand down her belly.

He pulled her head back and shifted so he could still pump into her and see her fingers go in and out of her pussy. Her fingers came back wet, and he almost came.

He tugged on her hair then fucked her mouth just a bit harder.

"Touch your clit, Shea. Pinch it." She moaned as she did. "Roll and pinch your nipples as you fuck your fingers, baby. I'm going to blow my load soon, and you have to come first. You got me?"

She nodded, eagerness in her eyes.

He watched as she fingered herself and played with her nipples, the sight intoxicating. Her breath came in pants around his cock until finally she moaned, her eyes rolling to the back of her head as she peaked.

"Relax and swallow, Shea."

Her gaze met his, and she nodded. He pumped into her mouth twice more then stayed there, his seed spilling on her tongue, down her throat.

Finally, he released her hair and pulled her into his lap. She curled into him, and he ran his hands over her body.

"You okay, baby?"

"Never better. You?" she whispered, her face in his neck.

"Heaven, Shea. Fucking heaven."

CHAPTER SIX

S hea swore the papers on her desk had multiplied over the weekend. She glanced at the stacks that hadn't been there on Friday and swore. Her co-workers were crazy if they thought she'd organize their mess.

Oh, *hell* no.

She might have rolled over and done it before, but not now.

Not since Shep.

Okay, so, according to Shep, it was all her and he'd had nothing to do with the fact that she was growing a backbone, but she'd take it.

He'd made her smile, lose herself and find herself, all in two weeks.

Two weeks.

She couldn't believe she'd known him for only two weeks. It didn't make any sense that she should feel what she felt about him—even if she wouldn't say the words—in such a small amount of time.

He made her laugh. He took her on the craziest dates. Who in their right mind would want to go to a cemetery in the middle of the night just to learn a bit more about their city and cuddle closer?

The image of just how close they got against the door, on the floor, in the bed, later in the shower, and then even later on the breakfast table, filled her mind.

She blushed so hard, she could feel the heat in her cheeks.

Oh yeah.

She liked the way he warmed her up in *every* way.

"There you are. Look at this mess. You chose to leave a perfectly good man for what? This squalor? I can tell from those piles on your desk you're behind. You're not even good at the job you left the family for, are you? God, what good are you?"

Shea froze at her mother's callous words.

What the hell was that woman doing here? She'd never once stepped foot inside Shea's office. Her place of work was too low class for a woman such as her mother—something Shea had secretly loved since that usually gave her a break from the bitch queen of all bitches.

"Mother?" she gasped, the flush from thoughts of Shep cooling faster than a plunge in the Arctic.

"Of course it's me. Who did you think it was? Is some other woman coming in here, knowing what I know? Of course you're probably disappointing other people just as you disappoint me, but just remember, you can *never* disappoint others like you disappoint me."

Shea had had enough.

"What is your problem, Mother? What have I ever done to deserve your scorn? You've beat on me since I was a little girl. Oh, you've never raised a hand to me. That would be too low-born. Yet you've never found me good enough. I've always been lacking. Tell me, Mother, what have I done?"

Her mother froze, her mouth gaping like a fish's before it thinned. "What have you done? Nothing!" She threw up her hands. "Nothing. You've always been a worthless leech. I've done all I could to ensure your place in our society. I've planned and perfected the perfect marriage, and yet look what you've done. You've thrown it all away. And for what? A tattooed thug who wouldn't be fit to lick my pumps."

Her mother knew about Shep?

"How the hell do you know about my boyfriend? And, for the record, don't talk about Shep like that. You know nothing about him."

"I know everything about him, darling. Don't you understand? I know all. It just takes a little money and a little shove and I know everything. I know about your trolling around town like a common trollop. He can't even take you on real dates. No. He takes you to places like cemeteries. God. He's an axe murderer waiting to happen, and you're cavorting with him? No. Not anymore, darling. Not anymore."

"You've had me followed?" Shea knew better than to assume her mother had followed her. There would be no way in hell her mother would lower herself to actually do the work on her own. Shea was surprised the woman had even taken the time to venture this far.

Something must be up the woman's sleeve.

Dread crawled up her spine, and she raised her chin, preparing herself.

"Of course I have. I've never stopped, Shea. You think you've left the family, but you haven't. We've let you take this break so you can *find* yourself, but now it's time to come back. Richard was understandably upset you couldn't make it to brunch, but he's still prepared to take you back. Of course we're compensating him for his trouble. It's only proper."

Shea blinked. "You've *paid* him to marry me? This isn't Regency England! I don't need a freaking dowry."

"Watch your mouth and keep a civil tone. Richard will have to strike that out of you if it continues."

Had her mother really just said her want-to-be-husband had to hit her? Jesus, the woman was certifiable.

"Mother—"

Her mother raised her hand, cutting her off. "No. I don't want to hear your excuses. You will leave this job immediately. You've already shown me that you can't keep up with the work. Just look at that messy desk of yours. A true Little would have at least excelled at their chosen profession. You couldn't even do that."

"That's not my work. I'm great at what I do. Stop cutting me down."

Her mother narrowed her eyes. "I don't like this new attitude of yours. At least when you left the family before, you did it with your eyes downcast like the little bitch you are. Now? Now I blame that tattooed thug for putting thoughts into your head. You're nothing, Shea. That thug is even less than you are. In another world, you two would be perfect for each other. Now? In this world, you're nothing. You're needed for the family, and you won't be allowed to slack on your responsibilities any longer. I won't have it."

Rage poured through her. "You won't have it? Who do you think you are? You're not my mother. You're just a shrewish bitch who doesn't understand she can't control me. Leave me alone. Can't you understand that I'm happier without the family? You'll notice not once have you mentioned Daddy's name. Why is that? Is it because he doesn't care one way or another? He's never cared, Mother. I don't care either. Just leave me alone."

Her mother flinched at the mention of her husband.

Direct hit.

Sadly, it didn't make Shea feel any better.

"Leave your father out of this. You've never been good enough for him either. You're the reason he ignores the things he does. You."

"Whatever you say, Mother. Now leave please. I'm tired and have work to do. Then I'm going to see Shep because I'm thirty-two years old and far beyond the age of caring what my mother says. Especially when all she spews is vitriol and hate. I'm done."

Her mother's lips thinned even more. If the woman wasn't careful, she'd run out of lips to thin.

"You can try, Shea. Oh, you can certainly try. But if you don't meet Richard tonight for dinner and say yes to his offer, I'll ruin that thug, *Shep*, and everything he touches."

Shea froze. "What the hell do you mean by that?"

"Watch your language."

"Fuck my language!" she screamed. "Tell me what you mean. You can't hurt Shep. He means nothing to you. He's not part of *your* circles and thank God for that," she spat.

Her mother raised her chin. "Oh, yes, he's certainly not part of that. He'll never be part of that. But what he is, is a lowlife with no college education who does something prisoners do in a jail cell."

"Shep's art is brilliant. You know nothing about him. Stop putting him down."

"He's *nothing*. With just a few phone calls, I can close that harbor of harlots, Midnight Ink. I'll make it so he can't even draw with chalk on the street without the police on his back for some crime or another. I'll ruin him, Shea. Don't think I won't. And if you still refuse to stay away from him, I'll ruin that other shop in Denver, Montgomery Ink. I'll ruin them all."

The determined glint in her mother's eyes made Shea want to throw up.

As it was, bile filled her mouth, and she fought to control her shaking.

Jesus.

Who *was* this woman?

"You...you can't do that," Even to Shea's ears, she knew her voice sounded weak.

Of *course* her mother could do that. The woman lived for things like this. She had connections through money and the family everywhere.

Shep could actually lose everything because her mother was a selfish, vindictive shrew.

Jesus.

"You know I can, Shea. You know I'd crush him under my shoe without even batting an eyelash. I'd enjoy it too."

Shea swallowed hard. "Why? Why do you want to do this?"

"We need Richard's family," her mother snapped. "We might have money and power in this state, but Richard's has it throughout the entire country. Together we can go even further. You know Richard has political ambitions. With you by his side, our family will be in the hallowed halls for generations. We will be remembered. Eternal."

The woman had to be crazy.

Certifiably insane.

"If you don't leave him, I'll take it all from him, Shea. You have until tonight."

With that, her mother turned on her expensive heels and left Shea standing alone in her office.

Broken.

Shea staggered back, her feet barely working as she bumped into her desk. A stack of papers fell to the floor, but she ignored them.

What was she going to do?

This couldn't be happening. Her mother couldn't just come into her life and try to regain the control she'd had for so long.

Shea closed her eyes, the tears she hadn't noticed before falling harder.

She'd lose Shep.

To ensure his life remained as he knew it, to ensure his happiness, she'd lose him.

Her arms went numb, her chest tingling.

God.

She couldn't lose him. She'd just found him.

She'd finally stood up to her mother with her chin held high, and it was for naught. Her mother always had the upper hand, the ace up her sleeve, and now she had what would guarantee the end of the life Shea wanted to build with a man she loved.

No matter how much she thought she could fight it, her mother would fight harder to punish Shea for the faults and wrongdoings she'd never actually committed.

That was the type of woman her mother was.

Shea didn't know how to fight against it.

Oh, she might have learned to fight for herself and would fight to the ends of the earth for Shep, but to risking hurting Shep beyond measure fighting against her mother when she knew she couldn't win?

No.

She couldn't do that.

She'd have to in order to make sure he could live without her.

She'd marry Richard and break completely in the process.

She'd do anything for Shep.

Even leave him.

She cleaned up the stack of papers she'd dropped and put them on top of the other stack of papers that she'd leave to the other accountants.

Hell. She was really giving up.

This was the person her mother had made her, the person she'd fought so hard not to be.

She hated it.

"Shea? I brought coffee."

The sound of Shep's voice startled her, and she dropped the papers in her hand on the floor. She cursed again—inwardly reminding herself she'd have to stop that when she married Richard—and bent to pick them up.

"Oh, I'm sorry, baby, for scaring you. Here, let me help with that."

Out of the corner of her eye, she saw Shep put down two coffee cups and a bag of something and walk toward her.

She had to turn away.

It hurt too much to face him.

She would just have to slink away like the coward she was.

"I've got it. I'm actually kind of busy right now. You've caught me at a bad time." Her voice was ice, just like it had been before she'd walked into Midnight Ink the first time and clapped eyes on the man she'd fallen in love with.

"Hey, what's up? What's wrong?" He put his hand on her elbow, turning her toward him. She lowered her head, unable to meet his gaze. "Talk to me."

"You need to go, Shep." The words were torn from her, bile rising in her throat yet again.

He lifted her head with a finger on her chin. "Why, Shea? Why do I need to go?"

"You...you have to leave. This has been fun. It really has, but I need to go back to my life. I've changed my mind about the tattoo. I don't want it anymore. I don't want you anymore."

She held back the tears, the agony unbearable.

Pain flashed across Shep's face before his expression went carefully blank. "What?"

"I...I can't be with you anymore. We're different people. You're so...you. So vibrant. So...Midnight Ink. I am ice. I've always been ice, and I will always be ice. You need to go, Shep."

"What the fuck are you talking about, Shea?"

"You need to go, Shep. We can't see each other anymore. It's over."

He looked down at her, wearing that same expression he'd worn when she'd first asked for her tattoo at Midnight Ink.

"No."

CHAPTER SEVEN

"**N**o," Shep repeated, keeping the anger—the anguish—at bay. "No. You don't get to do this."

"No? Why do you keep saying that? You can't just say no and get what you want." Her chin wobbled, and Shep clenched his jaw. Something was going on here, something more than fear of commitment or whatever he thought it might have been at first.

No, this was something much worse.

Shea was scared about something, and he'd be damned if he let her end it now because of it.

"I said no in the shop because you had no fucking clue what you wanted inked on your body, Shea. It's permanent. It's not a fucking dress or some shit like that."

Her head snapped back as though he'd slapped her, and he took a breath through his nose. Shit. He hadn't meant to lash out, but he was just so fucking angry that she was trying to leave him.

He'd never wanted a committed relationship before, yet now he wanted one.

With Shea.

She didn't get to leave.

Not when he knew she wanted the same thing.

Or least *had* wanted.

"I know a tattoo isn't a dress or pair of shoes, Shep. I'm not an idiot. Don't treat me like one."

"Then don't treat *me* like an idiot and lie to me. You're leaving because you're done with me? Fuck that. You're lying. Now tell me what the fuck is going on."

She swallowed hard, his gaze following the long lines of her throat. "I'm done, Shep. I don't want this." Her voice broke, but she didn't let the tears in her eyes fall. "Just go. Please."

He cupped her face, and she tried to move back. He tightened his grip, not enough to hurt, but to show her he wasn't letting her go.

Not without an explanation.

Maybe not ever.

"You don't get to leave me, Shea. Not when I know you're leaving because you're scared. If you didn't want me anymore? I'd know. You wouldn't be on the verge of breaking down. Something scared you. What was it, baby?"

She closed her eyes. "Let me go, Shep. I...I can't do this. I can't let you get hurt."

Hurt?

"Tell me, Shea."

"I can't."

"Is it your family?" Her eyes opened, and she nodded. Okay. He was getting warm. "You aren't who your family is, Shea. You aren't the person your mother wants you to be." She flinched. "Baby, you're so much fucking more. You're a breath of fresh air and so fucking amazing that I want to find every single layer of your soul and wrap myself in it. I love you so fucking much, Shea. Can't you see that?"

Her breath quickened. "Don't say that, Shep. You can't mean that."

"Stop it. You don't get to tell me how I feel. I love you. I've never loved anyone other than my family, so don't tell me I'm wrong. I fucking *love* you."

"You're trying to tell me how I feel!"

"Because you're lying to yourself! You aren't the person your family thinks you are, or should be, Shea. You aren't who *you* think you are."

She sighed.

He was getting closer.

"I want you, Shea. I want everything. I want the woman I went with on those nights. I want the woman in the prim dress and fuck-me heels. I want everything."

"Shep."

"No, let me finish. I want you to get that tattoo. I want to mark your body with your soul then mark you with me. I want you to look down at yourself and know I love you."

The tears started falling.

"Then, baby, I want your brand on my body. I want you to look at me and know I love you."

"Shep."

"I want everything, Shea."

She pulled away and tried to go around him. He wrapped his arms around her middle, pulling her close so her back rested against his front. He pressed his nose to her nose and inhaled.

"Baby, tell me what's wrong."

"I can't." Her voice shook, and he broke for her.

"Baby, don't be scared. I'll be there to catch you, though you're strong enough to catch yourself, too. You just have to believe it."

Silence, then a whispered, "I-I'm not strong enough. I'm a c-coward." The tears fell in earnest now, and he turned her, crushing her to his body.

He ran a hand down her back while murmuring his love and promises.

"Baby, tell me what happened."

"My mother," she whispered, her voice dead.

His grip tightened. "Your mother?" What the fuck had the bitch done now?

"She..." Shea stopped, took a deep breath, and tilted her chin until she met his gaze. "She told me that if I kept seeing you, she'd destroy you."

"Destroy me? What the fuck? Does she think this is some B movie or something?"

Shea shook her head. "You don't understand. My family has connections. No, not mob connections or anything." She paused. "Actually, I don't know if that's true. But the thing is, they have money. Lots of money. Mother uses that money to get what she wants."

"And what she wants this time is to break us up."

Shea bit her lip. "That and more."

"Why do I not like the sound of *more*?"

"She wants me to leave my job and meet Richard tonight."

"Richard. Your ex-fiancé, Richard?"

"That's the one. She says she's *paid* him to marry me. She *sold* me to gain more influence for the family."

He hugged her tighter. "Oh, baby. I love you, but I want to fucking kill your mom."

"You'll have to stand in line," she mumbled.

"Tell me about what she has on you for you to even consider this, Shea. I know you, baby. You left the family once, and yet you're going to go back to them?"

"Like I said. She's going to destroy you."

"How? Honey, she doesn't even *know* me. How can she destroy me?"

"She's going to have Midnight Ink shut down and make it so you can't work. Then she's going to hurt your family up in Denver, Austin and everyone. Shep, she's done things like this in the past. She had my third grade teacher fired and her license revoked because the woman stood up to her when Mother wanted me to do different work than the kids whose parents had less money than us."

"Jesus. What a fucking bitch. How the hell did she do that?"

"I don't know. Money solves a lot of problems for her. Shep, I don't want you to lose everything. I can't let that happen."

He kissed her. Hard.

When he pulled back, she looked up at him, her eyes dark.

"No. She doesn't get to do this. Fuck that. She might know people, but the people at Midnight Ink are even craftier than her. Fuck her. My family has influence too, baby. Not the same as her, but enough that she can't hurt us.

I'll find a way to keep us safe, baby. You don't get to run from me in order to protect me. Got it?"

"Shep. I won't have her hurt you."

"Well, you don't get to decide that."

"You tell me to be independent and fight for myself. That's what I'm doing."

"No. You're fighting for me and doing a fucked-up job of it."

"Well, fuck you!"

Shep threw his head back and laughed.

"This isn't a time to laugh, Shep."

"Jesus, baby, you just told me to fuck myself. You, the one who doesn't like using curse words except when I'm buried deep inside you."

A slow blush crept over her skin. "Stop bringing that up."

"Baby, you look beautiful when you come. You look beautiful every day. You do not get to leave me because your mom is a bitch. I'll call a few guys at Midnight and get this taken care of. She doesn't have the power she thinks she does. We're not high up in the echelons of power. We're down and dirty. She can't play our game."

"You promise?" she asked, her voice so full of hope he broke for her.

"I promise. Don't leave me, Shea."

"I didn't want to. I want to stay with you. I want it all too." The last part was whispered.

"Jesus I love you so much." He kissed her hard then pulled back. "Do you have anything to say to me?" he teased.

Shea smiled, the tears in her eyes now of happiness rather than the pain he'd seen before. "I love you so much. So freaking much."

"Damn straight, woman. Now, you have the office to yourself for a bit?"

Shea frowned. "Yes. I'm alone today. Why?"

"Because I'm going to fuck you on your desk while you're wearing those pretty pink heels. Got a problem with that?"

Her eyes darkened, and she squirmed in his hold. "Shep..."

"Got a problem with that?" he repeated.

"No," she whispered.

"Good. Take off your panties, Shea."

She gulped. "What about my skirt or shirt?"

"I want to keep you dressed. Doesn't that sound good? Me fucking you with us both dressed so when you go back to work later today, you'll be wearing my scent?"

She nodded and moved to slide down her panties.

What a sight.

Jesus.

He undid his jeans and took his cock out. Then he took the condom out of his back pocket—something he always had on him since meeting Shea—tore the package open, and slid it over his length.

"Bend over your desk, Shea."

She licked her lips and did what she was told. Her skirt was too long for him to see anything so he stood back and stroked his already hard cock.

"Hike up your skirt. Show me that pretty pussy."

Her arms reached around, and she slid her skirt up to her hips, keeping her cheek to the desk. Hell, his woman knew what he wanted.

The act left her ass and pussy bare for him.

"Spread your legs a bit, baby. I want to see all of you."

She did so, her legs shaky in her high heels, but she looked damn gorgeous.

Her ass was round, firm, yet with enough give that he always had a nice grip when he pumped into her. Her pussy was wet just from his voice, and he couldn't wait to sink his cock into it. Usually, he'd eat her out and go slow, but right now, he wanted her around his dick.

He stalked toward her and rested one palm on her ass. He moved and slapped it hard.

"Shep."

"Never leave me again. Don't even think about it. Not when it's for something as stupid as what happened."

She nodded, and he soothed the spot he'd slapped. They didn't play with spanking, other than a few here or there, but from the way she'd gasped when he did it, it would be something for them to look forward to in the future.

He let the tip of his cock rest against her folds, and she sighed. She tried to push back, taking more of him, but he held her firmly.

"Not yet, Shea. Let me control it."

"Anything, Shep."

God, he loved this woman.

He positioned himself then slammed into her with one thrust.

She arched back, a scream in her throat. Her pussy constricted around him as she came.

"Jesus, Shea. You came with just one touch. You're fucking hot, you know that?"

"You do it to me, Shep. Now, please, fuck me. Make me yours."

Well, if that's what she wanted.

He pulled back slowly then entered her just as fast as he had before. He gripped her hips and fucked her hard, pumping into her as fast as he could. Sweat beaded his forehead as he fought to keep from coming.

He didn't want this to end.

No, he wanted the image of Shea bent over her desk, his dick sliding in and out of her pussy, ingrained on his mind forever.

His balls tightened, and he cursed before pulling out of her.

"What?" she asked before he flipped her on her back and entered her in one stroke. "Oh," she gasped.

"I want to see your face when I come." He tangled the fingers of one hand with hers, the other on her ass to keep her steady. She wrapped her legs around his waist, heels and all.

He pumped into her as he kissed her, trailing his lips on every part of her he could reach. They were both still wearing clothes, and he knew as soon as he could, he'd strip them both so they could touch skin to skin.

His dick throbbed, ready to explode, and he took her mouth one more time.

"Love you, Shea."

"Love you, Shep."

He slammed once more into her, his come filling the condom as he groaned her name into her neck.

"Best. Ever," Shea panted.

He grinned against her. "You haven't seen anything yet."

EPILOGUE

"It rubs the lotion on its skin..."

Shep froze, one hand on Shea's side, the other on her bare bottom, keeping her in place. He repressed a shudder and closed his eyes.

"Shea, baby, stop saying that every time I put lotion on your tattoo."

She twisted around so he could see her face. The action brought her breasts closer to him so he leaned down to lick one peak.

He couldn't help himself.

Shea moaned and wiggled in his hold. He squeezed her ass then spanked her hard. "Keep still."

"You just spanked me!"

"You keep making that creepy movie reference when I rub you down with lotion."

She snorted and shook her head. "Sorry. It just comes to mind whenever you're lubing up my tattoo."

"And stop calling it lube. We've had to be careful for months so I wouldn't hurt you when I fucked you, so don't get me hard now."

Shea pouted, and Shep laughed. Oh yeah, he loved this new playful Shea. Sure, she could still be the ice princess when she needed to be, but whenever it was just the two of them, she was pure silk.

Pure *his*.

Together, they'd broken ties with Shea's family for good. That damn mother had no idea who she'd been trying to mess with. The Montgomerys and the people of Midnight Ink did not bow to anyone. It had taken only a few calls and they had enough dirt on Mr. and Mrs. Little to bury them forever. It was amazing what money for drugs and the need for kink—kink that wasn't within the boundaries of the law— could do to a family that prided themselves on being proper.

Apparently being proper was only for the cameras.

He'd chosen to keep that close to the vest though. There was no way he'd hurt Shea in the process of taking out her parents. He'd had the people at Midnight blackmail them. Yes, Shea knew everything to the last detail, even though she'd hated it, but nothing would blow back on her.

The Littles relented, and Shea had broken free.

She was free to be herself, to be with him, and to get her ink.

He ran a hand over the piece that had taken two very long sessions to complete. Shea had been a trooper, only wincing a couple of times before she fell into a rhythm with the buzz of the needle.

Oh yeah, he totally fucking loved this woman.

His finger traced the cherry blossom tree that ran up her entire right side and smiled. A branch curved under her breast and he knew that had hurt like a bitch, but she hadn't complained. Another branch ran up to her shoulder so it peeked out of dresses she wore. The tree's limbs tangled around the trunk and down across her hip, flowed across her lower back and ended right above her ass.

Seriously, it was his best piece of work ever.

Each bloom was a delicate form of pink, white, and shading.

The cherry blossom symbolized the end of winter, a difficult time, or a journey that had taken its toll. They'd chosen the cherry blossom tree because of her change and the way she wanted to live life.

Free.

She blossomed without her family's influence, so it was only fitting he'd done this for her.

What made that tattoo perfect for them were the carvings within the trunk of the tree. He hadn't gone for the normal fill and shading but had sketched markings that were special to them, leaving room in certain areas to add more when they occurred.

There was a Celtic marking for joy right on her ribcage. He remembered her laugh, her smile, her pure joy on their first date while listening to the bands play.

Another marking was Celtic for fearless. She'd run through the cemetery with him, jumped head first into his world, and brightened it for him. She'd gotten one of the largest tats he'd ever done on her first try because that's who she was.

The final marking was for freedom. That was the easiest thing to put on her body. She was finally free, though her freedom did come with him attached.

Not that she minded.

He rested his hand on her side and looked down at her. "I love you, Shea."

"I love you too, Shep. Though now that I'm fully healed, I'd love you more if you'd finally get down to business like you've been planning."

He threw his head back and laughed.

"Shush you. I was going to ask you something. Stop getting me hard." He looked down at his cock. "Or *harder*."

Shea snorted then sat up, her breasts jiggling when she did so.

He loved how she jiggled.

"What's up?"

He cupped her face, his heart racing. He took a deep breath and took the plunge. "I want to be with you forever, Shea. Forever. Marry me. Have lots of babies with me. Just *be* with me."

Shea's eyes widened, and she threw her arms around his neck, pressing her lips to his. Shep scrambled and pulled her closer.

He pulled back. "Is that a yes? I know we've only been seeing each other a few months but..."

"Shut up. Of course it's a yes!"

Shep smiled, joy filling him. "Fuck yeah. You're mine, soon to be Mrs. Montgomery."

Shea licked her lips. "Shea Montgomery? I love it."

"Not as much as I love you."

She ran a hand through his hair. "I love it when you get sappy, my sexy, tattooed, bearded man."

He leaned down and ran his scruff over her cheek. "Only for you, Shea. Only for you."

Shea had given him everything.

His future.

His happiness.

His inspiration.

Now he had a lifetime to pay her back.

Coming Next in the Montgomery Ink Series:

Sassy gets her story in a special bonus prequel,
INK REUNITED
The first full length novel, Montgomery Ink
Book 1, features Austin: DELICATE INK

Ink Reunited

A Bonus Montgomery Ink Novella

Ink Reunited

From the streets of New Orleans and the heat of Midnight Ink, comes the happy ever after for a character whose story was begged to be told.

Sassy Bordeaux is the Midnight Ink receptionist, honorary godmother, best friend to many, and matchmaker expert. In the past two months, she's watched eight couples fall in love, make mistakes, and find their happy endings. Though she might have had hand in each of those, she's yet to find the peace she's desired. When the men from her past come into Midnight Ink, she's forced to face what she left behind and what could happen if she lets go of her pain and finds a future she deserves.

Rafe Chavez and Ian Steele remember their time with Sassy like it was yesterday, yet have worked hard to move on. Or at least try to. Now they're both back in New Orleans for the woman they loved and for the connection they shared with each other. It will take more than the usual groveling, pleading and begging for these three to overcome their history, but once they take that step, the streets of New Orleans will never be the same.

CHAPTER ONE

"So, should I get a butterfly on my butt or a cobra on my hip?"

Sassy Bordeaux grinned at the just-turned-eighteen years old high school senior, and tapped her finger with a deliciously apple-red colored nail on her chin. The numerous bangles that adorned her wrists, covering yet still showing peeks of some of the tattoos she had on her forearms, jingled together with the movement. The sound mixed in with the echoes of motorized needles, laughter, music, and chatting within the shop.

The girl in front of her might have been eighteen, but she still had the baby face of a girl still growing. Normally, Sassy wouldn't have stepped in and told anyone that they weren't ready for a tattoo, but today she needed to step in.

Oh, who the hell was she kidding?

Sassy *always* stepped in and told it like it was. There was no use lying only to make a few bucks for the shop while the client ended up leaving with ink they really didn't want—or ink that didn't fit who they were—merely who they thought they should be.

She might have been the Midnight Ink receptionist and while most people on the outside thought her job was to make coffee and appointments, she and the crew knew better. She was the first line of defense for the artists' work and the clients' canvas.

It was a job she took seriously.

Even if she seemed like the crazy lady from the streets of New Orleans most days. That misperception by others led her to freedom.

Everyone underestimated Sassy.

Even Sassy underestimated herself sometimes.

Okay, totally the wrong direction for her thoughts.

Pushing away memories she'd rather not think about ever again, she placed her hand on top of the girl's hand and shook her head.

"Honey, is this really what you want?" she asked, lowering her voice, already smooth as honey, to a near-whisper.

The girl blinked up at her. "Uh yeah? I mean. I'm here aren't I?"

Sassy flipped her hair over her shoulder, the long brown waves tumbled down her back. Today, she had bright blue streaks in it thanks to the colored hair chalk she used. She liked changing it up daily and sometimes would change the color in the middle of the work day just to make people think twice.

The customers who didn't know her—and some who did—thought she was a little too crazy for them so she fed the fantasy and did nothing to change their minds.

Plus, the colors freaking rocked.

"What's your name, sugar?" she asked as she led the girl to one of the small couches they had in the guest area of Midnight Ink.

"Hannah. And you're Sassy. I've heard about you."

From the odd look on Hannah's face, Sassy wasn't sure she wanted to know exactly what the girl had heard. There were a lot of stories as to how she'd come to work at Midnight Ink. Between being a spy, a lost princess, and a former model who lost her way due to drugs, Sassy had heard just about everything.

It wasn't her fault the stories kept circulating. Okay, maybe it was considering she hadn't discredited any of them, nor had she told the truth as to where she'd come from.

No one needed to know that, and the fiction was more

exciting than fact anyway.

Sassy sank into the cushions of the couch she'd picked out for the shop and held back a sigh. Damn, she loved this couch. It was so plush yet didn't look it. It fit the look of Midnight Ink with its cream softness yet strong angles. The rest of the place had wood floors and dark black chairs, tables, and stools that gleamed under the warm lighting. The little reception area where Sassy could speak with clients, as well as have the artists relax was her zone and where her own magic happened.

At least that's what she *hoped* would happen in this case.

"So, Hannah, you've heard a lot about me?" Sassy asked, her tone casual. She needed to get out of her head and into this girl's. What the hell was wrong with her today?

Hannah rolled her eyes then bit her lip, as if she'd thought better of the action. "Well, you're...*The* Sassy. Everyone knows about you and your connection to Midnight Ink."

Sassy held back a snort at "*The* Sassy". Apparently her name was a title as well as who she was. She was special like that.

"Well, I am *The* Sassy, but that's not the important thing, is it, honey?" At Hannah's blank stare Sassy had to hold herself back from using small words. Damn, this girl was young. "Why do you want that tattoo?"

"Because I'm eighteen and it's my right as an adult." Hannah stuck out her lip in a pout that clearly said her words were a lie—at least the latter half.

An adult? Jesus, they made them younger and younger these days. Okay, so Sassy was only thirty-two, a baby in some respects but she'd seen enough to qualify her as more of an adult than this squeaky-clean teen.

"Okay, yes, ink is your right now that you're eighteen, honey. You need to remember, though, that ink is for life. It's not something to take for granted. Yes, a cobra on your hip would look kick-ass, in fact, I've seen a few that wrap around so beautifully, it's a work of art onto itself. Hannah, baby, if you get that though, it needs to mean something beyond wanting to prove you're older than what others think of you."

From the guilty look on Hannah's face, Sassy had hit the true reason for the girl's bout of rebellion.

No use stopping now since there wasn't a chance in hell any of the artists would lay ink on this virgin skin today. Hannah clearly wasn't ready and Midnight Ink cared about things like that. It's what made them who they were.

"Honey, go home and think about if this is truly what you want."

"But I want a tattoo," Hannah mumbled.

Sassy nodded. "Yes, I believe that you do, and I think that anything we put on you will look brilliant. Our artists rock, sugar, and they'll make sure you look fantastic, but right now? No, honey, that's not something you need. Wait until you're ready to get one for *you* and not what you think you need for *them*."

The girl let out a breath and ran a hand over her face. "I guess it was pretty stupid coming in here without an idea."

Sassy reached around and gave Hannah a one-armed hug. "No, honey. Actually, coming into Midnight Ink is the smartest thing you could have done. Somewhere else might not have listened to what you *needed* rather than what you said you *wanted*."

Hannah grinned up at her, looking much younger than her eighteen years if that was possible. "I guess that's why they call you *The* Sassy. You know all."

Sassy threw her head back and laughed. "Oh, I only wish I did, but it's fun pretending I do. Now let's get you a card just in case you decide to come back with a clear picture. When you do, we'll find you an artist, but I think Shep or Rosie would work for you."

Hannah ducked her head and blushed. "Shep's the really hot guy with the tattoos on his arms and shoulder in the corner right?"

Sassy held back a laugh and looked in the corner to where Shep was clearly holding back a laugh of his own. Apparently, he had ears like a freaking cat.

"Yes, darling, that's Shep. He's taken, but it's still nice to look and dream."

Caliph, the big bruiser of an artist and Shep's best friend, belted out a laugh and Hannah blushed even harder. Sassy glared at the man who smiled unrepentant, then let Hannah outside with a clear conscience.

She glided over to Caliph's station, the sway in her hips making her look like she was prowling even when she wasn't and waved her finger in her friend's face.

"I can't believe you laughed at her! She's just a teenage girl with a crush."

Caliph bowed his head and had the decency to look a little ashamed. A little. "Sorry, Sass. It was the idea of *you* fantasizing about dear old Shep that got me laughing, not the little girl who needed more time to think about her ink."

Sassy let out a breath then smacked his shoulder. "I would have thought since you found Jennifer you wouldn't be such a clueless brute when it came to girls."

"Hey, give him a break, Sass," Shep put in as he sidled up to them both. "He didn't mean anything by it and Hannah was smiling when she walked out of here. Why are you acting like it was bigger than it was?"

Sassy blinked and took a step back. Well, hell, she *was* blowing it out of proportion. All of Midnight Ink laughed and joked around. It was just what they did. They were a family and ribbed each other often. What the hell was wrong with her? And why had she asked that question more than once in such a short period of time?

Maybe she needed a break.

Or a man.

Nope. Not gonna think about that last one.

She patted Caliph's cheek so he would bend down. When he did so, she placed a small kiss on each one then sighed. "I'm sorry, hon. I think I just need a nap."

Or to get laid.

Stop it, Sassy.

Shep narrowed his eyes at her and she knew he didn't believe the words coming out of her mouth, but she ignored it. Her friends, as much as she loved them, didn't need to know everything about her.

"You should go home, Sass," Shep put in. "We aren't that busy and if you're saying you need the rest, then take it." He pulled her into a hug and she inhaled his spicy scent that did nothing for her other than remind her that he was family. "We love you, babe. You've taken care of us so now it's time to take care of yourself."

Sassy pulled back and pasted a smile on her face. Damn it. She knew that, yet the whole idea of taking care of herself was the reason she was in this rut.

Okay, so *that* was what was wrong with her.

"Shep, sugar, you don't need to worry about Sassy."

He grinned, his eyes dancing at her use of third person—exactly what she'd hoped for.

"Every time you talk about yourself in third person you freak me out. You know that right?"

Sassy nodded, her hair falling over her shoulders again. She never could make it do what she wanted most days. It seemed to like being even more free than she did. "That's why I do it, Shep dear. Now get to work on that stencil of yours. And you, Caliph, you left someone sleeping on your bench. How they could fall asleep getting a tattoo, I'll never know."

The big man grinned, then leaned down to kiss her cheek. "My hands are just that talented." He wiggled his brows and Shep made gagging sounds from beside her.

Boys.

They never grew up, even when one of them was rapidly approaching the big four-oh.

"You are a menace, but I'm glad Jennifer has you. Now get back to work. Shep? Don't forget that you need to bring in Shea for her next tattoo."

Shep smiled the smile that told everyone within a three block radius that he was in total love with the blue eyed woman who needed more ink. "I will, don't worry. She can't have anything on her arms or lower legs because of work—at least for now—but she's thinking of something for her other hip."

Shea met Shep within Midnight Ink when she had wanted a tattoo, and because fate was awesome like that, the two had fallen for each other in the process.

In fact, it seemed like love was in the air at Midnight Ink.

It had only been a month or so since the last of the love birds had found their match. All in all, eight couples—well, a triad in Eli's case—had fallen in love since the beginning of the year.

Sassy liked to think she had a hand in each of those.

Well, if she was counting, then yes, she'd helped each couple stagger through the murky waters of falling in love. After all, it wasn't all rainbows and unicorns. The best kind of love and happiness came after the parts where the couple had to work for it and find their way. Each of the couples who found love at Midnight Ink had been through their own unique forms of torture and now looked forward to bright futures and happy endings.

It didn't mean that Sassy would get hers though.

She closed her eyes and took a deep breath through her nose.

No, she wouldn't think about that.

Wouldn't think about *them*.

She hadn't thought about her past and those she'd left behind for so long that it was now just a distant memory. Sure, the taste of bitterness and regret still settled on her tongue once in a while, but it didn't rule her life, didn't rule her choices.

At least that's what she told herself.

With a shake of her head, she went to her station and made coffee. Sassy didn't make the usual coffee. Oh, no. She had a gift with it and those at Midnight Ink knew it. In a city filled with the most decadent coffees, Sassy could brew with the best of them.

See? That was something light and airy to think about. What else could she think of that had nothing to do with pain and regret?

Maybe she needed more ink.

She looked down at the spirals and flowers that covered her arms and smiled. Yes. More ink was definitely the way to go. She had a few pieces on her back and sides as well, and knew she had plenty of places for more.

Who would ink her though?

It had been her goal to get each of the Midnight Ink crew

to lay ink on her and so far, she'd gotten everyone at least once. Rosie had done a couple sessions with her. As the woman was her best friend, it only made sense.

Maybe she'd get Shep to work on her hip. The man knew exactly what to do with curves when it came to ink. She grinned as she thought of Shea. Okay, so maybe the man knew what to do with curves in other ways too, but that wasn't something she needed to think about.

Ever.

The shop's phone rang and Sassy moved to answer it. "You've reached Sassy at Midnight Ink. You desire it, we ink it."

The caller snorted and Sassy smiled. "Desire? Dear lord, Sass, you are milking it."

"Odalia!" Sassy squealed at her friend and Midnight Ink's client. "I'm so glad you called. Are you coming in for another session with that sexy, bad boy of yours?" Odalia and Jacques had been one of the couples she'd helped pair up recently and she couldn't be more happy for the cop and the bounty hunter.

"Since I'm planning on having Rosie finish up a couple pieces and I'll have to get partially naked to do it, yeah, Jacques will be there." Sassy could practically see the grin on the other woman's face through the phone. "You know how he likes to get me down to my skin."

"I'm sure you like to do the same, sugar. Now let me look through my appointment book to see when Rosie is available. You have any specific time you're thinking?"

They set up the time and Sassy penciled it in for Rosie who would make the final call. "Are you coming to the party we're holding in a couple weeks?" Sassy asked, speaking of Midnight Ink's Valentine's Day party.

The shop liked to hold parties of their own on certain holidays. Since the whole crew seemed to be in love, this party was only appropriate. It wouldn't actually *be* on Valentine's Day as most of the crew would want to be with their significant others, but it was near enough to it they could eat and drink, and for those who were sober, get inked.

"We'll be there. You know we love the shop and you,

honey."

Sassy opened her mouth to speak but suddenly came up short.

"Sassy." She heard the deep, achingly familiar voice coming from in front of her.

She blinked in complete disbelief at what she saw.

"Rafe."

"Nothing for me then?" Another voice, just as familiar, came from just beside Rafe, and Sassy swallowed hard.

"Ian." She shook her head. "What...what are you two doing here?"

She could have sworn everyone in the shop had stopped moving, stopped breathing. It was if they knew something was terribly wrong, and yet had no idea what to do about it.

She didn't know what to do about it.

"We're here for a tattoo," Rafe answered.

"And you," Ian put in.

With that, the phone dropped out her hand and her mind went completely blank.

Her past was back and standing right in front of her in all their sexy glory and determined faces. No matter what she did, she had a feeling she wouldn't be able to wish Ian and Rafe away.

It hadn't worked before.

It wouldn't work this time either.

Oh shit.

CHAPTER TWO

"**N**othing to say, Sass?" Rafe Chavez asked, his words sounding much calmer than he felt right then. He still couldn't believe he was there standing next to the man who had left him and in front of the woman who had done the same. A decade had come and gone, but right then, in that shop, it felt like mere moments since he'd lain eyes on them.

They'd been different people back then, he was sure, but damn it, he was here now and ready to face whatever the hell he had to in order to make his plan work.

She blinked up at him with those big brown eyes he once lost himself with no hope of escape. His fingers ached to caress the chestnut tresses draped over her shoulders and curled under her breasts. It was so Sassy that she had a couple blue streaks within the mass of waves that seemed to shout she was special.

"You can't be here," she breathed and Rafe held back a curse.

She'd been smiling and laughing on the phone, but now looked pale and shaky. He and Ian had done that, yet Rafe knew he'd do it again if it meant moving forward with what the three of them needed. Even if two of the three of them didn't realize they actually needed to do the same.

He didn't break eye contact with Sassy even though he wanted to risk a glance at Ian. If he was doing what Rafe thought, then Ian was also staring at Sassy, at a loss for what to do. Rafe could just picture the man, only an inch or so taller than he, giving Sassy that unwavering look with his piercing blue eyes, chiseled features, and onyx black hair that he'd tied back with a leather strap.

Rafe would have liked to think more about the man by his side but knew this wasn't the time or place. Now, it was all about Sassy. If they could get her to talk with them, maybe they had a chance for what Rafe wanted.

Since Sassy looked like she was about to bolt, he wasn't putting much faith in round one of their plan.

Crap.

"Sassy?" Ian said, his voice a low rumble filled with the elegant edge that Rafe had always secretly loved.

She shook her head once more then rolled her shoulders back. Well, hell, as much as he liked it when she got all sexy and angry at the same time, he'd much rather have had her not yell...and that was what she was about to do.

"What the *hell* are you two doing here?" she yelled.

Yep. Got it in one.

Rafe tore his eyes from her face and risked a glance at the people coming up behind Sassy. Most of the dudes were bigger than even he and Ian, and that was saying something. Plus, their looks of impending death and doom didn't bode well.

"*Cariña*, can we talk privately?" Rafe asked.

She narrowed her eyes at his name for her and curled her lip. "Don't call me that. You have no right to call me that."

While he understood her anger, which he knew he deserved, it took everything in his power not to remind her that *she* left *him*. That would be a discussion for a later time.

"I'm sorry." He wasn't. "We're just here to talk and get ink. We weren't lying about that."

She snorted. "Of all the shops, in all of New Orleans, you had to walk into mine?"

He grinned at the reference to their favorite movie then held back a frown at her reaction. The way she'd paled a bit after she'd said it, he knew she'd done it by accident. He'd take it however since that meant somewhere inside her she was still thinking of him, of them.

"Is there something wrong, Sass?" one of the dudes from the back said as he walked up behind Sassy. He put his hand on her shoulder and Rafe had to keep from yelling at the guy to keep his hands off his woman. He thought of Ian. *Their* woman.

Another man, this one even bigger than the first came up on her other side. He crossed his beefy arms over his barrel of a chest and glared.

Well shit, he didn't want to get in a fucking fight right there in the shop. He'd had enough of fighting as a teen and didn't want to do it again. Plus he didn't think Sassy would appreciate it.

"Need us to take care of these two for you?" the bigger man asked, his voice full of dangerous promises.

Sassy turned on her heel and put her fists on her waist. "Excuse me? Since when do I need the two of you to fight my battles? I'm not some damsel in distress who needs her white knight to slay the dragon. I'll slay my own fucking dragons." She glared over her shoulder at Rafe and Ian. "Or whatever the hell these two are."

The first man who'd spoken smiled warmly at her. "Sass, hon, we're just looking out for you. We all know you can take care of yourself. That doesn't mean you should."

Sassy let out a breath and Rafe sucked in one of his own, afraid of what she'd say. He knew the woman never liked to be perceived as vulnerable. He and Ian coming in like this and surprising her had been a bold move, and in retrospect, a not-so-smart one.

He just hadn't known what else to do.

"I'm fine, Shep." She patted his cheek then moved to the bigger man. "Thank you for defending my honor, Caliph. Now since I've made a scene where usually I only like to make my own on my own terms, I'm going to talk to these two...gentleman... away from here."

Rafe held back a triumphant fist pump but met Ian's gaze. The other man gave a small twitch of his lips, but otherwise didn't react to Sassy's words.

Well, it was better than nothing.

"If you're sure, Sass," Shep grumbled.

"I'm sure. They're not going to hurt me."

Rafe heard the odd note in her tone and knew what she was thinking. They'd hurt each other all those years ago but right then it was about overcoming all of that. It *had* to be.

"We really did come here for ink," Rafe put in, trying to ease some of the tension.

Sassy turned toward them and raised a brow. "Oh, I have no doubt that was one of your intentions. Now we get to see what your other ones are."

With that she moved around the desk, picked up her bag, and brushed passed them. That sexy wiggle in her step causing her hips to sway back and forth.

Damn, he'd missed watching her walk.

Ignoring the glares from Shep, Caliph, and the others in the shop, he turned to follow Sassy out the door. He heard Ian mutter something under his breath, then do the same.

"I don't know who you two are, but if you hurt Sassy, we'll hurt you," Shep said from behind them and Rafe stopped.

He looked over his shoulder and gave a slight nod. "We don't want to hurt her."

"Then don't be fucking idiots," Caliph put in.

Rafe gave one last look at the men who protected Sassy, then followed the woman in question out of the door and onto the street. Midnight Ink was located right on Canal Street and since it was just getting dark outside, the early dinner and cocktail hour crowd filled the streets. Since it was February, it was a bit chilly outside but nothing like what it would be back in New York where he'd lived for the past decade.

Sassy stopped in front of them and turned, her face expressionless. "I don't know why you're here and don't tell me it's for a tattoo. All three of us know that even though you might have wanted one, it was just a ruse to get me to talk to you. Well, now you've got me." She cursed. "For *this* talk only. I don't run away from my problems. Not anymore. So the three of us are going to go to my place and hash this out so I can go about my business. I don't like airing out my dirty laundry at work or in a public place. And that's what the two of y'all are. Dirty laundry."

While most men would have taken a hit at her words, Rafe knew he and Ian wouldn't. Sassy lashed out like a frightened kitten when she was cornered. Oh, he wouldn't back down. This kitten had claws, but damn, he missed the way she yelled and ranted.

Yes, he was a lunatic, but he'd long since gotten over that fact.

Going to her home would be a sweet torture for him since all he wanted to do was wrap his arms around her and never let her go. He wasn't an animal—barely—so he'd hold off doing something stupid like lie prostrate at her feet and beg for forgiveness.

However, that was the backup plan.

"That sounds like a reasonable plan," Ian put in, his voice smooth as silk. The man was like frost—ice, cold, and uniquely alluring—to others, but Rafe knew the man would thaw to reveal the fiery passion he and Sassy had fallen in love with that smoldered beneath the ice.

Rafe not only had to mend the frayed fabric of what he and Sassy had, but piece together the connection he'd shared with Ian.

He'd lost so much ten years ago and he'd be damned if he'd walk away now.

"Of course it's reasonable," Sassy spat. "It's *my* plan." She closed her eyes and rubbed her temples. Rafe held himself back from offering to help with that. "I need to stop snapping. We're adults and I'm sounding like a freaking teenager who lost her Edward doll." She rolled her shoulders. "Let's get this over with."

"Did you drive here?" Rafe asked. Though Ian and he had enough money to have hired private investigators and could call up data on Sassy at the snap of their fingers, they hadn't done so. They wanted to learn more about the woman in front of them on their own and be on equal footing.

Though where Sassy was concerned, she always had the upper hand; however, that was another matter.

She shook her head in response to Ian's question. "I

walked. I live close, and if it's too late by the time I leave, one of the guys from the shop walks me home."

Rafe ground his teeth. As much as he liked the fact Sassy wasn't walking alone late at night, he didn't like hearing about other men. She might not have been his for ten years, but that didn't mean he appreciated hearing about any other men in Sassy's life.

Damn it. He needed to stop acting like a Neanderthal.

Since they'd driven together in Ian's car, Rafe let him decide what they were going to do.

"We'll leave our car in the parking lot here, if that's safe," Ian said.

Sassy shrugged. "If you parked it behind Midnight in the gated area, you'll be fine. I have keys and can get you back to your car if they close up by the time y'all leave." She narrowed her eyes. "Though I don't think we'll be that long. Come on then. I'm right up this way."

They walked the two blocks to her place in silence. The tension rose with each step but Rafe didn't mind. Once they got over the first part, he'd be able to breathe again.

God, he'd missed them so much.

Not that he'd let anyone other than the two people near him know that. After all he was Rafe Chavez, badass mechanic and shop owner. He'd once been Rafe Chavez, badass high school dropout, but times had changed and so had he. Instead of boosting cars like he had in his youth, he repaired them and rebuilt classic ones on request. He was damn good at his job and everyone knew it. He now owned three shops, two in New York, and one right down here in New Orleans where he'd grown up.

He'd made something of himself.

In doing so, he'd lost what mattered.

Now he had a chance to rectify that. After all, he'd made himself who he was so he would take the chance and make his own future as well.

They finally made their way up to Sassy's loft apartment. Considering where she'd grown up, this place was small in comparison, but it definitely suited the woman in front of him.

From what he could see from the entryway, there was a living area, a large kitchen and two bedrooms. Every single counter and shelf had something on it. Colors burst from fabric, rugs, and little glass bottles. It would have been overwhelming if the owner had been anyone other than Sassy. Plants littered the area and were alive and flourishing, many with colored blooms. Knickknacks covered the spaces in between and yet what Rafe noticed the most was the lack of personal photos.

Not a single one of her friends from the present or the past.

That was telling...and something to think about later.

She set her bag down and sank onto her couch. "My feet are sore, my muscles ache from hot yoga this morning, and I have growly man friends at the shop I'll have to deal with later, so let's get this over with."

Rafe held back a grin at the word "friends". Well, that was one point for him and Ian. Plus he had to block the image of Sassy doing hot yoga. Talking over serious things while he had a hard-on probably wasn't the best idea.

"You look good, Sass," Rafe said as he slid his hands into his jeans pockets. Ian might have worn his suit and tie, looking like the billionaire he was, but Rafe liked the feel of well-worn denim. Plus, it was what Sassy had always seen him in, so he wasn't going to buck tradition and memories.

She smiled softly, even with the pain in her eyes. "You both look good, too." Her hands came up to her face and she sighed into them. "Jesus, what are you doing here? What are *we* doing here?"

He gave a nod to Ian, who unbuttoned his suit jacket and sat down on the couch next to her. He was ice and harnessed power where Rafe was fire and intense passion. Sassy was a blend of both with the manic energy necessary to handle the two of them.

That's what he loved about the three of them and what he prayed they would be again.

Rafe sat on the coffee table in front of her. They were essentially boxing her in on two sides, yet leaving her an escape with the third.

"We've missed you, Sass. No, don't yell. Please. Not yet. I'm speaking for Ian right now because I know he's felt at least that, but baby, *cariña*, you have to know this. We've missed you these past ten years. Not a day has gone by that I haven't thought about you and Ian." He smiled at the man who'd haunted his dreams right along with the woman in front of him. "We left things off all those years ago in such a shit way that I never thought we'd have a chance to fix it, but Sassy, we can."

She shook her head, those blue streaks in her hair waving wildly. "No. What we had? That was great when we were younger. Things like this, a triad, it only works when the stars are aligned and people don't give a fuck about what others say." She looked at Ian with a sad smile then at Rafe. "Y'all had so much to lose if we kept it up, and frankly, it didn't work because sure, we tried, but it wasn't enough. We were kids who wanted to have fun and now we're older and need to move on."

It hurt to hear the lies coming out of her mouth but he kept his face level. She was lying to herself just as much as to them. Sassy had to know they knew it as well.

"We're older, sure, but that means we know what we want." He nodded to Ian. "I'll let Ian talk about his own feelings and I'll talk about my own. We were kids, yeah. We were best friends from three walks of life and fell in love. Don't lie to me about that. Yeah, we fucked, made love, and had best sex of my life, but we also loved each other. Whatever we do from here on out, don't take that away. It wouldn't hurt so much now if it hadn't meant *everything* back then."

"Sassy, we've all made choices we regret," Ian said. "My biggest one is that while I wasn't the one to walk away physically first, I was the one who left emotionally."

Rafe sucked in a breath, shocked as hell that Ian would admit that. The man who never showed weakness as a young man had grown up.

Thank God.

Sassy growled then shifted away so she could stand. "No. Don't do this. I might've been the one to leave the two of you, but that was because y'all had already left me."

Tears streamed down her face and Rafe stood, unable to hold himself back anymore. He brushed her cheeks, and she pulled away.

"Don't," she whispered.

"I never left, Sass. No matter what you think, I never left." He'd deal with Ian in a moment, but right then, she had to know where he stood. He cupped her face and took his heart in his hands by lowering his head. His lips brushed hers ever so slightly as he fell into the memories of what they'd once been.

She tasted of sugar and spice, and he craved her more now than he ever had before. She pulled away again and sniffed.

"You have to leave. Both of you. I'm...I'm sorry I left the two of you before and broke everything, but I can't do this. I've moved on, and I know the two of you must have as well. Please. Just let me live my life without the two of you. I've done it for ten years, I can do it again."

Ian stood and moved to their side. "We'll leave you alone tonight." Rafe opened his mouth to speak and Ian shook his head. "No, we'll leave, Rafe. Sassy's been through enough tonight. It was a shock to see us. However, darling Sassy, we *will* be back. Or if you want to see us again before then, we're in my old loft."

Sassy's jaw dropped. "You...you're back?"

Ian smiled, but it wasn't nice, more of a determined promise. "Rafe and I are both back in New Orleans for good. We might have stayed away for our own reasons and were apart from each other for even more, but now? We're home now and we want you with us. Take your time. Think. But know that this isn't over."

With that, Ian laid a gentle kiss on her lips and walked to the door. Rafe gripped her chin and forced her gaze to his.

"I know it hurts, but we have to talk and tonight wasn't the time for more than just a few words and tears. I've missed you, my *cariña*. Don't run away. You'll only make me chase harder."

He kissed her once more then followed Ian out, leaving a

stunned Sassy in their wake. It hadn't gone as well as he had hoped, but he came away with far more than he bargained for.

The foundation had been laid, and it was time to see what happened. He'd come back to New Orleans for his future, and if he had anything to say about it, that future would include Ian and Sassy.

Rafe lost them before...he didn't want to do it again.

CHAPTER THREE

"Jesus, I can't believe we did that," Ian Steele mumbled again as he took a sip of his coffee. He'd slept for shit the night before, and combined with the fading adrenaline of seeing Sassy, his body needed the extra boost of caffeine.

He and Rafe had come back to Ian's home after leaving a fragile Sassy alone to find her strength—or at least that was what he hoped she was doing. Rafe had a place of his own in town, but both men had decided if they were going to find what they had before, they needed to remain together and learn who they were now.

Rafe had slept in the guest room, neither of them ready for anything more, and both had an unspoken agreement that they needed Sassy to come back to them first.

"You know, that's the tenth time you said something like that since we left her place last night," Rafe said as he sat down on the bar stool next to him.

"I'll keep saying it until it sinks in." He downed the rest of his coffee since it had grown cold while he'd been sitting there thinking and stood up to get another cup. He lived on the black elixir when he was at work so he knew today would be at least a half-a-pot day.

Ian looked at the man who had once been his best friend, lover and potential future, and sighed. He had no clue how he'd ended up here, but damn, he liked it.

Or at least he would when things worked out.

If they worked out.

Rafe grinned at him, that sexy-as-hell smile just as alluring as it had been when they'd been younger. The man had full arm tattoos that seemed edgier than Sassy's had been. Both sets of tattoos were new to him. The last time he'd seen Sassy and Rafe, the two had some shoulder and back ink, but that was then.

Time moved on and the ink had been laid.

Ian had a full back piece, but he'd gotten that after he left Rafe and Sassy. They hadn't seen his ink, and for some reason, he was nervous about that. He told himself he'd gotten the ink to remind himself that he was moving on, yet in retrospect, it was so he would never forget those he'd left behind.

Rafe stood up and walked behind him, careful not to touch, and Ian felt the pang in his heart at that. As much as the two of them had fallen into an easy rhythm since they'd come back to New Orleans, it had been so long since they'd seen each other that the barriers between them seemed monumental.

They'd been so fucking young when they'd met and thought they could handle a new and exciting relationship. At twenty-five, with the world at his fingertips because of who his family was, he'd thought nothing could touch him.

He'd fallen for Sassy, the bright and fiery woman with secrets he'd never been able to fully uncover, and Rafe, the man from a different world than his in almost every way that mattered.

While Ian was from old money and sophistication, Rafe had been in juvie as a kid even though he'd had a more loving family than Ian's. They'd met when Ian had gotten a flat tire and for some reason, didn't have a spare in his trunk. He'd never felt like such an idiot before that moment. His mother later confessed to borrowing his car, getting a flat, and not mentioning it to him.

He'd forgiven her quickly because he'd met Rafe that day. They had struck up a friendship, and when he walked into the tattoo shop and saw Sassy manning the reception desk, he'd been lost. He and Rafe had truly wanted tattoos when they walked into Midnight Ink. That hadn't been a lie. It had been a reason to get there, but it wasn't the real one.

Rafe had shown up in Ian's New York offices after ten years of not seeing or speaking to each other, surprising the hell out of him. Rafe and Sassy had been on his mind more than usual because Ian had been planning on moving back to New Orleans again. Rafe had come with the proposal that they try again for Sassy.

There really hadn't been a reason to say no.

In fact, it had taken everything in him not to walk around his expensive desk, slam Rafe into the wall, and sear their reunion on both of their minds.

He knew it had taken immense strength for Rafe to come to Ian after so long, but Ian had a feeling if the other man hadn't come to him, Ian would have found Rafe as soon as the move to New Orleans was complete so they could find Sassy.

It had been long enough.

When they had been younger, the three of them had been as thick as thieves and had fallen into bed quickly. It had never really occurred to him until much later that what they were doing was unheard of in most circles. They had simply been in the moment. He and Rafe had always been bisexual though they both preferred women and it had seemed like the next logical step to share each other as well as Sassy.

It hadn't seemed wrong then.

It hadn't *been* wrong then.

Ian, though, had been a fucking idiot and had let second and third thoughts about what they were doing take over his life. He'd let his family's and his own prejudices pull him away emotionally from the relationship that had been one of the only truly good things in his life.

They might have been young, but they had it right.

And he'd ruined that.

Rafe cupped his face and turned his body so they were standing chest to chest. Though they were both wearing shirts and sleep pants, Ian could feel the heat radiating off of the other man. They were practically the same height with Rafe being only an inch or so shorter than him. That meant Ian could stare into those honey colored eyes and sink into them fully.

He'd never thought of himself as a romantic. No, that had always been Rafe. Rafe with the warmth and smile for everyone he cared for, even with the badass persona he carried with him like a shield for others.

Ian on the other hand had been cool, remote. He'd always been that way because it was how he'd been raised. He was the only son of the Steele Empire and had the billions to prove it. He didn't even need to work and could let the Board do everything for him, but he liked the control, the power from making his own decisions and finding ways to make more out of what he had.

"Where are you, *mi corazón?*" Rafe asked, his voice that sexy rasp Ian had loved once and was starting to again.

Ian let out a breath and rested his forehead on Rafe's, needing the comfort even if he wasn't ready for the next step.

"Thinking about the past and what the hell we're doing now."

Rafe pulled his hands away and wrapped his arms around Ian's waist. Ian only hesitated a moment before doing the same. He rested his head on Rafe's shoulder, inhaling that spicy scent that had always been a dangerous drug to Ian.

"It's been a weird couple of weeks, that's for sure," Rafe mumbled into Ian's ear and Ian couldn't hold back his grin.

"What the hell are we doing?" Ian asked as he pulled back and leaned against the counter.

Rafe took a deep breath and shook his head. "I thought we covered this before we went to see Sassy."

"Then let's cover it again because we just shattered her peaceful world, and I feel like a fucking asshole about it."

Rafe narrowed his eyes. "This wasn't all me. I might've gotten the ball rolling, but you were right by my side."

Ian ran a hand through his hair and sighed. He needed to get a fucking hair cut but had been too out of his mind with worry about what he was about to do with his life to deal with it. Plus, he knew Sassy and Rafe liked it long.

"It's been ten years, Rafe. We both moved to New York when Sassy left us, and yet for all that time, we didn't speak to each other. Why was that?"

Rafe leaned against the other counter and folded his arms over his massive—and sexy—chest. Damn it, he needed to stop thinking with his dick and start thinking with his brain or he'd be in trouble.

Again.

"You never contacted me either, Ian. We wanted to cut ties when Sassy left, though you left us long before that."

Ian ignored the slice across his heart since Rafe wasn't saying anything he hadn't known already.

"I...you don't know how sorry I am for putting that distance between the three of us," Ian finally said after a moment of strained silence.

Rafe's eyes widened. "I never thought I'd hear you say that."

"What? You don't think I feel sorry? You don't think I can admit it when I make mistakes? I fucking acted like I was better than the two of you, like I was ashamed of what we had. Because fuck it all, I was."

Rafe looked like Ian had punched him in the gut and Ian cursed. Damn him and his big mouth for speaking without thinking first.

"Shit, that's not what I meant."

Rafe held up a hand. "You said it, and you never say things you don't mean on some level. You're ice, Ian. We both know that."

Ian ran a hand through his hair in a swift, jerky, motion. "Fuck. Yes, I was ashamed of what we had but not because what we had was wrong. Hear me out. You know that a triad in real life is almost unheard of. People don't see it as a legitimate relationship. They think of it as something for the bedroom, and even then, it should be behind closed doors— never spoken of. People don't understand that there are real feelings involved—at least there were for us."

"And by people, you mean your family," Rafe said dryly.

Ian grimaced. "Yeah, them and everyone else in my life

who weren't the three of us. I was a fucking idiot and we both know it. Sassy knows it too. Jesus, if I could turn back time and fix what I did, I'd do it. I hurt the both of you because I was too scared to figure out what the hell I was feeling and deal with it. I loved you both, you have to believe that."

Jesus, he'd never laid it out like that before, but damn it, he wasn't going to hold back like he had before. At least he hoped he wouldn't.

Rafe's features softened somewhat but he didn't smile. Ian missed that smile already, and because of that feeling, he knew he was already in deep. Did he care? He didn't know.

"Plus, Rafe, even ten years ago being in a relationship with you alone would have been cause for scandal in the world I grew up in. Things have changed for the better in that respect in the past decade, but back then it would have taken a strength I didn't possess to be honest with myself and you both. I'm so fucking sorry, Rafe, so very sorry I hurt you by pretending I was better than what we were and pulling back. I'm sorry I never introduced you or Sassy to my family and friends from that circle of my life. I've only ever been truly ashamed once in my life and it wasn't because of what we were, but how I handled it."

Rafe closed his eyes, his body tense and unmoving. Had Ian said too much? He knew that whatever happened from the point where Rafe had come into his office in New York to talk about their future that things would be beyond difficult.

He just prayed it would be worth it.

It *had* to be worth it.

"Again, you leave me breathless," Rafe whispered. "You should have talked to Sassy and me back then. You know it. I know it. And I'm pretty sure Sassy knew it. We were stronger together than we ever were apart. You pulled away and Sassy got scared and left us before we could hurt her. But you know, the truth is, we hurt her anyway. I might have been the one left behind by the both of you, but I made mistakes too. I never fought for you, never fought for Sassy. I just let it all happen and ran to New York with my tail between my legs. I didn't know what the fuck I wanted to do with my life, so I took a chance and ran away."

Ian cupped Rafe's face, startled that he'd taken the initiative this time. He had always been the one in control in the past, yet it had been a long time, and he didn't know where he stood. It would take a lot of trial and error between all of them to find their footing.

Ian was oddly intrigued about how that would all work.

"We're a couple of guilt-ridden wrecks, aren't we?" Ian asked, his voice a deep rasp. "What the hell are we doing, Rafe?" he asked again.

"We're trying to build a future," Rafe said after a moment. "We were young when we found and then broke each other just the same. We're older and hopefully wiser now, Ian. We each have our own lives, you with your business, me with the shops, and Sassy with the family she seems to have made. We're going to have to figure out how to fit into each other's worlds while building our own together at the same time."

"I came to New Orleans to make a life," Ian said. "I grew up here and in New York because of where my parents had homes. I made New York my home when I left here because that's where I thought I could do the best business...and I couldn't stay here after what had happened."

"And I've always had my family here, but I'm here for good now because I was tired of running. Tired of trying to be happy with what I had when I knew I used to have better." Rafe grinned. "Plus my mother wants grandbabies and wants them near her so coming home only made sense."

Ian choked. "Grandbabies?" Jesus. Were they at that stage? He hadn't even spoken to Sassy other than a few words and none of those had been the true apology she'd deserved.

Rafe threw his head back and laughed. "Grandbabies as in what all mothers—especially *my* mother desire most of all. You and I both know we are nowhere near ready to even think about that. Though, you know, we aren't getting any younger." He said that last part with a wicked grin on his face and Ian rolled his eyes.

"Let's take this one thing at a time, shall we?" He moved

away from the counter and went back to his stool. Rafe followed after he poured them each coffees.

"Shit, I forgot I got up to get coffee in the first place. Thanks." He took the mug and sipped. "My head doesn't seem firmly attached to my shoulders at this point."

"You're adorable when you're flustered," Rafe said and batted his eyes.

The coffee Ian had just sipped burned going down the wrong pipe and he coughed, his eyes watered. "Please, don't ever do that again," he laughed, wiping up the mess with a nearby dishtowel.

"You know you love me," Rafe said then closed his mouth as if he'd said too much.

Ian put down his coffee and the towel, then stood again so he was near Rafe. He widened his legs and Ian slid between them needing to be close. The hair on his arms stood on end as the heat and tension in the room rose, but he ignored it, his focus solely on Rafe.

He traced his finger over Rafe's bearded cheek then ran his hand over the other man's head, the short hair sliding between his fingers.

"I do, you know. Love you. I never stopped. Not really. I loved the man you were and from what I've seen, I love who you are now. I know that once we find out who we are since we've grown that I'll fall for you even more."

He licked his lips, scared as all hell that he'd just laid it out there plain for Rafe to see. He'd never said the words before. He'd been too afraid of what he was becoming to be honest with not only himself, but those around him.

Things were different now. If he was going to jump from that ledge he was going to do it on his own terms and put everything he had into it.

There was no holding back now.

He watched Rafe's throat work as the other man swallowed hard. He wasn't sure Rafe was ready for the words or the meaning behind them, even though Rafe had been the one to start it all, and decided to give the man some peace.

Or at least as much peace as he could give.

Rafe's eyes darkened, his breath quickened as Ian

lowered his head. Their lips brushed and Ian groaned, missing the feel of the other man's mouth beneath his. He licked the seam of Rafe's lips and his lover opened for him, groaning as well. Ian deepened the kiss, their tongues colliding, their tastes mingling. He drew back slightly to nip at Rafe's lips, soothing the sting with his tongue, then went back to the kiss he'd craved since Rafe had walked into his New York office with a plan.

He cupped Rafe's face needing to bring the man closer. Rafe's thighs tightened around Ian's waist, forcing him to rock his hips slightly at the pressure. Rafe pulled back with a gasp and Ian trailed his lips along the other man's neck, needing more, demanding more.

Rafe's hands went to Ian's ass, cupping him and Ian rocked harder, his cock tenting his sweats, brushing along Rafe's stomach.

Though they'd had each other in every way possible before, Ian knew they were going too fast right then. They needed Sassy to complete what they had and they both wanted to wait. Reluctantly, he pulled away, leaning his forehead against Rafe's.

They both breathed heavily, and Ian had to close his eyes for a moment to catch himself. God, he'd missed the way Rafe tasted, the way his kisses were always slightly rougher than what they had with Sassy. He loved both ways, and when the three of them came together, it was always so fucking explosive Ian could barely keep up.

"I...I've missed that so much."

Ian opened his eyes and drew back, turning to the sound of the cherished voice that did not belong to Rafe.

"Sassy..." he breathed, unable to comprehend what he was seeing.

She gave him a small smile, her hands clasped in front of her—the demure pose so unlike Sassy it startled him. Rafe stood beside him, almost knocking Ian over in his rush. Ian shifted slightly so Rafe had room, but still was touching him hip to hip.

"I'm sorry. I let myself in. Your doorman seemed to remember me and let me up."

Ian blinked. He had one of the nicer lofts in New Orleans and the doorman had been working for his family for over twenty years. Of course, the man would have remembered Sassy.

No one forgot Sassy.

Ian took a deep breath and nodded. "Don't be sorry. I'm glad he let you in." He could feel the blush creeping up his neck at what she'd walked in on. She might have said she'd missed it, but did she feel left out?

"Don't look like that, Ian. You either, Rafe. I was never jealous of what you two shared. Just like how you two were never jealous of what we shared with each other. God, guys. What you two just did? That sweet yet sexy-as-hell kiss? It meant *everything* to me. You guys used to hold back with each other at first, and it always killed me when you did that. But to see the two of you kissing and feeling that warmth from it makes me feel like the reason I'm here is okay."

Ian blinked then walked around the bar so he could be close to her. He felt Rafe on his heels and liked knowing that as he needed the man's inherent strength that Ian didn't seem to possess at that moment.

"What are you saying?" Rafe asked.

She looked between them both and took a deep breath. "I'm saying that I'm willing to stop hiding from what we were. I'm not saying I'm ready for a full commitment like what I think you both are saying, but I'm willing to take things one day at a time."

Relief slammed into Ian so hard he almost fell to his knees.

Rafe took a step forward and Ian almost followed but Sassy put her hand up. "Give me two weeks."

"What?" he asked.

"Two weeks where we just do coffee and maybe dinner. We can find out who we are now. I don't even know what you both do for a living. Not really. Give me two weeks where we don't touch, kiss, or give into the heat we all feel. I want to make sure that we actually like the people we've become rather than the people we were."

Ian nodded, liking that idea. Things were moving too fast

as it was. He was a planner and liked to have all his facts before he made a decision. Though he seemed to have already made one with his heart, the time to think would be good for his brain.

"Anything you want, Sass," Rafe whispered. "Just hear us out."

She gave them a shaky smile then rolled her shoulders back. "I hope you two know what you're in for. I'm *The* Sassy after all."

Rafe snorted. "There's a story behind that, isn't there?"

She smiled full out and Ian went weak in the knees again. "Of course. That's just one thing you'll have to learn."

If it took him a hundred years, he wasn't sure he'd ever find out every nuance of this woman, but he knew he'd do everything in his power to make it happen.

This was their second chance and he wasn't going to lose it.

CHAPTER FOUR

What was two weeks of celibacy compared to the months she'd been sex-free before this?

Sassy groaned and knocked her head against the wall. Well, considering for the past two weeks when she wasn't at the shop she'd been tied to Rafe and Ian, the lack of sex might just kill her. She'd not had sex with them for ten years; what was two more weeks?

Okay, so she hadn't exactly been in their vicinity for those ten years, so it made it easier, but still, she was a grown woman who could handle her urges.

Barely.

She was a confident, modern woman, so it wasn't out of character for her to take care of her own orgasms when she felt the need. It was just a coincidence that Rafe and Ian happened to be the center of her sweaty, naughty fantasies when she let her hand fall between her legs.

Damn it, she needed to stop thinking about sex and everything that came with it. Her nipples were constantly hard, and she was pretty sure her knees would go weak at just the thought of one of the men touching her.

She was *not* a weak-kneed school girl, and she refused to allow herself to become one.

In the two weeks since she'd walked in on Ian and Rafe in the kitchen going at each other like there was no tomorrow...

No, she couldn't think about the way the two of them had melded together in heat. She had to remain at least somewhat cool when the men arrived. If she looked all hot and bothered, they'd know.

They always knew.

It had been two weeks of coffees, dinners, and the occasional lunch with Rafe and Ian. She had been for coffee with Ian, to dinner with Rafe, and out with both of them, too. She liked that they were learning each other on their own as well as together. Plus, she knew Rafe and Ian would want to be together as well. It was always the three of them, even when they had their individual relationships as well.

She'd loved getting to know who the men were now, though she knew they were going to have to delve into the past again. If this - whatever *this* was - was going to work, they would have to overcome those barriers.

Barriers she'd helped put into place all those years ago.

The knock at the door pulled her out of her thoughts and she shook her head. After she smoothed out her dress, she opened her front door.

The zing that shocked her body just from seeing them never failed to amaze her.

They stood side by side, both dark in looks and in temptation. Ian had left his hair down, the sexy black strands brushing against his shoulders and begging for her touch. He shaved because of his job in the high-visibility world of real estate, but tonight, he'd left some scruff that made him look even more dangerously sexy.

Rafe too had a beard, but his was a bit longer. His honey eyes smoldered as he took in her body and she held back a delicious shiver.

Two weeks of casual dates with these two hadn't been enough.

Today was the end of that time limit she'd given them all. She would hold herself back from jumping them and rubbing all over them like a cat in heat for one more night.

Maybe.

Ian grinned at her and she blinked. Damn it. She loved when he smiled, and he didn't do it nearly often enough. "Are you going to let us in, Sassy?" Ian asked, his voice a raspy promise. "Or should we stand in your doorway for our date? I don't know as I'd mind that much considering I love the way you look in that dress. Those long legs of yours look fucking sexy, and I know they'd look even sexier wrapped around my waist. Rafe's as well."

The little moan that escaped her lips didn't surprise her, but the matching one from Rafe's did. It seemed both men were just as horny as she was.

Two weeks of temptation might have been a good idea for her heart, but her body wanted more.

Now.

She moved back, speechless, and annoyed with herself for being so.

She was *The* Sassy.

She was not an innocent little girl who couldn't speak around men.

She just happened to be *acting* like one at the moment.

Damn them both.

Rafe and Ian strolled into the room looking like jungle cats with all their sleek muscles. Ian wore a perfectly tailored, obviously custom-made designer suit that probably cost more than she made in six months, while Rafe was considerably more laid back and wore nice, high-end jeans and a button-up shirt. They were so different from each other, but the alphas living beneath the surface—and sometimes right out front—made her want to tilt her head and bare her throat, ready for her men to have her at their will.

And enough of that. "So, what's the plan today? It's the first time all three of us have a day off together."

Both men had taken the entire day off rather than waiting for an evening activity. She'd also taken the day off at Midnight Ink with everyone's enthusiastic encouragement.

Apparently, she'd been a little more snippy than usual.

It wasn't her fault she was deprived and moody.

Okay, so maybe it was partially her fault, but a woman never 'fessed up to that.

Rafe leaned against her couch while Ian stood beside

him, his gaze on hers. "Rafe and I didn't have set plans other than to walk around the historic district. It's been awhile since either of us lived here." He winced and Sassy felt bad for him. Referring to their shared past was like walking through a minefield.

She shrugged it off and walked to the kitchen, needing something to drink before they headed out. "I'm up for anything y'all want to do." And at this point, she might just mean, anything. "I'm getting a glass of water. Want one?"

Rafe shook his head. "If you don't want to head out, we can stay here and hang. I know we haven't had much time to spend together just the three of us in private." He walked toward her, following her into the kitchen area. She had an open space so all three of them could see each other no matter where they stood as long as they didn't go to the bedroom areas.

"It's hard to talk about the serious topics in public," Ian added and Sassy's hand clenched her glass.

Good. They were going to talk. Get it out in the open.

It was about fucking time.

"I've said I was sorry before, Sassy, but damn it, I'm so fucking sorry I walked away when I did."

Ian's confession startled her, the blunt words slicing through the lazy morning and bringing her back to the past. They'd already said their apologies but words weren't enough. They all knew that.

What the hell was she doing?

"This is so weird!" Sassy said as she put the glass down and threw her hands up.

Rafe blinked, but Ian didn't move.

"Don't you see that?" she asked. "We're grown ass people taking things slow like it's a fucking business deal and we're not talking about what matters. What the hell are we doing here?"

Rafe stood and strode toward her. "We're finding each other again," he said simply.

"We're forming a relationship," Ian added.

"Why are we doing this? Why now? Why can't I just quit you both?" The last part slipped out and she closed her eyes.

She hadn't meant that, not really, though it needed to be said.

Rafe cupped her face in a swift movement, the hard palms and calloused fingers tightening with great care.

"Why are we doing this?" he whispered. "Because we want to. Because we *need* to. We were a damn good thing ten years ago, and I know if things had been different, we would have made something of it. Can't you feel the chemistry between the three of us? Can't you feel the heat? We can't ignore that just because we're scared. That would make us fucking cowards. And you, Sassy, are not a coward."

Ian came up from behind her like he used to do all those years ago. His hands rested on her hips while his lips slid against her ear. "I'm scared too, Sassy. I'm so scared that we'll fuck this up again because we don't know what we're doing. But you know what? We're older now. Maybe even wiser. We're going to learn from our mistakes and be together again. It's what I want. It's what Rafe wants. And I hope to God it's what you want too."

Hadn't she told them this was what she wanted? Because she damn well did. Just because she wanted it, didn't mean it would be good for her.

She pulled away, needing air. She didn't like this wishy-washy version of herself and she knew if she didn't tell them exactly what had happened before, she couldn't move on.

"When I left you both, I had nowhere else to go," she started.

"Sassy..." Rafe's pained voice forced her to shake her head.

"Let me tell you what happened first. I need to get this off my chest. Then we can move on. Because, know this, I wouldn't be here with the both of you if I didn't want it. But what I want and my state of mind, it seems, are two different things."

"Then tell us, Sass," Ian said.

"I guess I should start earlier. You both know where I came from." God, she hated this part, but if she didn't start there, they wouldn't understand. *She* barely understood. Her men nodded. "I'm the Bordeaux princess. Or at least that's what my dad told me growing up." She gave a soft sigh, but it wasn't because of fond memories. Oh no, there weren't many good ones when it came to her father.

"I had everything I could have wanted, nice clothes, a nice house, fancy schools. We were *old* money." She spat the word and risked a glance at Ian. He too came from old money and merely nodded in understanding. "I was supposed to finish high school and go to college so I could have my degree to put on a pretty gold plaque on the wall of my husband's office like my mother had. I was supposed to marry the man my father chose for me who would have furthered his business and political plans. Then I would have two perfect children who would be raised by nannies, and I would lunch with other women of my ilk and never smile at the wrong person and never entertain an inappropriate thought."

"That wouldn't have been our Sassy," Rafe interrupted and Sassy smiled.

"Damn straight." She ran a hand through her hair and looked at a particular bright red streak. "Can you see this up in a bun or me wearing pearls?"

Ian cleared his throat. "I can picture the pearls."

Her pussy throbbed and she held back a moan. "Don't change the subject."

"I'll keep that in mind for later then."

Damn the man.

"Anyway, I didn't want all of that. I'd known it since I was ten, and yet I stayed there under my father's thumb for another five years." She closed her eyes, trying to fight off the memories. "God, I hated him. I don't know if I do anymore since he doesn't mean anything to me now, but I hated him then. Don't get me wrong, he never hit me, but he would have if he thought it would've worked."

"I'd have killed him if he did," Rafe's voice held a dangerous edge.

Sassy smiled. "You know I can handle my own battles, sugar."

Ian ran his finger down her arm but she didn't pull away, liking the touch too much. "You left when you were fifteen. I remember you saying that and thinking you were too young, but now? You were way too fucking young to have to deal with any of that shit."

She rolled her eyes. "Yes. I was stupid. I was this entitled rich kid who wanted to make my own choices, so what did I do? I ran away and had to learn the hard way that my issues weren't all that much in the grand scheme of things."

Ian gripped her wrist and tugged her so her body was flush against his. She could feel his half-hard cock against her belly, but it was his eyes that held her. The ice and determination nearly brought her to her knees in submission.

That was something she wasn't ready for, and she wasn't sure she would *ever* be ready for it.

"Never say your problems don't matter. Just because someone might have gone through something much worse than you, doesn't diminish your own past. It's not a competition, Sassy. It never had to be."

She closed her eyes, needing to break the connection from his gaze so she wouldn't melt at his feet. She rested her head against his chest and inhaled his musky scent.

"I met good people on the street, and they took pity on me. I learned the hard way how to take care of myself." She pushed away her memories of the cold and hungry nights she couldn't forget. They were part of what made her *The* Sassy. Without that edge, that pain, she didn't want to think about who she might have become.

Sassy turned in Ian's arms to face Rafe. "Then your momma found me," she said with a smile. "I was only eighteen and living in a commune-type thing doing odd jobs to make a living and your momma took me in."

Rafe came to her side and cupped her cheek. "I remember. You were all fire and anger and I knew we'd be best friends."

Sassy rolled her eyes but leaned into his touch, keeping her hands on Ian. "She gave me a job at your father's shop and I learned how to do something I was good at."

"You always ran us better than even my mom," Rafe teased. "She loved that you took up her role as the shop's receptionist."

"I loved it too," she said warmly, remembering how she'd learned to live in a family rather than in the cold mausoleum of her childhood. "I made friends, had a full stomach for the first time in years, and learned to take care of myself without having to fight for it." She turned to Ian. "Then you showed up at the shop with a flat tire a couple years later and I was lost."

Ian kissed her brow and leaned back. "It always surprised me that you and Rafe were never together before I showed up."

"She was too much a part of the family before you were there," Rafe explained.

"He's right. I was almost a sister at that point."

Rafe barked out a laugh. "Oh no, baby, I wouldn't say that. You were way too sexy, even at eighteen, for me to think of you as anything other than someone who was part of the family that I needed to stay clear away from if I wanted to stay on my mom's good side."

Sassy chuckled, already feeling at ease thinking of the good memories rather than dwelling on the painful ones.

Those would come eventually.

"As soon as Ian showed up, I don't know, it was like I couldn't hold back the attraction anymore."

"Thank God you went all in, because those couple years of living in the same house as you but having to act all good and not into you about killed me," Sassy teased.

Ian snorted and ran his hand down her back, soothing her. His hand brushed against her ass and she had to hold herself back from jumping him. As soon as she finished what she was saying, they could move on. It didn't make sense to leave everything unsaid where it could fester.

"Then the three of us were...us." She sighed. "I loved it. I loved you both as a young girl and I wouldn't have changed that year. It hurts so goddamn much to think about what happened at the end, but I wouldn't change anything about what led us there."

"We don't have to lose what we had," Rafe put in.

"No, we already lost it," Sassy countered. "But we can try

for something new. Building on the past and whatifs will only hurt us. I'm already liking the men you've become, and I sure as hell like who I am now. If we start again where we ended, we'd lose everything we've gained since."

"I was a fucking prick to step away. I've said it before and I'd say it again but I think you're tired of hearing it. I won't walk away because of fear." Ian gripped her chin, forcing her gaze to his. "I promise."

She noticed he'd tacked on the qualifier to his not walking away, and she put that back for later. None of them were talking marriage, babies and commitment. At least she certainly wasn't.

"One thing I will say though is that if I hadn't left, if I hadn't been forced to move on, I wouldn't have found Midnight Ink." She stepped away from Ian and Rafe and looked down at the ink on her arms. "I had only a few small ones when I met you and now I'm inked all over. I love it. I love my job and who I get to help daily. I love the family that I've made. So yes, what happened sucked. God, that's not even a good word for it. What happened shattered everything I thought I had and needed, but I grew up because of it. Each step I've taken has made me stronger and made me...Sassy. I love who I am, boys, and I'm not going to change that. What I will say though is this, who I am needs the two of you." At least for right now. She couldn't think beyond that or it would be too much.

Ian growled slightly and moved closer, Rafe on his tail. "This ink?" His finger traced her arm again and a shudder ripped through her at the promise of what was to come. "I want to see it all over. I want to see everything, Sassy. I want everything. That might make me a selfish man, but remember, I'm a Steele. I'm used to getting what I want."

Rafe's hand went down her back and cupped her ass. She moaned and rocked into him. "I might not be a Steele, but I know what I want too. I want you both. What happened is in the past and we're here now. We're going to move on together. You get me?"

She turned to face him and nodded. Oh yeah, she got him.

"Now you know where I'm at and where I've been," she said, knowing their time for talking was drawing to a close.

Thank God.

With a wicked grin, she took Ian's tie in one hand, and gripped Rafe's shirt in the other. "I think it's time for talking to be over. I'm not in the mood to go out today. Do you two have a better idea?"

She looked between the two men as their gazes heated and a little growl escaped.

"Oh yeah," Ian whispered.

"Oh, fuck yeah," Rafe growled.

This is what she wanted right then. Them. Her. No clothes. And a night filled with just the right amount of passion.

This.

CHAPTER FIVE

S assy licked her lips, loving the way both men's eyes darkened as their breathing became ragged. It had always been like this, hot, heady, and ready for anything. Her nipples tightened and her stomach fluttered thinking about what was to come. With two men, she never knew who would go first and set the stage.

Both Ian and Rafe had always been dominant in bed, but not Doms in the same sense that her friend's men were. They knew how she wanted it and gave it to her...after a tease or two. What she didn't know was which man would take charge first.

Ian and Rafe glanced at each other, as if having an unspoken conversation—hopefully deciding on what she'd just been thinking about. Rafe nodded and Sassy sucked in a breath as Ian took two steps toward her and reached around her head, wrapping her long hair around his fist three times.

She panted as he pulled, letting her head fall back so she could stare at him, wanting more.

"Mine," he whispered, then crushed his mouth to hers.

She moaned as his lips pressed against hers, his teeth nipping at them. She opened for him, his tongue tangling with hers. He tasted of mint and coffee, the taste mingling with her own. He tugged on her hair again, the sharp sting shooting right to her pussy.

"Don't forget me," Rafe said, his voice husky.

Ian pulled his lips from her and tugged on her hair again, this time forcing her gaze to Rafe. The act of Ian controlling her kiss with Rafe made her want to come right there. She loved it when they went all badass with her...and with each other.

Rafe cupped her face, then gently lowered his head. His kiss was soft, tempting, where Ian's had been fire and heat—so different from the personas both men showed the world. She closed her eyes, tasting his dark sweetness as she rocked into him and Ian at the same time, their bodies so close to her and each other, making it easy.

Ian pulled her away and brought his lips to hers again. She licked his lips and nibbled, loving the way both men's tastes mixed on her tongue, the heady combination reminding her that she'd missed this, that she'd *craved* this.

Both men took turns kissing her, their hands roaming her back, cupping her ass. She got lost in the moment, not knowing how much time had passed before they both pulled away and turned to each other.

No matter how hot it was to have them kiss her, it made her hotter to watch these two men go at each other. Their moans echoed in the kitchen as their kiss deepened. As rough as they were with her sometimes, they were so much more demanding with each other.

Hot. As. Hell.

She licked her lips again, watching and feeling part of their heat even if no one was touching her. Well, if *they* weren't going to touch her...

Her fingers brushed her nipples and she gasped, the sensation of that gentle brush rocking her. Damn, she was turned on and knew they had a hell of a lot more to do before she'd be sated.

She cupped her breasts, palming the large mounds while pinching her nipples. Her body swayed as she rubbed her legs together, needing the friction so she could come. If she could have just a little orgasm, she'd be able to go slow with her men.

As if they'd heard her thoughts, Rafe and Ian pulled away from each other and faced her.

"Trying to make yourself come without us?" Ian asked, his voice deep with need, his lips wet and swollen from their kisses.

"We should be taking better care of you, *cariña*," Rafe rumbled, his honey eyes dark with intent and promise.

Ian tilted his head. "Since she's been playing with herself, maybe we should let her continue. She doesn't need us, does she?"

She narrowed his eyes. "Hey, stop it with the *I'm a bastard* motif, sugar. You know I can make myself come but right now I want both of you to do it for me. It's only right."

Ian grinned but she wasn't sure she was about to get what she wanted. He always made her wait until it was the best possible. So while she hated him while she was squirming, she loved him when he filled her.

Tricky bastard.

"What do you want, Sassy?" Ian asked.

She licked her lips and glanced down at his erection tenting his pants then saw the matching one in Rafe's. As much as she wanted to come right there, what she *really* wanted was to taste her men.

"You," she whispered.

Ian grinned and Rafe chuckled. "On your knees, baby." He held out his hand and she placed her own in it as she knelt down in front of him.

Her breath quickened as she undid Ian's belt and undid his pants. While some women might hate it, she loved sucking cock. She loved having the power even though Ian and Rafe usually set the pace for her. *She* was the one giving them pleasure, and just the thought of it made her wet as hell.

Because when she was done with them, they'd reciprocate in the best way imaginable.

As quickly as possible, she pulled down his boxer briefs enough so she could grip his cock. He filled her hand, hot, hard, and ready for her mouth. Not wanting to leave Rafe out, she pressed a kiss to Ian's cock, then undid Rafe's pants.

Ian pulled at her hair, fisting it as he had before while Rafe held her shoulder. She pulled Rafe out of his pants and licked the crown while she wrapped her hand around the base of Ian's shaft.

She hadn't had a threesome since she'd been with Ian and Rafe, but the dexterity it took to pleasure them both at the same time apparently had never gone away.

With one last wink at her men, she got down to business, licking up Rafe's length, before doing the same to Ian's. Both men moaned and she smiled before sucking on the head of Ian's cock, letting her tongue brush the seam. He bucked into her mouth and she put her hand on his hip to keep him steady. She pulled away slightly to look up at him.

"Let me taste you both first before you fuck my mouth."

"I love that dirty mouth of yours," Rafe said and she rolled her eyes.

She went back to what she was doing and licked the drop of pre-cum on the tip of Ian's dick before doing the same to Rafe's. She held both of their cocks in her hands and she gripped them hard, rolling her wrists slightly as she pulled upward so she could glide along their lengths. Ian's dick was slightly longer with a curve to the left that hit a spot right inside her that used to make her eyes cross when he fucked her hard. Rafe's was thicker and stretched her in a sexy as fuck way whenever he pushed that meaty cock inside of her.

Damn, she'd missed these two.

Rafe cupped her cheek and grinned. "Let me watch you take Ian, Sass. Then you can have me. I love it when you suck on his balls when you go down on him."

She held back the moan in her throat then nodded before turning to Ian. Because she knew Rafe—and Ian—loved it, she pushed his cock up to his belly and sucked on his balls. She rolled one on her tongue, moved to the other and did the same. She could feel Ian's dick throb as she sucked, so she repeated the process. When she couldn't take it anymore— and had a feeling Ian was feeling the same—she moved to suck Ian down in one movement. His gasp of need and surprise was music to her ears. She pulled back, eager to continue once she found her breath.

"Let me help you," Rafe said and she looked up to see him standing behind Ian. He gripped the base of Ian's shaft and held it up to her lips.

She grinned, then sucked Ian down again. Ian's hand tightened in her hair and she froze, letting her jaw widen. With Rafe's help directing, Ian fucked her mouth. When he pulled out, she rolled her tongue, then swallowed on the tip as he sank to the back of her throat.

"Jesus," Ian grunted, but didn't stop moving his hips.

She hollowed her cheeks and hummed, looking up to see Ian's hand resting on Rafe's shoulder. Whenever her mouth would leave his dick, Rafe's hand would squeeze and run along his length.

Finally, Ian pulled away, his dick still hard since he hadn't come, and moved out of the way. Rafe stood there, his cock jutting out. She licked down his length as Ian came around behind her. She looked over and grinned as he shucked his clothes.

"What are you doing back there?" she purred.

Ian chuckled then gripped her shoulders. "Suck him off, then I'm going to eat that pretty pussy of yours, darling."

Well, that sounded like a plan.

She swallowed Rafe whole, bobbing her head up and down as she set the pace this time. Ian's hands came from around her waist as he knelt behind her. He cupped her breasts through her bra and pinched her nipples—hard.

She gasped around Rafe's cock as Ian pinched even harder and twisted slightly. The pain made her pussy ache, ready for either of their cocks, but she knew she would have to wait. She increased the pace, wanting to make Rafe lose control.

Ian's hands left her breasts only to go to Rafe's thighs. The sight of his strong hands on Rafe's even stronger legs almost made her come, but she held back. Ian rolled Rafe's balls in his hand as she hollowed her cheeks to suck him harder.

Rafe pulled back and she blinked up at him while resting on Ian's shoulder.

"I'm with Ian, here, *carina*, as much as I want to come down that pretty throat of yours, I'd rather make you come around my cock first."

She licked her lips, the salty taste of both men lingering. "Whatever you say."

Ian chuckled against her as he kissed her neck. "I like the sound of that."

Before she could blink, she found herself standing, both men pulling off her clothes, and then she was on her back on the kitchen island with Ian's head between her legs.

"Ian!" she gasped at the first swipe of his tongue. He licked and nibbled along her slit before honing in on her clit. She rocked her body against his face, wanting more.

"Let Ian taste you, Sassy," Rafe whispered as he pushed down on her hips, giving Ian more control.

She tried to keep her eyes from rolling to the back of her head, but it was damn hard with Ian licking her up like a cat with cream. It was even harder when Rafe sucked on one nipple, pinching the other with his nimble fingers. He bit down on the bud while he rolled the other and she came against Ian's face and around the two fingers he'd pumped into her.

Their names left her lips on a scream as they kept up their attack, not relenting until she found herself cresting another wave. She'd only ever had so many orgasms at once with these two and she thanked God some things never changed.

Her body went limp even though she still wanted to feel them both inside her. She felt Ian lift her up into his arms and carry her to the L-shaped couch with the deep cushions that were perfect for two people to cuddle on comfortably.

All three of them were soon naked and Ian was between her legs as she lay on her back so she was splayed out for them both. Ian stood over her, bending so he could reach her legs while Rafe stood behind him. Rafe reached around Ian's body and rolled a condom over his cock and Sassy about swallowed her tongue.

No matter how hot she thought she was with either of them, she loved watching them together because it made their heat rise even more. It might make her a dirty, dirty Sassy, but she didn't care.

She fucking loved it.

Ian turned to the side and she caught something that hadn't been there the last time they'd made love.

"Is that ink on your back?" she asked.

Rafe's eyes widened and he went behind Ian. "Holy shit, it's the Irish trinity. Dude. That's fucking gorgeous."

Sassy gave a watery smile. "You have a trinity on your back. Let me see?"

Ian gripped his dick, but turned for her.

God, it was beautiful. Heavy and dark, the three parts of the trinity were interwoven and carved in Gaelic. It was amazing.

The fact that he'd done that *after* they were broken up was telling, but she couldn't talk about that now. Not when she wanted him inside her.

Now.

"Ready?" Ian asked, his voice strained.

"Always," she whispered then moaned as Ian sank into her inch by agonizing inch.

He filled her up, their hips aligning, brushing against each other while she stretched to accommodate his length— just how she knew she'd have to stretch again to accommodate Rafe's girth.

"Jesus, you feel so fucking good," Ian gritted out then pulled out slightly.

Sassy moaned as her inner walls clenched, not wanting to let him go.

"Look over here, Sass," Rafe whispered. "And get up on your elbows."

When she was focused on Ian, Rafe had moved so he was standing on the couch beside her, his cock right at her lips. She opened for him, and let go. Both men fucked her hard, Ian in her pussy, Rafe in her mouth. Rafe's hands tangled in her hair, while Ian's gripped her hips.

Ian pumped his cock in and out of her at a steady, unending, yet exquisite pace, until he slammed into her hard once more and shouted her name. Sassy let go of Rafe's cock, and kissed Ian as he filled the condom. Ian pumped again, this time, his thumb thrumming her clit and she came, her moan covered up by Ian's mouth.

He pulled out even as her body still shook and Rafe slid inside her. She let her head fall back to rest on the couch as Ian went to dispose of the condom. Rafe must have covered himself with another one when she'd been coming because she could see it wrapped around him as he pulled out of her. His fingers dug into her waist as he pistoned into her, their gazes locked.

Ian came back into the room and sat beside her his hands roaming her body. He cupped her breasts, suckled on her nipples, and then moved his hand down to play with her clit as Rafe made love to her.

"Shit, every time you suck on her nipples, I can feel her clench around me," Rafe grunted.

Ian let go of her nipple with a pop. "Now you know how I feel, love," he said to Rafe, then went back to work on her breasts.

Needing to be connected even more than she was, she wrapped her hand around one of Rafe's wrists and tangled her free hand into Ian's hair. She closed her eyes, lost in the movements and sensations until she found the wave again and came crashing down once more, this time with Rafe as he jetted into the condom.

Rafe pulled out, jogging away to take care of the condom while Ian and Sassy laid down on the couch.

"I've missed that, missed you," Ian mumbled.

She smiled and sank into him.

Rafe came back and pulled a blanket off the back of the couch. Ian pulled her on top of his body as Rafe laid next to them. She rolled on her stomach so she could cuddle with both her guys, her limbs limp, her body sated.

"God, we have to do that again," she whispered.

Rafe patted her butt and chuckled. "Let me rest a bit before round two. I'm not as young as I used to be."

She smiled and waited for Ian's response only to find him passed out next to Rafe. "I guess we tired him out."

She looked at Rafe and laughed at both her sleeping men. With a happy sigh, she lay down on top of both of them and wiggled.

"Yep, still got it."

CHAPTER SIX

"Are you sure I look okay? Should I cover up my ink?"

Rafe closed his eyes and held back the retort that came to his lips. While he loved the woman in front of him, the fact she was even asking that question made him want to bang his head against the wall. She shouldn't have been as nervous as she was, and yet there was no stopping it apparently.

She'd put on nice slacks and a cute lacy top thing that made her breasts look fucking lickable as hell, but it wasn't the Sassy he knew and loved. She'd even put her hair up into this bun thing that only elongated her neck.

He walked slowly toward her and cupped her face. The worry in those sexy brown eyes of hers made him want to hold her and never let her go.

Not that she'd let him.

No, she'd push away and take care of herself because that's who she was. Or at least who she usually was. This Sassy in front of him wasn't that woman. He needed to fix that and alleviate her fears.

"Sass, stop it and breathe, *cariña*." He brushed his lips against hers and she relaxed. "We're just going to my parents' home for dinner. You've had countless dinners with them before. The only difference is that now we're a bit older."

She grimaced and he kissed her again. "It's not like it was before, Rafe. I used to be their ward or live-in or whatever. They knew I was dating you but I don't know if they knew we were with Ian at the time."

Rafe let out a breath. "I don't know either, baby. We kept it to ourselves because we were afraid of what everyone would think, but we aren't those people anymore. You know Ian would be here with us if he hadn't had to work."

They couldn't ignore the possibility of misconceptions like they had when they were younger. Their relationship wouldn't survive if they did.

He could sense her tension and see the uncertainty in her eyes.

They were doing this to her, turning the vibrant and sexy woman into a pile of nerves.

Damn it.

He ran his hand down her back and cupped her ass. The resulting flare of heat in her eyes made him smile.

There she is.

Sassy pulled back somewhat and looked down at her body before shaking her head. "What the hell am I wearing?"

Rafe held back, knowing if he smiled, she would hit him. Hard. "I didn't realize you owned that sexy secretary get-up."

She narrowed her eyes at him. "I believe they are called administrative assistants now."

He held up his hands in mock surrender. "My apologies."

"And if I were dressed as a sexy secretary, I'd be wearing a skirt so you could fuck me on top of the desk. Come on, now, you know that's how all the good porn does it."

Rafe threw his head back and laughed even as his cock hardened at the thought of Sassy in heels and a little skirt as he fucked her on top of his desk.

Or maybe Ian's desk.

Yeah, that would be better since Ian had a bigger office, and the whole suit and tie thing totally fit those fantasies. Maybe he and Sassy could fuck Ian over that desk too.

"Oh my God, stop thinking about sex right now, Rafe Chavez!" Sassy slapped his shoulder and Rafe snorted.

"You started it, babe." Well, maybe. This whole

conversation was a blur of angst and sexy as hell heels.

"We are on our way to go see your mother. She'll know what we've been thinking. She *always* knows."

Rafe grinned. He sure as hell hoped his mom didn't know *everything* that went on in his head. He wasn't even sure that she knew about him and Ian. He'd always been bisexual, but had never been out of the closet to his parents. He didn't know what they'd have thought about it.

What they would think now...

He'd been such a little shit as a teenager that when he'd finally found his way and learned to act like a man, he'd been afraid to break any trust he'd formed again. He'd hidden his feelings for Ian as anything more than his best friend from the family, and Rafe knew it played a role in Ian's departure.

Ian and Sassy weren't the only two who held blame for the demise of their relationship.

Rafe had his own failures and he knew he needed to redeem those.

Today was the first step in the right direction by bringing Sassy home. He'd hoped to bring Ian as well, but it might have been just as well he wasn't with them. Taking baby steps sounded like a good way to approach this.

Jesus, this was fucking complicated.

He shook his head, trying to clear his thoughts. If he went into the day thinking the worst, he'd just stress himself out just as he was sure Sassy had been doing from the way she was dressed.

Rafe looked down at his own dark jeans and button down shirt, then at Sassy. "*Cariña*, put on jeans and keep that sexy as hell top. It shows off the ink on your arms and when you bend over, I'll be able to see the ink on your back."

Her eyes widened. "I'm not bending over in your parents' house for you." She gave a saucy grin. "And no promises, but I might tease you if you annoy me enough."

He kissed her hard, sliding his tongue against hers. "Damn it. You get me worked up, Sass. But really, you're welcome to wear jeans and anything you want." He reached around and unclipped her hair. The long tresses fell over her shoulders in waves, and he sighed at the sight. Damn, his woman was fucking sexy as hell. He'd have to keep her hair up so he could pull it down again, but next time, she'd be naked.

Fuck. Yeah.

"You're thinking about sex again."

He licked his lips. "Hell yeah, but don't worry. I can control myself." Maybe. "Show your ink, let your hair down, wear what you want to in order to feel comfortable and be yourself. There's no reason to hide."

Her eyes filled with tears, and she blinked them away, but not before one fell down her cheek. His heart ached as he brushed away the moisture with his thumb.

"Sassy, baby, what's wrong?" He'd do whatever he could to make sure she knew she was special and *his*. God, give him strength.

"Other than you're acting all rough and perfect at the same time?" She shook her head then rolled her shoulders back. "I left them too, Rafe. What if they hate me for it? I didn't stay in contact because I was scared. I might've only lived twenty minutes away, but there could have been an ocean between us considering how it felt."

He closed his eyes and cursed himself. Of course that's what she'd be freaking out about. She'd lived with his family for a long time and walked out on them just the same. She'd done it to protect herself, and in doing so, she'd hurt his family. But not to the extent she must be thinking.

His family was very forgiving when it came to people they loved.

He should know.

"*Cariña*, stop worrying. They missed you, and yes, they were worried, but they knew you'd left for a reason. Let's go see them and get the hard part over with. They invited you over, Sass. They *want* you there. We'll talk, laugh, eat good food, and then when we get home, we'll make love, and hopefully, this time actually make it to the bed on the first try."

She laughed softly, exactly as he'd intended. "We always say we're going to make it to the bed and only end up sleeping there since we've tired ourselves out everywhere else."

He cupped her ass, bringing her flush against his body. His rock hard cock pressed against her belly and she raised a brow.

"You did this," he groaned.

Her hand went between them and ran along his length. "No, honey, you did this, but I'll take care of it. Later." She winked. "We're going to be late if I don't change now and head out. Two minutes!" She sashayed to the bedroom, his gaze following that generous ass of hers. He just shook his head.

Yep, that's the Sassy he loved. It only took her getting him turned on and turned inside out for her to come back.

By the time she'd changed into ass-hugging jeans that he'd enjoy peeling her out of later, and made their way to his parents' house, they were only five minutes late. Not bad considering Rafe had taken the time to make sure Sassy's jeans fit just right using the palms of his hands.

From the way Sassy glowed, he had a feeling his mom would know *exactly* why they were late, but he didn't care. He finally had the woman of his dreams next to him and the man of his dreams in his heart—and he hoped, waiting for them when they got home.

He didn't need much else.

Before they could even make it up the porch steps, his mother opened the front door and approached them with her arms opened wide.

"Sassy!" His mother pulled Sassy up the steps and enveloped her in those same strong arms that had held him countless times. Though his mother was at least a foot shorter and could practically fit in his pocket, she was stronger than anyone he'd known.

"Mrs. Chavez." Sassy's reply was a little stilted, but there was warmth there that went straight to Rafe's heart. This was her family too—he just had to make sure she understood that and didn't pull away.

Again.

His mom pulled back and frowned. "Mrs. Chavez? Do you think I'm my husband Carlos's mother and not Rafe's?

No, honey, you call me Juanita or Mom. I'll take nothing else."

Sassy grinned and Rafe pulled his mother away a bit so he could kiss her cheek. "Thank you, Mom," he whispered and she patted his cheek.

"You're a good boy, Rafe. Thank you for bringing Sassy home to us." There was a twinkle in her eyes he couldn't interpret. "And next time, I expect to you to bring Ian too. It's about time the three of you were together again."

Rafe stopped breathing, his feet frozen to the spot. "Wha...what?"

His mom shook her head, then wrapped her arm around Sassy's waist. "I knew then that the three of you were together. You can't fool me, young man. You all were so in love you couldn't hide it even if you tried. I know Ian thought he'd pulled off the cool and remote rich kid. He didn't, honey. He was in so deep with you, just as you and Sassy were with him, it was obvious."

Sassy reached and gripped his hand, but he still couldn't process what his mom was saying. She'd known? This whole time, she'd known. He thought he'd hidden it so well. Apparently he shouldn't have even tried.

"I don't know what you're thinking, Rafe, but know this, I've loved you since I first found out I was pregnant with you, and I will *always* love you. Your family feels the same. You have three sisters, two brothers, a father, and countless other members of the family in there waiting to see you and Sass. They love you and they won't turn their backs on you for loving who you love. And when you bring Ian by, we'll be the same."

Rafe lowered his head, but pulled his mom close, bringing Sassy with her. He wrapped his arms around his girls, the weight of what he'd been holding close sliding off his shoulders.

"I can't believe you knew this whole time," he rasped, his body shaking. From relief or the overwhelming urge to run to Ian and bring him there too, he didn't know.

"Honey, you can't slide things by me." His mom squeezed him one more time, then pulled away. "Now, let's get you two inside and fed. They're probably already pressed up against the window trying to see what the holdup is."

"I'm surprised they haven't come out yet," Sassy said as she tangled her fingers with his.

He gripped her hand, thankful for the anchor. She'd always been his anchor even when she'd been the one on the run. Without her...well, he hadn't been whole.

They walked inside and were greeted by his family, smiles and hugs bringing Sassy—and Rafe—into the fold. As much as Sassy had left them, he never forgot he'd done the same. Oh, he'd come back for holidays and births, but he'd made a home somewhere else.

Now he was back and he had to learn to blend with his family like he had before.

"Rafe," his father's deep voice pulled him out of his thoughts. The man had his arm around Sassy's shoulder and a grin on his face. "Good to see you could make it, *niño*."

"Dad," he said and hugged the man hard, bringing Sassy into it like he had with his mom.

His dad grinned but there was tension in his eyes like there had been at work—something Rafe had hoped would fade with time. "When you get time, we need to talk about the shop. There are things...*niño*, you know that I trust you with everything, but some things do not need to change."

When his father said everything, it didn't mean what it should, but this was neither the time nor place. His family might agree with his lifestyle—which was a surprise in itself—but having a father and son run a business together didn't always go smoothly.

"We can talk about it later," Rafe said with a smile, not wanting to cause an issue when today needed to be about Sassy—and later Ian. "For now, let's eat good food and show my girl off." He kissed Sassy's brow and she laughed.

"I can usually show myself off, sugar, but if you want to do the honors, I'm all yours."

He smiled and nodded at his father who got the message, then walked to the backyard where his family was partying.

It was odd how much he wanted Ian to be there with them, celebrating their time together as a triad. He knew Ian had planned on going public with the three of them and with the fact that Rafe's family accepted him. This just might work.

He looked down at the woman in his arms and sighed.

It better work because he'd do anything for her, anything for Ian. He just needed to make sure that it wouldn't be for nothing because if they ran away from him again...well...

He didn't know what he'd do then.

He'd been broken once before and if it happened again, he wasn't sure he'd be able to put himself to rights. Sassy and Ian had quickly become his whole world and that scared him.

Rafe would just have to prove to them that they could make it work. With the scent of his mother's cooking, the sounds of laughter and happiness, and the feel of acceptance surrounding them, it just might be possible.

Once dinner was over, they made their way to her place in record time. He barely had the engine off before Sassy was out of the car with him following. He chased her up the stairs, a grin on his face.

When she opened the door, he pushed her through it, held on to her wrist, and slammed her against it as it shut.

Her eyes widened and she grinned. "Eager, are we?"

He cupped her face. "Did I hurt you?" He hadn't meant to slam her into the door that hard, but damn, after hours of being with others and unable to be near enough to her, he couldn't hold back.

She squeezed his ass and rocked against him, the hard ridge of his cock digging into her belly. "I liked it. You held my wrist and used the other hand to hold the door so I wouldn't hit too hard. The door just made a loud sound, that's why it made it look like you were rough." She grinned. "Well, you were rough, but in the sexy-alpha-way. Now, go on and finish your plan. I hope you're going to fuck me against it."

He shook his head. This woman understood him so fucking well it scared him. "I'm going to eat you out against the door and then I'll make love to you in your bed because I promised."

Her eyes darkened and she gave him that little smile that always went straight to his cock. He tugged off his shirt and watched the way her gaze followed the lines of his abs and chest. He'd work out even more if he could keep getting her to look at him like that. He wrapped his hand around the back of her neck and brought her in for a kiss. He loved the way she tasted, all sweet and spicy at the same time.

He pulled back and tugged up her shirt. She lifted her arms and he took it off her then gazed down at her in her bra and sexy jeans. He'd told her that he loved the way they molded to her thighs and ass and he'd meant it.

God, he fucking loved her curves.

He undid the front clasp of her bra so her breasts were bare. Her rose colored nipples were hard and begged for his mouth. He lowered his head and sucked one into his mouth, using his hand to plump her breast as he nibbled and licked. He moved to her other breast and knelt down. She was just short enough that he could suck on her nipples and get a face full of breasts.

Seriously, he loved this part.

He moved down her body, leaving kisses and bites down her stomach until he came to the top of her jeans. He undid the button and zipper and pulled her pants down over her ass, bringing her panties with them.

"Rafe," she moaned as she wiggled out of her jeans and he threw them to the side.

"God, I love your taste," he said before he pulled one leg over his shoulder and licked her slit. She put one hand on his shoulders to steady herself and he lapped her up. He spread her and fucked her with his tongue and then two fingers. Each moan she made coincided with the sexy flutter of her pussy and he knew she was close.

He reached around with his free hand and probed her hole, knowing they hadn't done anal play yet, but it would be coming.

Soon.

"Yes, Rafe, just like that. My vibrator with the attachment doesn't do it like your fingers do."

He about came in his pants at her admission but kept his mouth on her clit, wanting her to come. His Sassy liked to play with herself all kinky like?

He was one lucky man.

He hummed against her clit as his fingers passed the tight ring of muscles. He only had her own juices as lube so he only put the tip in, not wanting to hurt her.

"Rafe!" She came on his tongue and he kept the pressure on her clit, knowing she liked it best that way.

With her eyes still closed, he stood up, keeping his hand on her hip so she wouldn't fall, then picked her up. He carried her to the bedroom like he'd promised before, her head on his shoulder, her body still shaking.

"How do you want it, Sass?"

"Fuck me on all fours. I love it when you go deep like that."

He grinned. "You're a dirty girl."

She rolled her eyes and he put her on her feet. "You're such a dude for saying that."

He slapped her ass as she turned and moaned even as she looked over her shoulder to raise a brow at him.

"Get on all fours in the middle of the bed, *cariña*. That way when you get weak-kneed, you won't fall on your face."

She laughed, exactly as he'd wanted her to, and he pulled off his pants after he took the condom from his wallet. He rolled it on his length, his cock beyond ready to sink in to that pretty pink pussy.

He slid into her in one thrust, and they both sighed at the same time. He pumped into her, his fingers digging into her hips as he fucked her. He leaned over her so his front was to her back, even as her hips lifted to meet his thrusts.

"Kiss me, my Sassy," he whispered.

"Mine," she said as she turned her head.

"Yours." He took her lips and came hard within her. He swiveled his hips so his groin slid along her clit and she shuddered. Her inner walls clenched around him as she came with him.

"Mine," he said back.

"Yours," she whispered, her voice heavy.

They both sank down to the bed, his cock still inside her yet he wasn't ready to move. He cupped her cheek and she looked over her shoulder at him once more so he could take her lips. Their sweat-slick bodies lay in a pile as their breathing finally evened and he swallowed hard, too overcome with the past and their future to speak.

This was what he'd wanted all those years and yet hadn't known he craved it. Sassy was his and Ian's. He just prayed to God they didn't leave him.

Again.

CHAPTER SEVEN

Ian ran his hand down his chest, smoothing out his tie. He had no idea why he felt so stiff and uncomfortable right then but it bothered him. He closed his eyes for a moment, taking a deep breath. If he didn't get his act together, he'd scare the other patrons of the restaurant. With his dark looks and even darker scowl, most people knew to comply to his demands.

That's how he'd made his way up the ladder of high-end real estate.

That and the Steele name.

Tonight he would use that name to get the table he desired but would do his best to lose the scowl. After all, he didn't want to scare away Sassy on their date.

"Ian? Are you coming?"

He blinked away the doubts that seemed to creep in when he least wanted them, and turned to his date, his Sassy.

It didn't matter to him if she wore cutoff jeans, a flowing hippy dress, or nothing at all—he loved the way his woman looked.

Right then though, her beauty made him so lightheaded he thought he'd pass out.

They were dining out at one of the nicer restaurants in New Orleans that night, and she'd apparently decided to go formal. Her long black dress hugged her curves in all the right places. The heart neckline accentuated her breasts but didn't make her look cheap. No, there was nothing cheap about Sassy and he loved that about her.

She'd left her hair down. Rafe told him she'd tried to put her hair up when they visited his parents and he'd taken it down. Ian sensed she left it down this time for him, something that not only surprised him, but made him fall for her all over again.

Her wild hair had one simple streak of black in it to match her dress, understated for what she normally did with it, but he still liked it. Rafe had mentioned how sexy she looked when he'd taken down her hair though, and Ian knew that they'd have to play with that sometime.

Right now, however, it was all about Ian and Sassy. They might have been a triad, but they were also comprised of three coupled relationships. That made it imperative that they not only spend time as the three of them, but on their own as well.

It wasn't that he liked one more than the other, he just knew that he needed both. He needed time alone with Sassy as much as he needed time alone with Rafe. When the three of them were together it was like they'd put all those pieces together forming a finished puzzle only they understood.

Complicated didn't even begin to cover it, but he didn't care.

He loved the two of them, and he'd be damned if he'd walk away again and lose it all.

"Ian, what is wrong with you tonight?"

He shook his head, then tucked her hand in his, bringing it to his lips. He brushed a soft kiss against her fingers and smiled.

"I'm sorry, love. I can't seem to get out of my own head tonight." They were standing in front of his car as the valet stood by them, his hand outstretched. Ian gave a cool smile and a nod to the younger man, as well as his keys, before taking Sassy's arm in his. "Now let me get you inside before I stand here all night woolgathering."

She frowned at him but followed, her arm tucked beneath his. "You can woolgather all you want Ian, but if you'd rather stay at home tonight, we can leave."

There was something in her tone that sparked a memory and he cursed himself. Before, when he'd pulled away emotionally, he'd acted aloof, locked inside his own head. If he wasn't careful, Sassy and Rafe would think he was doing the same now.

It wasn't even close to being the same mindset for him, but he understood their fears. It might have grated that they didn't trust him not to walk away, but he couldn't blame them.

The hostess sat them at a table in one of the secluded corners as requested. With a nod to the woman, he pulled Sassy's chair back and helped her sit.

"You know, I could have done that on my own, but I kind of like it when you act all old world manners on me."

Ian grinned, enjoying the fact that no matter what she wore, she was still Sassy.

"You might like it a little when I act old fashioned, but if I were to do anything more than what I just did, you'd have my balls in a vice in no time."

She winked, her eyes full of laughter. "Damn straight."

Their waiter brought the wine list and told them about the specials. Ian didn't care what he ate that night since he knew everything tasted great, and as long as Sassy was his dinner companion, he'd have the night he wanted.

He raised a brow in Sassy's direction. "Would you like to get one of each of the specials and call it a day?"

Sassy's eyes widened a bit before she smiled. "Sure. That makes things easy."

The waiter nodded and left while Ian took a sip of his water. "Why did it look like I surprised you with our order?"

Her brows furrowed as she thought about her words then licked her lips. "I don't want you to get the wrong impression of what I'm going to say."

He frowned. "You never have to hold anything back from me."

"I know that. Or at least I think I do now. Back when we were first dating, you used to take a while to pick your food. Like you needed it to be just right or something. And when we walked in here, I saw a few suits look in your direction for some kind of acknowledgment of their presence, but you didn't respond. You just looked at me the whole time. Don't get me wrong, I freaking love that you don't seem to care about what others think, but it's different than how you used to be."

Ian frowned, knowing she was right, but not liking who he'd used to be if that's what she thought. "Have I been that way in the past weeks?"

He hadn't thought he'd changed that dramatically since he'd seen her again. Yes, he *had* grown up in the past ten years, but this wasn't the first time they'd been out on a date alone together.

Sassy shook her head then reached out for his hand. "No, you've been great, Ian. I promise. I only mentioned it now because I noticed how different you are. Not bad different...just...I don't know." She sighed. "I like you, Ian. I liked the old you but I really like this new you."

He tangled his fingers with hers over the table and smiled. "I like you too, Sassy, both the old you and the new one. That's what happens when we grow up, I guess. We figure out if the new people can fit together as they used to." Images of how sexy she looked when they fit together a certain way filled his mind and he held back a groan.

"I know what you're thinking and, yeah, we fit together that way too." She winked and he threw his head back and laughed.

He could feel the stares from the people around them but he didn't care. This woman made him feel like he was something special for who he was, not for what he could do for her. He'd loved her all those years ago in a way he hadn't thought possible, but now it was even deeper.

He was one lucky bastard.

"Ian, I thought that was you."

Ian turned to the deep voice who'd spoken and gave a small smile. Dean was one of his father's friends and while the man had always been tolerable, he wasn't one of Ian's favorite people.

"Dean," Ian said as he stood. He glanced at Sassy who seemed as annoyed as he was that they were interrupted. The two of them had clearly been on a date and in the middle of a conversation, but people of his father's ilk, like Dean, didn't care about things like being considerate.

"I heard you'd moved back to town." The man didn't even look in Sassy's direction and Ian merely raised a brow.

"Let me introduce you to my companion, Sassy." He held his hand out for Sassy who stood on her own.

She held her hand out for Dean who blinked then shook her hand awkwardly. "Nice to meet you, Dean," she said politely.

"You as well, my dear," he said, clearly not quite sure what to make of her. After all, Sassy was unlike anyone Ian had dated in New York. While the ice queens Ian had tolerated in the city had been platinum blonde and almost frail, Sassy was lush and looked fucking delicious.

There was only one Sassy.

"Do you work with Ian or his father?" she asked, seemingly genuinely interested.

"I work with Richard, yes, but I hope that now Ian is back in town, we can do some business together."

Sassy smiled, her eyes warm. "You can't go wrong with Ian."

Dean smiled back, enchanted. "That I know. I'm sorry for interrupting your dinner, and I hope you two enjoy your evening. Ian, when you're settled, give me a call. I'd love to talk in a more...appropriate setting."

They said their goodbyes and sat down again. "Sorry about that," he said as their server brought their meals.

Sassy waved it off. "Don't worry about it. It wasn't like you could ignore him and he didn't outright say I wasn't right for you, so we're fine."

Ian raised a brow. "And if I'd said your last name, he'd put two and two together and figure out who you really are."

She shrugged, but he could see the spark fading in her eyes. Damn it. He shouldn't have brought it up.

"Whatever. I'm not that girl anymore and we both damn well know it. But he did seem like he didn't think of me like something on the bottom of his shoe or a hooker by the time he left."

Ian snorted. "Baby, you don't look like a hooker."

"I'm not as polished as any of the woman in here, but I don't really care."

He held her hand and brought it to his lips. "Do you think I care? I love you, Sassy. You know that. I love Rafe too." He'd whispered both, but if someone heard, it didn't matter to him. "Sassy, whatever happens from here on out, I'm not going anywhere. I made mistakes before. We both know this. I'm not going to make them again."

"And if people like Dean freak out about the three of us?"

"Then fuck them."

"Ian," she whispered, then shook her head.

"Really. Fuck them. They will get used to us. As long as they don't hurt you or Rafe, I don't care what happens outside of the three of us."

"You can't really mean that, can you?"

He let out a breath. "I'm not going anywhere. You're not going to truly believe that until you see it, so why don't we finish eating our meal, then go back to my place for dessert."

Her gaze heated and he had to adjust his pants. "Well, fuck, I'd actually meant caramel ice cream, but I like where your mind went just then."

She bounced in her seat. "Caramel ice cream? Can we have both?"

The image of licking the sweet mixture from her nipples filled his mind and he coughed. "Should I just ask for the check now?"

"Now, sugar, or I'm gonna run out of here on my own and have you follow."

The waiter quickly came when he was called and Ian left enough cash to cover the bill and then some. They made their way to his car and piled in before he drove like a bat out of hell to his place. He purposely kept his eyes and hands off Sassy the whole time or they wouldn't have made it in one piece.

By the time they made it upstairs and behind closed doors, they were both panting and his cock was going to have a permanent zipper scar.

"We're acting like teenagers," Sassy gasped as she tugged

his shirt off.

He pulled hers off too and they both took off their own pants. Their hands were shaking and Ian chuckled.

"Why do we want each other so much right now? It's like there was something in the wine," he mumbled, then crushed his mouth to hers, unable to wait any longer.

She smacked his ass and he pulled back. "Did you just say you needed drugs to get hard for me?" She had a grin on her face but still, one didn't anger *The* Sassy.

He gripped her ass in his palms and lifted her so she wrapped her legs around his waist. They both swallowed hard as his cock pressed against her pussy.

"I'm saying *you're* my drug, baby. Now, I'm going to put you down because holding you like this when I'm not wearing a condom was short sighted of me." He lowered her but she slid down his body slowly, and he had to suck in a deep breath not to bend her over and fuck her there. "Plus, I promised you ice cream." He smacked her ass like she had him and grinned. "Now go lay down on the floor in the bedroom and I'll be right there."

She raised a brow. "You're going to take a chance and ruin your expensive carpets for ice cream?"

How little she thought of him. No, how little she thought of how he *used* to be. "It'll clean, Sass. If I play my cards right, I'll be able to lick every drop off your nipples so it won't be problem. Now go lie down and spread out. I'm ready for my dessert."

Her eyes widened, and with a saucy grin, she sashayed naked as the day she was born into his bedroom. He took a deep breath, willing the control he'd honed, and went to the freezer for Sassy's favorite ice cream.

She lay on the ground, her hair splayed out around her. She rolled her nipple with one hand, while she slid the other in and out of her lower lips, her hips rocking to the motion.

He almost dropped the carton and spoons right there.

There was nothing sexier than a woman who knew exactly what she wanted and knew that she didn't need a hard cock to get it...yet when she saw his dick she smiled and winked.

"Took you long enough," she purred.

He fell to his knees, took the lid off of the ice cream, and scooped out a small bite. Before she could tell him what she wanted, he dropped it on her belly button—totally not sexy but she'd egged him on after all.

She rocked up and wiggled. "Holy fuck, that's cold."

"Let me warm you," he licked the cream over her stomach then swallowed so she wouldn't be too cold. She moaned as he pulled back and placed a smaller drop of the melting dessert over her breasts and gorged himself. The sweet taste of her skin mixed with the caramel made for a decadent combination that was as heady as any drug.

They played with the ice cream, taking turns licking and tasting until they were full. He found the small of her back the best place for a scoop and would have to make sure he let Rafe know that for later.

"I'm all sticky," Sassy said as they both panted. Neither of them had come and their ongoing foreplay made them both hot as hell.

"I'm going to grab a condom and then we'll make sure you don't get too much stickier."

He chuckled as he stood up. She wrinkled her nose and shook her head. "That was crude, but I liked it."

As he walked back to her, he slid the condom over his length, liking the way her gaze tracked the movement. In fact, she seemed to like watching him a lot.

"Get up, face the mirror on the dresser, and grip the edge," he ordered.

She grinned and did as she was told. He came up from behind her and placed his hands near hers so he could get a good grip but not crush her.

"Ready, my darling?" he whispered, then kissed the small spot behind her ear. She shivered in his hold and he rocked against her so his dick slid between her cheeks.

She bent for him slightly and he sank into her heat. He moved his hands so he could grip her hips and then pulled back. Their gazes met in the reflection and he grinned back at her.

"Ready, Ian. I'm ready for anything."

God, he hoped so, but those doubts weren't meant for then.

Their gazes in the mirror never wavered as he pumped into her. Their breathing synchronized, and he increased the pace. His balls tightened and the base of his spine tingled and he knew he was about to come.

He reached up and cupped her breast. She licked her lips and then they came together, their moans echoing in the room as he filled the condom. He couldn't wait to fill her up when he was bare, but that was for later.

Right now he had the woman he loved in his arms, his cock fully inside her, and her body pressed against his. He'd take that for now and pray that one day it would be more, that she wouldn't leave him. That she would trust him to do the same.

He shook of the melancholy thoughts and kissed her softly. "Mine," he whispered.

"Yours and mine too," she panted back.

"Yours, Sassy. Always yours."

CHAPTER EIGHT

"**S**o Sassy's working tonight?" Rafe asked though he thought he already knew the answer considering she wasn't in the loft with him and Ian.

Ian sat on the couch next to him, his tie undone and looking mighty sexy and disheveled. He took a swig of his beer and leaned his head back. "She closes tonight with Shep who is then taking her to his place so his girl, Shea, and Sassy can have a girls' night. His cousin, Austin, is in town again and they are going out so the girls can have some time alone."

"That's right," Rafe said then took a sip of his own beer. "He invited us along too, right?"

"Yeah, but I declined for us since I know we've both been working our asses off trying to acclimate to the move."

He closed his eyes, his head aching like a bitch after the day he'd had. His dad still ran the shop in New Orleans even though Rafe bought him out years ago since Rafe owned the other two in the franchise he'd made. The blend of two dominant men in one workspace wasn't working out as well as he'd hoped.

He'd run from Sassy and Ian—only to end up living near Ian for a decade anyway. He'd come back to New Orleans so he would quit running from his problems. When he'd been gone, he made sure he kept distant from his family because he'd shamed them.

Or at least he thought he had.

Damn. His parents were way more tolerant and accepting than he'd given them credit for. That, in itself, would have shamed him more for his lack of faith, but Sassy hadn't let him pile it on.

After all, they'd chosen to move on and find their own futures. However, working with his father was turning into a bitch all on its own. His old man didn't have the same visions as Rafe did, and while Rafe accepted his dad would never change, some things in life had to.

He'd work it out or open up a new shop as part of the chain if he had to. No matter what he wouldn't run away like he had before. He'd been young and stupid then.

He was older now and hoped to God not as stupid.

There was one dominant man in his life, at least, and things seemed to be running smoothly on that front.

He hoped.

He leaned over and rested his head on Ian's shoulder. Ian shifted so he could wrap his arm around Rafe comfortably. He took a deep breath and inhaled the sandalwood scent that was so...Ian.

"What was your plan for the night then?" Rafe asked, his voice a little drowsy. It was nice, sitting on the couch with the man he loved wrapped around him. They were just sitting there staring at nothing and he felt content. From the way Ian's body had relaxed around Rafe's, the other man was comfortable as well.

Ian ran a finger down Rafe's shoulder but didn't move otherwise. The tension in the room rose, but it was a heady one.

"I hadn't thought of anything beyond just staying at home. I'm too damn tired to go out there and pretend to party with the twenty somethings."

Rafe grinned. Ian had always been something of a homebody and older than his years when it came to being with people, but he wasn't going to bring that up. Not when they were getting along and just enjoying the evening.

They sat there in silence for another ten minutes or so until Ian shifted and Rafe sat up straighter. Ian let out a breath and then put his forearms on his thighs, his head bowed.

Rafe frowned and ran a hand up and down Ian's back. "What's wrong?"

"What are we doing?"

Four words.

Just four words and Rafe felt like the wind had been knocked out of him. He blinked, unsure of what to say. From the tone of Ian's voice, the set of his shoulders, Rafe knew they weren't talking about what they would do for dinner.

No, this was the conversation Rafe had been afraid to have...even though he thought they'd had it already.

Damn it. Now he was mad. "What the hell do you mean, Ian?"

Ian turned to him, his eyes wide. "Why are you angry? I wanted to know the next step so I wouldn't be behind." Ian stood, staggering back. "Fuck, Rafe. You thought I was going to leave again? You really fucking thought that after all of this, everything I've said and done, that I'd leave?"

Rafe stood so they were nose to nose. "You fucking left before!"

Pain arched through Ian's eyes before he shut it down. "Fuck you, Rafe. I thought we were past that. Have I given you any cause to think I haven't been here?"

Rafe narrowed his eyes but didn't say anything. He couldn't come up with a damn thing and that bothered him more than he wanted to say. His own insecurities were biting him in the ass.

"Ian—"

His lover held up his hand. "No, let me talk. I know I don't laugh and smile as much as you and Sassy do. I know I'm the one on the sidelines who just seems to be...there. But I like it that way, Rafe. I like watching the two of you joke around and smile at the oddest things. I like knowing that I'm there, even if I don't have to be *part* of everything at all times."

Jesus, Rafe was an ass. "Ian, you're always part of it. I know you're here. God, I'm so fucking sorry. I don't know what's wrong with me." And now he was sounding like a teenage girl. Or boy at this point for that matter.

Ian lifted his lips in a small smile before shaking his head. "I'm not going anywhere, Rafe. God, I made so many mistakes before and we all know it. I was so afraid of what my parents would think about me not only loving a man, but loving that man *and* a woman at the same time. I was so fucking stupid for not doing what was inside my heart rather than doing what everyone else expected of me."

Rafe didn't move, didn't speak, knowing this was important for Ian...and them.

Ian cupped Rafe's face, his strong hands an anchor when Rafe felt as if he were drifting, not knowing what was coming next.

"You and Sassy are my everything. You were before and I didn't understand what that meant. I'm in this for the long haul, Rafe. But I need to know what that long haul is. We're fucking crazy to just show up at Midnight Ink and want to start a whole life with Sassy without even talking about it with her first, but that's what we did. We made the big moment rather than waiting for something to happen."

Rafe turned his head to kiss Ian's palm. "I know. In retrospect, we could have gone about it a bit differently."

Ian grinned. "You don't say. It's been two months since we came back and tried to make this work and I'm not going anywhere. You've got to believe that or everything I'm doing isn't enough, Rafe."

"Jesus, I'm a fucking asshole."

Ian grinned. "Yeah, you are, but I love you."

"I love you too, Ian."

Ian lowered his head and captured his lips in a fierce kiss. When he pulled away he leaned his forehead against Rafe's. "We're taking this slow, Rafe." He snorted. "Well, as slow as we can since we're all already sleeping together."

Rafe grinned. "Well, we did have a past, so it's not *that* slow."

"I'm putting everything out there, Rafe. I'm in. I know you are, too, or you wouldn't be so scared of what could happen if I didn't."

"I know that. I do. I just had a panic attack or some shit."

"If you don't trust me, it's gonna make it fucking hard to move on. I know I deserve it in some respects, but I'm here. And I hope to God Sassy is too."

Rafe closed his eyes. "We have to give her the same benefit of the doubt we're giving each other."

"I know. We are. But you'll notice that while the two of us have said we loved each other, and Sassy as well, she hasn't said the words." The pain in Ian's eyes was too hard to take, and Rafe kissed him softly.

"It crossed my mind."

Ian pulled back and shook his head. "Look at us. It's been two fucking months of dating, the best sex of our lives and connecting in a way that means something and we're harping on the fact that she hasn't said she loves us."

"The words matter with Sassy."

"And that's what hurts so fucking much because I don't know if she'll ever say them. It's so much easier to go back to what she was doing before we came back rather than face the trials we're going to go through once the world finds out."

Ian wasn't being self-centered with that fear. He worked in a very public arena, and people had already been commenting that he was dating a secret woman named Sassy. It was only a matter of time before they found out about Rafe...and who Sassy was. They weren't hiding it in fear that they'd hurt each other. In doing so though, they'd allowed a new set of problems to creep up. They would deal with those problems, and Rafe knew it would be worth it.

He just prayed Sassy would feel the same.

"I'm not going to push her to say anything she doesn't mean...or if she does mean it, but isn't ready to admit to us, or even herself," Ian said.

"What do you want out of this?" Rafe asked. He knew what he wanted—the whole damn thing, vows, babies, and a way for the three of them to work and live together. The world could fuck itself for its views on what was right or wrong. They weren't hurting anyone with what they had, and everyone else could just get over it.

Easier said than done, but if Rafe's family was fine with it, that was their greatest hurdle. Ian could give a flying fuck about his parents, Sassy the same. Her true family at Midnight Ink was fine with ménages considering there was a triad at the shop already.

Ian ran his thumb over Rafe's cheek. "I want everything, Rafe. I want it all. Just like you. It doesn't mean I deserve it, but I want it. I don't know how it will work beyond what we can do as the three of us work together, but we will find a way."

"In terms of the three of us, it's just more communication if you think about it."

Ian rolled his eyes. "Yeah, we're not the greatest at that."

"Plus more sex since there are three of us."

Ian threw his head back and laughed—one of the sexiest things ever in Rafe's opinion. "There is that. And we're pretty fucking great at it."

Ian pulled him close and Rafe rested his head on his shoulder. They stood there for a while in silence, their bodies swaying to a beat only they could hear.

"We're going to be okay," Ian whispered.

Rafe closed his eyes and squeezed Ian's waist. "Yeah. Yeah, we will."

The only thing they had no control over right then that mattered —and no desire to *have* control over—was Sassy. She was a force unto herself.

As much as he and Ian loved each other, Rafe knew it wouldn't be the same without Sassy. She was the one who held them together and made their lives complete.

She hadn't left, but was she fully committed?

He didn't know, but he'd give her time. He and Ian both would.

She was their center.

They had to make sure she knew it.

CHAPTER NINE

"So is it different being with two guys rather than just one?" Shea's eyes widened and she slapped her hand over her mouth, shaking her head. "I can't believe I just asked that," she mumbled behind her hand.

Sassy ran her hand through her hair, her bangles jiggling as she tried to hold back her laughter at the question.

"Oh honey, you're family. You can ask those questions," Sassy teased.

Shep, the love of Shea's life and one of Sassy's best friends, came up behind Shea and put his hand on her shoulders. "Sassy, love, if she's family, maybe you shouldn't be talking about sex. And Shea, baby, I'm all the man you need."

Shea blushed hard and leaned into him. "You're more than I can handle most days, Shep, but I like trying to handle you just fine."

Sassy grinned as Shep pulled Shea into a steamy kiss then left her mussed, blushing, and looking sexy as hell. There was just something hot and sweet about looking at a couple—or triad—in love and knowing that there might be something for her as well.

Oh, she wasn't ready to come out and say that she'd found her bliss, but she was definitely on the right track.

She purposely kept her feelings from Ian and Rafe, after all they'd only been reunited for a couple months. They still had time to find their rhythm and figure out how each piece of their particular puzzle would fit together. However, that didn't mean she hadn't been thinking about it.

God, some days it felt like it was the *only* thing she thought about.

Things were going well though. Great even. She had moments with each of her men and moments with both of them at the same time. It wasn't lost on her that she constantly thought of Ian and Rafe as *her* men.

That's what they were.

They were hers as much as she was theirs.

Shep went back to his notepad, working on artwork for a design for Shea, leaving her and Sassy to talk about what they loved best.

Their men.

Of course, Sassy had to answer the phones and do all of the other thirty-thousand things that went with being the Midnight Ink receptionist, but today was a rather slow day thankfully. It was mostly just the artists working on upcoming projects with only two clients in chairs getting inked. The buzz of the needle was a gentle hum, sliding up and down Sassy's spine.

Oh yeah, it was totally time to get new ink.

Maybe she'd get that ink Rafe and Ian had wanted when they'd first come in to the shop a couple months ago. It was hard to believe it had only been two months since they'd walked in and scared the shit out of her. God, she loved them, but she was waiting to tell them.

Something was holding her back, she didn't know what, but she wasn't ready to let them know.

"What are you thinking about that's giving you that serious face?" Shea asked, pulling Sassy out of her thoughts of love and her men.

Sassy shook her head and smiled. There was no use talking about things she couldn't even fully form in her mind. She'd rather talk about the good things—like sex and the fact that Shep and Shea would be getting married soon.

Well, by soon, she meant within the next year, but that was still pretty freaking cool.

"So, are you excited about your new ink?" Sassy asked, changing the subject. Shea raised a brow but didn't point it out.

"I just finished my first piece with Shep, but he's planning number two. I think it'll be a while before I get to it though. I want to make sure I don't go crazy and get twelve tats in twelve months."

Sassy tilted her head. "You know, if they were small ones, that could be a good promotion."

Shea rolled her eyes. "Oh God, look what I started."

Sassy grinned and turned to the front desk so she could write down that idea. Someone had left the morning paper on top of her legal pad and as she moved it out of the way, something caught her eye.

"The Bordeaux Whore Is Back In Town. What Does Daddy Have To Say About That?"

Sassy blinked as the buzzing in her ears grew louder and louder. She opened her mouth to speak but nothing came out. She put her finger on the column on the society pages and licked her lips.

"Sassy? What is it? Oh God, you're pale. Are you sick? Shep!"

She heard Shea calling out but it was from somewhere far away and moving even farther away.

They'd found out.

Someone had figured out who she was and how she was connected to Ian. She glanced at the words, *whore, sodimist,* and *threesome,* standing out and making her want to vomit.

They'd found out about Rafe too.

Strong hands pulled her around and she looked into Shep's eyes, unseeing.

"Sassy? What's wrong, honey? Talk to me. Austin, get her some water."

Sassy had forgotten Shep's cousin Austin was back in town. She'd have to make sure she teased him about his ink like she always did. That was, if she could ever think again...or face these people again.

Oh God, what would they do when they found out she'd lied to them all this time?

"Oh my God, Sassy," Shea gasped beside her and Sassy closed her eyes.

Damn it. She'd seen the article.

"Oh honey, that stupid bitch Vivian is such a fucking asshole when she writes in the gossip column. They put me and Shep in there when we were first dating because of my dad, but it blew over."

Sassy felt Shea's hands on her back but she couldn't speak. She could only think of what she needed to do and who she'd have to protect. That was her job.

She was *The* Sassy.

She'd have to give it all up to make sure Rafe's family, Ian's people, her crew, all of them, would be okay.

There was no other choice open to her.

Because no matter how scandalous it was for Shea, the golden girl, to date an inked tattoo artist, it was nothing like being the lost Bordeaux princess who found herself in a threesome with one of the most eligible men in the United States and another man with no breeding according to her parents' society circles.

That's what they'd tear them down to. It didn't matter that she loved Ian and Rafe or that they were both more than a label. Nothing mattered in the world where she'd grown up, that same world she still fought so hard to leave behind.

The public face was the only thing that mattered in that world.

Living the ultimate sin in their eyes would only harm Ian and Rafe.

She couldn't do that.

No matter what she thought of herself, she wouldn't hurt the men she loved.

Damn it.

Tears threatened, but she fought them back. She wouldn't break down in front of her friends—the family she'd made with ties she hoped to God were stronger than blood.

"Shit, Sassy, there's a crew out here with a camera saying they want to talk to you," Austin said from behind her and Sassy held back a shudder. "I locked the doors. This is private property and they can go fuck themselves."

"I need to get out of here," she whispered, her voice broken.

Her *everything* broken.

Shep ran a hand through her hair, but she barely felt it. Barely felt anything.

"Okay, honey, we'll get you out of here."

She shook her head and pulled away. She could feel the stares of everyone in the room. People she loved walking toward her, trying to help, but she couldn't do it, couldn't take it.

"I need to be alone. I'm going to go out the back, but I don't have my car."

Austin threw his keys at her and she caught them without thinking. "It's my rental. Take it. I can hitch a ride with Shep, easy."

"Austin, I don't think she should be driving right now," Shea admonished.

"I think she's stronger than any of us. If she needs to get the fuck away, we need to let her," Austin countered.

God, even a man she'd only known for a couple months thought she was stronger than she really was. She hoped she could live up to it because she was about to do something that would take everything out of her.

"Sassy," Shep snapped and she blinked out of whatever daze she was in. "Get it together. I know you can do this. You need to leave? Okay, we can do that for you. But you don't get to drive out there and hurt yourself because you're locked in your head. Get me?"

She nodded, grateful for her family. "I'm going to be okay," she lied.

She'd never be okay with what she had to do, but she'd do it anyway. Strength didn't come from the easy choices, but from the very difficult ones that she was being forced to make now.

"We'll hold the fort," Shep said. "Then you can tell us what happened. We're not going to pry."

She kissed him on the cheek then ran out the back door. She couldn't see any reporters around, but she didn't trust them not to ambush her. She put her brain on autopilot as she drove to Rafe's garage. Ian would be there too. It was his day off, and he was helping out Rafe's family and forming those connections she craved. They were supposed to go out for lunch, the three of them, in another hour and then Ian would spend the afternoon at Midnight getting to know her family.

At least that had been the plan.

Not anymore.

A few spiteful words in a newspaper gossip column had ruined that.

She pulled into the garage and shut off the engine. The tears still hadn't fallen. It was as if she were frozen in time, watching everyone around her moving around like nothing had happened. Like her world hadn't just shattered into a million tiny pieces and would never be whole again.

"Sassy? Are we late?" Rafe asked, a smile on his face. He had grease stains on his coveralls and looked strong enough that he could hold her with his will alone.

It wasn't enough.

"Baby?" Ian came out from the other room, dressed in jeans and a t-shirt making him look more casual than she'd ever seen him. He looked like he *fit* in the family.

Something she'd never be part of.

"What's wrong?" Rafe asked as he came up to her.

She took a step back when he tried to reach for her. The shock and pain on his face was like a blow to the chest, but this was how it needed to be.

"Can we find a private place to talk?" She could see Rafe's father walking into the garage and she couldn't face him, not when she was going to disappoint him and his family again.

God, she'd done this before but then it had been to protect her own heart.

No, it was to protect them.

There was a difference.

There had to be.

"Yeah, we can go to the back," Rafe said, the fear in his voice shooting straight through her.

Funny, she'd thought she'd be numb by now.

She followed them both and stood between them, knowing this would be the last time she'd do so.

"Have you seen the papers?" she asked, her voice devoid of emotion. If she broke down then, she'd never stop and wouldn't be able to get it out.

"Not yet," Ian said. "I read the front headlines, but haven't looked at the rest. What is this, Sassy?"

She shook her head. "Look at the gossip column when you get a chance, or don't. They know."

Rafe blinked. "Who knows?"

"Everyone. They all know. They know the Bordeaux whore is in a threesome and the lost princess is a shame to her family."

Ian's face grew stormy. "What? What name did you just use?"

She shook her head. "That's not important. You'll read all about it. What they wrote? It's not true. We know that, but it doesn't matter. What does matter is that we're hurting people being together. Ian, you'll lose so much by doing this. You too, Rafe. Your family might agree with what we're doing but will they once they're hounded by my past and the future we thought to make?"

"Fuck the world, Sass," Rafe barked. "We've been through this before. We're not losing you."

She shook her head. "We've never done this before. I've spent my life trying to find out who I am, and if I stay and hurt the people I love because I wanted something I can't have, then I've lost myself as well."

"Nothing we are is *wrong*," Ian whispered.

She closed her eyes tight to keep the tears at bay. "I know that. I *know*. We've never been taboo in my head. I've never thought anything was wrong with loving two men. That isn't it. It's the fact that others would be hurt because of what I want. That's what kills me. That's the difference. If I could love both of you and never have it harm the people we love too, then I'd leap at the chance. But I can't be selfish."

"Stopping this now isn't the answer," Rafe said, his voice hard.

"Stopping this now might make me a coward, but it saves

the people around us. I was happy before you came back and maybe, just maybe, I might find that again. If I don't? Then I never deserved it in the first place."

The first tear fell and she knew she was running out of time. "I love both of you. Please know that, but I can't go on living something that will only hurt us all in the future."

Neither man spoke, their faces hard, and she nodded.

There.

She'd done it.

She'd broken it all.

Again.

She turned on her heel, got in Austin's rental, and drove off.

The tears fell in earnest now, but she drove on, not knowing where she was going. Home would be too much, too much Rafe, too much Ian.

For as much as others had claimed she was strong, she knew it was a lie.

No matter how strong she acted, no matter what she did to help the others in her life, she was weak. *The* Sassy wasn't destined for a happy ending.

CHAPTER TEN

"You're just going to let her leave?" Rafe's father barked, and Ian took a deep breath.

He nodded at Rafe then faced the man who would one day be his father-in-law if Ian had any say in it. "No, we're not. She might need time to breathe, but she doesn't get to leave us when she just told us she loved us."

"Perfect fucking timing," Rafe bit out.

"Language, *niño*."

Rafe growled beside him and Ian ground his teeth.

"She left because of what she saw in the paper. So, let's see what it is she saw and then we fix it."

Rafe stepped in front of him as he took a step toward the office. "Fix it? How are we going to do that? Fuck, Ian, we just let her walk out of here."

Ian cupped Rafe's cheek. "And if we'd forced her to stay, she'd resent the hell out of us. So we're going to look at the real issues here—the media and who leaked this story—and fix it. Then we're going after her. We should have done that ten years ago and we're not going to make the same mistake again."

He'd be damned if he'd act like he did before.

He kept running Sassy's words over and over in his head, fixating on those that meant they had a chance at a future. She'd never told them she loved them outright, not before, but the words were out there now and she didn't get to take them back.

She didn't get to run away for good.

When he pulled up the gossip column on the damn society pages, he let out a roar. Rafe jumped and looked over his shoulder before letting go with a particularly vile curse that surprised Ian in its vehemence.

"God, they were vicious to Sassy," Carlos whispered. "Who would do such a thing?"

Ian ground his teeth. "They were petty and cruel to her while saying that she's a disappointment to her family. Notice they didn't mention Rafe and me beyond who we were."

"The attack was directed specifically at her," Rafe said.

"And who would want to hurt her the most and have the ties to make it happen?"

"Fuck. That fucking prick."

"Her father?" Carlos asked, ignoring his son's language. "*Mierda.*"

Ian's brows rose in confirmation. He looked at Rafe and let out a breath. "Let's deal with him once and for all. He's always been in the background of our relationship with her. We've chosen to put it aside because acting on it could hurt her, but right now, we're going to fix it."

"You really think she's going to like us going in and fixing the problem for her?"

Ian shook his head. "No, she's going to hate it. She should face him but not before she's ready. If we want to make our future work, we need to make sure that bastard isn't part of it. He needs to know he can't show up when he wants to hurt her. The only reason he even knows about us is because of who I am and the people who follow me. I'm going to use that to crush him."

"And when she resents us because we took care of it for her?"

Ian shook his head. "Then she can confront her father too. Right now though, this is something *we* need to do. That fucker isn't the only thing that's bothering her and once we assure her that we can make this work, then she's part of it as well. We're not doing it only for her, we're doing it for *us*."

He wasn't just rationalizing. No matter how much Sassy might *need* to confront her father, it wasn't going to happen right then. The SOB didn't matter enough in the long run, and Ian would do what he could to make sure he no longer mattered at all.

They hopped into Ian's car and drove to the Bordeaux estate on the other side of the city. He'd never been there, although because of his family connections, he'd been invited. The Steeles and Bordeauxs would have made a perfect match in snob heaven. Too bad Ian and Sassy found each other the way they wanted to, not how their parents desired.

He pulled up to the gate and lowered his window.

"Can I help you?" the guard asked.

"Tell Donald Bordeaux that Ian Steele is here, and he'd better let us in. Now."

The guard's eyes widened at the mention of Ian's name, and he scrambled back to the phone. Ian rolled up his window and put his hands on the steering wheel, gripping it like a lifeline.

"It's good to have your name sometimes," Rafe said, though Ian could hear and sense the underlying anger and fear.

"My name fucks us over more times than it helps it seems, but I'm done worrying about what others think. This man is going to know he crossed the wrong family, the wrong people. Then we're going to go to Sassy, get down on our knees, and beg for her to come back because I'm through waiting."

Rafe snorted. "Sounds like a plan. Easy. Concise. And full of what-the-fuck."

The gate opened and Ian pulled through. A butler walked out of the front door and nodded toward them as Ian parked in front of the colossal house. Where Ian had chosen to live in a modest loft and was planning on buying a bigger home for the three of them, Donald's home was a fucking monstrosity that screamed wealth and privilege.

Just one more thing Ian couldn't stand about the bastard.

The place dripped money yet looked cheap at the same time. Sassy had more class in her little finger than the entire place and the people who lived there combined.

Ian and Rafe walked through the place and Ian had to grin at what they were wearing. Instead of his usual suit, he had on jeans and a t-shirt while Rafe still had his work coveralls on. Their current wardrobe choices weren't particularly power-driven, but they would work for what Ian had in mind.

He could pull off power and absolute control in a suit at the drop of a hat, but even in the jeans and t-shirt, he managed to convey a dangerous anger and the power to back it up.

He left no doubt that he would obliterate the man who tried to crush his own daughter.

"Well, good afternoon, Ian. I wondered when you'd drop by for a visit." Donald walked through the archway into the foyer and blinked at their attire before looking like he flicked them off like a piece of lint.

Good.

Bordeaux had made the first mistake in a power play, underestimating your opponent.

"You're a fucking asshole," Ian growled.

Donald's perfect eyebrow rose. "Such an attitude from a man who is standing in my home in ragged clothes beside a man who must be your mechanic. Or is that your lover?"

"Stop it with the archetypes," Ian spat. "You leaked Sassy's name to the press."

Though it wasn't a question, Donald answered anyway. "That little bitch thought she could come back to New Orleans and defile our name? Fuck her."

Ian's body moved before his brain could engage. His fist slammed into the bastard's face and Donald went down hard.

"Well, I could have done that," Rafe said dryly.

Ian shrugged. "You get the next one."

"Gee, thanks."

"You bastard!" Donald scrambled to his feet, clutching his obviously broken, very bloody nose. "You'll pay for that."

"No, I won't. You'll back off from Sassy. You'll publish a

detailed retraction *and* an apology. You'll stay away from Sassy, Rafe, and me. You'll stay away from the families we've made. You *will* back the fuck off."

"And just why do you think I'll do that?"

Ian leaned in so he was inches from Donald's face. "Because while you have a few dollars, I have billions. While you have some power in New Orleans, I have more everywhere else. And even if my relationship takes me out of the forefront of my company, I still have everything else. You have nothing. You come at me and what's mine again, and I. Will. Destroy. You. Utterly, and thoroughly.

Donald paled a bit, the truth hitting home.

Rafe slid up to Ian's side and gripped the man's chin with bruising force. "And what Ian can't get to, I can. You think I'm gutter trash? You haven't got the first clue, asshat."

"Oh, and for the record, Sassy's been here all along. Your daughter has hidden in her own city for over ten fucking years and you never noticed until you thought it could help your masquerade as the poor victim. Well fuck you and fuck the morals you think you have. Stay away from her or I'll hunt you down like the swine you are."

"Do you get us?" Rafe asked and Donald nodded.

Ian pushed the man away then strode out of the house. "You drive to Sassy's. I need to make a few calls." He'd ensure Sassy's future regardless of cost or consequence. He had the money, the privilege, and the connections. He'd just make a few calls to those he worked with and they'd have so many eyes on Donald, he wouldn't be able to scratch his ass without an audience.

Sassy was more important than anything he could ever lose.

"You really think she'll be there?" Rafe asked as they drove.

Ian ran a hand through his hair. "It's a place to start. I'm not giving up until we find her."

"No shit," Rafe snorted. "I can't believe you punched her dad. She's gonna be pissed."

"No, she's going to be annoyed she missed it."

"That's what I meant."

Ian smiled and put his hand on Rafe's knee, needing the connection. God, Sassy had walked out on them. With everything that had happened, it still hadn't clicked that she'd left them.

They parked at Sassy's place and got out. They each had a key and rather than knock and wait for her to not answer, they walked in, unprepared for the sight that greeted them.

Sassy sat in the middle of her L-shaped couch, her face pale, tear stains on her cheeks, her eyes vacant.

"Oh, sweet Jesus," Ian whispered, then hurried to her.

She just looked at him and closed her eyes. "I ran away. How stupid am I?"

Rafe came to her other side and pulled them both close. "That's not stupid."

"It was a knee jerk reaction apparently, and then I spent the day crying and wanting my boyfriends. God, I'm a fucking teenager."

Ian took Sassy's chin between his fingers and forced her gaze to his. "Stop it. You're not a teenager. You're allowed to cry and fight and act however the hell you want when someone who you are supposed to trust, someone who is supposed to love you betrays you."

She licked her lips and pulled back. "So it was my father then? I didn't figure it out until after I left you."

"Honey, you were thinking about the pain and others, not about who could have caused it," Rafe said. "You aren't required to be all things to all people all at once."

"What did you do?" Sassy asked.

Ian blushed. "Uh…"

"Oh my God. You went to him? Without me?"

Rafe glared at Ian but Ian knew he'd have to roll with it. "Yes, this first time. Next time we go over there to confront him, you'll lead the charge. I promise we didn't go over there to act like Neanderthals."

Rafe coughed.

Sassy looked between them and then at Ian's swollen knuckles. "You hit him. Didn't you? Oh, my God! I missed it!" She punched him in the shoulder, and Ian was relieved to see the color back in her face. "I can't believe I missed *Ian*

Steele punching my dad."

"I'll do it again just so you can watch."

Sassy smiled like he hoped she would and wrapped her arms around his neck, pulling him down for a kiss. He obliged, missing the feel of her beneath him. She pulled away and did the same to Rafe before hitting them in the arms again.

"Don't handle my problems."

"Hey, they were our problems, too," Rafe said.

"I told your dad to fix it in the media or I'd make life tough for him. You know I can do that."

Her eyes widened. "Ian! But what about your company? What about Rafe's family? What about Midnight? It's not all about that one article. We could hurt a lot of people."

Ian narrowed his eyes. "How? How could we do that? The only people we care about love us and support our relationship. Nothing else matters."

"But Ian—"

"Sassy, it will be okay," Rafe interrupted. "My family can handle it. They already knew things might get iffy for a bit at the shop if people start to care, but they don't. Not really. And if things change? Then I can take a back seat and let my brother and father take care of things. My family isn't going to leave me, and our shop won't go under because of who I love."

"And my company and its people are financially secure. That won't be an issue. It's *in* right now to be different in certain circles, and I can use that if I need to. Those people I trust aren't going to leave me because of who I love. As for my parents? They don't like me as it is, Sass. Nothing I do will change that and I don't really care to. You're my family now. You and Rafe."

Her eyes filled and she blinked quickly. "I'm not going to cry again. I cried enough for the day."

Ian cupped her face. "Okay then. Now about that last part. About Midnight? You made that family at the shop and those people fucking love you. They stand strong no matter what happens around them. There's even a fucking threesome in the group as it is. I think we'll be fine."

Sassy blushed. "Okay, so I was reaching with that one."

"Stop fighting us, Sassy," Rafe whispered. "It's okay to be happy."

"It's okay to take a chance," Ian added. "Take a chance on us, Sass. Take a chance on our future."

She bit her lip and blinked up at him. "I promise not to run away again. I'm in. I'm sorry I ran."

Ian shook his head. "I'm going to spank that pretty ass pink for scaring me like that, but I believe you, baby. You're allowed to get fucking pissed at what you read, but we'll handle it together."

"That's what we're here for," Rafe whispered.

Sassy pulled Ian down for a kiss, her tongue brushing his, and he moaned. "Love me," she whispered against his lips.

"Always," he answered.

"Take me to the bedroom," Sassy demanded and Ian nipped at her lip.

"I thought I was the alpha one."

She rolled her eyes. "If you two don't know by now that I call the shots, there's really no hope for you."

Rafe stood, bringing Sassy to her feet. "We'll see about that." He picked her up and carried her to the bedroom as she squeaked.

Ian took a deep breath and smiled.

Finally.

She was theirs.

He stripped off his shirt and pants as he made his way into the bedroom, not at all surprised that Sassy was already naked and Rafe was between her legs, licking that sweet pussy of hers.

Her hands were tangled in Rafe's hair and she grinned at him. "Told you," she whispered.

"Really? You're in control?" Rafe asked, then pumped three fingers into her heat and she bucked against him. "Pass me the lube, Ian."

Ian chuckled and got the bottle and a few condoms from the nightstand. He squeezed a few drops on Rafe's hand and cupped his dick as he watched Rafe fuck her ass with his finger, nice and slow.

"See? I'm totally in charge," Rafe mumbled against her thigh.

"You win!" Sassy gasped.

"No, I win," Ian murmured as he stood behind Rafe and dipped his own lubed finger between his cheeks.

"Holy shit, that's cold," Rafe shouted.

"I'll warm you up," Ian promised.

He rimmed Rafe's hole with his finger then slowly pressed against it, the feel of the tight ring of muscles intoxicating. He couldn't wait to feel it around his dick.

"That feels so good," Rafe moaned.

"I know *exactly* what you mean," Sassy panted beneath Rafe.

Ian worked Rafe until he knew he was ready. He slowly rubbed small circles over Rafe's prostate and his lover shuddered.

"Don't do that yet. Fuck. I'm going to come and I'm not even in Sassy yet."

"Then saddle up," Ian teased.

"Did you just compare me to a—oh my fucking God that feels good!" Sassy screamed as Rafe slid into her pussy.

Ian gripped Rafe's hips to steady him. "Let me know if I need to go slower," he said, then pressed the crown of his condom covered cock at Rafe's entrance. He pushed, the pressure giving way as he slid past that tight ring.

Both men—and Sassy—moaned as Ian moved. Inch by inch, he sank into Rafe's ass, the tight feeling so fucking hot he knew he'd have to be careful or he'd come right then. Finally, at fucking last, he was balls-deep and ready to move.

"Ready?" Ian gritted out.

"Ready!" Sassy and Rafe yelled together.

Ian pulled out, the motion forcing Rafe to move back as well, his own cock deep in Sassy. Ian set the pace, each thrust thereby thrusting inside of Sassy. He pushed hard, his balls tightening as he forced himself not to come.

Sassy writhed under them, her fingers digging into Ian's arms. He loved that she was touching him as well, connecting them in body, soul, and future.

"I'm going to come," Sassy breathed, and then her body flushed, her nipples darkening as Rafe leaned back to rest his head on Ian's shoulder.

Rafe pounded into her and Ian pushed the man down on top of her so he could do the same. Rafe shouted, his ass tightening around Ian's cock as he came and Ian followed soon after, his body going lax as he filled his partner's ass inside the condom.

Ian pulled out then laid on the bed beside Sassy with Rafe lying on her other side.

They rested there for a few moments before each man got up, took care of their condoms, then came with warm, wet towels. They took turns cleaning Sassy and each other up before throwing the towels near the hamper and lying back down on either side of their woman.

"I've missed that," Ian panted. "God, I've missed that."

Sassy laughed between them and patted both of their chests. "Next time I get to be the creamy center of our cookie. Then Ian can be. We'll switch it up."

Ian closed his eyes. "I think I need a nap first."

Rafe snorted. "You're getting old, man."

Sassy reached down and cupped him, his dick hardening. "Naw, you're both getting hard at just one touch. But don't worry, I'll let you rest. We're not going anywhere."

Ian turned on his side so he could look down at them both. "Never, Sassy. I'm not leaving you. I love you, both."

Rafe turned as well. "I love you both, too."

Tears filled her eyes and she smiled. "Happy tears. I promise. I love you both so fucking much. So. Fucking. Much."

Ian let out a breath and took her mouth.

That's what he'd waited to hear and knew that no matter what had happened, what *would* happen, as long as they had those words, they'd be fine.

They'd be better than fine.

They were together again.

Finally.

EPILOGUE

"Yes, Ian, darling, getting a tattoo hurts. Suck it up," Sassy teased. She laid on her stomach as Shep inked her ass with the same tattoo Caliph was putting on Rafe, and Austin—their guest artist for the time being—drew on Ian.

While Rafe was smiling as Caliph inked their tattoo on his lower hip, Ian kept closing his eyes and gritting his teeth.

"What's the matter, dude? Don't like someone touching your ass?" Caliph snorted.

"I have a preference for who touches my ass, thank you very much," Ian gritted out.

Austin threw his head back and laughed. "I'm touched that you're letting me ink you then. I know your ass belongs to Rafe and Sassy. I promise to leave your dignity intact."

"Fuck you," Ian mumbled.

"I think we just said I wasn't going to that, bro', but thanks anyway. And you have this whole piece on your back. You'd have thought you'd already be used to ink."

Ian let out a breath. "I'm relaxed. I promise. I just don't like seeing Sassy wince."

Sassy grinned as the men let out a collective "Awww". "That's sweet baby. Yeah, it hurts, but its okay. Shep's hands are magic."

"They better not be too good with the magic," Rafe pointed out.

"Fuck you, Chavez," Shep said and flipped him off. "Don't let Shea hear you say that or she'll kick you in the nuts."

"And since I like his nuts, I'll be sure to keep him from acting like an idiot," Sassy put in. "How's it looking?"

Shep grunted. She knew he didn't like talking about how his work looked until it was done. He was temperamental that way. Between him, her men, and Austin, and Caliph, they'd come up with a design that would work for the three of them.

They'd finally found something small, but perfect. It was a ring of fire interlocking with a ring of ice encircling a red lily in the center. It was mostly black with subtle color shading so the red really stood out, and Sassy freaking loved it.

It was perfect for them.

They wanted the ink because after all, it's what Rafe and Ian had come in for in the first place. Now she was part of it. And because they weren't planning on a wedding until they could work out the details of their own lives and the legalities of it, the ink would represent their promises.

Their devotion.

She turned to look at her men as they got their ink and smiled.

Her second life began at Midnight Ink and she'd never forget that.

Her second chance at a true happily ever after, walked through Midnight's doors ten years later. They were three in one, united and loved.

They were reunited and yet still themselves.

There really wasn't anything else in the world she could have wanted.

Midnight Ink had given her love, life, and happiness.

Rafe and Ian were her center.

This was her future. After all,

The Sassy always knows best.

The End

Want more Ink? The first full length novel of the Montgomery Ink series, Delicate Ink, is out now. Follow Austin back to Denver and meet the rest of the Montgomery Clan.

Delicate Ink

A Montgomery Ink Novel

Delicate Ink

On the wrong side of thirty, Austin Montgomery is ready
to settle down. Unfortunately, his inked sleeves and scruffy
beard isn't the suave business appearance some women
crave. Only finding a woman who can deal with his job, as a
tattoo artist and owner of Montgomery Ink, his seven
meddling siblings, and his own gruff attitude won't be easy.
Finding a man is the last thing on Sierra Elder's mind. A
recent transplant to Denver, her focus is on opening her own
boutique. Wanting to cover up scars that run deeper than her
flesh, she finds in Austin a man that truly gets to her—in
more ways than one.
Although wary, they embark on a slow, tempestuous
burn of a relationship. When blasts from both their pasts
intrude on their present, however, it will take more than a
promise of what could be to keep them together.

CHAPTER ONE

"**I**f you don't turn that fucking music down, I'm going to ram this tattoo gun up a place no one on this earth should ever see."

Austin Montgomery lifted the needle from his client's arm so he could hold back a rough chuckle. He let his foot slide off the pedal so he could keep his composure. Dear Lord, his sister Maya clearly needed more coffee in her life.

Or for someone to turn down the fucking music in the shop.

"You're not even working, Maya. Let me have my tunes," Sloane, another artist, mumbled under his breath. Yeah, he didn't yell it. Didn't need to. No one wanted to yell at Austin's sister. The man might be as big as a house and made of pure muscle, but no one messed with Maya.

Not if they wanted to live.

"I'm sketching, you dumbass," Maya sniped, even though the smile in her eyes belied her wrath. His sister loved Sloane like a brother. Not that she didn't have enough brothers and sisters to begin with, but the Montgomerys always had their arms open for strays and spares.

Austin rolled his eyes at the pair's antics and stood up from his stool, his body aching from being bent over for too long. He refrained from saying that aloud as Maya and Sloane would have a joke for that. He usually preferred to have the other person in bed—or in the kitchen, office, doorway, etc—bent over, but that wasn't where he would allow his mind to go. As it was, he was too damn old to be sitting in that position for too long, but he wanted to get this sleeve done for his customer.

"Hold on a sec, Rick," he said to the man in the chair. "Want juice or anything? I'm going to stretch my legs and make sure Maya doesn't kill Sloane." He winked as he said it, just in case his client didn't get the joke.

People could be so touchy when siblings threatened each other with bodily harm even while they smiled as they said it.

"Juice sounds good," Rick slurred, a sappy smile on his face. "Don't let Maya kill you."

Rick blinked his eyes open, the adrenaline running through his system giving him the high that a few patrons got once they were in the chair for a couple hours. To Austin, there was nothing better than having Maya ink his skin—or doing it himself—and letting the needle do its work. He wasn't a pain junkie, far from it if he was honest with himself, but he liked the adrenaline that led the way into fucking fantastic art. While some people thought bodies were sacred and tattoos only marred them, he knew it differently. Art on canvas, any canvas, could have the potential to be art worth bleeding for. As such, he was particular as to who laid a needle on his skin. He only let Maya ink him when he couldn't do it himself. Maya was the same way. Whatever she couldn't do herself, he did.

They were brother and sister, friends, and co-owners of Montgomery Ink.

He and Maya had opened the shop a decade ago when she'd turned twenty. He probably could have opened it a few years earlier since he was eight years older than Maya, but he'd wanted to wait until she was ready. They were joint owners. It had never been his shop while she worked with him. They both had equal say, although with the way Maya spoke, sometimes her voice seemed louder. His deeper one carried just as much weight, even if he didn't yell as much.

Barely.

Sure, he wasn't as loud as Maya, but he got his point across when needed. His voice held control and authority.

He picked up a juice box for Rick from their mini-fridge and turned down the music on his way back. Sloane scowled at him, but the corner of his mouth twitched as if he held back a laugh.

"Thank God one of you has a brain in his head," Maya mumbled in the now quieter room. She rolled her eyes as both he and Sloane flipped her off then went back to her sketch. Yeah, she could have gotten up to turn the music down herself, but then she couldn't have vented her excess energy at the two of them. That was just how his sister worked, and there would be no changing that.

He went back to his station situated in the back so he had the corner space, handed Rick his juice, then rubbed his back. Damn, he was getting old. Thirty-eight wasn't that far up there on the scales, but ever since he'd gotten back from New Orleans, he hadn't been able to shake the weight of something off of his chest.

He needed to be honest. He'd started feeling this way since before New Orleans. He'd gone down to the city to visit his cousin Shep and try to get out of his funk. He'd broken up with Shannon right before then; however, in reality, it wasn't as much a breakup as a lack of connection and communication. They hadn't cared about each other enough to move on to the next level, and as sad as that was, he was fine with it. If he couldn't get up the energy to pursue a woman beyond a couple of weeks or months of heat, then he knew he was the problem. He just didn't know the solution. Shannon hadn't been the first woman who had ended the relationship in that fashion. There'd been Brenda, Sandrine, and another one named Maggie.

He'd cared for all of them at the time. He wasn't a complete asshole, but he'd known deep down that they weren't going to be with him forever, and they thought the same of him. He also knew that it was time to actually find a woman to settle down with. If he wanted a future, a family, he was running out of time.

Going to New Orleans hadn't worked out in the least considering, at the time, Shep was falling in love with a pretty blonde named Shea. Not that Austin begrudged the man that. Shep had been his best friend growing up, closer to him than his four brothers and three sisters. It'd helped that he and Shep were the same age while the next of his siblings, the twins Storm and Wes, were four years younger.

His parents had taken their time to have eight kids, meaning he was a full fifteen years older than the baby, Miranda, but he hadn't cared. The eight of them, most of his cousins, and a few strays were as close as ever. He'd helped raise the youngest ones as an older brother but had never felt like he had to. His parents, Marie and Harry, loved each of their kids equally and had put their whole beings into their roles as parents. Every single concert, game, ceremony, or even parent-teacher meeting was attended by at least one of them. On the good days, the ones where Dad could get off work and Mom had the day off from Montgomery Inc., they both would attend. They loved their kids.

He loved being a Montgomery.

The sound of Sloane's needle buzzing as he sang whatever tune played in his head made Austin grin.

And he fucking *loved* his shop.

Every bare brick and block of polished wood, every splash of black and hot pink—colors he and Maya had fought on and he'd eventually given in to—made him feel at home. He'd taken the family crest and symbol, the large MI surrounded by a broken floral circle, and used it as their logo. His brothers, Storm and Wes, owned Montgomery Inc., a family construction company that their father had once owned and where their mother had worked at his side before they'd retired. They, too, used the same logo since it meant family to them.

In fact, the MI was tattooed on every single immediate family member—including his parents. His own was on his right forearm tangled in the rest of his sleeve but given a place of meaning. It meant Montgomery Iris—*open your eyes, see the beauty, remember who you are*. It was only natural to use it for their two respective companies.

Not that the Ink vs Inc. wasn't confusing as hell, but fuck, they were Montgomerys. They could do whatever they wanted. As long as they were together, they'd get through it.

Montgomery Ink was just as much his home as his house on the ravine. While Shep had gone on to work at Midnight Ink and created another family there, Austin had always wanted to own his shop. Maya growing up to want to do the same thing had only helped.

Montgomery Ink was now a thriving business in downtown Denver right off 16th Street Mall. They were near parking, food, and coffee. There really wasn't more he needed. The drive in most mornings could suck once he got on I-25, but it was worth it to live out in Arvada. The 'burbs around Denver made it easy to live in one area of the city and work in another. Commutes, though hellish at rush hour, weren't as bad as some. This way he got the city living when it came to work and play, and the option to hide behind the trees pressed up against the foothills of the Rocky Mountains once he got home.

It was the best of both worlds.

At least for him.

Austin got back on his stool and concentrated on Rick's sleeve for another hour before calling it quits. He needed a break for his lower back, and Rick needed a break from the pain. Not that Rick was feeling much since the man currently looked like he'd just gotten laid—pain freaks, Austin loved them—but he didn't want to push either of them too far. Also, Plus Rick's arm had started to swell slightly from all the shading and multiple colors. They'd do another session, the last, hopefully, in a month or so when both of them could work it in their schedules and then finish up.

Austin scowled at the computer at the front of shop, his fingers too big for the damn keys on the prissy computer Maya had demanded they buy.

"Fuck!"

He'd just deleted Rick's whole account because he couldn't find the right button.

"Maya, get your ass over here and fix this. I don't know what the hell I did."

Maya lifted one pierced brow as she worked on a lower back tattoo for some teenage girl who didn't look old enough to get ink in the first place.

"I'm busy, Austin. You're not an idiot, though evidence at the moment points to the contrary. Fix it yourself. I can't help it if you have ape hands."

Austin flipped her off then took a sip of his Coke, wishing he had something stronger considering he hated paperwork. "I was fine with the old keyboard and the PC, Maya. You're the one who wanted to go with the Mac because it looked pretty."

"Fuck you, Austin. I wanted a Mac because I like the software."

Austin snorted while trying to figure out how to find Rick's file. He was pretty sure it was a lost cause at this point. "You hate the software as much as I do. You hit the damn red X and close out files more than I do. Everything's in the wrong place, and the keyboard is way too fucking dainty."

"I'm going to go with Austin on this one," Sloane added in, his beefy hands in the air.

"See? I'm not alone."

Maya let out a breath. "We can get another keyboard for you and Gigantor's hands, but we need to keep the Mac."

"And why is that?" he demanded.

"Because we just spent a whole lot of money on it, and once it goes, we can get another PC. Fuck the idea that everything can be all in one. I can't figure it out either." She held up a hand. "And don't even think about breaking it. I'll know, Austin. I *always* know."

Austin held back a grin. He wouldn't be surprised if the computer met with an earlier than expected unfortunate fate now that Maya had relented.

Right then, however, that idea didn't help. He needed to find Rick's file.

"Callie!" Austin yelled over the buzz of needles and soft music Maya had allowed them to play.

"What?" His apprentice came out of the break room, a sketchbook in one hand and a smirk on her face. She'd dyed her hair again so it had black and red highlights. It looked good on her, but honestly, he never knew what color she'd have next. "Break something on the computer again with those big man hands?"

"Shut up, minion," he teased. Callie was an up-and-coming artist, and if she kept on the track she was on, he and Maya knew she'd be getting her own chair at Montgomery Ink soon. Not that he'd tell Callie that, though. He liked keeping her on her toes. She reminded him of his little sister Miranda so much that he couldn't help but treat her as such.

She pushed him out of the way and groaned. "Did you have to press *every* button as you rampaged through the operating system?"

Austin could have sworn he felt his cheeks heat, but since he had a thick enough beard, he knew no one would have been able to tell.

Hopefully.

He hated feeling as if he didn't know what he was doing. It wasn't as if he didn't know how to use a computer. He wasn't an idiot. He just didn't know *this* computer. And it bugged the shit out of him.

After a couple of keystrokes and a click of the mouse, Callie stepped back with a smug smile on her face. "Okay, boss, you're all ready to go, and Rick's file is back where it should be. What else do you need from me?"

He bopped her on the head, messing up her red and black hair he knew she spent an hour on every morning with a flat iron. He couldn't help it.

"Go clean a toilet or something."

Callie rolled her eyes. "I'm going to go sketch. And you're welcome."

"Thanks for fixing the damn thing. And really, go clean the bathroom."

"Not gonna do it," she sang as she skipped to the break room.

"You really have no control over your apprentice," Sloane commented from his station.

Because he didn't want that type of control with her. Well, hell, his mind kept going to that dark place every few minutes it seemed.

"Shut up, asshole."

"I see your vocabulary hasn't changed much," Shannon purred from the doorway.

He closed his eyes and prayed for patience. Okay, maybe he'd lied to himself when he said it was mutual and easy to break up with her. The damn woman kept showing up. He didn't think she wanted him, but she didn't want him to forget her either.

He did not understand women.

Especially this one.

"What do you want, Shannon?" he bit out, needing that drink now more than ever.

She sauntered over to him and scraped her long, red nail down his chest. He'd liked that once. Now, not even a little. They were decent together when they'd dated, but he'd had to hide most of himself from her. She'd never tasted the edge of his flogger or felt his hand on her ass when she'd been bent over his lap. That hadn't been what she wanted, and Austin was into the kind of kink that meant he wanted what he wanted when he wanted. It didn't mean he wanted it every time.

Not that Shannon would ever understand that.

"Oh, baby, you know what I want."

He barely resisted the urge to roll his eyes. As he took a step back, he saw the gleam in her eyes and decided to head it off at the pass. He was in no mood to play her games, or whatever she wanted to do that night. He wanted to go home, drink a beer, and forget this oddly annoying day.

"If you don't want ink, then I don't know what you're doing here, Shannon. We're done." He tried to say it quietly, but his voice was deep, and it carried.

"How could you be so cruel?" She pouted.

"Oh, for the love of God," Maya sneered. "Go home, little girl. You and Austin are through, and I'm pretty sure it was mutual. Oh, and you're not getting any ink here. You're not getting Austin's hands on you this way, and there's no way in hell I'm putting my art on you. Not if you keep coming back to bug the man you didn't really date in the first place."

"Bi—" Shannon cut herself off as Austin glared. Nobody called his sister a bitch. Nobody.

"Goodbye, Shannon." Jesus, he was too old for this shit.

"Fine. I see how it is. Whatever. You were only an okay lay anyway." She shook her ass as she left, bumping into a woman in a linen skirt and blouse.

The woman, whose long honey-brown hair hung in waves down to her breasts, raised a brow. "I see your business has an...interesting clientele."

Austin clenched his jaw. Seriously the wrong thing to say after Shannon.

"If you've got a problem, you can head on right back to where you came from, Legs," he bit out, his voice harsher than he'd intended.

She stiffened then raised her chin, a clear sense of disdain radiating off of her.

Oh yes, he knew who this was, legs and all. Ms. Elder. He hadn't caught a first name. Hadn't wanted to. She had to be in her late twenties, maybe, and owned the soon-to-be-opened boutique across the street. He'd seen her strut around in her too-tall heels and short skirts but hadn't been formally introduced.

Not that he wanted an introduction.

She was too damn stuffy and ritzy for his taste. Not only her store but the woman herself. The look of disdain on her face made him want to show her the door and never let her back in.

He knew what he looked like. Longish dark brown hair, thick beard, muscles covered in ink with a hint of more ink coming out of his shirt. He looked like a felon to some people who didn't know the difference, though he'd never seen the inside of a jail cell in his life. But he knew people like Ms. Elder. They judged people like him. And that one eyebrow pissed him the fuck off.

He didn't want this woman's boutique across the street from him. He'd liked it when it was an old record store. People didn't glare at his store that way. Now he had to walk past the mannequins with the rich clothes and tiny lacy scraps of things if he wanted a fucking coffee from the shop next door.

Damn it, this woman pissed him off, and he had no idea why.

"Nice to meet you too. Callie!" he shouted, his eyes still on Ms. Elder as if he couldn't pull his gaze from her. Her green eyes never left his either, and the uncomfortable feeling in his gut wouldn't go away.

Callie ran up beside him and held out her hand. "Hi, I'm Callie. How can I help you?"

Ms. Elder blinked once. Twice. "I think I made a mistake," she whispered.

Fuck. Now he felt like a heel. He didn't know what it was with this woman, but he couldn't help but act like an ass. She hadn't even done anything but lift an eyebrow at him, and he'd already set out to hate her.

Callie shook her head then reached for Ms. Elder's elbow. "I'm sure you haven't. Ignore the growly, bearded man over there. He needs more caffeine. And his ex was just in here; that alone would make anyone want to jump off the Royal Gorge. So, tell me, how can I help you? Oh! And what's your name?"

Ms. Elder followed Callie to the sitting area with leather couches and portfolios spread over the coffee table and then sat down.

"I'm Sierra, and I want a tattoo." She looked over her shoulder and glared at Austin. "Or, at least, I thought I did."

Austin held back a wince when she turned her attention from him and cursed himself. Well, fuck. He needed to learn not to put his foot in his mouth, but damn it, how was he supposed to know she wanted a tattoo? For all he knew, she wanted to come in there and look down on the place. That was his own prejudice coming into play. He needed to make it up to her. After all, they were neighbors now. However, from the cross look on her face and the feeling in the room, he knew that he wasn't going to be able to make it up to her today. He'd let Callie help her out to start with, and then he'd make sure he was the one who laid ink on her skin.

After all, it was the least he could do. Besides, his hands all of a sudden—or not so suddenly if he really thought about it—wanted to touch that delicate skin of hers and find out her secrets.

Austin cursed. He wouldn't let his thoughts go down that path. She'd break under his care, under his needs. Sure, Sierra Elder might be hot, but she wasn't the woman for him. If he knew anything, he knew *that* for sure.

CHAPTER TWO

Sierra Elder threw her handbag on the counter and stomped her heels on the tile. The nerve of that man. The freaking *nerve*.

Seriously? That bearded mountain of a man thought he had the right to judge *her*? What right did he have to sneer at her and look down on her with those gorgeous blue eyes, and make her feel like she didn't belong in *his* shop?

Wait.

Gorgeous blue eyes?

What the hell was wrong with her? He'd judged her and found her wanting, and yet she thought he had pretty eyes?

She was twenty-nine for freak's sake. Not a teenager. Pretty eyes shouldn't matter. But they were gorgeous.

Apparently, she needed to eat since she was clearly lightheaded and not thinking straight. That man had thrown her off her game, and she wasn't in the mood to deal with him. It had taken all her courage to walk across the street and into the black and hot pink shop.

Dear Lord, the courage.

She'd lived with the consequences of her actions, of Jason's actions, for ten years, and in some respects, it hadn't been long enough. Not enough time to wash away the taint, the nightmares.

She couldn't think about that. Not now. Maybe not ever.

That Montgomery, Austin, according to her friend Hailey, had pushed her back, and now she knew she needed to buck up and figure out her next step. If she was honest with herself, she would say that she'd just been looking for an excuse to run away from her plans of ink and recovery, but she didn't want to be honest with herself. She wanted to blame Austin of the gorgeous blue eyes for her problems and fear. If only for a moment. It was the coward's way out, but she'd take it for the afternoon.

Then she'd find a way to walk back in and talk to the sweet apprentice, Callie, about finally getting her tattoo. Until then, she'd think of interesting ways to beat the crap out of Austin since she was too small to actually do it herself. Plus, violence wasn't always the answer. Not always.

Great. Now she didn't know what to think, but she was still hungry. She looked around at the almost finished shop she loved and shook her head. She was too angry, confused, and hungry to deal with the little details that remained until her opening in a few days. What she needed was a sandwich, fresh iced tea, and the smile of her new friend, Hailey.

Luckily, Taboo, Hailey's café, sat right across the street from her own boutique, Eden. That also meant that Taboo was right next to Montgomery Ink, but that couldn't be avoided. Sierra thought the café even had a side door right into the shop, which must be nice for the artists. Lucky bastards.

Lucky Austin Montgomery.

Nope. She wasn't going to think about him anymore. Not even her rabid curiously about just how much ink he wore and where it led would move her from her position. She did *not* want Austin Montgomery, and she did *not* want anything having to do with his tattoos, thank you very much.

And enough about bearded mountain man's tattoos.

It wasn't just the tattoo, however. Just his presence made her yearn for things she'd long since buried.

She picked up the purse she'd thrown on the counter and left her shop, locking it behind her. After a good meal and a pick-me-up conversation, she'd get back to it. There were numerous details left for her to handle, but she'd mapped out a whole afternoon off so she could talk with a tattoo artist.

Now it seemed that would all be for naught, but she wasn't going to think about that. Not until she talked with Hailey and had a turkey and provolone club in her belly. She'd been so stressed for the last few months working on getting Eden ready, putting all her hopes and dreams into a store that could crash and burn on the streets of Denver, that she hadn't been eating as much as she should. Luckily, Hailey took care of Sierra and made sure that she had food in her system, at least when she was downtown.

Sierra didn't have the curves she'd always craved when she was younger. She might have filled out some from her all-limbs and flat-chested youth, but not much. She still had harsh angles and barely a handful of breasts, though Jason had never complained.

No, she wasn't going to think about Jason.

Not twice in one day. There was only so much she could take without trying to find a drink before five at night. She had standards and rules after all.

She purposely kept her gaze from the front of Montgomery Ink. Their large windows made it easy to see in and watch the artists at work. She couldn't trust herself not to find the one man she shouldn't find in the first place, so she kept on walking. The man angered her, made her feel like she wasn't wanted, and yet her damned libido still wanted him.

It was just her dry spell, and he happened to be an oasis in the desert.

A mirage.

That was it.

"There you are," Hailey called out from her place behind the counter. "I was about to call you and make you come over here for food. God knows you haven't eaten yet." Hailey smiled, her red-painted lips bold against her pale skin and white-blonde bob with blunt bangs. The other woman always reminded Sierra of a starlet of a forgotten era mixed with the undeniable energy and spunk of the current one.

Hailey also made kick-ass soup and sandwiches. The woman was a dream with coffee, despite the fact that during peak hours, when she didn't have time to wait in line for better coffee, Sierra went to the other coffee shop that sat right beside Eden. She'd seen Austin meander in with those long legs of his to the place next door to Eden as well.

Not that Sierra watched him move.

She disliked him, she remembered. Disliked him and his attitude.

"I'm here, and I'm starving. Your famous club, please." Sierra leaned over the counter to brush a kiss on the other woman's cheek, the soft scent of Hailey's perfume calming her. Hailey might have secrets that Sierra could never pry out of her, but she listened and helped Sierra move on from the pain she'd so long hidden from the world.

When she thought about it, she knew their friendship would seem one-sided. However, Hailey knew that Sierra would be there for her when the other woman shared her past. Sierra herself had only just recently done so. In fact, Hailey was the only person in her new life that knew even a fragment of the journey that had sent Sierra from Boulder down to Edgewater and Denver, Colorado. The miles down the highway might not seem long to some, but the mileage and wear on her body and soul were far from short.

Hailey set the sandwich and iced tea in front of Sierra then walked around the bar to sit down next to her. "Tell Momma Hailey what's wrong, darling."

Sierra snorted her tea then wiped her chin. "Warn a girl before you start calling yourself Momma Hailey."

Hailey wrinkled her nose and stole a sweet potato fry. "Yeah, that so doesn't work. I was trying out a new thing. Maybe if I dye my hair a different color and nod sagely it would work."

Sierra tried to think of the other woman with a hair color darker or even brighter—if that was possible—than what she currently had and came up empty. "You're a bleach-blonde girl, Hailey. I don't think that's ever going to change."

Hailey tugged on a strand of Sierra's hair and frowned. "I would try something like yours, that darker chestnut with honey highlights, but I don't think that's me."

"The highlights aren't natural; I've paid good money for them, but I like them." She squinted and tried to picture Hailey with the color of her own hair. "I can see you in them if you tried, Hailey. You'd be beautiful no matter what color your hair is. The blonde, honey, that's your personality as I know you."

"Did you just call me an airhead?" Hailey winked, and Sierra rolled her eyes.

"Yes, that's exactly what I meant, dork."

The bell above the door tinkled, and Hailey stood, wiping her hands on her apron. "I've bothered you enough. Now eat while I take care of these customers. Then you can tell me what's going on in that head of yours and why you look so lost."

Sierra nodded, unnerved that Hailey could read her so well, though Sierra had tried to hide her nerves. Sure, it could be because of Eden's grand opening in a few days, but she had a feeling she looked as if it was something more. After all, it *was* something more.

When she took a bite of her sandwich, Sierra's eyes almost rolled back in her head. The burst of spicy mayo on freshly carved turkey and cheese made Sierra want to kneel at Hailey's feet. She might have knelt at another's feet in her past due to more personal reasons, but she'd never done it for food before. Hailey would be so worth it.

Wow, she had no idea where that memory came from, but she needed to bury it like she had all the others. Jason was gone, and she was moving on. She'd even looked into finding a way to cover up the evidence of her past that afternoon.

"You're scowling," Hailey remarked, thankfully pulling Sierra out of her thoughts.

Sierra took another deep gulp of her tea then cleaned off her mouth, surprised to find she'd eaten every last scrap of her sandwich and sweet potato fries while she'd been lost in the tangled web of her thoughts.

"I'm not scowling," she lied. She may have been scowling for all she knew. She'd been thinking of men with blue eyes and a lost love she didn't want to remember.

"You were, but I'll let you think otherwise if it helps. So, I might have gone off track when you first walked in with that Momma Hailey stuff, but I'm here now, and people are taken care of. What's wrong, dear?"

Sierra licked her lips, surprised to find herself nervous about telling Hailey what had happened that day. The other woman didn't know *everything* that had gone on in Sierra's past but knew enough that whatever Sierra said next would hold meaning rather than pleasant nothings and murmurs. That, above all else, told her to let it all out. Maybe not then, not in Taboo, but soon. She needed friends, needed confidants. She needed to step away from the cage that was Boulder and her own memories, and find a new way to live.

That, after all, was why she was opening Eden in only a few short days.

"I went into Montgomery Ink for a tattoo and met that oaf of a man, Austin." She hurried through her sentence and looked over Hailey's shoulder to ensure the door between Taboo and the tattoo shop was indeed closed. The last thing she wanted was for that bearded crazy man to walk through and listen to her speaking of him.

Thankfully, the door hadn't opened, and she was in the clear.

"A tattoo! Really?" Hailey squeezed her arm, once again bringing Sierra's thoughts out of delicious scruff and into the present. Maybe she needed more caffeine. "What are you going to get?"

Sierra blinked. "So we're just glossing over the oaf-of-a-man part of my statement?"

Hailey narrowed her eyes as she pursed her lips. "If you want to only talk about Austin, we can do that. I don't quite think of him as an oaf, so you'll have to elaborate."

"He's a rude, inconsiderate oaf." And she wanted to crawl up his body. Damn it. She would not allow herself to think like that. Not again.

Hailey frowned. "What did he do? Do I need to go kick his ass? I might work right next to him and have known him longer, but that doesn't give him the right to be rude. What did he do?" she repeated.

Sierra closed her eyes, annoyed at herself for even bringing it up. Hailey was a good judge of character, and if she hadn't had a problem with Austin before, it was probably just Sierra. Oh goody, she just brought out the best in people, didn't she?

"I went in for a tattoo, something I'll talk about with you later—when I'm ready." Hailey gripped her hand, and Sierra opened her eyes to see the other woman's knowing gaze. "I promise. It took enough for me to even walk over there and try. I'll explain it all eventually. That's if I go through with it. As soon as I walked in, Austin was there, glowering at a woman talking about their sex life. I mean, really."

Though she didn't want to press it, that odd kernel of something akin to jealousy had rankled her. That was why she'd been as rude as she had at first. She hadn't meant to talk poorly about the shop. No, she'd heard great things about it, so that wasn't her intent. The woman with the sultry walk and plump lips had annoyed her. Before Sierra had opened her mouth, she'd seen the same emotion running through Austin's eyes. Not that she'd given either of them time to understand it.

Crap. Maybe it was all her fault that Austin had acted like that—dismissing her without just cause. To him, her careless words could have been construed the same way. Damn it. She wasn't going to apologize. Not when Austin was worse. She might apologize to that nice girl, Callie, but that was it. She didn't need to speak to Austin. Ever.

"That would be Shannon," Hailey said then raised her brow. "The woman talking about their sex life. They broke up months ago, and from what I hear, it was mutual."

"Then why is this Shannon walking into his place of business discussing the lack of flair in their sex life?"

Hailey snorted, her grin wide. "Oh really? She said that? That's a whole different tune than what she was singing when they were going out. It was all 'Austin's hung like this' and 'Austin can get her off in two seconds flat.' "

Sierra's eyes widened. "She said that? To you?"

Hailey stood and cleared off the counter, a spring in her step. "Hell, yeah. She said it to any woman who'd listen. After all she was with *the* Austin Montgomery."

"He's a *the*?" She could see that. No. No she couldn't. Damn it, that man needed to get out of her fantasies.

Hailey looked over her shoulder and smirked. "Oh, honey, he's *the* the."

An uncomfortable wash of envy...or something much worse filled her. "Did you and he ever..."

Hailey threw her head back and laughed. "Oh, God no. I wouldn't say he's like a brother to me, not like he is with Callie or his three sisters, but he's like a first cousin or something. So not on my radar like that." An odd look crossed her face, and Sierra perked up.

"Is someone else on your radar that I should know about?" Hailey was notoriously single and quiet about it. Sierra just wanted her friend happy. After all, one of them should be.

Hailey shook her head, stopped, and then shrugged. "Maybe. It doesn't matter anyway." Her gaze went to the closed door between the shop and Taboo, and Sierra's interest sparked.

So, it was someone at Montgomery Ink that had captured Hailey's heart. It if wasn't Austin, it could be any one of the other artists or apprentices there. Sierra wouldn't push and pry. At least not then. Maybe when they were liquored up, she'd pry it out of her.

"Also, we were talking about sexy Austin," Hailey said, her eyes too bright, her smile too wide. Yes, there was something there, something that Sierra would do her best to help with when she could.

"Sexy Austin?" That bad-boy biker look had been in her past, and she'd thought she'd gotten over it. Apparently she hadn't. Not by far.

"Don't tell me you don't see it. I saw your eyes light up even when you called him an oaf. But I digress. Back to

Shannon. The two of them broke up, and I thought everything was fine. Shannon, from what I can tell, doesn't like to let anything go. She probably went along with the breakup because she thought she could find someone with deeper pockets or a bigger cock. It looks like she didn't find it."

Sierra's mouth hung open at the description then laughed with Hailey. "Well then. That's good to know."

"Is it?" Hailey teased.

Blushing, Sierra stood up and left money on the counter. "Shut up. And take the money, Hailey. You can't keep forcing me to keep my money and not pay for my meal."

Hailey curled her lip in a snarl. "If I want my friends to eat for free in my own shop, then I should be able to. You need the money for Eden anyway."

True, but that wasn't the point. "You need the money for Taboo as well. Just come over and buy a sexy bra and panty set when we open."

Hailey raised a brow. "It seems to me that's quite a bit more than a sandwich."

"Then I guess I'll have to buy a few more sandwiches. Now I'm off to the store to work on a few last-minute displays before I go into inventory again. Thanks for talking to me and for the food."

"We really didn't talk about anything, Sierra." Hailey met her gaze, and Sierra saw the concern there.

"I know, but it's exactly what I needed. I'm going to work my tail off for the next few days to make Eden ready for the best opening ever. Then I will go back into Montgomery Ink—Austin Montgomery or no—and get my tattoo."

"That's the spirit. And when you do get yours, let me know, and I'll hold your hand. You're not alone, Sierra."

Sierra nodded then left on her way to Eden. Hailey might be in her corner, but Sierra knew the other woman was wrong.

She *was* alone.

And that was the way it was meant to be.

CHAPTER THREE

I want to suck your cock. That big, meaty dick that filled me up so much I couldn't walk for days. I miss the sound of your voice as you come inside me. I miss the feel of your silky, white cum in my engorged pussy.

So not the message he needed to be reading during the Montgomery family outdoor barbecue. Engorged? Can we say *hell, no*?

Austin deleted Shannon's text and groaned. That woman just wouldn't take a hint and leave him the hell alone. He thought they'd broken up because they were bored with each other. Apparently he was wrong. No matter how many times he told her they were over—something he was pretty sure had been her idea in the first place—she kept coming on to him. She texted him shit he certainly didn't want to see or read, came by his house and shop, and was on the verge of stalking him in every sense of the word.

He wasn't worried she'd hurt him, or anyone else around him; that wasn't her style, but he was getting tired of it. Plus, if he wanted to actually move on and date another person, well, he didn't want to think about what she'd do about that. She'd always been jealous when it came to his past. He hadn't thought about how she'd react to his future.

That would teach him to try to have a good time rather than settle down.

He closed his eyes as he put his phone back in his pocket. Settle down? Was that what he wanted to do? The idea held merit considering the way Shep smiled and laughed every time he was near his Shea, but Austin also saw the strain of marriage on two of his siblings. Sure, his parents made it look effortless, but Alex's and Miranda's respective marriages never made it look like it was something he wanted to do.

Though he didn't know the whole story, he never saw either of them as an incentive to getting married in the first place.

He was getting old. He'd thought he'd be married by now with a couple kids. That hadn't happened, and as forty quickly approached, he was afraid he'd lost his chance at that forever.

Images of honey-brown hair and big green eyes filled his mind, and he had to swallow hard. Sierra might not be his usual type, but she wouldn't leave his mind alone. That didn't mean he wanted her. Not like that. She wasn't the answer to whatever marriage questions he had on his mind. She was just a woman who might want a tattoo and probably thought he was some dirty biker tattoo artist.

That was fine with him.

"Why do you look like you just smelled something rank?" Wes, his brother closest in age, asked him. Wes might have been only three minutes older than Storm, but he'd used that small time frame like no other for the past three or so decades.

"One word. Shannon."

Wes raised a brow and tucked his hands in his dress pants. Though they were at their parents' house in Westminster, Wes hadn't changed into jeans and a T-shirt like the rest of the family. He still wore a long-sleeved button-down and his work attire, but he'd at least taken off the tie. Wes was a contractor and head of Montgomery Ink. Yes, his twin, Storm, also ran the company with him, but Wes was the idea man. Storm liked to hide in the background. If anyone asked the two of them, they'd say their administrative assistant, Tabitha, was the glue that held them together, but that was another story altogether.

"Did someone say Shannon?" Storm asked as he walked up to the two of them, three beers in his hands. He handed them off and took a sip of his own. Wes and Storm were identical twins. Years and personalities had made them easy to tell apart. Storm had the rugged look down pat with his long hair, never-quite-shaved face, worn jeans, and bulkier frame. Both men were strong as hell to do their jobs, but Storm had filled out more over time. It didn't matter that he was the architect of Montgomery Inc. He used his hands more often than not.

"Yeah. She keeps texting me and shit," Austin explained after he took a sip of his beer. Storm had brought Fat Tire to the party, and Austin couldn't have been more grateful. Nothing like a Colorado beer to make him feel better.

"I told you she'd be trouble," Wes said sagely.

Austin flipped him off then leaned against the side of the house, his back aching from a six-hour session on his client's back piece. Maybe he'd get a massage from the spa down the street. He'd long since given up on the idea it was sissy. They worked wonders on his back—and nothing else, unlike what his brothers teased him about—so he could work long days and do what he loved.

Maybe if he was lucky, he'd find a woman to massage him at home as well.

He closed his eyes, cursing himself. Dating just for the moment was what got him into this mess with Shannon. He needed to keep a tighter rein on his dick it seemed. Maybe he'd head to the club with Decker and find a sub to help. That might relieve the tension. But even as he thought it, he knew it wouldn't be good enough. He wanted long-term, though he'd never admit that out loud at this stage. Helping a sub for only a night or two wouldn't be enough for him.

"You never said Shannon would be trouble," Storm argued. "You said she would wrap Austin around her little finger and fuck him over." His brother grinned at Austin. "Well, maybe that means trouble after all."

"You're a laugh riot. Both of you. Now I'm going to go and bug Meghan about the tattoo she wanted, and still hasn't gotten, and leave the two of you to your own devices. God help us all."

Sasha, Meghan's daughter, squealed as her brother, Cliff, chased her around the backyard. Maya followed them both with her friend Jake trailing behind her. Between the eight siblings, extended family, various friends, spouses, children, and neighbors, the barbecue was in full swing and loud as hell. He loved it. This was his family, his home. Sure, he was about fifteen minutes away from his real home, but this was where he'd grown up, where he knew he'd always have a place to return to even after living away for twenty years.

The six-bedroom house was a two-story dream for anyone with a large family. Since there were more kids than rooms, everyone, at one point or another, had shared a room with someone. It was just the way it was, and despite the fact they complained and yelled as kids do, it hadn't killed them. His dad had built on to the house as time passed, expanding the kitchen and living areas and giving his mother the deck of her dreams. Well, that wasn't exactly right. She'd done some of the building as well. She might have started out as Montgomery Inc.'s administrative assistant, but she learned to use a hammer and nails like the rest of them. The basic structure had remained the same, and it was perfect for them. They were on the end of a cul-de-sac but were far enough away from the actual street that they, like Austin, had plenty of land around them—something coveted in the suburbs.

Austin grinned and left his two knucklehead brothers talking to each other—most likely about him—and found Meghan in a quiet argument with her husband, Richard. Sadly, this was not the first time he'd seen it, and he knew it wouldn't be the last. She wouldn't like him to interfere, but that would be her problem. His little sister, the eldest of three Montgomery daughters, was his blood, and that meant he had the right to protect her from the world. Even if the world included herself.

"Hey, little sister," he said as he wrapped an arm around her stiff shoulders. "I've missed seeing you around these things. You've been missing a few." *Subtle, Austin.*

Meghan gave him a look that would have felled most men, but he was not most men. Seeming to catch herself from showing too much, she gave him a fake smile and leaned into him for a hug. She was the tallest of the M&Ms—the nickname their father had given his three daughters, Meghan, Maya, and Miranda—but still didn't come up to his nose.

"Cliff's soccer practices and Richard's business parties have happened to be running at the same time as the folk's barbecues. So we've been missing a few, but we're here now." She gave her husband a pointed look that didn't seem to help the situation.

Richard smiled coolly at his wife before nodding toward Austin. "Yes. We're here at the Montgomery clan barbecue. As you have enough of them, I assumed it would be fine to miss a few. Plus, we're Warrens now. It's okay to not show up to all of them."

Austin clenched his teeth at his brother-in-law's words. The bastard had been married to Meghan for eight years, and yet Austin never learned to like the man. What was there to like? A smile too fixed, hair too gelled, a look of disdain that never quite went away. In fact, Richard blatantly looked down on tattoos, blue-collar workers, and anything that remotely resembled honest manual labor.

Not that Austin would give the other man a piece of his mind. He was the father of his niece and nephew, and husband to one of the women in his life Austin loved more than anything. It wouldn't do any good to beat the shit out of him.

It might help Austin's mood, so he'd put that off as a maybe for later.

"Once a Montgomery, always a Montgomery," Austin shot back with a bite.

Meghan elbowed him in the gut, and Austin let out an oof. She was stronger than her slender frame implied.

"Can you give Richard and me a moment, Austin? We were just finishing up a discussion." Her eyes pleaded with him, and he leaned down to brush a kiss over her brow.

"Anything for you, Meghan. Remember that."

He glared at Richard as he left and nodded at Maya and her friend Jake on his way over to Griffin and Alex. Griffin was the quietest one of the Montgomery clan, but since he *was* a Montgomery, he wasn't all that quiet. Alex had recently been giving Griffin a run for his money in the quiet department. Austin didn't know how to fix that. As the oldest Montgomery sibling, Austin felt it was his duty to take care of and protect his brothers and sisters—no matter the cost.

"What are you two doing on the sidelines of all the action?" he asked in greeting.

Alex just shrugged, his gaze off in the distance, a tumbler of whiskey in his hand rather than a beer. It was just shy of five o'clock, but considering the day his brother could have had with his job as a photographer and his wife, who hadn't even bothered to show up, Austin wasn't going to judge. Yet.

"We're just watching the action," Griffin responded, taking a drink of his own beer.

"Where's Jessica?" Austin asked, speaking of Alex's wife.

Alex's jaw tightened, but he still didn't turn to meet Austin's gaze. "Not here. As you can see."

Austin raised a brow, and Griffin just shook his head slightly. Well, hell. Austin didn't know how to fix this— whatever this was—but he knew if he had a chance, he'd try. He didn't like to see this cold version of his brother, the only one who looked alone in a sea of people, which, when she was there, included his wife and high school sweetheart.

"Well, look who just showed up," Griffin said with a smile.

Austin turned to see their friend—Griffin's best friend in fact—Decker stroll into the backyard. His beat up leather jacket looked like it had seen better days, and his hair brushed his collar. He wasn't a Montgomery by birth, but he was one by heart.

"Decker!" Marie Montgomery ran across the backyard and jumped into Decker's arms.

Decker's face broke into a smile and caught her with ease.

Austin couldn't hear what they said to one another, but Austin knew it was only for the two of them. His mother loved Decker like one of her own, and when Decker's father had been in prison, he stayed with the Montgomerys more often than not. Sure, Decker's mother was still alive—barely, it seemed, after Decker's father got through with her—but she hadn't been strong enough to raise a boy on her own. The Montgomerys had taken him in when the law allowed, and if they could have, Austin was sure they'd have adopted him to make nine instead of eight.

"Did someone say Decker?" the youngest sibling, Miranda, asked as she came up to Austin's side.

Austin automatically lifted his arm so she sank into his side like they'd done since she could stand. Even before then, he'd placed her on his hip and taken her around the house, the age gap between them creating a stronger bond.

"Mom found him, so don't worry, he'll have food in his belly soon," Griffin teased.

"He works for Montgomery Inc. so I don't know why you're acting like you haven't seen him in ages," Alex grunted.

Miranda stuck her tongue out at Alex, acting like they were children again rather than grown and out of the house. "He's been out of town for six weeks working on that satellite project for Wes. Now he's back. Plus, I'm finally back from school and starting my new job, so it will be nice to have him around."

Something about the way she said that made the hair on the back of Austin's neck stand on end, but he didn't have a chance to think about it too hard, as his mother let out a sharp whistle that made his teeth ache.

Well, she had to do something to wrangle eight rowdy children.

"Now that we're all here, I want to make sure you all enjoy your food, drink, and conversation," his mother boomed, her hand firmly in their father's hand. "Stay as long as you'd like, eat as much as you can, and live life. Now, for my own children, we're having a family meeting at the end, so you don't get to go. You know I love you, so stay." She gave them a bright—almost too bright—smile then lifted her drink. The others around them lifted their drinks in unison then began talking again—albeit a little nervously.

Austin frowned. There was something in the way she spoke that put him on alert. He looked at their father and let his gaze trace the lines on the large man's face. Something was up, and Austin didn't like it. He wanted these other people to leave so he could find out exactly what this family meeting was about. It wasn't unusual to have one at these things, as it was the one time they were all in one place other than a holiday. Since it was the first one where they were all together in a long while, he hoped it was just a family meeting to reconnect, but he had a feeling it was something more. He met his siblings' gazes one by one and knew they were feeling the same thing.

Something was off, and he didn't know what.

It took less than two hours for people to leave, yet Austin felt like it had been years. He hadn't been able to pry anything out of either parent, no matter how hard he tried.

He found himself wedged between Meghan and Decker on one of the couches in the living room. The rest of the family sprawled on the various other pieces of furniture while Miranda and Maya sat on the floor together, their hands firmly clasped as if they, too, knew something was wrong. It didn't surprise Austin to find Decker within the group as he was as much a Montgomery as anyone, just as it didn't surprise him that Richard had left with the children. Richard made it clear he wasn't a Montgomery, but the children were Montgomerys by blood. Sure, maybe the kids didn't need to be there for a family meeting for other reasons, but this seemed different.

"Why did Richard take the kids?" he whispered to his sister.

Meghan narrowed her eyes at him and shook her head. "Don't, Austin. Not now." He opened his mouth to speak, and she shook her head again. "Please."

He sighed then nodded. "For now, baby girl." He gripped her hand, and she tangled her fingers with his.

Dad came in, his body larger than life, but something was off in the way he carried himself. Something that Austin would have caught on to sooner if he hadn't been focused on illicit texts, a honey-haired woman he shouldn't want, and his siblings, who meant the world to him. Harry folded himself into his armchair that had been part of the house for as long as Austin could remember. Mom followed quickly, concern in her gaze, then sat in her own chair right beside her husband.

"What is it, Mom?" Maya asked. "You're scaring us."

Murmurs of agreement sounded around the room, and Meghan's pressure on Austin's hand tightened.

Marie gave them a sad smile. "I'm so happy to have my babies home."

Austin swallowed hard. "Tell us, Mom."

Harry cleared his throat then leaned forward, his hands clasped in front of him, his forearms resting on his thighs. Both of his parents were forces of nature. Neither would let the other stand alone; they either took turns in the lead or led together. That's what made their marriage as rock solid as it was. The fact that they both looked uneasy and couldn't form words made Austin want to bolt. He wasn't sure he wanted to hear what they had to say.

Harry met each one of his children's gazes, one by one. "Well, kids. I have cancer. Prostate cancer in fact."

Austin's world broke in half, the silence in the room an overwhelming vacuum of confusion, pain, and loss.

"What?" he breathed. Or he thought he had. No sound had come out, and from the lack of voices around him, his siblings were as shocked as he.

It couldn't be. This strong man, this man who had raised them with a strong back and open heart couldn't have cancer. Cancer killed. He knew that. Cancer couldn't take his dad. Not now. Not ever.

"What's the prognosis?" Decker asked, his voice devoid of emotion. Austin looked over as his friend leaned down and ran a hand over Miranda's hair. His sister leaned into Decker's hold, tears streaming down her face.

In fact, there wasn't a dry eye in the room other than his and Decker's.

He didn't know why he wasn't crying. It didn't make sense. The words coming out of his father's mouth about prognosis, treatment, and what it would mean to the family didn't compute. He'd ask later in detail and find out how he could help, but right then, he couldn't think. Couldn't breathe.

His father, the center of the Montgomery family, had cancer.

Nothing else mattered.

CHAPTER FOUR

"Thank you and enjoy your night out," Sierra said with a smile. Her two middle-aged customers grinned and blushed at each other as they made their way out of Eden. Sierra held back a happy sigh at the sounds of laughter, teasing, and murmurs.

Eden was officially open for business.

It had been only two days, but those two days had been some of the best of her life. Sure, she wanted to scream, throw up, or shake uncontrollably whenever she thought of the monumental chance she was taking in opening a slightly above average boutique in the middle of downtown Denver. She'd read the statistics for opening a small business in the metro area and knew the risks and pitfalls. That didn't mean she could just walk away. She hadn't come from money, but she'd come from comfort. It wasn't naive of her to think she could provide that for herself in the future as well.

Eden sold clothes for the city girl in Denver. It wasn't a New York boutique with the odd angles and daring choices that some could pull off, but not those here in the wild west. She grinned at that. Contrary to popular belief, the only horses in the city pulled carriages and there wasn't a five-gallon hat to be seen. Okay, maybe on that last part she lied a bit. There were a few cowboys, but none of them had said darlin' to her in the past twenty minutes. Most of them worked the land and didn't come near her boutique.

The clothes, lacy undergarments, and scents she sold were things she'd wear herself. Or things her two assistants, Jasinda and Becky, would wear, as they were a few years younger and had slightly different taste and body shapes. She did her best to sell clothing in a wide variety of sizes, colors, and styles. So far, from the steady stream of people who had entered her doors, she knew she'd struck a chord. If that chord continued to ring for longer than a few days, she'd happily do a jig right on the 16th Street Mall.

Her phone chirped, and she bit her lip. The morning had passed too quickly, and now her scheduled afternoon off—one the girls made her take—was upon her. She'd worked that morning and would work late into the night to make it up. Maybe she'd cancel her appointment and work some more. She couldn't leave Eden alone when it was in its infancy. It would be irresponsible.

"Go, Sierra," Becky said from beside her. "Jasinda and I can handle whatever comes our way. Plus, if we need you, you'll be right across the street. You haven't left the store but to sleep and hopefully eat for almost a week. You need to see sunlight for a moment and then do what you need to so you can feel like a human again."

Sierra opened her mouth to start her excuses, but Jasinda, with her big red hair and her smoky eyes, shook her head. "Don't even try to say we can't handle it, darling. Go get your tattoo, piercing, or whatever you're planning since you won't tell us what it is and let us handle the register for a few hours. We all know you'll be back in the morning to lead the charge."

"I can't leave Eden as soon as I opened it," Sierra complained. "What was I thinking?"

"You're thinking that if you don't leave this building right now, you're going to tire yourself out to the point you won't be any use to us." Becky crossed her arms over her chest. "Get a coffee from Hailey since it's after the lunch rush then go take your appointment."

"But what if—"

"Go, woman," Jasinda cut her off.

She threw her hand up then picked up her purse. "Fine, but you need to come to me if there is *anything* wrong. You understand? Eden...Eden's my baby."

Jasinda gave her a small smile then leaned into her to brush a kiss over her cheek. Becky did the same on Sierra's other side, and Sierra relaxed.

"Go," Becky ordered. "We'll care for your baby. It's what you hired us to do after all."

With one last look at her happy customers and the store that was the result of her blood, sweat, and tears, she walked out into the sunlight and made her way across the street to Montgomery Ink. She didn't stop for coffee at Hailey's, as she was already running on enough nerves and any caffeine would make it worse.

Sierra took a deep breath and rolled her shoulders. She wasn't on her way to the guillotine or about to walk the plank with a smarmy pirate at her back. It was only a consultation with an artist. Nothing too drastic. She wouldn't even have to take her clothes off.

Okay, so that sounded odd even to her, but she let it go. It had been six days since she last stepped into Montgomery Ink, and once again, she found herself on the precipice of something more—something that scared the crap out of her.

Since she last saw Austin and the others, Eden had opened to the public, running her ragged. The man with blue eyes and a beard she wanted to feel on the intimate silk of her thighs filled her mind more often than she wanted him to, but she did her best to push that aside. Eden needed her full attention, and any life-altering decisions—whether about men or tattoos—had to be put on hold so she could live her dream.

Eden had been up and running for two days—and would hopefully run for much, much longer—and Sierra had an appointment with an artist she hoped could help her deal with the part of herself she'd tried to hide for so long.

When Callie put her name in their electronic appointment book, Sierra hadn't asked which artist she'd have. From what she'd heard about the shop, she trusted all those who worked there with her skin. Or at least she tried to. Hopefully, she would find out who her artist was today and she'd start the next step in her healing. Just the thought of showing them where she needed her ink made her shudder. She wasn't quite ready for that, but she knew she would have to be soon.

She wasn't a coward, but dear God, she wanted to be. Just once.

"Sierra! You made it."

Callie's welcoming voice soothed Sierra's nerves immediately. The other woman had such a young, vivacious energy about her, though when Sierra looked closer, she could see a bit of an old soul in those bright eyes.

She'd learned the last time she was there that Callie was Austin's apprentice, learning art and technique, and gaining experience from, as Callie put it, the best of the best. With the way Callie seemed to bounce from word to word, Sierra thought that Austin had the best of both worlds. He could stand in the back and act all broody and rude while Callie brought in all the clients. No, that wasn't nice. She knew from her research that Austin was a very talented artist, sought after from all over the world if reviews could be trusted. His sister Maya was much of the same.

Sierra licked her lips nervously then gave in to Callie's exuberant hug.

"Nice to see you, Callie," she said, trying to keep it polite considering the war within her made her stomach want to heave.

"It's good to see you too. Your artist is almost ready for a consult, so go ahead and take a seat on one of the comfy leather couches. Can I get you a coffee or water? Maybe a juice?"

Sierra tilted her head, amused. "I'm good, thanks. Are you the Montgomery Ink receptionist as well?"

Callie blushed, shaking her head. "We keep running out of those. We hire college kids mostly who need to pay for their tuition at UCD or the other Auraria campuses right off Spear Boulevard, but they get flaky over time between deadlines, parties, and the fact that the campus just built a freaking dorm right off the highway." Callie rolled her eyes.

"Anyway, we're between receptionists right now so I'm doing my best. Hopefully, Austin and Maya will hire someone soon so they don't have to deal with the Mac of Doom."

Sierra's eyebrows rose. "Mac of Doom?"

Callie gestured toward the computer on the corner desk, leaning over to whisper. "Maya bought that because she wanted everything on the desk or whatever instead of a whole tower, and now no one knows how to use it. If you ask me, you should say goodbye soon because, between Sloane and Austin, there might be an 'accident'."

Sierra snorted then took a seat. "Poor guys."

"Hey, poor me. I'm the one who has to fix whatever they mess up. Now if you're sure you don't need anything, I'm going to go work on a sketch for tomorrow's client. Your artist will be by in a bit."

It wasn't lost on her that Callie still had not mentioned the artist's name. Maybe it was an artist-temperament thing. Sierra's gaze traveled over the large room where eight stations sat against walls filled with artwork—photos, paintings, sketches, and a few ceramics and metal sculptures. There were a couple of people Sierra didn't immediately know, but she'd seen Sloane and Maya around enough to know them by their faces. Each of them was working intently on their client. Sloane had his head down over a middle-aged man's thigh, working with a red color that mixed with his blood. The sight made Sierra a bit queasy, so she turned her attention to Maya. Austin's sister flicked her tongue ring in and out of her mouth as she focused on the line work on her client's foot.

Just the thought of someone digging a needle into her foot made Sierra wince. No thank you, not for her first tattoo. First? Was she planning on getting a second or third? Maybe she should just focus on getting through this first one without passing out or weeping uncontrollably.

"Callie?" she asked before the other woman headed off completely. "Who is my artist?"

"That would be me."

Sierra's heart sped up, and she clamped her thighs together at the deep rumble of Austin's voice. Oh no. Austin couldn't be her artist. She wouldn't know what to do with herself if this man had his hands on her. She didn't him want to see exactly where she wanted her ink. That was too personal. Too personal for a man that invaded her space by just breathing. She also reminded herself she didn't even like him. He was a rude, overbearing oaf. It didn't matter that her body seemed to want him.

Her mind did not.

"Okay then, I'll leave you both to it." Callie ran away, and Sierra narrowed her eyes at the woman. Oh, Callie knew *exactly* what she was doing.

Great.

"I thought you told me to leave," she whispered. She hadn't meant to whisper, but it was all she'd been able to force out.

Austin nodded, his eyes full of pain. Pain she hadn't seen before in those deep blue eyes. She would have remembered.

"I apologize for the way I acted before. Shannon, the woman who was leaving as you came in, put my back up, and I acted harshly."

Surprised he admitted to his rudeness, she could only forgive him. After all, she wanted—no, needed—to know what had put that broken look on his face. She wasn't vain enough to think it was about her and his need to apologize. No, this was about something far deeper.

"I'm sorry for my words when I first walked in. I've heard great things about Montgomery Ink, and I want a tattoo, not to judge who gets one." There. She'd said it.

Austin nodded but didn't smile, didn't do much of anything. "Come on to my station in the back, and we can talk about what you'd like." Again, his voice was devoid of emotion. No, that wasn't quite right. There was something there, something that made her yearn to reach out to him and make it better.

She took a seat on the bench he offered her as he sat down on a stool, picking up a sketchpad and pencil. "Tell me what you'd like."

Sierra searched his face, unable to focus on any type of design. "What's wrong, Austin? What's put such sadness in your eyes?"

She cursed herself for asking such a deeply personal question of a man she didn't know, but there was something there, a connection she had no right feeling.

Austin blinked then swallowed hard. Her gaze traced the long line of his throat and his beard. "What do you mean?"

She shook her head. "I'm sorry. I shouldn't have asked that. You just look so sad, and I wanted to know if there was anything I can do. Silly, right? I don't even know you."

Austin set down the sketchpad and pencil, resting his forearms on his thighs. "I'm not in the right frame of mind to draw anyway. Or, rather, I'm in the perfect mindset if you think about it. I know you came here for a consult, and I'll get to that. Soon. Okay." He met her gaze, that agony a sharp slice across her heart. "My dad has cancer. He told us the day after you walked out of here, and I haven't been able to deal with it. I don't know if I can."

Sierra sucked in a breath and gripped his hand, the shock of the connection surprising her, but she pushed past it, thoughts of Austin's family in the forefront of her mind.

"I'm so sorry, Austin. Oh God, I had no idea it was something like that. I know my words are paltry, but I'll be thinking of your father and the rest of you. I'm so sorry," she repeated. Her eyes filled with tears for the man in front of her and the man who'd raised him, a man she'd never met but knew Austin cared for a great deal.

Austin cupped her cheek, an action that startled them both. "Thank you, Sierra." He pulled back quickly, clearing his throat. "He'll be okay. He has to be. And if I only focus on just him and what's going on, I won't be able to function, so let's talk about your ink."

Her cheek was still warm from his touch, and she wanted more. Wanted his hands on her, wanted his gaze on her as she undressed for him. She wanted to kneel at his feet as he brushed her hair back, letting her know everything was okay.

She pulled back at that thought. That wasn't her anymore. Those thoughts weren't hers. They couldn't be.

She'd grown from the woman she'd been with Jason, and she couldn't, no, wouldn't, be that woman with Austin. He was the one who would lay ink on her skin, not lay claim to it.

That was if she could find the courage to do so in the first place.

"Sierra? Your ink? Callie said something about flowers, but that means so many things. I need to know more."

She sucked in a breath, her lower lip trembling. "I...I want daisies on my right side. I don't know how many, or how large or even what color, but I need them to...cover up, or rather go around, something."

Austin furrowed his brow. "I'm covering up other ink?"

She shook her head. "This is my first tattoo."

Austin gripped her hand softly, his touch soothing, calming, an anchor. "What am I covering up, Sierra?" His voice had lowered, as if he was talking to a frightened lamb on the edge of a precipice.

Though that was an apt description at the moment, she didn't want to be that person.

Not anymore.

"I have a couple scars." Oh, what a lie, but she'd tell the whole of it soon. She'd need to. "I'm...I'm not ready to show them to you yet, so I know you can't design anything."

Austin squeezed her hand, and she cursed herself.

Jesus she was an idiot.

"I'm wasting your time today, Austin and I'm sorry for it. I thought I'd take it one step at a time, but that was stupid. You'd need to see my side so you can design."

Austin nodded then pulled back. "If you're not ready to show me, then we can take it one slow step at a time. I don't mind, Sierra. I will say that doing a cover-up on scars isn't possible, not in most cases. It's an art form in itself that we don't do too much of here unless we know the scars and can trust your ink won't fuck up in the future because of them. The skin that's scarred is too different and puckered usually, and the ink will end up spreading out over the scar, rather than being where we wanted it in the first place. However, we can do something *around* the scars."

"I researched that. But your time is valuable."

"So is your recovery and healing."

Touched, she blinked up at him, licking her lips. "Then what can we do today?"

He grinned at her then, his eyes filling with a touch of laughter for the first time since she'd walked in. That alone made her feel as if coming in that day was worth it.

"If it's okay with you, I'll trace your side so I can get an idea of the size of canvas we'll be working with. Then I'll work on a few daisy types and show you the next time you come in. Hopefully by then, I'll be able to see exactly what you mean by scars, and then we can move on to the next step."

Her hands shook, but she nodded, knowing in order to fully do what she wanted she'd need to show him. It was a no-brainer, but it still didn't make it any easier.

"That sounds like a plan then."

"I can tell you want ink, Sierra. If you didn't, then we wouldn't be sitting here. I don't mind waiting until you're ready. And when we do start actually tattooing, and even when you show me your scars, I'll put up the curtain we have so it's just you and me. No one else. What do you say?"

That idea appealed more to her than it should have, and she nodded readily.

"Okay then, stand up and lift your arm. Show me exactly how large you're thinking and then I'll trace you. Like I said, I won't know exactly what I will be doing until I see everything. Even if this is just for show today, it's still a step. You know?" He met her gaze. "That means I'll have to put my hands on you. You okay with that?"

More than okay.

Instead of saying that, she nodded again and stood.

She turned so her side faced Austin and she wouldn't have to meet his gaze. As soon as he put his hands on her, she jumped.

"Steady, Legs, I'm not going to bite," he teased. "Well, not unless you ask me to."

Despite herself, she snorted. "Stop calling me Legs." It was insulting...and made her want to dissolve in a puddle at his feet. Damn the man.

"I like the look of your legs, so I'm going to keep doing it. Now, how big are we thinking?"

Big. Thick and long.

Wait, that wasn't what he was asking.

Austin gave a deep chuckle. "I can see from your face where your mind went, and yes, big is a good word for it. However, I was talking about your tattoo."

Sierra refused to meet his gaze but lifted her chin. "Confident of yourself. And I'm thinking the entire ribcage, side of my stomach, and down over my hips." Her scar covered most of that, but since she would have to have ink around it, she wanted something to remember. Something that was worth the pain and memories.

"That's big, but I think with your curves there, it's going to look great. So hold tight and let me trace you."

The pencil traced over her side, and his hand brushed the underside of her breast. They both gasped, but neither commented. They needed to stay professional for both their sakes. His calloused fingers pressed through her shirt and she held back a sigh. She had recovered most of the feeling in her side, and his hands were so large, so...male...that she new she'd never forget his touch.

"Ride with me."

Sierra turned, confused. "What?"

Austin gazed into her eyes, intense. "Ride with me. On my bike in the mountains."

Sierra broke out into a cold sweat. Visions of flames, the squeal of tires, and the smell of burnt flesh caused her knees to give out.

"Shit, baby, I'm sorry," Austin murmured, his hands on her hips then her cheeks. "You don't have to ride with me, not if you're going to react like that. You don't have to tell me why, but you can if you want. I'll listen."

She sucked in a breath, embarrassed for reacting like that. "I'm sorry."

"Don't be, Sierra."

Damn it. She didn't want to be locked away in her past, unable to take a step into any kind of future. Eden had been a step, as had coming into Montgomery Ink, but it wasn't enough. Not yet.

She needed to be a big girl and learn to breathe again.

Her gaze met Austin's concerned one, and she swallowed hard. "Yes, Austin. Yes, I'll ride with you."

He looked like he didn't believe her, but she'd show him. She was ready to move on, even if she had to force herself. She wouldn't be hidden and caged. Not anymore.

If Austin could help her, well, then she'd take that step. Finally.

CHAPTER FIVE

S hep Montgomery ignored the dagger eyes aimed at him, taking it as par for the course with this particular client. When Lisette came in for any ink, her man, Mathieu, came with her. And by came with her, Shep meant guarded her like a pit bull and practically growled at Shep for daring to touch *his* woman.

With a roll of his eyes, he cleaned off leftover ink and plasma so he could finish the shading on the koi fish. Lisette had come in with those flirty eyes of hers and her easy smile, begging Shep to draw a koi surrounded by a field of flowers and cool water over her hip and thigh. Shep loved working with her since she was so easy to please once they got the right design.

Shep guessed that Mathieu would cheerfully rip Shep's arms off for where he had to place his hands during the process. And Shep knew his own wife, Shea, would probably do the same thing if anyone touched him like that. Actually, Shep might hurt anyone who thought they could ink Shea too, so he didn't blame Mathieu in the slightest.

"You feeling good, Lisette?" Shep asked, his attention on his final shading and not on the man looming over the both of them. Seriously, Mathieu was one big motherfucker.

"Mmm," she hummed, and Shep had to smile. He loved it when his clients fell into the bliss that was tattooing rather than tensed up the entire time. Lisette was a pro at this.

He added one last stroke then wiped the area, sitting back to appreciate his work. "All done. You need help up to see it in the mirror?"

"I've got her," Mathieu grumbled.

Shep held back a brighter smile. He'd known that's what the big man would say, but he liked to egg him on anyway.

Lisette let out a little gasp, and Shep knew his work was done. They went over the aftercare instructions that he knew she was aware of since she had a half sleeve of flowers already, but he never let anyone leave Midnight Ink without hearing it and agreeing to it on Shep's terms. As he watched Mathieu carefully walk his woman out of the shop, Shep bounced on his feet, antsy to get back to his own woman. Lisette was his last full client of the day, and after he finished the next consultation with Chavon, one of his favorite people in the world, he'd be able to go home to his wife.

His wife.

He'd never get used to that, but God, he loved the sound of it. They'd courted quickly, got engaged even faster, and then married at the justice of the peace because they couldn't wait any longer. He'd thought Shea would have wanted the big wedding with the even bigger dress, flowers and all the trappings, but he was wrong. It'd been Shea who wanted the small wedding in the little office so she could call him her own. She'd been the one to pull him from the coffee house on the warm day with a smile on her face. He couldn't ask for anything better.

He'd do anything for her, and saying 'I do' in that cramped office was only the small part of it.

By the time he finished the consult for Chavon's latest ink—this one *not* on her ass contrary to what her man thought Shep did only when it came to her—he was beyond ready to head home to Shea.

"Say hi to Shea for me," Sassy, the Midnight Ink receptionist and one of his closest friends said as he packed up.

"Will do," he said back. "And don't tire your men out too much." Sassy was engaged to not one man, but two—Rafe and Ian—who thought she was the center of their universe.

"Let me know when you have a date for the wedding. Shea's been asking."

Sassy nodded, an odd light coming into her eyes, and turned away. He sighed, knowing he'd have to deal with that if she'd let him. That was a big *if*.

He said goodbye to his 'family' at Midnight, then headed home, that odd gnawing in his gut coming back. There was something up with Shea, and he couldn't figure it out. They hadn't been married long enough for him to learn every tic and look, but he was enjoying figuring them out. However, he knew something was wrong. She didn't act any differently. She'd still smile brightly at him, but sometimes, it would be a little too bright. Her normal, quiet personality hadn't changed, and she truly let herself go only when it was just the two of them. She was ice to his fire, and he wouldn't have it any other way. But he needed her to be happy.

He'd figure it out. He always did.

As soon as he stepped into the house, he opened his arms, and Shea rocketed herself against him like she did every evening. Seriously. Best. Thing. Ever. He hoped this would remain something they did every day no matter how old or busy they eventually became. Okay, so maybe when he was older, he might break a hip doing it, but it'd be worth it. He worked later hours than Shea because he started later in the day, so she was always home first. If it had been the other way around, he knew they'd end up in the same embrace. He inhaled that sweet scent of hers, crushing her to his body then slanting his mouth over hers. She tasted of tea and grapes.

"God, I love you, Shea Montgomery."

He'd never get over hearing her new last name. The name, however antiquated the practice of her taking his name, reminded them both that she was his...and he was hers.

Shea pulled back, breathless. "I love you too, Shep."

She smiled, but it took a second longer to reach her eyes than it should have.

There. There was something in her eyes. Something wrong. He'd asked her about it before, and she'd waved it off, saying he was just seeing things. He wouldn't ask again. No, he'd find it out on his own. He'd just do his best to make her happy no matter what. He'd hate to think he was failing at this marriage thing right out the gate. That was not something he would allow.

"I was just getting everything out for dinner. Want to help?"

He kissed her nose then nodded. They cooked dinner together most nights, the dance around the counters as their bodies brushed against one another a type of foreplay that made the rest of their nights even better.

His phone buzzed in his pocket, and he took it out, one arm still around Shea. "It's Austin," he said after looking at the screen.

"Answer it," Shea said. He'd introduced Austin to her when they were dating, and the two of them hit it off easily.

"Hey, bro', what's up?" Shep kissed the top of Shea's head as they made their way to the kitchen.

"Hey, do you think you can come up to Denver for a bit? You and Shea."

Shep froze, squeezing Shea's arm at Austin's tone. The other man's voice didn't sound like the warm, yet broody man he'd grown up with. Something was off. Shea looked up at him at his touch, worry in her gaze.

"What's wrong?" he asked, his throat choking up.

Austin sighed. "I...shit. I don't know how to say this. Damn it. I shouldn't have to say this at all. It's not fair." He took a deep breath while Shep held his. "Dad has cancer, man."

Shep staggered back, using Shea as support. "What? You're serious?"

"As serious as it gets," Austin said softly. "He's starting treatment soon, and I think he'd like you there. You and Shea. He's never met her, you know," he said, stating the obvious.

He swallowed hard, blinking away the tears in his eyes. Shep's parents had moved to Oregon when he moved to New Orleans over a decade ago, but he'd grown up in the big mess of Montgomerys in Denver. The idea that bigger-than-life Harry was sick just didn't compute.

There really was only one answer to give.

"I'll be up there as soon as I can, for as long as I can, Austin. You can count on me."

Austin let out a breath, and Shep wanted to reach through the phone and grip his cousin hard. "Thanks, man. You can stay at Griffin's place since he has the guesthouse. You and Shea. That way you both have some privacy for as long as you need it. I have the guest room, but I know y'all are newlyweds and all that shit. I don't know why I'm even rambling on like this, but fuck. I'm lost, man. I...I know all the siblings are here, but I could use you too. You know?"

Shep sucked in a breath then kissed Shea's temple. "Anything, Austin. You know it. We'll make the arrangements, and I'll get back to you on the when."

"Thanks, Shep."

"See you soon, cousin, and breathe, okay? Harry...Harry's stronger than all of us."

"That's what I thought too. See you soon."

His cousin hung up, and Shep stared at the phone in his hand. Shit. Harry had cancer. Fucking cancer. That didn't make any sense. Cancer wasn't supposed to touch his family. It was something that happened to others and he donated money for treatments and cures. Crass and cruel, but that's how his mind dealt with the things that made no sense while tearing a hole in his gut. He didn't know how to work with this.

"I heard most of that, baby." Shea cupped his face, her eyes filling with tears. "I'm so sorry. Let me call work and take time off. What I can't take off, I can do from my computer anywhere I go. Then I'll look up plane fare and all of that. We'll stay in Denver as long as we can. Okay?"

He kissed her then, his lips a soft caress before sinking into her fully. She moaned into him even as their tears mixed together.

"I love you, Shea. Never leave me. Please. Just be by side forever."

His wife licked her lips even as that odd light shot over her eyes again before she blinked, clearing her gaze. "Of course, Shep. I love you. I'm not going anywhere."

He held her close, knowing that he needed to be strong for Austin, for Shea, for Harry, for the lot of them. He might be only a cousin in this, but he was family. He and Shea would head up to Denver and do what they could. And while he was there, he'd find out what was up with his wife. There was only so much a man could take, and he didn't want there to be anything between them that could harm their relationship.

Life was too short for the kind of pain that could be healed.

CHAPTER SIX

Austin gripped Sierra's hips, keeping her steady as she blinked up at him, her gaze drunk with pleasure, but still on him. Only him. He licked his lips and could practically taste her sweetness on his tongue. God, he couldn't wait to have the sweet cream on his taste buds.

"I'm going to fuck you hard, Legs," he growled, his body shaking as he fought for control.

"Take me." She lifted her chest, her breasts standing out like a succulent feast. Her nipples looked like fucking ripe berries in the clamps he'd put her in, begging for his tongue.

Austin let his cock drag along her swollen pussy, taking in that quick catch of her breath. His gaze traced her breasts then up to where he'd tied each of her arms to the bedposts using the brand-new rope he'd bought her.

Seriously the best image ever.

He couldn't wait to plunge deep within her and have that tight pussy of hers clench his cock, milking him down to the last drop. Just as he pulled back, his eyes opened, and he cursed himself.

Great. A dream. Another fucking dream.

And he spent on his stomach before getting to the good part.

Austin rolled out of bed, his body groaning from a restless sleep and vivid dreams. Thankfully, he slept naked so there would be less clean-up, considering he dreamed like a thirteen-year-old boy. He staggered back, his body not quite awake and in desperate need of coffee. He pulled on the sheets, careful not to get any of his mess back on him.

He stumbled naked to the laundry room and stuffed the sheets into the washer, starting it and adding the soap with one eye open. He'd probably regret doing this half-awake later, but he had enough experience cleaning his own clothes he was reasonably sure he wouldn't end up with water and soap on the floor. Maybe.

Damn it. He couldn't believe he'd come in his dreams like a young kid first learning the shape of a woman. He was almost forty for God's sake. Apparently he didn't need a little pill to put a hop in his step and a mess in his sheets when he had Sierra and those long legs of hers on his mind.

At the moment he'd rather have them around his hips as he drove into her.

His cock filled again, and he cursed himself. Really? It wasn't even seven in the morning, and he already had another hard-on after coming in his sleep because of a fucking dream. It was just one more reason he needed to get laid and get a rein on that control he was so famous for.

With a sigh, he jumped in the shower, ignored his aching cock, and then made a cup of coffee. Thankfully, today was his day off and he didn't have anywhere special to be. Normally he'd go for a ride on his bike up into the mountains and maybe even to Estes Park, but he wasn't in the mood. Decker would be over later that day for food and beer, and on any other week, his brother in everything but blood would ride with him on his own bike. This week, this month, though, was different. Neither of them had gone riding since they heard about Harry's cancer.

Shit.

Cancer.

Austin still couldn't wrap his head around that. He'd buried his head in the sand actually. While the rest of his family had either tried to not leave his folk's sides or done as much research as they could, Austin had stayed away, saying he'd be there if anyone needed him.

Fuck, that made him an ass.

He was just too freaking scared to look up things like treatments, prognoses, and other medical terms that left him in a cold sweat at just the thought. He was the oldest brother, the oldest Montgomery kid, yet he was failing.

Austin rubbed the area over his heart with his fist then went to his porch to watch the sun finish rising. He loved his house and his views. He had a wraparound porch so he could see the sun rise or set depending on where he sat. Here, he could ignore what went on around him and focus on absolutely nothing, a fucking ridiculous way to live.

He needed to get his head out of his ass and think about what was actually going on in his family. He needed to stop dreaming about a woman who looked so scared at having anyone touch her skin she practically bolted like a frightened rabbit at his gaze alone.

Austin sat there for another hour, finishing his coffee and feeling the cool mountain air slowly warm as the sun rose higher.

His phone buzzed on the corner table on his deck, and he picked it up, his heart racing. What if it was his parents telling him something worse? Shit. Thinking about what was coming rather than actually putting together a plan was making him crazy. First thing after Decker left, or maybe even when the man was there, he'd do his research. It wasn't like him to be so out of it when things mattered. He hated himself for putting himself into this situation in the first place. There was no point in worrying himself sick over nightmares with no evidence. He had a feeling that once he really went into it he might have even more nightmares.

His father deserved every ounce of Austin's strength and determination, however. And hiding in his house wasn't what Austin had been raised to do.

Without looking at the screen, he answered the phone and immediately regretted it.

"Austin, baby."

He was so over this. So fucking over. "Shannon. Stop calling. I tried to be nice, but we broke up months ago. A mutual decision I might add. I'm not normally such an asshole, but if you don't stop clinging and practically stalking me, I'm going to have to take action." Calling the cops for a stalker? Not what he wanted to do, but Shannon wouldn't leave him the hell alone no matter what he'd done to stop her. He'd never fight with a woman physically, so he'd have to give up and have someone else deal with it for him.

"We had something, baby. Please. Please don't leave me, sugar."

Austin closed his eyes and pinched his nose. "No, we didn't, and we both know it. You loved me even less than I loved you. Which was next to nothing." Harsh, but the truth. "Find yourself someone you can actually love and care for, and find that future you want, Shannon. It's not me." At her silence, Austin sighed. "Goodbye, Shannon."

He pressed *End* on his phone, but he had a feeling he wasn't through with whatever she wanted. He just hoped she didn't take it any further than she already had.

His morning even more tainted now, he got up off his chair on the deck and made his way inside. His house was situated on the edge of a small ravine; even though he couldn't really see his neighbors, they were there. He actually lived in a cul-de-sac with a dirt road at the end that led to his two-story house. Well, two stories and a full basement that could be seen on the back end since his house was on a slope. The entire two top floors on the back end that faced the ravine were all glass so he could see a closer foothill, some of the Rockies, and any wildlife that found themselves walking about.

He loved it. He got city and country all in one with just his house. Plus, he could blare his music up as high as he wanted and not have a problem.

After he ate breakfast, he went through his normal day off routine of cleaning and puttering around. He might live alone, but he didn't want to deal with the mess of it all. He wasn't as much of a clean freak as some of his family members, but he liked to be somewhat clutter-free.

As he checked his mail, he put the bills aside for later then went through the rest of it, throwing out the junk mail that seemed to accumulate faster than even the bills. On top was a thick envelope from a company he didn't recognize, and he frowned. A lawyer? Maybe it was for the shop or even Montgomery Inc. Given all the Montgomerys, sometimes people sent things to the wrong addresses. Luckily his immediate family lived close enough that it wasn't a problem to hand the mail to whomever it belonged.

"Austin, you around?"

Decker walked in without knocking, and Austin set the mail aside. He'd deal with whatever it was later.

"I'm in the kitchen. You want coffee?"

Decker strolled in, wearing his worn jeans low on his hips and a black cotton T-shirt that looked like it'd seen better days. Austin looked down at his own clothes and snorted.

Apparently they'd be twins that day.

Black T-shirts and worn jeans were their uniforms—days off or no.

"Coffee. Please. I only had enough for one cup at home and wasn't about to spend five dollars on bitter coffee on the way here."

Austin rolled his eyes. "You drink Starbucks and Hailey's coffee all the time. Don't know why you're complaining."

Decker's brows rose. "I did not just hear you call Hailey's coffee bitter."

Austin winced as he poured a cup for Decker. "No, that's not what I meant. I meant Starbucks. Crap. Don't tell her I said that."

Decker grinned, taking the cup then blowing over it. "What'll you give me for my silence?"

Austin flipped him off. "I won't kick your ass."

"You can try, old man."

"You're getting closer to the big number, too."

Decker grinned. "I'm twenty-nine. You're thirty-eight. Those are two different big numbers, bro. Just saying."

"Fuck you."

"No thanks. I prefer my bedmates with a little less chest hair."

Austin grinned. "Only a little less? Is there something you should tell me? You know we'd all love you no matter your preference."

Decker groaned. "Shut up."

Austin rolled his eyes then went to his living room, knowing Decker would follow when he wanted. There would be a game on so they'd relax and do nothing. Maybe research if he got up the nerve, but nothing too taxing.

In reality, Decker was Griffin's best friend, but Austin got along with the younger man just as well. Decker had been living with his family off and on for most of his teens so he'd become close to every Montgomery. As evidenced from that conversation that had changed their lives, he was included in family meetings as well without a second thought.

"So I hear Shep and Shea are on their way to Denver?" Decker asked after a few moments of peaceful silence.

"Yeah. I called him up and asked for them to come." He shrugged as if it didn't matter, but it clearly did to all of them more than they wanted to admit. "Dad hasn't met Shea yet, and though Shep's parents are in Oregon now and he's been in New Orleans for going on ten years, Denver is home."

"I get it, man. He's needed here, even if it's just for a smile and a hug. Besides, I can't wait to meet the woman who tied Shep down."

Austin ran his tongue over his teeth. "I would've thought Shep would be doing the tying."

"Ha ha," Decker said dryly. "You know he isn't into kink as much as we are. But I meant with the marriage thing."

Decker wasn't wrong when it came to kink, but the idea of marriage being a burden? Austin wasn't sure about that anymore. Not that he'd recently had a good experience with women, considering Shannon was his latest girlfriend.

Sierra came to mind, and he frowned. He hardly knew the woman, and yet her face came to mind when he thought of forever. Not something he wanted to think too hard about. Or did he?

"What's that frown for?"

"Just thinking."

"About?"

"Marriage, I guess."

Decker whistled softly. "Thinking about giving up the single life then?"

Austin slid Decker a look. "You're complaining a bit much about marriage if you ask me. Don't tell me you're planning on living the single life forever?"

Decker shrugged then looked away uncomfortably. "You know where I came from, Austin. You think I really want to force that on a woman I love?"

Austin cursed under his breath. "You won't become your father if you marry someone, Deck. Your dad's a drunk, abusive asshole, but you aren't. You've never raised your hand to a woman, and you never would."

Decker shook his head. "And that's the crowning example of what a man I am? Or why I should be married? Mom always said Dad never hit her when they were dating. It came afterward."

Austin stood up, towering over Decker. "You've got to be fucking kidding me. Your dad was always a mean son of a bitch, and you know it."

"You weren't there."

"No I wasn't, but you don't just grow into that kind of mean overnight." Austin sighed then gentled his voice. "You're not your father, Deck."

Decker met his gaze. "And you're more yours than you know. Have you talked to Harry since he told us he was sick?"

Austin looked away, the twisted ball of guilt in his stomach rolling at the change of subject. "No," he muttered.

"Fuck, Austin. Talk to him. He's going to be okay, damn it. We aren't going to lose him to this. He's starting treatment in two weeks since they had to wait until the next cycle started and had to get him ready for it. He's not alone, not with all of us around him, but you can't hide from him. Got me?"

Austin nodded then went to the couch, resting his head in his hands. "What if he doesn't make it, Deck? What if he's not strong enough?"

"He's the strongest man we know."

"Yeah? Did you see him in that living room? I've never seen him look like that. He looked so...small."

Decker let out a breath as they sat there in silence. Austin hadn't voiced his fears to anyone yet, though he'd almost done so to Sierra in the shop when she'd begun to voice her own. Decker would listen to him and not rail on him too hard. Or maybe just hard enough for what he needed. If Austin spoke to any of his siblings about his thoughts, well, he wasn't sure what would happen. He needed to be the strong one like he'd always been, and right then, he wasn't acting like it.

And he hated it.

"Don't kill your father, Austin. He's not dead. He's not going to fucking die. We're going to beat this, and then we're going to kick your ass for putting him in the grave before you even talked to him."

"Fuck you, Decker. I'm not killing him. How could you even say that?"

Decker met his gaze, a fire in his eyes Austin didn't quite understand. "You're thinking about the worst before letting what's in front of you happen. That's a kind of killing in my book."

Austin ran his hand over his face. "I'm an idiot."

"Yes. Yes, you are. But you're also a scared idiot. What do you say for dinner we head to your folk's? You know they won't care if we just show up. We can talk to them about plans and things. You know they'll want to see you, and I'll be there if you need to run."

Austin raised a brow. "I'll call Mom just in case. They might not care if we just show up, but she'll like us better if we give her notice."

"Sounds good to me. So, you want to tell me what else is going on? You're wound tight like a spring right now."

Austin shrugged. "I'm fine."

"You're not fine. What's up? Is it that Shannon woman? She still giving you shit?"

He groaned, thinking of her phone call that morning. "That's part of it. She won't take a hint. Hell, that's not right. I've given her more than a hint. I don't know what her problem is. She didn't like me this much when we were dating, and the fact that I have to keep telling her no is making me feel like an ass."

"You *are* an ass."

He flipped his friend off. "Shut up. She'll find someone else she actually likes and get off my case soon. I just don't like feeling like I did something to hurt her when we were dating when we all know that wasn't the case."

"She's just bored, and we all know it," Decker added. "You said she was only part of it. So what else is there? Oh wait, is it that honey-brown-haired woman who opened... What's the name of that shop? Eden?" At Austin's arch look, Decker grinned. "Maya was telling me about her. She said while you started off as your normal, overbearing self, the second time this woman came in, you were all soft growls and soothing words."

"Your words or Maya's?" He didn't like the idea of Maya talking about him and Sierra as if there was a him and Sierra. Thankfully, his sister didn't know about the date or ride or whatever they had called it coming up. For some reason, he wasn't ready to share Sierra.

That made him a bit uneasy, but he'd live through it.

"Maya's of course, and from the look on your face, you're not ready to talk about her. Well, shit, I had planned on coming over here to talk to you about the scene, and now you're in knots over a woman. Very cool."

"I'm not in knots over her." Lies, but he wasn't about to tell Decker that. "And what about the scene? I haven't been to a club in ages, Decker. and I know you haven't either. That's not really me."

Decker leaned forward. "I thought you just needed to get laid or at least use that pent-up energy to help a sub in need. But maybe I was wrong."

Austin ran a hand over his face. He and Decker, as did other Montgomerys and their friends, had a kink of their own. When he was younger, he used to take to the scene and help subs who wanted subspace for the night or to feel his floggers. It was a connection that worked inside the club alone, and he'd never had a sub outside the place. That wasn't for him.

Austin sighed. "I'm not the club guy. I'm not a Dominant in my every day life. I'm my own type of man. I like sex how I like it. If that happens to be with me telling her what I want, sure. If that means I want to flog her because that's what she wants, perfect. That's who I am. I like what I like."

"I know, man. But it's something to think about."

Austin let out a breath. Yeah, it was. But he couldn't get Sierra out of his mind, and she couldn't even show him the skin she wanted inked. He wasn't sure what he wanted, and he damn sure didn't know what she wanted.

What he *was* sure of was he needed to get off his ass and start being the Montgomery he was meant to be. That meant taking care of his family and, if things worked out, Sierra as well. He had a feeling she wasn't going anywhere, and for some reason, Austin perked up at that thought.

Only time would tell, but Austin couldn't wait.

CHAPTER SEVEN

The dream started out like it always did. In each instance, Sierra knew when she was dreaming, just like she always knew she'd never be able to pull herself out of it. She lived through each agonizing cry, each burn, each break over and over again then woke up screaming.

Her dream-self wrapped her arms around Jason's waist, her head resting on his back. Her helmet blocked the feel of him from her cheek, but that was okay. She could still feel his warmth through their leather jackets. That alone calmed her.

It shouldn't have.

Sierra knew that.

The dream never ended well.

He reached down with his free hand and squeezed her hands clasped on his belly. She sighed happily, even as, in the back of her mind, she knew this was it. This was how it all ended.

The screech of tires came first then the pounding along her head, the searing pain on her side. Screams came from deep within and around her. She didn't know which was which anymore. Fire licked across her skin, and even though this was a dream, the memory of each nerve ending bursting in pain came back, and she felt it all again.

She sucked in a breath, reaching out to Jason's limp form, praying this time it would be different. Praying this time he'd wake up.

Only it wouldn't happen.

It never did.

Two figures stood above her, their faces in shadow. They hadn't been there the night she died inside and didn't play a part in every dream she faced.

They poured gasoline over her body, the smaller shadow lighting a match. In that instant of light, she saw the narrowed eyes, the rage and pain held within that gaze manifesting into a nightmare she'd never shake.

As the match dropped and her body caught fire, she woke up, her chest pounding, her sweat-slick body shaking so much she thought she'd fall out of bed.

On unsteady legs, she made her way to the bathroom. She barely had time to flip open the toilet lid before she emptied her stomach, the acid burning up her throat. By the time her nerves settled, she was sure she'd lost any food she'd had the day before and the only thing she'd do next was dry heave. God, how she hated that.

She flushed the toilet, wiped the lid with a bleach wipe she had on hand, then stood on somewhat steadier legs. After she brushed her teeth and washed her face with cool water, she was finally ready to wake up fully.

The nightmares had plagued her for years with the latter part of the dream showing up more often than not recently. Those shadows had been the reason she'd left for Edgewater and Denver to begin with. Not that she'd voice that aloud. She didn't want to say she'd run from her problems, but staying there and taking them with no ability to defeat them hadn't helped her. It had only made things so unbearable she'd been unable to heal fully.

Not that she was sure she'd ever be able to heal.

Her fingers skimmed the puckered skin and pale white lines along her side, but now that she was free of the chains that had bound her for so long, she might be able to find a way to live with the scars that marred her body as well as her soul.

She met her gaze in the mirror and cursed herself for trying to push herself too hard too fast. Wasn't it enough that she'd moved to a new place? She'd opened a business, one she loved that would hopefully succeed. She even went to her consult with Austin for a tattoo to help ink around the scar that had marked her for so long.

Yet Austin was precisely the problem.

He'd stepped on her toes and pushed something within her to the front. She wanted him, and she didn't know what to do about it. She wasn't ready for a man so large, so strong when she knew she wasn't sure about anything anymore.

Then he'd asked to take her for a ride, and she panicked like someone had thrown her into a tank full of sharks. He'd seen the pain in her eyes, the panic in her gaze, and hadn't thought twice about taking back his offer. He must think she was weak, though he hadn't said as much. She hated being weak. She'd been that way for so long she wasn't sure how to be anything else.

At least that's how it seemed.

Damn it. She wasn't that person anymore, but she also knew her limits. Going on a ride wasn't on the list of things she *needed* to do right then. The nightmares had gotten worse in the days since Austin mentioned it. Maybe once she got her tattoo and Eden had been open for longer than a week, she'd be able to do it. Throwing herself into fifty changes at once wasn't helping anyone. She might be the type of person who needed to raise her chin and get on with life, but she knew better than anyone when enough was enough.

She'd just call Austin and cancel the ride.

The sliver of disappointment that slid through her surprised her. Was it the idea of riding itself that she wanted? Or the fact she'd have to wrap herself around Austin's strong body in the process?

Her breasts ached at the thought, her nipples hardening.

Austin was a big man with an even bigger presence. The idea that after so long being alone and not finding another man she wanted made her think. Throw in the fact this man was so attractive physically and emotionally that she wanted more than a casual date or two and she was a goner...

It wasn't that Austin wasn't good enough for her—God no. She wasn't the type who thought beards, tattoos, and the dangerous look of leather were somehow a representation of who a person was. In the grand scheme of things, it honestly didn't matter, but she also knew that Austin had more hidden depths than she was ready to deal with.

In her mind, she could feel his calloused hands on her skin, the roughness of his beard on her inner thighs as he feasted on her. She let out a shaky breath. She needed to keep Austin out of the forefront of her mind. She had so many other things to think about, to worry about, that wanting Austin in her bed and in her life shouldn't be so high on the list.

She also knew Austin had his own worries. She'd never met the senior Montgomery, but her heart ached for him and his family. Cancer was such a scary word, and even though the media talked about it now more than they had before, the public still didn't know enough about it to truly understand.

She'd done some research on prostate cancer when Austin told her about his father. She knew it was so far out of her scope and probably very invasive of her, but she wanted to know what Austin would be going through as a son and what Harry would be going through as a patient. Not that reading a few lines on a computer connected her to the family in any way, but it was a step in a direction she wasn't sure she should take.

Austin had said he didn't know much about the prognosis or even what stage his father was at because he'd been too dazed to really comprehend. She just prayed the cancer had been caught early enough that the Gleason grading was low. If Austin was still too worried to research or deal, then she'd be able to help him that much anyway. It was the least she could do for him after she freaked out over the ride and his hands on her skin.

Speaking of the ride, she needed to call Austin and cancel. It hurt to think about, but she wasn't ready, and she knew it. Sitting on the back of a bike while having a panic attack would be downright dangerous, and no matter how slow Austin might go for her, she wouldn't risk their lives because she had to push herself.

She quickly showered and dressed for her day. She didn't open that day because it was Jasinda's turn to open and Becca's to close, but Sierra never had a true day off from Eden—even in the planning stages. And she loved it.

It gave her purpose.

She glanced down at her phone then stuck it in her purse. Instead of calling, she'd tell him face to face that she couldn't go. He deserved that much, and then she'd be able to see him.

Damn it, she needed to stop acting like a dreamy-eyed schoolgirl.

Once she finished her makeup and put her hair up in a bun at the base of her neck, she headed out to Eden. She lived in Edgewater, a little square 'burb of Denver that sat right against the city proper. If she stood on her street, she could even see downtown easily. While the small 'burb was nice, her apartment wasn't. In fact, the building was rundown, sketchy, and full of drug dealers who were very nice to her for some reason, but it was cheap.

She'd put her heart, soul, and bank account into Eden, and the rent in Edgewater was all she could afford. Hopefully after the one-year lease ended, she could find a better place to live where she didn't feel the need to lock her windows at night even when the air conditioner was broken.

By the time she made it to downtown and parked in the special lot behind Montgomery Ink—how they'd lucked into that she'd never know—she had convinced herself she'd meet with Austin for two minutes and leave without feeling anything special.

She didn't want to want him; she didn't have time for that. She barely had time for her daily life to begin with. Instead of heading directly to see Austin, she went to Eden first. She'd talk to him during the lunch break the girls forced her to take daily. That way she had an excuse to rush back afterward and not get caught up in his gaze. Not that she would get caught up in his gaze. She was stronger than that.

Maybe.

The girls weren't surprised she was there an hour earlier than scheduled. A couple hours passed quickly as she rang up purchases and helped customers find their perfect outfit or special nightie. Her goal was to be as personal as she could get without freaking her guests out. She had a gift, as the girls called it, to find out exactly what someone needed. Whether it be a scarf, a cocktail dress, or a special push-up bra that a woman's partner could take off with their teeth, Sierra could usually find the perfect match. There was nothing better than watching a pleased customer leave her shop with a hop in their step. That meant not only were they happy, but they might come back and shop again. Perfect.

Her phone chirped quietly and she excused herself from the counter where Jasinda was ringing up a purchase. She'd set the alarm to force herself to go over and speak with Austin. Jasinda had already taken her break while Becky had just arrived, so it would be Sierra's turn.

She said her goodbyes, telling them she'd be right back. From the looks on her girls' faces, she had a feeling they knew exactly where she was heading first. How they could possibly know that, Sierra wasn't sure, but she ignored them. She had a job to do. First, she'd say no to Austin as calmly as she could and back out of their date. Because it was a date. From the sparks between them and the look in his eyes when he'd asked—no, *told* her that he would take her for a ride on the back of his bike, their outing couldn't be construed as anything *but* a date.

The bell over the door rang as she walked in. Callie sat on a stool behind the computer, a sketchpad in her lap, her head bent over her drawing. She looked up with a scowl that turned into a bright smile.

"Hey, Sierra. Austin is in the back sketching. He just finished with a client, so he should be free for you."

"He's free," Maya said on Sierra's other side.

Sierra studied Austin's sister and couldn't tell if Maya was happy he was free or not. The woman didn't smile, but smirked, her eyes twinkling. Sure, that could be happiness in there, or maybe she wanted to push Sierra over a bridge or something. The other woman came off as abrasive, but from the way Austin had spoken of her, Sierra knew there was more to her than the piercings, tattoos, and attitude.

"I'll just head on back then," Sierra said coolly. When she didn't know how to act in a certain situation, she always reverted to the ice princess. It never failed to keep people at a distance—well, *almost* never failed. Austin was another matter altogether.

"Do that then, princess," Maya said, just as coolly.

Well then. Sierra knew exactly where she stood. And, honestly, she didn't care.

"Stop being a bitch, Maya," Callie called out. "You're just in a mood because Jake is out of town."

"Is Jake your boyfriend then?" Sierra asked and could have immediately smacked herself. Why was she asking personal questions of a woman who clearly didn't want Sierra to have anything to do with her brother?

"He's just a friend," Maya said with another smirk. "Jake and I don't need to have sex to be in the same room. Unlike some people I know."

"Bitch," Callie sneered then smiled. "Go on back, Sierra. He's just in the office."

Sierra looked between the two women then made her way to Austin. She didn't know exactly what was going on, but she had enough on her plate as it was. When she made it to the office, she stopped and held back a sigh.

Austin had his head bent over his sketch, his forearm flexing as he drew. His side was to her, and she could see the long lines of his body bunched in the chair—a lion ready to strike.

His head whipped around to face as her as she let out that sigh. When his gaze reached hers, he smiled, and another bit of that sadness that had been present in his eyes when he told her of his family went away. If she could do that for him, then maybe it would all be worth it.

"Hey, I didn't know you were stopping by today." He stood up, those long legs of his stretching out his jeans nicely.

Not that she was staring at his jeans. Much.

She licked her lips, holding back a blush as his eyes darkened when she did so. Damn it. She wasn't some naive virgin. Oh, hell no. The things she'd done, the things she'd craved...well, she wasn't an innocent. She shouldn't be blushing at a man when he stared at her. She was stronger than that.

Centering herself, she rolled her shoulders back. "I just came by to say in person that I don't think I'll be able to ride with you." Why hadn't she done this over the phone? It would've been so much easier, but she wanted to do it face-to-face so she wouldn't be rude. Plus, she wanted to see him because she couldn't get his face out of her dreams and his presence out of her system.

Damn Austin Montgomery.

Austin frowned, moving toward her. She forced herself not to take a step back. She wouldn't run. Not anymore. But she didn't know if she could keep up the denial if he got any closer.

He ended up standing right in front of her, so close she could feel the heat of his body. The act reminded her of her dream of Jason, and she held back a shudder. It wouldn't do her any good to compare the two men. Her past and her...whatever this would end up being.

His hand came up so he gripped her chin. He searched her face, and she just stared up at him, unsure of what to do or say next. He hadn't spoken, and it threw her for a loop.

"Okay, Sierra," he said finally, his voice low, deep. So deep it went straight to her core, and she had to keep from sighing. Again. "If you don't feel like you're ready to ride yet, then we won't."

She let out the breath she wasn't aware she'd been holding. "Thanks, Austin. I'm sure we'll see each other around then." What was she doing? That hadn't been the plan. Or had it? Honestly, she didn't even know what her plan was anymore. She wanted him, she was clear on that much, but she wasn't sure she could handle more. This wishy-washy thought process wasn't doing her any favors. She needed to buck up and either give in fully or step back.

Taking half steps would only hurt her in the end. Didn't she know that? Hadn't she lived that?

"Oh really? I don't think so. That's not how this is going to play, Legs."

"Excuse me?" The ice was back in her voice, but she didn't know how to control it, not when he was so large and...Austin around her.

"You don't want to ride? Fine. I get that you aren't ready, and I don't want to force you into something you aren't comfortable with. Hopefully, you'll be able to talk about it soon, and we can figure out how to get you on the back of a bike. Because, Sierra, you want to. I saw the look in your eyes after the fear. You want to ride again, and we'll figure out a way to make that happen."

She narrowed her eyes. "So, you know what I'm thinking, do you?" She didn't like it when people made decisions for her. Not at all.

"Yeah. In this case, I do. I'm not saying I know everything. Far from it. But I get this. Now, on that note, just because we aren't riding doesn't mean you're out of my life for good. You get me? We're going to date, or whatever, or find a way to see each other again because I want you, Sierra. And from the way you licked your lips and looked at me when you first walked in, you want me too. I get that, right?"

"Bastard," she mumbled. "I don't like this alpha thing."

He brushed his thumb over her lips. "Yeah, Legs. Yeah you do. Now, I'm going to pick you up tomorrow for lunch. Sound good? A real date and all that shit."

"So romantic." Yet she didn't pull away. *Couldn't* pull away. "You think you can just tell me we're going on a date?"

He grinned at her. "I asked you, didn't tell you. I could have told you, and I think from the look in your eyes, you might have liked it just as much."

How could he see that deep inside? How could he know what she'd been in the past? It had to be just her imagination. That wasn't who she was anymore anyway.

"Fine. Dinner. I'll text you my address."

He smiled full-out then, leaving her breathless. Damn man. "Good, baby. Good." He lowered his head; she knew what he was going to do.

And she let him.

His lips brushed hers, once, twice. She closed her eyes, melting into him. He reached up and cupped her neck and the back of her head. She moaned, parting her lips. His tongue tangled with hers as he deepened he kiss.

This kiss, this man. Oh, God was he potent...dangerous.

He pulled back when she would have begged for more. Only the promise in his gaze stopped her.

"We'll do that again soon, Legs. I promise you."

That was exactly what she was afraid of.

CHAPTER EIGHT

Austin winced as his phone buzzed on the kitchen counter. He hadn't heard from Shannon in four days, and it was starting to scare him. Hopefully she'd back off, but who knew with her? He hadn't thought she was that possessive and monumentally crazy when they'd gone out, but apparently, he hadn't looked too deeply beneath the surface.

A mistake he wouldn't be making again.

He looked at the readout and saw a text from Miranda letting him know that dinner was off because she had a date.

A date?

Seriously? Who the fuck was dating his sweet, innocent baby sister? She was only...wait, she was twenty-three. He didn't even want to think about what he'd been doing at twenty-three, but, shit, Miranda shouldn't be dating.

He closed his eyes and prayed for patience. Meghan was married and had kids. Maya was out and doing only God knew what since she was proud of her body and sexuality. Her words. Not his.

He should get over it and let Miranda date. Not that she needed permission, per se...

Austin rolled his tongue over his teeth. Nope. Not gonna happen. He quickly texted back that no, that would not be okay, and she should cancel her date. He didn't add that she could cancel *all* dates, but that would be implied.

He was a force to be reckoned with and authoritative. She would listen.

When his phone buzzed again, and he looked at the response, he cursed.

No can do, big brother. I'm dating. Get over it. Love you! XoXo

Didn't his sister know anything? He was the eldest brother. His siblings should listen to him. He closed his eyes and knew it would be a lost cause. Plus, now he could see if his lunch date with Sierra could turn into something more.

It was Sunday, and they both had the day off, meaning they'd planned to spend the afternoon together. He already had plans with his sister beforehand or he would have made a dinner date with Sierra in the first place.

Now he had a chance to do both.

He quickly called her to set it up, just in case she'd thought of getting out of it. He didn't know why he was so nervous about this. At his age, he'd dated countless women—not that he ever wanted to really think about that vast pool. He should have been on familiar ground, but when it came to Sierra, nothing was common, and nothing was at all familiar.

For some reason, he truly liked that.

"Hey you. I was just about to call."

Her voice, usually a soft purr that went straight to his cock, sounded distracted. "What's up, Legs?"

"I wish you wouldn't call me that," she said absently. What was up? She usually put more effort into her denial of his nickname.

"What's wrong, Sierra?" There. He could learn. Besides, she didn't sound like she'd appreciate his teasing.

"I'm going to have to cancel lunch."

He frowned. He'd let her cancel their ride because she wasn't ready for that—frankly, he didn't blame her—but he wasn't about to let her cancel again. Not when they had something. He knew they did, and he knew she knew it, too.

"Why?"

She sighed. "Because some kid broke my window. It was an accident, and his mother already made him come over and apologize, so I know it could have been much worse considering where I live...I mean..."

He clenched his jaw. He knew she lived in Edgewater, and while it wasn't the nicest 'burb of Denver, it wasn't the worst either. From the sound of it, he should have been much more worried.

"Are you okay? Were you near the window when it broke?"

"Oh, no. I'm fine." She gave a rough chuckle. "I was in the bedroom, and the broken window is in my kitchen. I cleaned up the glass, but maintenance said they couldn't fix it until next Friday so now I'm stuck having to figure out how to put a board up or something. I can't leave my house because of the broken window, you know? So, no, I can't make lunch, but it's not because I don't want to. You get that, right?"

He was already grabbing his keys and passed by the mail that he'd, once again, forgotten to check. He needed to get on that. Damn.

"I'm on my way. Stay where you are, and I'll bring a sheet of plywood I have in the garage. Then I can work on the window myself once I do some measurements."

"Austin. You can't come and fix my window."

She kept telling him not to come over and help, so he mumbled and grunted as he went to his garage for supplies. He jumped in his truck after putting the sheet of wood in the back. "Yes. I can. You said yourself you can't leave your house to go find something to block it, and this way I can still see you."

He hadn't meant to say the last part, but from her happy sigh, maybe it was a good thing he had.

"I'll be there in less than twenty minutes. Don't walk out of your house to get away from me or something. Okay?"

"Okay. Austin?"

"Yeah?" He put his phone on Bluetooth and sped up the driveway. She'd given him her address the day before so he had a relative idea of where she was. He knew Denver well enough it wasn't a problem.

"Thank you," she whispered sweetly.

"Anything, babe."

He hung up and drove on, antsy to see her and help.

Damn. He had it bad, but right then, he wouldn't have it any other way.

When he pulled up, he wanted to curse, then pick up Sierra, pack all her shit, and head back to his place. Why the hell was she living here? Sure the place didn't look dirty, but it was a hell of a shithole compared to Eden and his own home. There were couches on lawns, people smoking weed out in the open. It might be legal state-wide to own it, but smoking it out on the street corner wasn't the smartest idea.

However, in Sierra's neighborhood, apparently, it didn't matter.

He pulled into what served as her parking lot. Well, it was mainly a lot filled with beat-up cars and potholes, but he found a spot near her car anyway. He got out, locked his truck, then pulled the plywood out of the truckbed. He knew she was on the first floor and cursed yet again when he saw the window.

Austin needed to get her out of this neighborhood as quickly as he could. However, telling her, not asking her, to move into his house before they'd officially had their first date would probably be pushing it. Plus, he knew she was saving for Eden. He could remember the lean times he and Maya shared when they'd first opened Montgomery Ink.

Yeah, it rankled that he couldn't fix everything for Sierra, but he had to live with it. He'd just find a way to get her to stay at his house more often than not. He had two extra bedrooms, and she could stay in one if she didn't want to sleep in his bed.

The image of her in his bed went straight to cock, and he took a deep breath. There was no way he could fix her window and find a way to get her to his place when he had a hard-on the size of Texas.

She walked out onto her back porch—more like a cement slab she shared with four other units—her feet in sandals and a frown on her face. "You got here fast." Her gaze searched his, and he wished to hell he had free hands to brush that lock of hair from her face.

"I'm not too far away." He said that part loudly in case of any of her banger neighbors decided to poach on Austin's territory. Call him an alpha asshole, but Sierra was his now, and they'd all just have to deal with him if they got too close.

"Thank you." She walked closer and put her small hand on his chest. He sucked in a breath. "Really. Thank you. I honestly wasn't sure what to do since I don't even have a vehicle to put the wood into anyway."

There was a dirty joke in there somewhere, and if Sierra had been one of his siblings, he would have been the first to call it, but he held it back.

From the way Sierra's eyes widened, she thought it too.

"Uh, I mean... oh, whatever. Now, what can I do to help?"

Austin grinned. "I've got this. It's pretty easy here. Just make sure all the glass is cleaned up since you'll be walking around barefoot in your house, I presume." Unless he got her to move in. Nope. He had to stop thinking along those lines.

"It's all cleaned up. Are you sure there isn't anything I can do?"

"We're good. My brothers are contractors, remember? They do this for a living." He started to work, grateful the board was the right size, so he wouldn't have to cut it down with the tools he had in the back of his truck.

"Yeah. *They* are. You're a tattoo artist."

He looked over his shoulder and scowled. "You saying I can't fix something like this? I learned with them, right alongside Dad. Just because I went into ink doesn't mean I can't work with my hands."

She blushed hard then, and Austin's cock filled. Again. Damn dick.

"You're great with your hands. Oh, shut up. I get it. Hands. Sex. Whatever. You're an artist, Austin. I don't want you to hurt your hands and not be able to work."

He finished up quickly, shaking his head as he did so. "If I bang my thumb, it won't kill me. I'm good at what I do."

"Don't I know it," she mumbled, and Austin grinned again. "Want something to drink?"

"Sounds good to me." He followed her into her small apartment, not surprised that she had nice furniture in a shitty place. From the way she walked and talked, he figured that she hadn't always lived in a place like this.

They drank in silence for a bit before she finally let out a breath.

"I just don't want you to get the wrong idea about me asking you here."

Austin tilted his head. "Wrong idea? I asked you on a date, and I came here to help on my own accord. Not sure what wrong idea I can get."

"I don't know what you're looking for here. Relationship-wise. I mean, I don't even know what I want."

He set down his glass on the high counter then brushed his lips over hers. "One day at a time, Sierra. One day at a time."

"What does that even mean?" She scowled then set down her own glass. "One day at a time? For what? What are we even doing, Austin? I thought we didn't even like each other when we first met. Now you're asking me to ride with you, kissing me, and fixing my window."

Austin frowned then took her chin in a hard grip. Her eyes widened a bit before her pupils dilated. Ah, that's what he wanted to see. So she liked him in control, did she? He'd have to be clear about what he was and what he liked before they went further, but if his instincts were right, she'd be perfect for him.

Fuck. He couldn't wait.

"I'm too old for games, Sierra."

She didn't pull away from his hold. Good.

"I'm not playing games. I'm honestly confused and wondering how we got here. How are you in my apartment with your hands on me? I don't know what happened."

He took his other hand and collared her throat as he let her chin go. She sucked in a breath, her pulse fluttering beneath his thumb.

"I want you, Sierra. That much is obvious. Tell me you want me to." He lowered his voice at the end, putting as much order in his tone as possible.

"I don't know," she lied. Oh yes, he could tell it was a lie.

"Be honest. Don't lie to me."

"I...I want you too. But I don't know what that means. Want you for how long? For what? We need to talk it out first because I'm not jumping into bed with you only for you to leave right after and never see me again. I'm not that person."

He brushed his thumb over her pulse again, narrowing his eyes. "You think I'd leave you right after I've tasted you? You don't know me as well as I thought."

She finally pulled away, and he let her. She crossed her arms over her chest, and shook her head. "See? That's exactly the point. I'm not going to lie and say I don't feel this heat between us. That much is obvious, but I don't know if I can handle more. Do you understand that?"

He nodded, getting a clearer picture of the woman he wanted in his bed, and from the direction things were going, in his life as well.

"You don't want this to be only for a night, but you don't know if you're ready for everything that comes with it if we last longer."

She let out a breath, her shoulders sagging. "I didn't come to Denver for a relationship. In fact, I've done my best not to be with another person in so long that I don't even remember what it's like to *be* in one."

He let out a breath, then brushed her cheek with his knuckles. She leaned into his touch, and he held back a groan. Oh yes, she would be perfect under his dominance. He only hoped she knew that. Or would at least be open to it.

"I've tried to be in serious relationships, but they haven't worked out. I'm not the kind of person to love 'em and leave 'em, but I haven't been serious about anyone truly."

"And do you want that? A serious relationship?"

He nodded even as her eyes widened. "Yes. That's what I want. But me saying that doesn't mean we have to jump in headfirst. Sierra, it's okay to start off as exclusive then work our way toward what we become rather than focusing on the end and dreading the way there."

"So you're saying we see each other and find our way, knowing it might end up in tatters because I don't know what I want?"

He shook his head then cupped her face. He brushed his lips against hers, craving her taste. When he pulled back, her eyes had darkened again. "I'm saying that we take it one day at a time. Stop worrying. Just know that I'm not going into this with an end date in mind. I'm not going to leave like a fucking bastard. I'm not that man."

"I don't believe you are," she whispered, and he held back a fist pump. Well, at least he was getting somewhere.

"Then we can date, get to know one another, and find our way. Freaking out about a future we can't control won't help us."

She rolled her eyes then ran her hand through her hair as she pulled back. "Tell me about it. I've been trying to control my destiny for so long, it seems like no matter what I do, life happens the way it wants."

He wanted to know more about what she was saying and find out all her secrets, but he knew it wasn't the time for that. He'd find out. Soon.

He was done with the Shannons and Maggies of his past. He'd known that before he went to New Orleans to see Shep. Now he had a future with Montgomery Ink, a fucking scary path to travel with his father, and now this.

If he was saner, he'd pull back from Sierra and focus solely on his job and his family, but he never claimed to be sane. Although he was through burying his head in the sand when it came to his dad, he wasn't ready to face it fully. Not without someone by his side. That was fucking crazy to think, but for some odd reason, he was ready for that.

Now he just had to get Sierra to agree.

"I'm going to feed you, and then we can come back here and...talk."

Her eyes widened before she threw her head back and laughed. "Talk, huh? Is that code for something?"

Well, he needed to talk to her about his needs and what he saw of her needs as well, but yeah, code worked. He didn't answer, merely kissed her again, this time a bit harder. He nipped at her lip, and she sighed and flowed into him. He nibbled at her jaw, wrapping her hair around his fist so he could tilt her head to gain better access. She shivered in his hold, her breasts pressing against his chest. Her nipples pebbled, and he held back a groan. He couldn't wait to feast on them, biting and licking until they reddened. Maybe she had darker nipples that would fill to a nice plum color. As soon as he could, he'd make a study of her breasts and explore every inch of her.

Austin damn sure needed to know the color of her nipples.

The color of the blush of her pussy.

He couldn't hold back a small groan at that thought and pulled back, his chest heaving. Sierra breathed hard as well, her cheek resting on his forearm since his hand was still tangled in her hair.

"We need to do that again," she whispered, and he chuckled deeply.

"Yeah...yeah we really do." He pulled back, releasing her hair. The tousled look made her look even sexier. He couldn't wait to see what she looked like after a long night of him buried deep inside her.

"Lunch."

Austin blinked, his gaze moving from her mouth to her eyes, which were filled with need and humor. "What?"

"Lunch. Take me to lunch, and then we can come back and...talk."

He grinned then. "Lunch it is."

He took her hand, and she stepped readily into his space. This could be good. Fucking good if he let it. He just hoped when they talked for real his needs didn't screw it all up. He might not need to be in control every time he was in bed, but with Sierra and this connection, he knew he couldn't ignore it.

Only time would tell, and from the way his cock tented his jeans, he knew lunch would be a fucking long one.

She smiled up at him even as she raised a brow at his hard-on.

Yeah, the wait would be worth it.

CHAPTER NINE

L unch at Gregorio's was surprisingly relaxed. Sierra had expected to sit through an achingly long lunch while shifting in her seat. She'd been aroused, yes, her body begging for release even from the small touch of Austin's hand on her chin, her neck, her lips, but Austin made lunch...pleasant.

He hadn't touched her under the table beyond tangling his legs with hers. They sat across from one another, the distance helping cool her down slightly.

Not that she'd ever be completely cool when she was around Austin. Oh no, that ship had long since sailed. Sure, she could be the serene, put-together owner of Eden with others, but as soon as she got near the bearded man, she wanted to melt.

Or kneel and lower her gaze.

That had been ingrained in her from her time with Jason, and it seemed that her inner need found what it wanted in Austin.

There was no denying Austin was a Dominant. While that should have scared the hell out of her, she found herself curious as to how he'd handle the situation.

How he'd handle her.

While she'd never be a twenty-four/seven sub who trusted her Dom to make all of their choices, she had enjoyed giving Jason control while they were in the bedroom. She liked being his first priority and the way he cared for her before, during, and after their scenes.

They'd never visited a club or ranch or anything like that. They preferred to do things in private, and that was exactly how she liked it. They also didn't play every time they had sex. Sometimes it was just the two of them and their own needs. She hadn't needed to give up control and relax—if one could call it relaxing—each time they made love.

Everyone's kink was different. Needs changed as the person changed. As long as it was safe and consensual, it could work.

However, she hadn't participated in anything like that in ten years. It had taken five years after the accident for her to even have sex again. Even then, it hadn't been worth it. Yeah, it scratched an itch, and the two men she'd slept with since were nice but nothing to do cartwheels over.

If she let herself think about it, then she'd worry it was her and her lack of heat, but she'd been good to herself. It was a lack of chemistry, a lack of true desire beyond a need to comfort that led her to those mediocre couplings.

Austin, however, would be anything *but* mediocre.

They made it back to her place after having, in her opinion, the best burritos in town. They had reached an unspoken understanding that whatever needed to be said, whatever would be done, would be in her place first. She might not love her place—she hated it—but it was *hers*. For their first time—even if it was just talking about what they wanted—she needed it to be in her own place.

Yes, that was clearly her not giving up the control, but it had been so long since Jason...

She mentally slapped herself. This wasn't about Jason. This was about her and Austin. No matter where their future ended up, she needed to keep Jason firmly rooted in the past. He was gone. Austin was not. The girl she was all those years ago wasn't the woman she was now.

She was stronger, scarred, and had finally come into her own.

And now she was alone in her living room with Austin Montgomery of the gorgeous blue eyes that saw far too much.

"Where did your mind go just then?" Austin asked, pulling her out of her thoughts.

"Everywhere and nowhere," she answered honestly.

He raised both brows then sat on her old wood coffee table, pulling at her wrist so she sat on the couch directly in front of him. Their knees brushed, and she wanted to pull away and scoot closer at the same time. Yes, they truly needed to talk.

"That is an oddly cryptic answer, but I'll let that go. We need to talk anyway."

If anyone else had said those words she'd have thought it was the clear sign of a breakup. However, they hadn't been dating for more than an hour. Well, maybe longer considering she'd been territorial over him since the first time she saw him, but that wasn't something she was going to think about. She had a feeling she knew what he wanted to discuss.

There was no hiding the alpha in Austin Montgomery.

"Okay, then. I'm ready."

He searched her gaze. "I think you are." He cleared his throat then took both of her hands in his. "Do you know what BDSM is?"

He looked so worried. Yes, his face was set and relaxed, but she could see in his eyes he wasn't.

She squeezed his hands. "Yes, I know. And before you start to worry if you're scaring me away, I was in a D/s relationship before."

The shock that crossed his face wasn't a surprise, but the jealousy was. Seriously?

"Really?" he growled out.

She sighed but didn't pull her hands back. She had been the one to jump right in, so she'd have to deal with the consequences.

"Yes. It was over ten years ago. I haven't played since."

He pulled his hand back, and for a moment, the loss made her ache until he cupped her face. "Not in ten years?"

She swallowed back the pain, the memories of what she'd lost because of one careless action. "Jason—that was his name—and I were a couple, and I was his submissive while in the bedroom. We weren't twenty-four/seven, and that's how we both preferred it. I can't give up complete control, but I think you know that about me."

He narrowed his gaze, his thumb running along her cheek. "On the one hand, it's good to know that you're aware of the lifestyle and have experience. I could tell you were a sub, but not about all of your experience. That's probably because it's been so long."

Ignoring the memories, she rolled her eyes. "You have sub-dar, do you?"

His grip tightened on her chin, and she sucked in a breath. She hadn't realized how much she missed this. Damn him if this went sour. Damn them both.

"Sub-dar? It's a thing, but it's not like you glowed or I heard little pinging sound when you were near me."

She snorted then rolled her eyes. "Good to know. I think I'd have to get that checked out."

"Insolent," he muttered then leaned closer. She could scent him, the musk that was Austin and pine. "It's the way you lowered your eyes when I touched you, the way you came closer in certain ways and pulled away in others. Your body, your soul was made to trust a Dom to take care of you in bed."

"Not all the time," she added in. She needed to make that clear.

He nodded, understanding filling his gaze. "I understand. I'm wired the same way." He grinned then, and she held back a sigh. He really was a gorgeous man. Not that she'd tell him. He was already too sure of himself as it was.

"So it seems we're on the same page," she whispered.

"It seems. But we're not done talking yet. Open communication in any relationship is important, but even more so in this case. I don't need to inflict pain or control on my partner unless they desire it. That need is what drives my own. So every time we're making love—because Legs, we'll be making love soon—we don't need to be together in a D/s way. We won't need the flogger, the nipple clamps, or the way I want to tie you up each time."

She shuddered out a breath, her pussy growing slick at his words alone.

Dear God, she wanted all of that.

She hadn't known how much she wanted that.

"Sometimes, Sierra, sometimes I'll want you to be on top as you ride me, rocking your hips as you take my cock deep inside that pussy of yours. Other times I'll be soft and on top, pumping into you as we just let ourselves go, no control, no dominance, just us." He paused, and she held back the need to squirm. "Does that sound like something you'll need? Something you'll enjoy?"

She nodded.

He shook head. "Say it, Sierra."

"Yes...Sir?" She wasn't sure what he wanted her to call him.

He grinned then, cupping her face. "I'm just Austin, Sierra. I don't need to be called Sir or Master for you to be under my gaze. That works for some, but it's not my kink. If you need to call me that, then you can, but I want to hear my name on your lips as you come."

She licked her lips. "Austin."

He grinned. "Good. Right now, since I don't have any of my things and I know we both want to ease into that part of our relationship, I'm not going to tie you up, flog you, or make you scream." He paused. "Oh, I might make you scream, but only when I'm thrusting inside you."

"What if I make you scream?" she teased.

He snorted. "I intend to shout your name, Sierra. I promise you. Now, before we start, we need a safe word."

She raised her brows. "I thought you said we weren't starting that part yet."

He shook his head. "But it's always good to have one. You know that."

"I think the standard red, yellow, and green will work." It was what she'd used with...no, she wouldn't think of him. Not here.

He narrowed his eyes. "You need a strong one, Sierra. There's a ghost between us. One you're not ready to talk about."

She sucked in a breath.

"Pick a different safe word."

There was only one word she could use, and they both knew it.

"Motorcycle," she whispered.

Austin nodded, his eyes carefully blank. Had she hurt him? Maybe, but he'd asked for the safe word. It was something they'd both have to deal with when they were ready.

He stood then, holding out his hand. She took it and stood so her chest brushed his, her body flush to him.

"I want you, Sierra Elder. Say you want me too."

She knew this was big. A step she hadn't been sure she was ready to take as late as that morning. However, she'd been hiding for so long, neglecting what was inherent to her being that she knew she needed to take this risk.

"I want you too."

"Good."

He crushed his mouth to hers, and she moaned. His hands were in her hair, forcing her head to stay in one place as he devoured her mouth. His tongue pressed against hers, controlling the kiss, and she gave in. They might not get into the truly D/s things this first time, but she wanted—no, *needed* to let herself give in and see if she could trust him.

Not fully.

Not yet.

But soon.

His lips trailed along her jawline, and she closed her eyes, reveling in the feel of his lips, teeth, and tongue on her skin. He bit her earlobe then placed small kisses right behind it, sending delicious shivers down her spine, her knees going weak.

"Austin," she whispered.

"Yes, that's my name," he growled against her neck, one hand on her head, the other on her lower back. "You're going to be saying it over and over again soon."

Before she could respond, his mouth was on hers again as he cupped her breast. She gasped as he rolled her nipple hard between his thumb and forefinger. It didn't matter that she still wore her shirt and bra, the exquisite pain and sweetness went straight to her core, and she shuddered.

Oh, how she missed this.

"I want to suck your nipples, learn their taste." He pulled up her shirt, and she lifted her arms, letting him strip it off her head, leaving her in her tank and bra. "Earlier, I was mesmerized by just the thought of them. I wanted to know their color and what they'd look like after I'd sucked and nibbled on them. Then my thoughts went to your pussy, and I wanted to know what you'd look like swollen and wet, ready for my cock."

"If you don't stop talking like that, I'm going to come without you touching me."

He grinned and sucked her bottom lip between his teeth. "That would be fine with me. After this first time. I need to see you." He pulled back, meeting her gaze. "All of you."

She licked her lips and felt her whole body stiffen. In all of this, she'd forgotten her scars. How could she forget what had plagued her for so long?

"You don't have to tell me right now how it happened. I don't want to ruin what we have at this moment, Sierra." He pulled up the bottom of her tank, and she let him, knowing if she didn't do it now, she'd never do it at all. "No matter what scars you have, Sierra, you'll always be beautiful. No amount of ink or scars will make your skin anything but perfect to me."

Tears filled her eyes at the beauty of his words, and she refused to close them as he looked down at her side. She sucked in a breath as his fingers gently traced the puckered scars and fine white lines that used to be so much worse.

He knelt before her, and she choked on a sob.

That this man would kneel before her...

She would never get the image of his dark head at her stomach, her scars, out of her head for as long as she lived.

His lips brushed the nearly numb areas on her skin, and a tear slid down her cheek. Her hands rested on his shoulders as he kissed every inch of her marred skin , caring for her in a way no other had ever done before. He finally looked up at her, his eyes dark and full of promise.

"Beautiful," he breathed.

And she was lost.

He stood then, cupping her face so he could kiss her. He tasted of warmth and strength, and she wanted more. Oh, how she wanted more. His denim-clad erection pressed into her belly, and she grinned at the size of it. Yeah, it would hurt at first, but she couldn't wait; she wanted it badly.

Austin pulled away from her mouth but didn't let his lips leave her body. Instead, he gently set her down on the couch so he could kneel between her legs. At some point, he'd pushed the coffee table back so he had more room. How had she missed that?

His lips moved to her collarbone, her sternum, then over each breast through her bra. She sucked in a breath as he licked along the lacy edge of her cup.

"Let's see what color your nipples are, shall we?"

His hands expertly undid the clasp at her back, and he slid the straps off her shoulders His gaze met hers as he removed her bra, letting it fall to the floor at her feet. She swallowed hard as he lowered his eyes, his gaze on her nipples. As if they knew they were the center of his attention, they hardened into sharp points, ready for his tongue.

He reached out and caressed her breast. The globe slightly filled his palm. The sight itself was one of the most erotic things she'd ever seen.

"Jesus. Like little pink berries. You're going to redden up so fucking nice when I suck on them. One day, when I use clamps, they're going to be so hard they'll beg for my tongue." His gaze met hers. "Are you going to beg for me, Sierra? Beg for my tongue? My cock? You want my dick between your tits as I fuck those then your mouth?" She licked her lips, squirming for release.

"I love your voice." It was so deep, so rough. It went straight to her clit, and she knew if she tried she could get off on the sound of it alone.

"Don't move, Sierra. Save your clit for me."

She froze at his tone, her body as tight as a bowstring. She ached for him, but on another level, she knew if she sat still for him, he'd make it better soon.

That was the kind of trust she held for him so early in their relationship. It boggled her mind, but she pushed it to the side. She wanted this. Wanted it right then.

"Good girl." Then he pinched her nipple.

Hard.

The sting shocked her system, and she sucked in a breath, using everything within her power not to move. If she moved, he might stop, and she didn't know if she could take that. She wanted his touch, his everything.

She'd worry about the consequences later.

"Get out of your head, Sierra." He pinched the other nipple just as hard then laved the sting with his tongue. "It's just you and me. Nothing and no one else. Just think of me. That's all you have to do. I'll do the rest. You get me?"

She nodded.

He pinched her nipple again. "You get me?"

"Yes, Austin."

"Good girl."

He lowered his mouth to each breast and feasted, his tongue and teeth devouring one as his free hand palmed the other, rolling and pinching her nipple. She let her head fall back as he gave special attention to each nipple, she loved the way the scrape of his beard made it even more erotic. Each scrape, each lick sent waves of pleasure through her body, pooling in her clit so that it hummed, needing just a little more pressure so she could get off.

Still, she didn't move her hips.

She wanted Austin to do it.

Trusted him to take care of her need.

He pulled back, his gaze dark. "Just like I thought. Red berries. So fucking hot. Ass up."

She blinked, confused.

"Ass up, Sierra. I'm taking off your pants so I can eat your pussy before I take you into your bedroom and fuck you hard. Ass. Up."

"Yes, Austin," she said and smiled as his nostrils flared. Oh yes, he liked it when she said that. She'd be sure to say it again...or not if she wanted his hand on her ass.

Well, it seemed that this hidden part of her, the part she thought she'd buried so deep, wasn't so hidden after all. She lifted her hips and bit her lip as he undid the button on her jeans and slowly unzipped her zipper. Then he gripped her jeans and panties in his fists and pulled. She helped him with each leg, keeping her ass above the couch, her weight resting on her forearms.

Austin groaned. "Fuck, you're beautiful. You can rest now, baby. "

She sank into the cushions, her legs spread around Austin as he studied her. She could have felt self-conscious, but she didn't, not with the look of pure pleasure and thirst on Austin's face.

"Gorgeous," he whispered before lowering his body and licking the long line of her pussy straight up to her clit.

Her body rocketed off the couch, and he clamped his arm over her waist. "You were doing so good, baby. Don't move."

She licked her lips. "I need to, Austin. I need..."

His gaze met hers. "I know what you need. And if you keep still, I'll give it to you."

Well now, *that* was incentive...

With that intensity of his, he lifted the hood then lowered his head again, sucking her clit into her mouth. She almost moved off the couch toward his face but stopped herself. He flicked it against his teeth before stroking her entrance with his finger. When he breached her, she sucked in a breath. It had been so long, and a vibrator wasn't as good as Austin's hand...or anything else on Austin for that matter.

He pumped one finger into her then two, slowly, then faster as he teased her. He kept his mouth on her clit, humming and growling against her. The feel of his beard scraping her thighs was the last straw, and she came.

Hard.

Her pussy clamped around his fingers, but he didn't relent. Instead, he curled his fingers on her G-spot and massaged the bundle of nerves until her body shook and she came again, this time screaming his name as her eyes rolled to the back of her head.

By the time she opened her eyes, Austin stood at her feet, licking his hand, one finger at a time. Her juices coated his beard, his hand, his fingers, yet he looked so pleased she didn't care. God, she wanted to do that again.

If she could walk.

"You taste so fucking good, Sierra. Like nectar I can't get enough of. Now I'm going to fuck you until we both pass out, then wake up for dinner, fuck you again, and repeat. How does that sound?"

She licked her lips, her body languid even as it thrummed for Austin. "I just hope I have enough condoms." She'd bought a whole box before on a whim and was damn glad she'd done so.

He grinned at her then. "One day we'll talk about other forms of birth control and getting tested so I can make love to you bare and feel every sweet inch of you. For now, I hope you have enough rubbers, too."

He lifted her up, her naked body resting against his clothed one. She smiled up at him. "It's not fair you're not naked you know."

When he kissed her brow, she sighed contentedly. "Give me a moment, and I'll be just as naked as you."

He sat her on the edge of the bed then stood in front of her. When he stripped off his shirt, her jaw dropped.

Dear. God.

Ropes of corded muscles, hard lines of strength, sex, and everything in between covered his body. He had some chest hair, enough to enhance the beauty of his ink, but not too much.

And, sweet baby Jesus, his ink.

Tribal, skulls, flowers, and other symbols covered his arms and chest. A dragon went down his side to his hips, flaring out over part of his back.

And the nipple rings.

How on earth had she missed those in those tight shirts of his?

He grinned down at her. "Glad to see you like it."

"You're like a rock, Austin."

He looked down at his cock then raised a brow. "Seems so."

"I meant your body..." She looked down at his crotch. "Oh. Well then." She licked her lips. "I didn't realize you had nipple rings."

He reached up and flicked one, and she wanted to do the same with her tongue. "I don't always have them in. Sometimes I just have the spacers."

"I like them."

"Good." He undid his pants then shucked them and his boxer briefs down his legs. His cock jutted out, so erect it brushed his belly.

Without giving it a second thought, she slid off the bed and knelt at his feet. Her legs were spread, and she put her open, up-turned palms on her thighs, the submissive pose so ingrained in her she didn't have to give it a second thought.

Austin's nostrils flared, and he took the two steps between them toward her. His hand cupped her chin to raise her eyes. His cock brushed her cheek, and she had to hold back from turning and sucking the thick head into her mouth.

"That is the most achingly beautiful thing I've ever seen in my life. I'm honored, Sierra. Honored." He stroked her cheek then pulled away. The loss was almost overwhelming before he held out his hand.

"Let me lay you on the bed and make love to you. I want to feel you wrapped around me as we both come. We'll explore everything else next time." She stood up, using his arm as support. "There *will* be a next time."

"Yes, Austin. Yes, there will be."

He walked her backward then laid her on the bed. She scooted so her head was on the pillow, and he hovered over her.

"Condoms," he bit out.

"The nightstand."

He nodded then left her to get the box from the drawer. The whole box.

Ambitious.

He tore open a packet and rolled one over his length. She swallowed hard as he worked his cock, the girth of it a little intimidating. When he came over her again, her body shook, from anticipation or nerves she didn't know.

"Ready?" he asked, his body shaking as well.

"Yes, Austin. Please."

He lowered his head, kissing her softly. She could taste herself on his lips and was only disappointed she hadn't been able to taste him as well. *Next time*, he said. She couldn't wait.

"Put your hands on the headboard," he ordered, and she shuddered.

When she did so, keeping her hands close together, he wrapped his hand around both of her wrists. God, he was big everywhere.

He settled between her legs, his body pressed against hers as he kept his weight on his other arm. Then he pressed against her opening, his cock sliding through her juices. Thank God she was so wet for him because, hell, he was big.

Much bigger than anything she'd experienced before.

He slowly stretched her, filled her inch by inch until they were both sweat-slick and panting. "Jesus, baby, you're so fucking tight." He let his hand drop from her wrist as he moved to his knees. The action brought him that much deeper, and she cried out in pleasure, not in pain. It must have shown on her face because he slid his hands down her sides, gripping her hips.

Then he moved again, thrusting in and out of her slowly at first, then harder.

Her gaze met his, wanting that connection like her next breath.

"You feel so good around my cock, Legs. I can't wait to take you from behind and push even deeper. Then, one day, you'll be above me, your tits bouncing as you ride me. Maybe I'll tie you up, your ass in the air, and fuck that sweet ass of yours. You want me to do that? You want me to fuck your ass like I'm fucking your pussy?"

She couldn't speak, couldn't think.

He lifted her hips up with one hand even as he continued to fuck her, and then he slapped her ass. Hard.

"You want that, Sierra? Answer me?"

She nodded. "Yes, Austin. I want it all."

"What do you want, Sierra?"

"I want everything. I want you to tie me up, spank me, fuck my ass. I want it all." Later she might blush at her words, but right then, with Austin's intense gaze on hers, his cock deep inside her, she wanted nothing but him and everything he had to offer.

"You'll get it all, baby. You'll get everything." He lowered himself again, his body resting over hers as he put his weight on his forearms. He kept thrusting in and out of her, the sensation of his cock hitting her in just the right place sending her over the edge even as she stared at him.

She couldn't breathe, but she could see him, see the way his jaw clenched, and then he growled her name as he came, filling the condom. He kept thrusting, pushing them both over the sweet edge of ecstasy into the warm comfort of afterglow and contentment.

More than contentment, so much more.

When they became more aware of things around them, he pulled out, took care of the condom, and came back to bed. He wrapped his body around hers, pulling the sheet over the two of them.

She wiggled closer, turning to rest her head on his chest. He held her shoulders to him, his head buried in her hair and his other hand on her ass, patting and massaging almost as if he couldn't stop touching her.

Sierra couldn't blame him because she was doing the same to him.

"Perfect," he rumbled before falling asleep.

She smiled, pushing away all thoughts of the trials and complications to come that had been forgotten in the moment.

"Perfect," she whispered back.

Perfect.

CHAPTER TEN

S hea Montgomery might be a new Montgomery, but she was part of the family nonetheless. At least that's what she told herself as she stood on Harry and Marie's porch, her hand firmly in Shep's.

"You ready for this?" Shep asked, his face a little paler than normal.

She wanted more than anything to pull him into her arms and never let him go. She had no idea how to make things better, and she wasn't sure there was a way to begin with. Someone Shep loved more than anything in the world might be dying, and there was nothing she could do.

Shep had grown up in Denver with the rest of the vast Montgomery clan. He had three sets of cousins, plus his own siblings. Sure, many of the cousins and others had moved away from Denver over the years, but the core group, Harry and Marie's, all still lived within the Denver limits. Shep said they were noisy, loving, and always into each other's business.

He loved it.

Shea wasn't so sure.

She'd grown up in a family where being in another's business meant telling them what to do and belittling them while they did it. Her father had cheated on her mother for years, using mistress after mistress to bury the pain of being married to her mother. Her mother? Well...her mother was an icy bitch of epic proportions.

It had taken years for Shea to feel free enough to even think that, let alone say it.

She'd finally gotten out from under her mother's thumb—she'd never truly been on her father's radar since she wasn't a son.

Now, she had a job she enjoyed, a husband she loved to the depths of her soul, and a new large family she was about to meet. Yet she felt like she was out of control, on the verge of something she couldn't name, something she couldn't vocalize, not when there were more important things to worry about—namely Harry and Shep.

Her own fears and secret desires would have to wait. She'd tried to hide from Shep what was going on in her own mind, but she wasn't sure she was doing a very good job of it. In fact, she knew she sucked at it. Hiding things from her husband was nearly impossible. It wasn't as if she was hiding something truly horrible; it was a dream and a nightmare at once that she couldn't control, not the end of the world. She knew she was being irrational, but she couldn't stop the damn worrying.

Strong hands cupped her face, and she blinked.

"Shea? Baby? I asked if you were ready."

She licked her lips and leaned into his hand. "I am. Just lost in thought I guess."

His gaze searched hers, and he sighed. Damn it. She was doing this all wrong. It was getting harder and harder to conceal her worry and concerns. Without thinking, she put her hand over her stomach, praying everything would be okay.

"I wish you would tell me what's wrong."

"I'm fine. Just a little tired. We should go inside or knock or something. Standing out here loitering probably isn't the best first impression I can make."

He frowned then kissed her softly. "I love you, Shea. You can tell me anything."

She smiled at him then, loving him more than she could ever have thought possible. "I know. I love you too."

The door opened, and Austin stood in the doorway. "You two done making out on the porch, or should I let you keep at it for a bit?"

Shea turned in Shep's arms, blushing, with a small smile on her face. Austin grinned at her, his expression lighter than she'd ever seen it. Something had happened to him since his time in New Orleans, something good that might not completely outweigh the bad, but good nonetheless.

"It's good to see you, Austin," she said as she slid from Shep's arms into his cousin's. He wrapped his arms around her, hugging her close.

Austin was the only Montgomery she'd met, and she liked the fact that he'd be a familiar face in what would surely be a sea of people, whose names she would never get right.

He kissed the top of her head then moved back, his arm still around her waist. "It's good to see you, too. I don't know why you didn't let me pick you up from the airport."

Shea rolled her eyes as Shep shrugged then went in for a hug with Austin. Shea moved away for them to embrace in a hug that wasn't one of those male hugs where they clapped each other on the shoulder and all that crap. No, this one was one between brothers and cousins who were both in pain.

"We wanted to rent a car since none of you have an extra one," Shep explained. "We have all our crap in the back, so we'll just head to Griffin's place after dinner with the folks."

Her husband looked as exhausted as she felt, and she sighed. This was going to be a very tiring trip, but they needed to be there. Austin had asked, and they had come with no second thoughts. It didn't mean it would be easy.

"Are you going to make them stand in the doorway for the rest of the night, or are they allowed to come in?"

Shea turned to see an older version of Austin—sans beard and visible tattoos—walk toward them. He didn't look sick. That surprised her. Austin had told Shep that Harry looked smaller than he had before, sicker.

That could be the case, but Shea didn't see that. She saw a man who looked vital and ready to fight.

Good for him.

Harry held his arms out with a smile on his face that didn't quite reach his eyes. There. That was what Austin must have been talking about. Well, okay, she'd do her best to be there for all of them. They were her family now, and she'd be damned if she'd be the weak link.

"Well, girl, come here to your Uncle Harry and give him a hug."

She couldn't hold back her smile as she did as he asked. He wrapped his arms around her just as Austin had, holding her tight. The man might be in his sixties and in the early stages of cancer, but he hadn't lost his strength yet.

"You look good, Shea." He smiled down at her when they pulled apart. "I'm sorry we couldn't make it to the wedding."

She bit her lip. It had been her idea to not wait for a large wedding and forego having family there. She just wanted Shep to be her husband, and he hadn't complained. She thought now that she might have made a mistake.

"Hey, don't look like that, dear," Harry said as he tilted her chin up. "You get married for yourself and your partner. You don't do it for others. We didn't need to be there, but you're here now. That's all that matters." He cleared his throat, and Shea held back tears. "You're here now," he whispered.

Shea pulled away as Shep said hello to his uncle, blinking quickly so she didn't cry.

"Shea, honey, I'm so glad you're here," Marie said as she came into the room, wiping her hands on a towel. She set the towel down on the side table then opened her arms as Harry had.

Shea sank into the other woman, the softness over a steel will not surprising her in the least. Marie was a mother of eight and countless strays. It was no wonder she was so strong. As Marie ran her hand down Shea's back, Shea relaxed, that little ball of anxiety in her belly soothing.

God, was this what it should have been with her own mother? A hug that took out some of the sting, some of the pain?

She was officially an emotional mess, but at least she'd held back her tears. So far.

"Well then, darling," Marie said as she wiped her own eyes. "Now that we're here, let's have some food, get settled, and then we can visit a bit."

"That sounds like a plan," Shea said. "Is there anything I can do?"

Marie shook her head. "No, I've got this down to a science. It's on the table, and we're ready to go."

Shep came over and took her hand, leading her into the dining room. Soon, she was eating a generous helping of roast chicken stuffed with oranges, plus mashed potatoes, and lemon asparagus. She hadn't been eating enough recently and, in the mornings, had been having trouble keeping things down. Right then, she ate every bite and relaxed for the first time in weeks.

Shep ran his hand over her knee, and she leaned into him. Yes, she'd tell him what was going on soon, but first she needed to figure out what was wrong with herself emotionally and how to help Shep's family.

As dinner wound down, they made their way into the living room. She sank into the couch, her body relaxing against Shep's. Austin sat on the other side of her, as if he knew they all might need the comfort.

"So...we're here," Shep started, running a hand over his face.

"You're here," Harry said. "You're here because Austin asked that of you, and I'm grateful." He met Shea's eyes then Shep's. "As you know, I have prostate cancer. We caught it early because my wife makes me go to the doctor to catch things like this." He let out a breath then gripped Marie's hands.

Shea let a tear fall. It would be no use holding them back now.

"Can you tell us more about it?" Shep asked. "Where you're at? What treatments? I want to make sure we understand so we can help out and know all we can."

Harry nodded. "I'll tell you everything I can. I don't want to hide this from you, nor do I want you to go in thinking the worst...or even the best. I'm in the very early stages of the disease with a slow-growing, low-grade tumor."

"That's good, right?" Shep asked and Shea squeezed his hand. "Shit. I mean better. Not good. There's nothing good about this."

"He caught it early, and that's a good thing," Austin said quietly.

"Yes, son. That's exactly it. It's low-grade, as I said. That means we're looking at external beam radiation therapy and not a radical prostatectomy. However, if the doctors think I need that, then we'll do it. I'm not going to risk my life and forego treatment because of cost—not yet."

Shea didn't think Harry meant the cost in terms of money.

"Sierra and I were looking at the types of radiation and how it would work while we were researching," Austin began then coughed. "I hope that's okay."

For the first time, Harry looked truly bright. "Sierra, is it?"

"We're just starting out, Dad."

Shea smiled as Austin squirmed in his seat.

"Why didn't she come tonight?" Harry asked.

"She had to work at Eden, her shop across the street from Montgomery Ink. I'll bring her next time, okay?" Austin grinned a bit, though he looked like he'd rather not be subjected to his parents' stares.

Good for Austin.

"Good," Marie said sweetly. "I want to meet this woman that Maya speaks of."

Austin groaned. "You know better than to listen to what Maya has to say."

"Austin Montgomery, you be nice to your sister," Marie ordered with a smile. She looked over at her husband and sighed. "Now where were we?"

"They're still prepping me for radiation," Harry said after he let Austin sweat a bit. "I start it in three days, and it will probably kick me in the ass, but I'm not going to let it keep me down."

Shep let out a shaky breath, and Shea ran her hand down his thigh.

"We'll be here for a couple of weeks or so," Shea said. "I can do most of my work from home at this point, and Shep's coworkers at Midnight Ink don't mind picking up the slack while we're here. That means we can help with whatever you need."

"You rented a car, did you?" Harry asked, and his brow rose.

"Yes, we wanted to be mobile," Shea answered.

"Well, you can return the damn thing," Harry said. "Take my car. I'm not going to be able to drive anyway." Shea knew it had taken a lot for Harry to admit that, and she wanted to hug the man hard.

"Uncle Harry..." Shep began then shook his head. "Thank you."

"You're welcome, now let me hug that wife of yours again because it looks like she needs it."

She did, but it looked like Harry needed it more. She hugged him again hard then pulled away as Austin and Shep did the same. Marie wrapped her arm around Shea's shoulder and both women stood off to the side, still as stone.

It was clear to anyone that Harry was the center of the Montgomery family. If they lost him...well, Shea didn't want to think about that. She put her hand over her stomach again, that worry sliding through her like it'd never left.

One thing at a time, she whispered to herself. One thing at a time.

CHAPTER ELEVEN

Miranda Montgomery might be the youngest in the family, but she wasn't a kid anymore. Getting that idea into the thick skulls of her brothers and sisters, on the other hand, might take a miracle.

Forcing the man she'd loved for years to see that would be even harder.

Well, considering she was currently on a date with someone else so she could get that other man out of her head probably wasn't helping things.

But there was only so much little-sister babying she could take.

She was twenty-three, done with school, and on the prowl.

She couldn't help the grin at that thought. On the prowl? More like on a slow, steady march toward what she wanted. Right then, she was on a pit stop to make sure she wasn't being an idiot though.

Just because she happened to love her big brother's best friend didn't mean he had to love her back.

Oh no. Decker Kendrick didn't do anything he didn't want to do, and loving her wasn't in the cards. Seeing her as an adult woman with needs seemed so far out of his scope that Miranda was just about to call it a lost cause.

"Miranda, darling, are you listening?" Edward, her date, asked, that pleasant smile on his face getting on her nerves.

It wasn't that he tried to be annoying; he couldn't help himself. Everything about him was pleasant. His not-too-tight and not-too-bright smile, his suit that wasn't designer—but neither was it bargain priced—his job as an accountant that was middle of the road, his voice that wasn't too deep, wasn't too high, or anything else she could name. He was just...pleasant.

What had she been thinking when she'd agreed to this date?

Oh, yeah...that Decker hardly looked at her as anything more than a little sister and she hadn't been on a date in months.

Miranda shook her head then calmly put her napkin down on the table. They'd gone out to a nice dinner that wasn't too fancy, nor was it all that casual, either. The man had a theme for sure, and he wasn't about the get off course.

"I'm sorry, Edward. I'm not feeling well. I think I'm going to go home so I can make sure I'm ready for work in the morning."

A Thursday evening date. Seriously? What had she been thinking? She had class in the morning and would have even more papers to grade after that. But she was trying not to be a homebody, and Thursday night dates with pleasant, boring Edward had been her answer.

Or not.

Edward frowned but not too deeply. "I'm sorry to hear that. You drove in. Are you able to drive yourself home?"

She'd driven in because she'd had a feeling she'd have to cut the date short. Also, her brothers would have killed her for going on a first date without an escape route.

"I'm good. Thank you for the evening." She stood up, and he stood as well, gently kissing her hand.

And *nada*.

No spark.

"Rain check?" he asked, his eyes hopeful.

Instead of answering, Miranda gave him a small smile then said goodbye. She wasn't about to crush his hopes in the middle of a restaurant, but she couldn't go out with him again. Not when she was beyond bored.

She made her way home, then kicked off her heels and flopped on the couch. She'd get out of her dress and makeup in a bit. It was only seven thirty, so she had plenty of time.

Seven thirty.

Dear Lord, what a dull evening.

Miranda shouldn't have said yes when Edward asked her out, but she'd wanted to get out of the house and get her mind off of the torment that wouldn't go away.

Her dad had cancer, and she didn't know how to deal with that. Others had made lists, done research, made food and brought it over, even though Mom could cook just fine at the moment. Miranda had hugged her dad and said she'd be there no matter what. Just tell her what to do.

It still scared the hell out of her.

She looked down at her phone and bit her lip. Austin might be done with dinner at the folks' house with Shep and Shea. She'd just see how it went. Her big brother always knew what to do. She sent him a quick text asking how it went and smiled as he answered right away.

Good. As good as it can get. We just got to the house now, and I'm settling Shep and Shea in for the long haul. They'll be here for a bit.

Miranda had to roll her eyes. For a man with fingers as big as his, her brother sure did type a lot in a text. Even as she smiled, she warmed. Shep was Austin's age, so she hadn't grown up with him as a sibling, but he'd been in her life for the whole of it. He still joked that he'd helped change her diapers.

Not something she liked to hear about, considering he'd once said it in front of her prom date.

I can't wait to meet Shea.

You'll like her. She's tiny but powerful. We'll be around, hon. Get some sleep. You have school in the morning.

Once a big brother, always a big brother. It didn't matter that she was the teacher, in this case, and not the student. School came early in the morning anyway.

However, it wasn't even eight yet, and she wanted to talk to her family. She dialed Meghan's number, knowing the kids would be in bed by now and she'd have a better chance of reaching her sister.

"Hey you. What are you doing on the phone? I thought you'd be on your date."

Miranda sighed at her sister's words. "Edward was dull and boring. I'm home now."

Meghan gave a soft laugh. "Honey, his name was Edward. You told me yourself you only thought of the sad sparkly vampire when you said his name."

Miranda chuckled. "He wasn't emo, Meghan. He was just...boring."

"Well, you're home now. I'm sorry it didn't work out."

I'm not. Edward wasn't Decker, but Miranda wasn't about to tell Meghan that.

"What are you up to tonight?"

"Oh, the usual...cleaning up vomit off the floor of the bathroom because Boomer decided to try to eat one of my shoes, and it didn't agree with him."

"Oh, poor Boomer," Miranda said through held-back laughter.

"Don't you laugh at me, Miranda Montgomery. That puppy might be the cutest thing ever, but he's a devil. And Richard has had it up to—"

Her sister cut herself off, and Miranda wanted to scream. She hated Meghan's husband, but she couldn't voice it. She'd done it once, and her sister had told her not to judge what she didn't understand.

So, she'd be the good sister, hold back, and be there for her no matter what. She'd just say bad things about Richard in her head...or to her other siblings.

Someone yelled on the other end of the line, and Miranda winced.

"Crap. Richard just found another puddle. I need to go. Love you, honey."

She hung up before Miranda could say it back. Damn it. She was worried about Meghan just as she was about her dad. It sucked being the little sister where she couldn't help, only stand back and pray that things would work out, being there if needed.

If only she was what Decker needed.

No, she wouldn't think about that. Not now.

She knew love was hard. She'd seen it her whole life...but she'd been in love just as long. What was one more day?

CHAPTER TWELVE

Sierra fell onto her back, her body sweaty, shaky, and sated. Her eyes threatened to close, but she forced them open. Morning sex—even great morning sex—meant she needed to get out of bed and rush to get ready if she wanted to make it to work.

Morning sex with Austin... Well, thankfully, he woke her up early pumping into her from behind; there was nothing quick and easy about the man.

"Don't fall asleep, Austin," she mumbled, her own body ready to rest again. She wouldn't allow herself to curl into him for petting and care because she needed to get up and get ready for work. If she hurried through her shower—solo— she'd have time to eat before she went.

He sat up, running his hand over his beard. She blushed as she remembered the feel of his beard on her breasts and her pussy just a few moments before.

Dear Lord, she loved that beard.

His gaze caught hers, and he raised a brow. "I thought you said you needed to be at work. If you keep looking at me like that, we aren't getting out of bed any time soon."

She tried to jump out of bed but staggered since her legs were still a little jelly-like from that thorough wake-up call.

"Yes. Keep your hands off of me. I can't think when you touch me."

"Aw, Legs, that's one of the best compliments you've given me."

Sierra rolled her eyes then strolled naked to the bathroom, picking up her overnight bag on the way. She wasn't ready to leave clothes or anything else at his house, as they'd only been dating for a couple weeks, and she wasn't ready for that step. Packing an overnight bag, however, was good enough for her. There was no use lying to herself and saying she wouldn't be sleeping over and then dealing with the fact she wouldn't have any of her things the next morning.

"I'm going to jump in the shower and then blow out my hair." She narrowed her eyes. "And, no, you can't join me because I want to eat before work so the girls don't yell at me, and if we shower together, we'd take twice as long since you can't keep your hands off me."

Austin grinned then stood up, naked and so freaking sexy Sierra had to keep her mouth closed lest she start drooling. His cock was only semi-hard considering they'd just finished coming less than five minutes ago, but, damn, he was big. Lucky her.

"You know, we'd save water if we share. Think of the planet, Legs."

She rolled her eyes even as she walked into the bathroom to turn on the water and get about her morning business. She closed the door behind her, but he walked right in. Well then, apparently they were past privacy in their relationship.

That was fast.

She jumped in the shower while he did his own business, and Sierra thought about where her life had been and where it was now. Here she was in a pretty freaking serious relationship even though neither of them said it, and now she was sharing a bathroom with the man.

"By the way, Legs, the girls aren't the only ones who'll be pissed if you don't take care of yourself and eat."

"I'm going to eat as soon as I get out. Promise." Her body warmed at the thought he cared for her in more ways than just in bed. They were slowly becoming more entwined in certain ways outside the bedroom. They ate lunches together during the day and had meals together at night. He'd fixed her window, and she helped him pick out curtains for, of all things, his living room. He made sure she ate, and she made sure he had a game plan when it came to helping his father deal with what was to come.

They were a couple, and there was no way she could deny it.

Not that she was sure she wanted to anymore.

By the time she got out of the shower and blew her hair out so it was decent for work, Austin was in the kitchen wearing only a pair of jeans and pouring oatmeal into bowls.

She smiled then walked up behind him, wrapping her arms around his waist.

"Hey, Legs, you smell good," he rumbled as he added fruit to hers and brown sugar to his. "I figured oatmeal would be better than bacon and eggs. I don't have any yogurt, or I'd have made that for you."

Sierra took the pot from his hands, set it down, and then stood on her tiptoes to cup his face. "Thank you."

His gaze traced her face, then he lowered his lips to brush along hers. "You're welcome, Legs. Now eat so we're not late."

"Don't you need to shower?" she asked as she sat at the bar next to him.

"Yeah, but I can do that quick while you put on your makeup or whatever you need to finish up."

They sounded so much like a married couple that Sierra had to take a step back. They hadn't been together that long, but they sure were acting like it. One day at a time, she reminded herself. She wasn't ready for marriage and babies—she wasn't sure she'd ever be—but sitting there that morning she thought it could be a possibility.

"Did I fuck up the oatmeal?" he asked, and she blinked. "What?"

"You just went pale for a second. You okay?"

She shook her head to clear it then smiled. "I'm fine." Really. She was. For the first time she thought she could be. "What are you plans?"

"I have a couple consultations, then I have to work on a client's leg for most of the day. I'll be free at noon for an hour or so for lunch and then will be busy until I get off work. You?"

She nibbled on a strawberry. "I need to go over the books while I'm not up front. I'll have lunch off, but I'll probably be working late since books take forever."

Austin licked his spoon then stood up, taking their empty bowls to the sink. "I should be done by seven or so for a late dinner if you just want to come over here. I'll pick up Chinese, and we can just relax."

"Two nights in a row?" she asked.

"You got a problem with that?" He stood right in front of her, his body big but his presence bigger.

She thought about it then shook her head. "No. Actually, I like it. Pull me out of the books when you get done, or I'll end up there all night. I'll have to stop by my house and pick up another change of clothes while you get the food."

"You know, it would be easier if you just left things here."

She let out a breath. "True, but I'm not ready for that. Okay?"

He nodded then kissed her again. "Okay. I'm going to go jump in the shower. I'll be quick."

She smiled up at him and wondered how the hell she'd ended up here and, at the same time, didn't want to leave.

By the time lunch rolled around, Sierra's nerves were fraying. It had been a non-stop morning with customer after costumer needing one-on-one care. While that normally would have made her feel like she was on top of the world, her books were calling her name. Jasinda had the flu, and that meant Sierra was on her own for the day.

Not something she could have handled if it wasn't for sheer perseverance.

Lunch with Austin had been hurried since they both had to get back to work. She ignored Hailey's pointed look followed by mouthing the word "oaf" over Austin's back. So, Sierra had gotten it wrong before. Whatever. She'd judged, and so had he, but they were past it.

Now, thankfully, there was a lull, the store being empty, and Sierra could catch her breath. Eden was still going great in this first month of opening and she knew she'd have to hire another person soon so she wouldn't burn out. There was only so much she could do.

The bell over the door rang, and Sierra turned to see who it was, only to have her smile freeze on her face

She remembered that woman and her prey.

Shannon.

Austin's ex.

Oh, goodie.

"Good afternoon, how can I help you?" she clipped out through a false smile. The ice princess was back, but she didn't give a damn. From the gleam in Shannon's eyes, the other woman wasn't there for a scarf or dress.

No, she was there for another reason entirely.

Whatever.

Shannon lifted a lip in what might have been a smile but was more of a smirk. "I'm just browsing. I'm not sure you'll have anything that appeals to my...taste and quality here."

So it was going to be like that, was it? Good to know. Sierra really didn't like jealous women who gauged their self-worth by the men they snared in their web. Shannon was one of those few who gave women a bad rep, and she had no use for her.

"I'll be around if you need me then. Enjoy."

Shannon lifted a red-tipped finger. "Actually, sugar, I have something to say."

Sierra folded her hands in front of her. "Yes?"

The other woman's eyes narrowed. Sierra wouldn't back down though. This woman meant nothing to her other than being in Austin's past. In fact, if it wasn't for Shannon being who she was and Sierra's muttered comment when they'd first met, she and Austin might never have met the way they did. Who knows what would have happened otherwise?

"I don't know who you think you are walking into my town and acting like you're the shit, but you're not good enough for him. You'll bore Austin in another week or less, and then he'll be back to me. He always comes back to me."

Well, that was a lie in so many ways that Sierra wouldn't even bother to contradict her. "If that's how you feel, you can keep thinking that, *sugar*. However you're boring me, so you can go now if you're not going to purchase anything. Claim whoever you'd like, but you won't be chasing me away."

She'd done enough running in her lifetime as it was.

"You're an ice-cold bitch, you know that?"

Sierra raised a brow. "I've heard that a few times in my life." From Jason's parents actually, but she wasn't going to think about that. "If we're done, I have a business to run."

Shannon snarled then stomped out of the store. Well, that was dramatic and not worth her time. She'd have to tell Austin about it so it wouldn't come as a surprise later, but it wouldn't be worth the time. The other woman had thrown away something special, and Sierra was just now beginning to realize what she could have if fate worked her way.

Fate hadn't worked her way in the past, however, so she knew better than to get her hopes up.

Becky ran through the door at that moment, her face red. "I'm here. I'm here. Traffic was horrible. Accident on 70, but I'm here now. Go in the back and work on the books, and I can handle it here."

Sierra snorted then hugged the woman hard. "Thanks, honey. I don't want to think about numbers right now, but I don't have a choice."

Becky wrinkled her nose. "I wouldn't want to either, but that's why you're the boss and I'm the lowly peasant."

"Peasant my butt." The bell rang again, and Sierra stepped away. "Have fun; I'm going to go drown in numbers."

"Better you than me," Becky mumbled before sighing and greeting the two women walking in.

Sierra went to her small office in the back, sat down, and took off her shoes. She stretched her toes and cursed the person who invented stilettos. It must have been a man.

Her cellphone buzzed, and she picked it up, not looking at the caller ID. "This is Sierra."

"There you are. I knew we'd find your number. There's no use hiding from us. We will *always* find you, you murderer."

Sierra almost dropped the phone at the cruelty and anger in the voice.

The voice that shouldn't have been able to find her so quickly, but there was a restraining order in place for this.

"Marsha, you know you shouldn't be calling me." She swallowed hard, her palms clammy, her vision blurring.

"You think I care what a little piece of paper says? You killed my *son*, you little bitch. You killed him, and yet you get to walk away free and open your little shop like you don't care. You weren't good enough for Jason, and you turned him into a freak with your trollop ways."

Sierra closed her eyes, trying to find the strength not to yell back, not to do anything but hang up and call her lawyer. Marsha and Todd couldn't hurt her anymore. They couldn't take anything else from her that she hadn't already lost because of one careless action.

"You need to leave me alone, Marsha. Jason is gone, and we can't bring it back. But I didn't kill him." If she kept saying that, maybe she'd believe it.

"You killed my son!" Marsha screamed into the phone, and Sierra couldn't hang up.

She deserved some of the taint on her. The scars on her body hadn't been enough.

The familiar echo of thoughts she'd thought she destroyed went on a loop in her.

Murderer.

Killer.

Slut.

Freak.

Tainted.

Whore.

All the words Marsha had used over and over again when they'd lost their son would never be banished from Sierra's memory no matter how hard she tried to scrub them clean.

She'd always be dirty.

Scarred.

"Sierra, this is Todd."

She held back a sob at Jason's father's words. The man never yelled, never showed any other emotion except clear indifference.

"Yes, Todd?" God, why was she subjecting herself to his? Why was she allowing this man and woman to ruin her life again?

She didn't deserve it. She tried to tell herself...but it didn't ring true.

"Marsha made the unfortunate decision of allowing her emotions to rule her call today; however, none of what she said was false. You are the one who laid false claims on the memory of our son. You were the one who led him down the dark path of the sickness that is Dominance and submission. I realize now you're truly mentally ill and need a man to tell you what to do to live. In order to do that, you ruined our boy. You made him believe he had to hit you, and in doing that, you hurt him. That would have been cruel enough, but then you killed him that night."

Sierra's body shook, the familiar refrain slamming into like a lethal blow. It didn't matter that she didn't believe Todd's words. The fact that the man and his wife believed them beyond any degree of doubt made it matter.

"We are not done, Sierra. We will never be done until we have justice."

He hung up then, and Sierra stared down at her phone, her body going numb. She'd thought she'd been so safe, so free. She'd tried to find a place to call her own, a man to do the same.

Yet it would never be enough.

Damn it. She wasn't this person. She wasn't weak or something to be spat on because people didn't understand. What they thought was evil and tainted they fought against.

After she wiped her face with a scarf she had in her drawer, she called her lawyer, ready to fight. Or at least put on a brave face when she lied to herself.

A woman answered the phone, and Sierra cleared her throat, holding back the tears that would take over if she didn't find the way to be stronger than the person others had made.

"I need to speak to Mr. Trust," Sierra said, surprised that her voice was so clear. Flat maybe, but not shaky.

"He's in a meeting at the moment. May I take a message?"

"Tell him it's Sierra Elder, and I need to talk to him immediately."

"Oh, Ms. Elder, Mr. Trust told me you might be calling. He said to put you through right away. Please hold."

Well, it seemed that Rodney was expecting her call. What could she make of that? Clearly. something was going on that meant Jason and her past were far from over.

"Sierra, damn it. I was going to call you after I got more information, but from this call, I guess I was too late?"

Rodney was a middle-aged man who'd never been married because he'd married his job long ago. He might have put on a little weight around the middle, but other than that, he still looked like he was her age. He'd been on her side from the beginning, her only friend when everything had gone to hell.

If she had been ready for a lover when they'd first met, she knew they'd have found each other in bed. By the time she was ready, though, they'd passed into the stage where they needed each other more as friends than a causal fling.

The man worked like a dog and had protected her when no one else would.

Now it seemed he'd have to do it again.

"Marsha and Todd called me," she whispered. She didn't need to be as strong for Rodney...much like she didn't need to be around Austin.

She'd deal with that thought later.

"Damn it. You have the restraining order in place."

She shook her head. "It doesn't matter. They didn't call from their number, and I didn't record it. What can I do? I don't care anymore, Rodney. I just want to move on."

He let out a breath, and Sierra wanted to throw the phone. "They're not going to make that easy, honey."

"What are they doing now?"

"They've tried criminal suits out the ass, and that hasn't worked. They don't have a leg to stand on. Now they're going through the civil courts and trying to find a way to make you pay. If they can't get you in jail, they're going after everything else you have."

"Eden," she breathed.

"Eden. Damn it. I'm sorry. I'm working on what I can, but I don't know if I'm going to be able to stop this one from going to court. If they base it on emotional damage to themselves rather than what happened to Jason and get a sympathetic judge, they could find a way in."

Her stomach revolted, but she held down her lunch. God, her lunch? It seemed like ages ago that she'd sat with Austin and seen his face and those gorgeous blue eyes.

"What are we going to do?"

"I'm going to try to find a way to fix this, Sierra."

"And if you can't?"

"Just because they might get it to court—honestly, they don't have a legal leg to stand on—doesn't mean they'll win."

"They lost their son, Rodney."

"You lost him too," he snapped back. "You lost so much more." He let out a breath. "I'm sorry. I'm working on it and will keep you posted. Live your life, Sierra. Try to find a way to make it. Okay?"

"I'll try." They said their goodbyes then hung up.

It seemed the past would never leave her. It would always lurk in the corner like a shadow. She looked down at her books and shook her head. She wouldn't be able to think tonight. They would have to be put off until tomorrow.

She would just go home, take a bath, drink a glass of wine, and try to forget it for a moment. Wait, no, she couldn't do that. Austin was expecting her at his place.

"Sierra?"

Speak of the devil.

She looked up at Austin and lost it. Tears spilled down her cheeks, and she let out sob. He was on her in an instant.

"Oh, baby, what's wrong?" He picked her up like she was nothing and held her to his chest before sitting down in her chair. It creaked, and she prayed it didn't break under their combined weight.

He soothed her while she cried, kissing her softly and running his hands down her side.

"I'm sorry," she whispered when she was done.

"Baby, tell me what's wrong."

"I..." She would she realized. She'd tell him everything. He'd seen her scars, yet he'd never asked her about it. He'd trusted that she'd tell him eventually and now that time had come.

"I don't want to talk about it here. Let's go to your place, and then we can talk."

He searched her face then nodded. "I don't want you driving though, okay? I'll have Maya and Jake take your car home when they get done, if that's okay. We'll get your stuff and then head to my place."

She nodded, feeling drained. "I'll tell you, Austin. I'll tell you everything."

He tucked a piece of hair behind her ear. "Okay, then. Let's get you home."

Home.

She liked the sound of that.

She just prayed that when she told Austin her story he wouldn't ask her to leave.

The world might have shattered around her before, but if Austin sent her away, she knew she'd find only a broken piece of herself left behind.

CHAPTER THIRTEEN

Austin let the wheat taste of his beer slide down his throat as he watched Sierra out on his deck while he leaned against the opening of the sliding glass doors. She stood at the railing, her hair free and blowing in the wind. The sun was just setting, and the orange and pinks in the sky reminded Austin of why he loved his home and his city.

He was surrounded by nature even though he could drive two minutes and find civilization.

Right then he wanted to clutch Sierra to his side and protect her from the world. Something had scared her today. Something so bad she'd easily given in to his orders and control. She hadn't batted an eyelash when he took her car keys away and drove her to her place. He'd packed up her things while she told him what she wanted. He hadn't wanted her to lift a finger.

The fact that she let him spoke volumes.

They ordered Chinese and had it delivered, though both of them only picked at their food. He didn't want to pressure her to tell him what had spooked her since lunch, but if she didn't start talking soon, he just might do it.

He dominated in the bedroom, not in everyday life, but when she looked so lost, so broken, he'd do what he had to in order to keep her safe.

Sierra Elder had come to mean more to him than he'd thought possible in such a short amount of time.

To hell with it.

He set his beer down on the outside table then went to her. When he pressed his front to her back, caging her in, she leaned into him. She tilted her head up, and he took her mouth in an easy kiss.

"What happened after lunch, baby?"

She turned in his arms then wrapped hers around his waist. He didn't hesitate and hugged her close, resting his cheek on her head.

"I don't know how to start."

He pulled back then tugged on her hand, picked up his beer and led her to the living room. He sat down on the couch and pulled her into his lap.

"Start with right after lunch. Who bothered you?"

She blinked at him then snorted. "Oh, well, before I go into what the, shall we say, bad part, someone *did* come in after lunch and bothered me."

Austin narrowed his eyes. "Who?" he growled.

"Now don't freak out because I handled this part on my own. I just thought you should know."

"Who?"

"Shannon."

"That fucking bitch. What did she say to you?" Hell. He'd call the cops and get a restraining order at this point. He could take it just fine, but no one was allowed to bother Sierra. No one.

"She did her whole song and dance about how you're hers and all that crap. It didn't bother me other than it happened in my place of business. I handled it, Austin. I honestly think she's just bored and will go away once she finds something new. She just needs something—or someone in this case—to do. Don't worry about it."

He rubbed her cheek with his thumb, pissed that his past was coming out to bother his present. "I don't have *that* many exes, but it seems one I do have is trying to fuck it all up."

"Trying, but not doing it. It's fine. She'll get bored when she gets ignored, and we'll move on. On that note, do you have any other exes I should hear about?"

Austin blushed a bit. "Uh, not really. I haven't heard from any of them. I think Maggie is in town, but it's been years since I've seen her. Most of them are married, I think. I mean married now. Not that they were married when we were together. You know what I mean."

Sierra kissed his bearded cheek. "I get it." She let out a breath, and Austin tensed. "Now, about my ex."

"Jason?"

She nodded. "Jason. Damn it. Okay, so you know about my past with him a bit in terms of our relationship, and you've seen my scars."

She closed her eyes, and Austin held still. If he moved or breathed loudly, she might stop speaking, and he knew she needed to get this out.

Not only for him, but for herself as well.

"They're connected."

"Did he do this to you?" he ground out.

Sierra's eyes opened, and she shook her head. "Not in the way you think. We were in an accident. And it was my fault. I killed him."

Austin's heart stopped.

"You what?" He shook his head. "Just tell me it all. Tell me about what happened and why you think you killed him. Then tell me how that relates to how I found you in your office today."

"He had an old Harley he loved," she said then licked her lips.

"Riding," he muttered. "Oh damn."

"Yeah. Damn."

Her gaze met his, and he had to suck in a breath. The strength he saw there made him want to hold her close and never let her go. She might feel she was weak, but she was wrong. He'd do whatever was in his power to make sure she understood.

"We rode everywhere," she started again. "We were young, in love, carefree. You know how that goes."

Not exactly, but the burning knot of something he'd rather not delve too deeply into started to tighten. "How old were you again?"

She gave him a sad smile. "Nineteen." When his eyes widened, she snorted. "Yeah. I know. Nineteen and in love. We were both in college going for business degrees. He was going to work for his father, and I was going to open my own boutique, and we'd have babies and ride into the sunset. Damn, those dreams were so big for teenagers, but I thought it could happen. I truly thought we could take over our part of the world and live happily ever after."

Jason had been the center of her life back then. Sierra was a full nine years younger than he, something Jason never really thought about, but she'd been in love and lived in a way Austin would never understand.

Now that she was in his life, though, Austin was just starting to comprehend that kind of feeling, that kind of need, but this wasn't the time to dwell on it, not when she was in the past with the man she'd loved before him.

"We worked well together. At least I thought we did."

"What do you mean?"

"My in-laws, well, those people I thought of as my in-laws since Jason and I were only engaged and not actually married, hated me."

He cupped her face. "How could anyone hate you?" The irony that he'd tried to hate her before he even met her didn't escape him, but that had been his own prejudice.

She rolled her eyes. "I wasn't good enough for their precious baby boy. They had money. Lots of it. I didn't. I came from the middle class. My parents worked their asses off to get me money for college, and I worked on the side to pay for room and board as well. CU is expensive."

Austin nodded. He knew that, though he'd never gone to college. All of his siblings who'd gone to school went there. He'd taken business classes at UCD, the offshoot of CU, so he could be ready for Montgomery Ink, but that was it. He'd never felt like he needed more, and honestly, he still didn't.

"My parents were older when they had me and died about five years ago. Well, my dad did from a heart attack and my mother three months later with a brain aneurysm. So now I'm all alone, but I've moved off track."

Austin cupped her face. So much loss in such a short time. "I'm sorry, baby. So fucking sorry."

She closed her eyes and leaned into him. "I'm okay now. I know they're together, and I had started to move on, but now I'm really off my story." She took a deep breath. "So Jason. Him. We rode together on the weekends when I wasn't working. He didn't have to work since his parents took care of him. I hated it a bit at the time since he could go off and do what he wanted and I had to work my ass off serving tables, but it really didn't bother me too much. Money didn't matter to me other than to save it. Jason was always a little spoiled, I get that now, but he couldn't help it. Not with the kind of parents he had." Her mouth twisted into a wry smile.

"They hated me. God, how Marsha and Todd hated me. Still hate me. Not only did they think I wasn't good enough for him, but right before he died, they found out about the D/s part of our relationship."

"Shit," he mumbled. He could only guess how they'd reacted. A lot of people didn't understand the lifestyle. He wasn't out in the open with it unless he trusted people because he didn't want it to hurt his family and business.

"Yeah. Shit. They called me a whore and said I was abusing him. They said that I was some sick pervert that needed to be hit so I must have tainted their poor son and forced him to flog me. They even went to the cops and said I made Jason choke and cut me." She narrowed her eyes at him. "I was never into breath or blood play. I'm still not, but they went to the cops with the most taboo things they could find on the Internet and tried to get me out of Jason's life."

"Fucking bastards." To take something so precious between a Dom and sub and turn it out into the public like that? Fuck, he didn't know what he'd do, but it wouldn't be pretty.

"Pretty much. The cops couldn't do anything, thankfully. Jason and I were open and honest with them, and we got lucky in the fact that one of the cops was also a Dom. He took care of us and kept an eye out just in case Marsha and Todd tried a different tactic."

"Thank God for him then."

"I know, right? So, the bad part." She shook her head as if trying to clear the cobwebs. "We took a day off to ride up to the edge of Pike's Peak. We didn't like to ride all the way up because that's freaking dangerous and cold, but we liked the drive through the Springs and such."

"I get it." If he kept her talking, she'd eventually get to the bad part and then to why she'd freaked out when he saw her in her office. Jesus, even with what she'd told him, it was enough to make anyone have a breakdown.

"So we were on our way back, and the sun had set so we had our lights on and our night glasses on for the wind and glare. We even had helmets on, though Jason hated his. I wouldn't let him on the bike without it or his leathers if we were going for a long ride. I was a little mouthy back then, so I got my way."

He didn't mention that she still was, but he liked her that way. He didn't want a doormat in his life; he wanted fire and ice.

"What happened, baby?"

She closed her eyes and flinched, as if she was reliving whatever had happened. He brought her closer, letting his lips rest on her brow. His hand caressed her back, letting her know he was there.

"We were on a side street on our way to the highway since we didn't want to deal with all back roads in the dark. There were a couple of cars, but not that many since it wasn't rush hour and it was the weekend. It had been an amazing day and ride. We'd stopped for lunch and even made love in the forest on the way up there. We almost got caught but got lucky. It was seriously the perfect day. I had just wrapped my arm around his waist and yelled that I loved him. You know how you can't hear a thing over the wind, so I yelled. Right in his ear."

Fuck. He didn't want to hear the rest because that meant she'd have to tell it, but they both had to go through with it."

"Jason turned to me and yelled it back. He shouldn't have, but we weren't thinking. We were just...happy."

A lone tear slid down her cheek and he kissed it away. He didn't want to see her cry and didn't want to see her in pain, but he couldn't kiss it all away.

"We didn't see the train tracks until it was too late."

"Fuck, did you..."

"There wasn't a train, but the tracks were at an angle to the street. So instead of going at the ninety-degree angle you need to on his bike at our speed, we hit it awkwardly. The bike went down, and we both flew off of it. I skidded down the right side of the road and shredded my leathers. Jason ended up in oncoming traffic."

Dear. God.

"A semi on the way to the highway hit him at full speed. He didn't have a chance. The back tires slammed into the bike and caused an explosion. I had just turned over to see my fiancé die, hit by a truck, and then parts of the bike that were on fire slammed into my side. It was only a small part, but the burns and impact crushed three of my ribs and tore into one of my lungs. I don't remember much after that."

"Oh baby, oh fuck." He gently held her close, as if she was still as broken as she'd been the day of the accident ten years ago.

She wrapped her arms around him and hung on tight, tighter than he held her. Taking that as encouragement, he gripped harder, never wanting to let her go.

Her shoulders shook as she sobbed in his arms, and he felt his own tears track down his face into his beard. She'd been so young and so fucking lucky that she'd lived through that. To have to watch her fiancé die like that...hell...he didn't know how she survived.

"You're so fucking strong, Sierra. You lived, and you're still here. To do that...baby, you're so fucking strong," he repeated.

She pulled back, confusion in her gaze, before she kissed him softly. "Thank you for that. I don't always feel it, and back then, I knew I was weak. That's what I kept telling myself over and over again. That's what Marsha, Todd, and their lawyers kept saying."

"You were *never* weak."

"Thank you," she whispered then cleared her throat. "Jason died on impact. He was still alive when the semi came because I remember him looking up at me one last time, but he would have died quickly after that according to the doctors. I was in a medically induced coma for four days before I finally woke up."

He ran his hand up and down her back, feeling incompetent. He didn't know how to take her pain, but he could do his best to comfort her.

"It took months of surgeries, skin grafts, and agony before I was able to leave the hospital and not have a home nurse. By then, I had dropped out of college and moved back in with my parents."

Sierra bit her lip then shook her head. "I eventually went back and got my degree, but it took a hell of a lot longer than I'd planned. My parents died before they could see me graduate."

"Oh, baby."

"I know, but they were there for me when I really needed them. Not with just the healing and PT stuff. You see it was an accident according to the cops. At first."

She met his gaze, and Austin held back a curse.

"I told you Todd and Marsha had money. Well, they used that money to stir their grief and found a judge who looked into the case. They did all they could to find me criminally responsible for his son's death. They even tried to sue the semi driver, though he'd done nothing wrong. He called the police and saved my life by putting pressure on my wounds, but Jason's parents didn't care. In fact, I think they blamed the man for saving my life."

"You're kidding me."

She shook her head. "No. No I'm not. They told me flat-out to my face that I should have died in that accident and not him. They told me, and had the judge convinced, through money or idiocy, that if I hadn't forced Jason into the lifestyle, he would have been in the right mind never to get on the death trap of the bike in the first place. They told everyone they could that I must have done something on the back of the bike—sexual or violent depending on who spoke, Marsha or Todd—to cause the accident. They went on and on, trying to get me in jail."

"None of that would have brought back their son," he bit out.

"I know that. The cops knew that. The other judges knew that. We never went to court, thank God. They didn't have a case. It took years and many threats, but I was finally able to move on. By then, my parents were dead, and I had scars on my body that weren't as deep as the ones on my heart. The cops on the scene ruled it an accident, and though it was, it took me a long time to see that myself. In fact, I still don't believe it some days. I still feel like I'm the one who killed him."

He cupped her face, anger running in his veins at the situation and the idea that she'd think that and blame herself for something so far out of her control; it was crazy.

"You did nothing wrong. You loved a man, and you both had an accident."

"That's not all," she whispered, the darkness in her gaze forcing Austin to hold himself back.

"What?"

"I was pregnant when we went down."

"Fuck," he grunted then tugged her close. "Oh, baby. I'm so fucking sorry."

"I didn't know it at the time and lost the baby due to the trauma. When Jason's parents found out—I'd been drugged up because of the pain and let it slip—they blamed me for that death as well. I lost my baby and Jason all in one day and yet they compounded the whole situation."

"I'm so, so sorry, Sierra. There are no words, and yet all I want to do is hold you and try to make it better."

"I know. And the fact that you're here holding me makes it better in some ways. I've never told anyone about this, not the girls at work, not even Hailey, though she knows some of it." She met his gaze, her shoulders squaring. "I don't know if

I'll be able to get pregnant again, Austin. I don't know if babies are in my future."

He let out a shaky breath. Yeah, he wanted kids, and the more time he spent with Sierra made him think that she was the one for him, but there were other ways.

"When, and if, we come to that, we will deal with it," he said softly. "There are other methods of having children, and I'm not going to leave you because of something that might not happen. You get me?"

"I get you," she whispered.

"Good. Now tell me how this connects with how I found you at work today."

She sighed then told him about the phone call and what her lawyer had said. Each new piece of information set Austin's teeth on edge. It took all in his power not to clench his fists and end up bruising Sierra in some way because he couldn't control himself.

"You've got to be fucking kidding me."

"No. It's not over, and that pisses me off."

"Good, an angry Sierra is better than the one who thinks she can't do anything. I like it when you're all icy and have your chin up. You can take on the world then."

Her eyes filled with tears, and he wished he could take those words back. Maybe he'd been too honest.

"That's one of the nicest things you've said to me." She snorted. "I know that sounds crazy, but the fact that you believe in me means so much."

He kissed her softly then pulled back so they were eye to eye. "Of course I believe in you. You've been through so much, and you've never given up. And one thing, you're not alone. You get that? You've got me and the Montgomerys on your side. We're not letting these bastards hurt you. You're mine, Sierra Elder, and I'm not letting go."

He'd never said those words to another person before, and he knew one day soon he'd also tell her the other three words he'd never uttered to someone who wasn't his family.

"I...thank you," she whispered.

"Anything, Sierra. Know that. I'll do anything you need me to do." Including kill those bastards who thought they could hurt her.

She looked him straight in the eye, her chin rising. "Make me yours in truth, Austin."

He froze. "What?"

"You've done so much for me, but I've never done anything for you."

"Sierra, just you being you does it for me."

She shook her head. "No, I mean I've never *served* you. I want to take our relationship to the next level. I want to care for you the way we both need. I want you to do what you need as well. I want to find that trust and work toward something more."

No sweeter words had ever reached his ears.

There was only one thing to say.

"Kneel."

CHAPTER FOURTEEN

Sierra startled for only a moment—the fact she hadn't done this is in so long was almost jarring—before sliding off Austin's lap to the floor. He'd ordered her to kneel, and just that one word sent shivers down her spine.

She'd opened up to him in a way she'd never opened up to anyone, and now she wanted more. From the look in Austin's eyes, he wanted the same.

It should have been fear or anxiety running through her veins at the thought of giving herself body and soul to another man, but it wasn't. Instead, the need and desire burning through her body ignited a torch she prayed would never be extinguished.

Still clothed, she sank to her knees on the floor, her legs spread and her hands palms up on her thighs. She kept her chin raised and her gaze downward. Normally, she would do this nude, but as this was starting something new for the both of them, they'd take it one step at a time.

Her breasts ached for his touch, her pussy wet and ready with just that one word from him. She would have thought that after everything she'd just told him she wouldn't be ready for him so quickly, but she couldn't help herself.

She wanted Austin Montgomery.

Now.

Austin stood up so he was in front of her. He cupped her cheek, bringing her gaze to his. "You look beautiful, Sierra.

This gift you've given me...I'm going to take care of you. Do you understand me?"

She nodded.

"You understand?"

"Yes, Austin. I do."

"Good. Now you say you want to serve me? Tell me exactly what you mean. This first time, while we're still understanding each other, we'll talk about each thing before we do it. We will eventually get to know each other well enough that words won't be necessary, but for now, I need you to tell me what you want."

"Yes, Austin." She licked her lips. "I want to suck your cock and serve you."

He didn't smile, but his eyes danced. "Good. I want your mouth on my dick. What else do you want? What do you want me to do with your body?"

Everything? No, she couldn't say that. She needed to be specific.

"I want you to play with my nipples."

His hand went to her breast, cupping her softy even as his gaze remained on her. "I can do that. You want to go harder?" She nodded. "Good. I'm going to put you in nipple clamps. I want to see those reddened nipples. I want to see your eyes widen as I take them off and have to suck on them to help with the sting."

Dear Lord, this man was good at dirty talk.

"What else, Sierra?"

"I...I want you to flog me."

There. She said it. After all they had talked about, she needed the feel of leather on her skin. Austin had told her he was a master with the flogger, but they'd never played that way. Oh how she wanted his attention solely on her as he delivered those sweet lashes.

He growled slightly, and she grew wetter.

"I want to see my mark on your body." Her eyes widened and he narrowed his. "My mark isn't the same as your scars, Sierra. My mark will be something for the both of us, something to desire, to *feel*." She let out a breath and he nodded. "I'll flog your back, your sides, your ass. I want to see how red you get before I soothe your aches and fuck you hard. Tonight we'll do both of those things after you suck my dick and swallow my come." He pulled his hand back from her cheek, and she felt the loss.

"Undo my pants and take my cock out. Hold it in your hand but don't let your lips touch it."

Nervous, she looked past him at the open windows that covered the wall floor to ceiling.

Austin's hand went to her hair, wrapping it around his fist. He pulled. Hard. "Don't look at the windows. I didn't tell you to do that. I told you to get my cock out. No one can see inside here even when it's dark and I have the lights on. The windows are specially tinted so we can see outside, but they can't see in. If you think I'd let anyone else see you on your knees in front of me, you're disrespecting me."

Tears shimmered in her eyes at the thought that she'd already messed up. She was out of practice, and Austin was so different than Jason.

Damn it.

Jason wasn't allowed in her mind anymore. He was gone, and she wanted to serve Austin. She quickly undid the button on his jeans then slowly slid the zipper down. He was wearing boxer briefs, and because he already had an erection, she didn't want to hurt him.

Her hands went to the waist of his jeans and slid them down over his ass so she could get a better angle. Then she took his boxer briefs and did the same. His cock sprang out, almost hitting her in the face.

If it had been any other situation, she would have laughed, but all she wanted was to taste him and have him fill her. She loved Austin's cock. Loved the look of it, the feel of it in her hands, in her pussy. She wanted to know his taste. He'd yet to let her do that, and now she'd have a chance.

Sierra licked her lips then wrapped her hand around his erection. Her thumb and middle finger couldn't touch, and her eyes widened. She knew he was big, had felt it, but hell.

"Good girl. Now run your hand up and down that way. Feel all of me. Then take your free hand and cup my balls."

Eager, she did as he said, loving the soft feel over hardness.

"Let the head of my cock sit on your tongue. Just the tip."

Yes. This was what she'd been missing. She opened her mouth and let the crown of his cock lay on her tongue. She kept her hands on him as well since he hadn't told her to do otherwise.

"Suck on it."

She closed her mouth and sucked, running the tip of her tongue around the edge then along the slit. Austin sucked in a breath so she knew he liked that.

"Swallow as much as you can then pull back. Then keep going. Get me as hard as possible and almost to the point of coming. Serve me."

She held back a groan then opened her mouth, letting her jaw hang open. She swallowed as much of him as she could, even taking some of him down her throat, but she couldn't take all of his cock. When she slid back up, she let her teeth gently graze him, but not too hard. Austin hissed, and she held back a smile.

"You don't have a gag reflex?" he grunted out.

She pulled away, letting him go with a pop. "Not really."

"Fuck, we're going to have so much fun."

She met his gaze then smiled. "I'm counting on it."

His hand was still wrapped in her hair, so he pushed her closer to his cock. Taking that as a cue, she swallowed him again then pulled back. She licked, nibbled, and kissed down his length before repeating the process. Then she pushed his dick up so it pressed against his belly to give her better access to his balls. She let them fill her mouth one at a time, rolling them on her tongue. When he groaned, she went back to his length and sucked some more. She increased her pace and hollowed her cheeks, using all she could to get him going. When the first spurt of come hit her tongue, she squeezed his cock with her fist then opened her mouth wider. He shouted her name and came down her throat. She slurped him up, missing a few drops, but not caring. They slid down her chin, and she'd never felt more naughty.

Well, maybe, but right then, she didn't care.

When he was done, he pulled away then stripped off his shirt. He wiped her chin then bent to kiss her.

Hard.

"You're such a good girl, Sierra. You're mine."

"Yours, Austin."

He stood straight then tucked himself back into his pants before holding out his hand. She put hers in his then stood up. "Follow me."

He led her to the basement, each step she took sending shivers and aches down her spine right to her clit. When he took her into a room she'd never seen before, she held back a gasp. He had everything they would need in his small, personal dungeon. It wasn't fancy or too expensively done, but it looked safe and sexy as hell.

"Stand in the center while I undress you."

She did so, clasping her hands in front of her. Her chest hurt from her heart beating so hard. He stripped off her shirt, and she had to put her arms up to help him. Then he undid her bra and took off her pants, leaving her naked to his gaze.

He walked around her, inspecting her. She'd never felt so naked, bare in front of another person, yet so cared for at the same time.

When he came around again so he stood in front of her, he smiled. "You're beautiful, baby. I love that you don't shave your pussy but trim it. Your scars only make you look stronger. And your breasts? Fuck, I can't wait to see them in clamps."

Her knees shook as he left her to get the clamps from one of the drawers on a side table. He came back, and she felt like she could climax right then. He lowered his head, taking one nipple in his mouth. He sucked and teased until it was so hard she felt like she was breaking. When he put the clamp on, she sucked in a breath. Oh, God, it hurt, but in the best way possible. He did the same to her other breast, and she had to hold herself back from squirming. She was so wet she knew that if he looked he'd see it. That alone pushed her to the edge.

He kissed her again, a fierce show of strength and caring, nibbling on her bottom lip as he pulled back. "Go stand in front of the cross, facing the wall. Do you need me to tie you to it? Or are you going to be a good girl and hold on tight?"

Both ideas made her warm. "I can hold on."

He raised a brow. "If you don't, you'll be punished."

Right then, she'd take it, but she wanted to see if she could do it.

She went to the cross and put her arms on the slats, facing the wall. She could hear him looking through something, but she couldn't look back and see. He hadn't told her she could.

When the tail of something soft and smelling of leather brushed along her back, she gasped, but didn't let go of the cross.

Austin came to her side and gripped her chin so she could face him. "This is our first time, so instead of surprising you or letting you tell me what things are just by touch, I'm going to show you. This is elk hide and buttery soft." He held up a yellow flogger that looked almost brand new. She must have given something away because he nodded. "It's new. Everything I will touch you with will be new. You're the first woman I've brought here in ten years.

She nodded, her eyes filling with tears.

"Now we're going to go slow today. I won't go too hard. I don't break the skin nor will I use anything different than what is in my hand right now. Do you know your safe word?"

"Yes, Austin."

"Good girl. Face the wall."

She did so and heard him move to her back. She closed her eyes, waiting.

The first touch of leather against the meat of her shoulder stunned her, the quick sting of pain receding into pleasure. He did the same to her other shoulder, then her lower back, ass, and thighs. He increased the pace slightly, never striking the same spot twice in a row. The pain gave way to warmth that went straight to her clit. Her breathing slowed, and she knew her pupils had dilated, the sweet pain becoming bliss.

Soon, she couldn't remember how much time had passed until she felt his hands on her back, and her ass.

"Let go of the cross," he whispered.

She let go and swayed on her feet, leaning into his hold. He soothed her, kissing her softly, running his hands over her body. He released each nipple clamp, sucking the nipples into his mouth before the hurt came.

"Come on, baby girl. You did so well. You look so fucking hot right now with my marks on you."

He picked her up and pulled her to his chest. She closed her eyes, letting her body relax even further in his care. When he set her on the bed, she laid down, her legs spreading of their own accord.

She felt so *good*.

Austin came back and wiped her down with a cool cloth, caring for her like she was the most precious thing in the world. He brought a glass of water up to her lips, and she drank greedily.

"I've never seen anything as beautiful as your submission to me, Sierra. I want to fill your pussy and make you come. Are you ready for me?"

She blinked up at him, her mind finally regaining focus. She hadn't come yet because he'd been careful not to touch her clit.

"Yes, Austin. Make me come."

He lowered himself to her, kissed her hard, and then spread kisses down her body until he reached her clit. He licked her once, and she came.

Her eyes shot open, and she bucked off the bed. He held her down and lapped up her juices. She was so wet that she could even hear him feasting on her. It was so fucking sexy that she was already on the verge of coming again. He nibbled on her pussy, spearing her with his tongue before fucking her with his fingers.

She came again when he pressed on that inner bundle of nerves, the muscles clamping around his fingers.

When he pulled away, she whimpered.

"Face down and on your knees. I want that ass in the air."

She rolled over as he went for a condom. When she laid her cheek down on the mattress, she gripped the blanket. Before she could ask him for more, he filled her to the hilt in one stroke. They both called out and froze.

"Fuck, you're so tight. I'm going to fuck you hard. You ready for that?"

She moaned and then gasped as he smacked her ass. "You get me?"

"Yes, Austin."

"Good girl."

He pulled out then slammed back into her. She screamed his name, her pussy clenching him. Austin pumped in and out of her, his grip punishing on her hips. Before she could come, he left her for a moment then flipped her on her back. She bounced once, and then as she hit the bed again, he was in her.

"Austin!"

He pistoned into her, his eyes on her face. "Say my name again. Say it."

"Austin. Austin. Austin," she chanted his name then gasped into his mouth as he crushed it to hers.

He rotated his hips once more, and she came, her body shaking under his. He threw his head back and shouted as he filled the condom. When he could, he rested his head on hers, their breathing heavy.

"Best. Ever," he mumbled.

"Yes, Austin," she agreed.

He smiled against her cheek then held her close. "My good girl."

Yes, she was. She was his.

And nothing could take that from her.

Nothing.

CHAPTER FIFTEEN

"Again," Austin shouted. "Say my name again."

"Austin," she panted, her body bowing as she came one more time on his cock.

His hands came to her breasts, rolling her nipples between his fingers. "You're mine, Sierra. Your pussy is like a fucking vise on my dick, and I'm going to come. You ready for that?"

"Please, please come inside me."

He pushed up once more, and she gasped as he filled her. This time without a condom. Their first time without a condom.

They'd stayed up for hours after their time in the basement, making love and talking. They'd both discussed protection, and since she was on birth control and they were both clean, they were ready for him to go bare with her. Now Austin had woken her by making her sit on his cock.

She fell on top of him, and his arms went around her. One hand tangled in her hair, the other grasped her hip.

"I love being in you without a condom, Legs. Best. Feeling. Ever."

She smiled against him. "I love it too."

It was the first time they'd used that word in any way when it came to one another, and she wasn't about to take it for granted.

"Let me stay here for a bit then I'll pull out and clean you up."

"I can just jump in the shower."

He smacked her ass, the sting forcing a gasp out of you. "Let me take care of my woman."

"Yes, Austin."

"Good girl."

Their exchange had almost become a joke between them, the way he always praised her for serving him. The joke had turned into something warmer inside her, and she knew she'd have to focus on that soon. Not right then. For now, she wanted to be lazy and enjoy their day off.

In fact, she had a plan for that, but she needed to build up the courage to ask Austin about it. It wasn't bad, just something monumental in her life. As if anything monumental could be "just".

Finally, Austin got up, pulling out of her. She clamped her legs closed, trying to keep him within her. It made no sense, but some primal part of her wanted him inside her. So weird.

He came back into the room with a warm washcloth and cleaned her up, his gaze never leaving hers. "Feel good?"

She smiled. "Yes. You take good care of me. Let me make you breakfast after I help you shower."

He leaned down and kissed the side of her mouth. "You take good care of me too, Legs."

She warmed at his words then took his hand as he led her to the bathroom. They took a *very* thorough shower, then she let him go make his calls for work as she went to the kitchen to make breakfast. She wasn't the best cook in the world, but she could take care of her man's needs.

All of his needs.

She blushed as she thought about what she and Austin had done the night before. She hadn't let go like that, trusted another person, since Jason ten years ago. Even then, though, she wasn't sure she'd fully let go.

If she was honest with herself, she would say that she'd never fully given in to Jason. There had always been that residual resentment between the two of them. He'd never held a job but had one promised to him since birth. She had to scrape every penny together just to go to school so she could have a future that didn't include waiting tables for the rest of her life.

No matter how much distance Jason had tried to put between them and his parents, they had caused rifts throughout the relationship. He never did cut ties because it simply never occurred to him to do so. She didn't trust him enough to make it an ultimatum. Now that Sierra truly thought about it, she knew it would have strained their relationship to the point they might not have made it. The idea that they would have brought a child into the middle of that worried her, but she would have shouldered that pain to have her baby back. She must have known something was off between her and Jason all along because she'd never trusted or given in to him as she had with Austin in just one night.

That might scare her, but she would just take it in stride. She'd had it.

She was finished with running.

She'd been a child with Jason, but she wasn't with Austin.

Strong arms wrapped around her waist, and she leaned against her man. "Good morning," she murmured as he kissed up her neck, his beard scraping her delicately.

"Good morning," he growled into her ear. "Breakfast smells amazing. Omelets?"

She nodded then pulled away so she wouldn't burn either of them when she finished plating everything. She couldn't quite think straight when Austin's arms were around her.

"You have the single coffee maker, so I didn't start your cup. I did put the little cup in there so all you have to do is press a button."

He smiled at her and did just that. "Always thinking. So, what's the plan for today? I know you have to do the books and I have some things I need to do paperwork-wise, but I honestly don't want to spend the whole day cramped indoors."

She brought their plates to the breakfast bar then sat down as Austin pulled out her seat. "I was thinking about that. What do you say we work for a couple hours since it's only six? We woke up early so that will give us until eight or eight thirty to work until we go out."

Austin took a bite of his omelet and groaned. "This is good, Legs. I'm going to have to keep you around just for these."

"I live to serve," she said dryly, then almost choked on her coffee at the heated look he gave her.

"Good to know," he whispered.

She cleared her throat. "Anyway, at nine or so, I thought, if you were ready, we could go on a ride to Estes Park."

She looked down at her plate instead of at him so she couldn't gauge his reaction. The memory of how she'd freaked out at the shop when he'd asked her the first time was not lost on her.

Austin's big hand went to the back of her neck, and she sucked in a breath before facing him.

"You sure you're up for that, Legs?"

She nodded. "I think so. I mean we'll know before we even leave the driveway, right?"

"You don't have to prove anything to me."

She smiled at that. No, she didn't. Not with Austin. He took her as she was, and she wouldn't trade that for anything. "I know. I have something to prove to myself. Plus, I miss riding, Austin. I used to do it weekly, and now I haven't been on a bike in a decade. I'm ready."

He searched her face, for what she didn't know, but he must have found it. "Okay then. I don't have that much paperwork to do, so I can get the bike ready for us when you're finishing up. A ride to Estes Park isn't that far, but it's not around the block either."

"I know. I want to go in big."

He leaned down and brushed his lips over hers. "We will, baby. I have an extra helmet that my sisters use when they ride with me, so you'll be good there. We'll have to stop off at Maya's and get you a leather jacket because it might get cold up there on the mountain in some spots."

Sierra thought of Austin's sister and the fact that the other woman didn't seem to like her. "Why Maya?"

Austin winked. "Because she lives the closest, and since I know she's not home because she's working at the shop today, we can just go in and take it."

Sierra held up her hands. "Oh no. I am not going to steal from your sister. A sister who doesn't like me."

His eyes widened. "Why would you think that?"

"Uh, because she's always a little snarky to me."

"She's Maya. She lives on snark. It's like oxygen to her. She likes you. If she didn't, she wouldn't have let you in the back with me." He grinned at her. "Not that I think that would have stopped you. You've got nerves of steel."

"If that's what you think, sure. But why are we stealing her jacket?"

Austin shrugged then started on the dishes. "Because she won't care. I'll text her just in case, but she'll be fine. She's not wearing it today because Jake is out of town, so she's not riding."

"I thought Maya would want her own bike." She seemed the type of woman who wanted that kind of power between her legs. In fact, in the past, the idea of owning her own bike had crossed Sierra's mind a time or two. She wasn't sure she was quite ready for that right then.

"She'd rather daydream without having to deal with steering and all that. I see that look on your face. You want a bike of your own?"

She lowered her eyes then sighed. "I used to. I didn't know if Jason would have liked it though."

Austin put a wet hand under her chin. "If you feel like you can handle a bike, then get one. Let's get through actually seeing if you can ride on the back of mine first. I think you owning your own bike would be fucking sexy, honestly. I'm not that much of a caveman."

"Sure you aren't."

"Me Austin. Me want you."

Sierra threw her head back and laughed. "Oh my God. Never do that again. Please. I beg of you."

He rolled his eyes then smacked her on the ass. "Go get some work done while I finish the dishes. I'll text Maya and see if I can get her jacket. If not, I have two more sisters and a mom who would have one to fit you. The only one of us without a jacket is Alexander's wife, but seeing how she's never even been on the back of a bike, there isn't a problem there."

Sierra caught his tone and raised a brow as she pulled out her work. "You don't like her?"

He shook his head. "Can't stand her. She's a bitch, and since I try not to call women that name, that should tell you how much she bothers me. She treats Alex like shit and thinks our family is a bunch of inbred losers. Between her and Meghan's husband, Richard, we Montgomerys haven't had much luck with spouses."

He left it at that, and she was glad. If he had made a joke about changing that, she might have freaked out. They hadn't been dating long enough for marriage, but the idea that she could spend forever with Austin didn't scare her as much now.

They worked side by side for an hour, and surprisingly, Austin's presence didn't hurt her concentration. She'd taken her bag with her when they went to his place, so she had her things with her to work on. Since they were both focused, she didn't have time to worry about being nervous or anything like that. It was just...comfortable.

And nice.

Austin left her alone for a bit to get things ready for their ride. She finished up one set of numbers and felt good enough to call it a day. She packed everything up and then looked down at her clothes. Thankfully, she had on jeans and a tank and had brought boots, so she'd be properly clothed on the bike. Once she had a helmet and jacket, she was all set.

Yet her stomach threatened to revolt.

She could do this.

She wasn't going to crash.

There wasn't going to be fire and pain and screams.

She'd ride with Austin and be safe.

Austin would be safe.

He walked in, his boots squeaking on the kitchen tile. "We can back out, Sierra. We don't have to do this."

She shook her head. "No. I'm ready. Just having a little pep talk. Do we need to bring anything?"

He gave her a look then held out his hand. She went to him without question, sinking into him. "I have food and water and extra supplies in the saddle bags. It's not that far of a ride up there, and it's a tourist area so we can grab lunch and just hang out. We had a tough winter so the river and streams are going to be swollen. It should be a nice view. I have my camera in the bag, too, in case you want to take photos."

The man thought of everything, and he was doing his best to make the destination worth it, rather than focusing on the ride to get there.

"Let's go."

"My bike's out front. All we need to do is get on and leave."

She let out a breath. "Okay."

He cupped her face. "I'll be there the whole time, and I won't take my eyes off the road. You get me?"

She smiled softly. "I get you."

"Okay then. Let's ride."

She followed him out of the garage, and he hit the panel on the side to close it. He put on her helmet then his. When they both had their sunglasses on, he leaned down and kissed her quickly.

"We'll head to Maya's then up to Estes Park." He got on first and started the bike so she would literally just have to get on. The sound of the pipes roaring didn't send her into convulsions, so she took that as a good sign. And his bike was freaking sexy. All black and chrome with the Montgomery Ink logo etched on the side. So very Austin.

She took a deep breath then walked over, careful not to touch the hot pipes. She put one hand on Austin's shoulder then took another breath.

316

She could do this.

This was Austin.

He would protect her.

And she would protect herself.

She put one foot on the footrest then slung her leg over quickly so she didn't knock the bike over. She needn't have worried though considering Austin had his feet firmly planted on the ground.

As soon as she sat down behind him, she felt the vibrations of the bike. Where she thought she might have been scared, instead she was invigorated.

God, she'd missed this.

Missed the feel of the bike and its power between her legs. She'd missed wrapping her body around a man as they rode. Missed the air on her face.

Though the last thing she remembered doing on a bike was wrapping her arms around a man, she did just that now and wrapped her arms around Austin's waist.

The world didn't end.

She didn't pass out.

Thank God.

Austin patted her hand but didn't look back.

She was falling in love with him and didn't want to stop.

He took off slowly up the driveway and into the neighborhood. Her grip tightened as they moved. It had been a long time since she'd ridden; it was like riding a bike.

She grinned at her little joke then let her body remember the motions. She leaned into the turns, didn't throw her weight around, and let Austin have the control, just like she needed.

The disappointment when they had to stop at Maya's to pick up the jacket surprised her, but she didn't have to wait long. Austin ran in to get it, and then they were on their way up to Estes Park.

The road underneath them and the mountains to their west soothed Sierra in ways she hadn't thought possible. She leaned against Austin for some of their ride, his body warm, large, and comforting. He never turned toward her, never turned to look at the mountains or land around them.

Usually people could take a quick look at their surroundings and immerse themselves, but Austin didn't.

He kept his eyes solely on the road for them.

For her.

She smiled, holding back tears, this time the truly touched and happy kind. When she leaned back—her hands were still on Austin because, frankly, she couldn't stop touching him—she let her head fall back, and the sunlight and shadows danced across her face.

She'd missed this so freaking much, yet she hadn't realized *how* much until they started out. Yes, there was still the little ball of nerves in her stomach, and she didn't think it would be going away any time soon. When they first started out and were on the highway to get through Boulder, she'd tensed. Not only because Boulder was where her past wouldn't go away, but semis would pass them and she'd have minor flashbacks. Thankfully, Austin didn't pull his hand from the handlebars to soothe, nor did he look behind him, even when they stopped at a stoplight in the middle of the city. He did lean back, pressing his body against hers, showing her he was there.

He really knew how to care for her, and the fact that she felt like she was fumbling to take care of him in the same fashion made her want to try harder. He was her Dom. There was really no other way to put that. She trusted him in and out of bed, and he took care of her. She needed to be fully into being his sub. It wasn't that she wanted to do exactly what he said outside of the bedroom and kneel at his feet when they were causally sitting in the living room—that wasn't their kind of kink—but she wanted to ensure she was - *his* the best way she knew how.

She'd just have to work on that.

When they moved into the mountains, Sierra was grateful they'd stolen—or borrowed she supposed—Maya's jacket. The sun still beat down on them, but the wind was cooler, the air thinner. There was still some snow on the highest peaks. When they pulled into Estes Park, Sierra sighed.

The place really was a dream.

There was a large body of water and streams everywhere. The town played to tourists and history alike, so all of the buildings had a quaint feel to them that made her want to come back again and again. Austin quickly parked in one of the lots, and she got off the back of the bike, her legs a bit achy.

Austin took off her helmet then leaned down to kiss her softly. "You did good, Legs."

She smiled up at him. "Thank you. I couldn't have done it without you."

He shook his head as he put their helmets away and got out two bottles of water. "I don't know about that. You're strong on your own, but I like being here if you need me."

Smiling, she put her hand on his chest and leaned in. He had to lower his head but brushed his lips over hers. "Thank you," she whispered.

"You're welcome. Now how about a walk and then lunch?"

"Sounds good to me."

He took her hand then led her toward the taffy place first. He knew exactly what she wanted.

Of course he did. He was Austin.

Now she just needed to figure out what to do with that.

CHAPTER SIXTEEN

I f one more crazy-assed motherfucker walked into his shop, Austin was going to throw the damn chair at them. It had been one stupid idiot after another wanting shit ink that morning. These assholes were determined to ruin his good mood from the ride with Sierra the day before.

Fucking pricks.

The first person who walked in that day hadn't had an appointment, and usually that was fine. Each of them tried to put an hour or two in their day for walk-ins and cover-up emergencies. If those hours weren't filled, they could sketch or work on the other million things they had to do. What they needed was a damn receptionist, but they couldn't seem to keep one for longer than a month.

No clue why, but the lack of one was killing his schedule.

That first person had wanted a dragon on his back. Sure, Austin could have done it, but the kid had wanted to start right then. A full dragon piece would take at least three or four sessions of three hours each. Probably more considering the kid kept shifting from foot to foot as if he couldn't sit still. Moving during a tattoo meant Austin had to stop and start numerous times or bash the kid's head in.

Not that he'd ever do that, but he'd thought about it.

So the kid had yelled and bitched about time and demanding it right then for a hundred bucks. Yeah, totally not happening. The next one that came in was some really skinny chick who wanted the undersides of her obviously man-made breasts inked up with Playboy bunnies.

Austin wasn't even going to touch that one.

Well, to be sure he wouldn't have to deal with her, he showed her what he'd be working with. The woman freaked out when she saw the needles and left. Considering all the needles that must have touched her skin when she'd had the surgeries to make her body the way it was, her phobia made no sense.

Besides, what did she think they used, *Paint By Numbers?*

It had continued on like that with idiot after idiot until Austin said enough and locked himself in the back. He would just sketch until lunch and then deal with his scheduled clients. Sierra couldn't make it for lunch since she had to cover Jasinda, who found out it wasn't the flu but a baby making her ill.

Seriously, Austin wanted to just go back home, throw Sierra on the back of his bike, and forget his troubles.

That wasn't going to happen though.

His dad had treatment that day, and he wasn't allowed at the house until the next morning. His parents didn't want a crowd, and since there were so many Montgomerys, they would be nothing *but* crowd.

Jesus.

He didn't think he could take another bomb, not after Sierra telling him her story and his dad dealing with the big C. His siblings were all dealing with their own shit, and their stress was bleeding into him.

Austin closed his eyes and pinched the bridge of his nose. He needed to stop freaking out about things out of his control. He couldn't fix everything, though he wanted to damn well try. He sucked in a breath then let it out slowly.

He would do what he came in here to do.

Work on Sierra's ink.

He had an idea for the daisies on her scars, and since he knew her body under his hands now, he had a better place to start. They would put her ink on hold with her job and their new relationship, but he wanted to start on it soon. It might take a couple sessions, considering he didn't know how her skin would react to the ink. They would have to play it by ear and work on it slowly.

He just hoped he didn't hurt her too badly. She'd been through enough as it was.

Just as he bent over to start focusing, Maya slammed the door open. "What the fuck are you doing back here? We have people coming in, and I need you to get off your ass and actually work."

"Fuck off, Maya."

"No. I'm not going to fuck off. You're in here pouting over some shit, and I can't do everything out there alone."

"Imagine that, you saying you can't do something. And you're not alone. You have Sloane out there."

Maya stomped to his side, but he didn't get up. "What is with you?"

"What's with me? I had to deal with fucking idiots all morning, I can't see Sierra until tomorrow most likely, and Dad is in the fucking hospital right now getting treatment that might kill him before the cancer does. So sorry if I'm not in the mood for fucking company."

Maya hiccupped a sob, and Austin stood quickly. His sister *never* cried.

"Oh, honey, I'm sorry. I'm an ass. Come here." He opened his arms, and she threw herself into him.

"Dad can't die, Austin. He's not allowed to. He's the strong one. Well, other than Mom, but they're a pair. You know?"

He kissed the top of her head, rubbing his hand up and down her back. "I know, Maya. I know. He'll be okay. I'm just freaking out and taking it out on you."

"What do you think I was doing?"

He snorted then squeezed her hard before letting go. "We make pretty good punching bags for each other."

She rolled her eyes then wiped away any remnants that she'd been crying. "That's why we work so well together. We can yell and beat on each other without hurting feelings. Sorry I cried. I know you hate crying females."

"Yeah, but if you need to cry, do it. I'm good at holding them when they need to let it all out."

Maya tilted her head. "Sierra?"

"I can't talk about it, Maya. If you want to know more about her, maybe you should actually get to know her. You know, instead of giving her the side eye whenever she walks in."

"I didn't think she was good enough for you."

"Seriously? What the fuck, Maya? If anything, I'm not good enough for her. You've got a lot of nerve."

"Hey, I didn't say I still thought it, did I? She makes you happy, Austin. Anyone with eyes can see that. If she hurts you, I'll kick her ass, but now? Now she's cool."

"She'd be cooler if you actually spent a few minutes with her not scowling."

She rolled her eyes again then punched him in the shoulder. "I'll try. If she's going to be around, I guess I'll have to get to know her."

He met Maya's gaze and nodded. "I think she's going to be around for a long while, Maya."

His sister's eyes widened. "No shit?"

"No shit."

"So...uh...she doesn't think your kink is weird or anything? Not like that Maggie chick?"

Austin closed his eyes and groaned. How his little sister knew this, he didn't know. Nor did he want to talk about it with her. "We're good, Maya. And that's the last we're talking about that."

"What? We all have kinks." She winked.

He put his hands over his ears. "I'm not listening. La la la."

"You're a riot. I'll leave you in here to work then get back in. We'll just be closed to walk-ins for a bit since the crazies seem to be out in full force."

"Thanks, Maya."

"Welcome, big brother."

She left him to sketch, and he felt better just for having said all he had out loud. His sister got him better than most people, and he knew he should have just told her what was on his mind to begin with.

He wanted the daisies to flow down Sierra's side, delicate like her skin. It was going to hurt like a bitch, but he'd make it up to her. Maybe he'd let her help him sketch his next tattoo. That way she was a part of him always.

Always?

He liked the sound of that. Scary as hell, but good. He could see her at his side as they grew older, raising children—whether through adoption or through the usual method. Even a month ago, he wouldn't have thought it possible he'd find someone he could potentially spend the rest of his life with. Sure, he'd had an itch to settle down because he knew forty was quickly approaching, but it had been only a dream, not something as concrete as thinking of Sierra as a Montgomery.

Maybe she'd even get the Montgomery Iris tattoo like the rest of his family. Richard and Jessica had never gotten the ink. Richard because he didn't think of himself as a Montgomery—and he was an asshole. Jessica because she hadn't wanted to mar her figure—and she was a first class bitch.

Come to think of it, bringing Sierra into the mix was only a good thing. He'd be increasing their clan in a good way, rather than bringing in the idiocy Alex and Meghan did.

Well, that was just cruel of him to think. His siblings had each found someone they loved; just because their partners didn't fit in with his family didn't make them bad people. In Austin's opinion, it was the way they treated their significant others that made them sketchy and not good enough for his family.

Sierra treated him right and trusted him with her past and her body. He had an inkling she trusted him with her heart and soul as well, though neither of them had said the words. Those would come though; he was sure. They were on the good path, and he just prayed nothing pushed them off.

"Yo, Austin, you have a visitor."

Austin blinked at Sloane's words and shook his head, clearing his thoughts. Damn it, he had to stop woolgathering. He'd never get this sketch done for Sierra at this rate.

Wait. Visitor? If it was Sierra, she'd just walk back, so who could it be?

A knot formed in his belly. Fuck, he hoped it wasn't...

"Hello, Austin," Shannon purred.

"I'm out of here," Sloane said as he fled.

Fucker.

"What do you want, Shannon?"

She stood in the doorway, her dress too tight, her eyes too bright. He didn't want to deal with her and was thankful they weren't still together.

"I wanted to say I'm sorry."

Austin almost cleaned out his ear with his finger at her words. He couldn't have heard right. Sorry? Really?

"Seriously? You're sorry?"

She stuck out her bottom lip and pouted. "Yeah. I shouldn't have gone to your girl like that. She didn't do anything wrong but get the toy I wanted, and I acted like a brat."

"Did you just call me a toy?"

She blushed. "I'm just using the words Tony used."

"Tony?" She made no sense, and he wanted her out of his office, but if she got whatever she needed to off her chest, then hopefully he wouldn't have to deal with her again. He'd take the little pain to be free.

"My new man."

Well, that was fast. And exactly what Sierra had said to him about Shannon needing a new man to get off Austin's back. He'd just have to kiss his woman when he got to see her again. Hard.

"Good for you," he mumbled.

She smiled. "Thanks. Tony is just so...well, you don't care, and I won't take up more of your time. So I'm sorry for coming in here, calling you, and bugging your girl. I just don't like being alone, and I took it out on you. So, sorry for being a bitch."

Austin let out a breath. "You weren't a bitch, Shannon. You were just...clingy."

She snorted and shook her head. "I'm a bitch, and I know it. I'm going to try and not be."

Austin wasn't too sure she could stop so quickly considering it had been all of two days since she'd acted like that. She couldn't have been with Tony for long, but if he was going to change her for the better, then good for him.

Good luck with that, Tony.

"Thanks for apologizing," he said. There really wasn't more he could say, and he'd rather she left. Call him an ass, but he was over it all.

"Thanks for listening. I would go apologize to your girl, but I don't think either of you would appreciate that."

He nodded. "I'll let her know."

Tired of sitting at his desk and getting nothing done, he followed her out of the office; he wanted to make sure she was actually gone. Call him a cynic, but he didn't trust many people these days. Apparently Maya felt the same way, considering she kept her eyes on Shannon until she was out the door. As soon as the door closed behind her, everyone in the room let out a collective breath—including the clients in the chairs.

"She gone for good then?" Maya asked, her focus on the man's arm in front of her now.

"Yeah. So she says, but it might actually work this time. She apologized."

"We know," Callie said with a wink. She sat near Sloane, watching him work on shading for the day. "We had the music down so we could hear what she had to say."

Austin opened his mouth to yell then closed it, snorting and shaking his head instead. If he'd been in their shoes, he would've done the same thing. The crew of Montgomery Ink was a nosey one.

"Brat," he muttered as Callie fluttered her eyelashes.

"I try."

He went back to his station and started getting ready for the next client. By the time he was done, they were in an odd lull where they had no clients waiting or in chairs. The next big rush of appointments would be soon, but for now, it was just him, Callie, Sloane, and Maya.

The door opened again, and Austin counted to three before turning. If it was Shannon or another idiot, he was going to scream.

Instead, a man in a nice suit and a briefcase stood in the doorway. God, he hoped they weren't getting sued for ink. It hadn't happened to him but it had to others in his profession. Some people were never happy no matter how hard others tried.

"Mr. Montgomery?" the man asked.

Austin frowned. Well, shit. "I'm Austin Montgomery. There's a few Montgomerys around so you'll have to be specific."

The lawyer nodded. "Yes, you're the one I'm looking for. In fact, it's been pretty difficult to find you, Mr. Montgomery."

Something icy went up his spine. "What do you mean?"

Maya came to his side, her arms folded in front of her. Sloane stood up with Callie by his side. They were united against whatever came, but Austin had a feeling they wouldn't be enough.

"I've sent you a letter with what I need to talk to about."

Austin racked his brain then cursed. There had been that letter from lawyers that he'd put aside because he hadn't recognized it. Things had been so crazy with dad and Sierra that he'd forgotten about it. Fuck. What had he missed?

"Sorry about that, we've been a bit crazy here. What can I do for you?"

"We also couldn't reach you by phone because your number seems to have changed in the past ten years."

Ten years? What the hell was this about?

"And now that circumstances have changed, I needed to see you face to face, rather than discuss things through mail or over the phone."

"Out with it already," Maya muttered.

"And you would be... miss?" the man asked, his eyebrow raised.

Yeah, they were all tattooed freaks in his eyes, but what the fuck ever. "This is my sister Maya and my co-workers Sloane and Callie. They might as well be family, so say what you need to say. You don't need to wait for them to leave."

"If you're sure. This is quite personal."

Austin's stomach clenched, but he didn't let his nervousness show. At least he hoped not. "They're family, so they'll find out anyway. What's going on? Why are you here for me?"

The lawyer nodded then walked forward, putting his briefcase on the counter. "You might want to sit down, Mr. Montgomery."

"Call me Austin. Mr. Montgomery is my father, and I'm fine standing."

"Okay then, Mr. Mont—I mean Austin." He cleared his throat, and Austin was ready to throttle the man. "Do you remember a Miss Maggie Forrester?"

Maggie. Damn, her name had come up a lot in the past few weeks.

"Yes, I remember her. We dated over ten years ago. I haven't heard or spoken to her since. What's up with Maggie?"

Maya's hand went to the small of his back, and he realized his body was shaking. Something was wrong, and he wasn't sure he wanted to hear what it was.

"I'm sorry to say Maggie Forrester passed away three months ago."

Austin blinked, an odd shock going through his system. He hadn't thought about her often since she'd broken up with him after calling him a freak, but it still hurt to hear she'd passed away.

"Damn. I'm sorry to hear that. What happened?"

"Car accident. She died on impact."

"Again, I'm sorry to hear that, but I don't know what that has to do with me. I haven't seen her in years."

"Well, she left something behind, Austin."

Maggie had left him something? Why they hell would she have done that? It made no sense. His confusion must have played on his face because the lawyer gave him a sympathetic smile.

"Austin, she left behind a son."

He blinked then took a step back, then another. Sloane came up from behind him and helped him sit on one of the stools.

"A son?" he croaked. No, it couldn't be. Maggie would have told him if he had a son. Wouldn't she?

Images of her face when she'd screamed at him and called him an abuser filled his mind and he cursed. Maybe not. She might have hidden it from him because she'd been afraid.

Holy fuck.

"I can tell from your face that you understand. Leif is ten years old, and according to his birth certificate, he's your son. Are you telling me you never knew?"

"Of course he didn't know, you asshole," Maya bit out. "You think he would have just stayed away if he thought for a second he had a kid out there."

"I've seen a lot of terrible things in my line of work, Ms. Montgomery."

"Well. your line of work sucks," Callie said, tears in her voice.

"Leif?" Austin asked, his voice hoarse.

"Yes, his given name is Leif Forrester Montgomery."

Montgomery. "She gave him my name? Why?"

"I can't begin to go into the decisions people make, Austin. Right now, we don't have DNA to certify her claims, but as you're listed on the birth certificate, you do have rights."

"Rights? Wait. Where is he? Where's Leif? Is he with her folks?"

The lawyer shook his head. "I'm afraid they passed away when Leif was born."

"So she's been on her own this whole time. Raising a kid, my kid, this whole time. What the hell? Why didn't she tell me?"

Tears filled his eyes, and he tried to come to terms with what the lawyer was saying, but he couldn't comprehend it.

"Where's Leif?" he asked again.

"We have him in a group home for now. Unless you claim him—and that's not as easy as it sounds—he will have to find a foster family and stay in the system. As I said, it's really your choice. Since your name is on the birth certificate, we can make the process easier. However, I don't want you to make a decision now. Take your time, but remember, the life of a child is at stake."

Austin couldn't breathe. Couldn't think.

"Give us your number and how to contact you," Sloane said, taking charge. Everyone else seemed to be in shock. "We'll figure it out and let you know. Do you need anything right now for the DNA test?"

"We can do a swab right now and get started."

"Austin?" Sloane asked, standing right in front of him.

He blinked. "Okay, yeah. Let's do that." The kid was his. He knew it deep down in his soul though he'd never met him.

The lawyer swabbed his mouth, and he sat quietly through it. The lawyer said he'd be in touch and left, leaving a broken and confused trail in his wake. Austin didn't like the idea of Leif staying in a group home while he had plenty of room at his place, but things hadn't connected in his brain yet. He needed to tell his folks, needed to tell Sierra.

Fuck. Sierra.

Dear God.

What was he going to tell her?

"What are you going to do, Austin?" Maya asked. "Want me to get Sierra?"

He shook his head. "No, let her work. I need to think."

"You sure that's the best thing? This affects her too."

"I know that, but I need to breathe. I can't just let my kid, if he really is mine, be alone there when I can take him in, but what do I know about kids? Fuck."

Maya shook her head then walked to the door, flipping the sign to closed. "Callie, call our appointments and reschedule. We're going to go take Austin home and figure it out. Then when you're ready, we'll call the family. Mom and Dad will be at home, but they'll be strong even with the treatments."

"Fuck, the treatments."

"I know, big brother, but we can do this. One step at a time, Dad."

Dad.

He ran his hands over his head. Dad? What the hell was he going to do? There was only one thing he *could* do.

"I need to call Sierra."

Maya frowned. "You can just go over there."

"No, I can't see her right now. I can't...I need to talk to her, but I need time."

He knew he was messing this up, but he was floundering. He dialed her number and sighed when it went straight to voicemail. Maybe it was for the best. She had enough to deal with without his drama.

He had a kid.

Everything had been looking up, and now it had all crashed down. Life certainly knew how to throw punches, only Austin didn't know if he'd be able to get back up after this one. Not this time.

CHAPTER SEVENTEEN

Austin hadn't called again. He'd left a weird message saying that he would see her later then hadn't called back all night. Sierra didn't want to think it was a bad sign, but she was certainly worried. It had now been over twelve hours since that phone call, and Sierra had a bad feeling about it.

Something had happened, she just knew it, but Austin hadn't answered his phone when she called, so now she didn't know what to think.

The day before, she'd spent almost all of her time either on her feet dealing with a mad rush that might have made her pocketbook happy but not the arches of her feet, or she'd been in the back, bent over her books.

Being a business owner was not for the weak.

Well, being a successful one anyway. And she wanted to be successful damn it.

By the time evening had come around, even though she'd need to work for another few hours, she'd gone home with the beginnings of a headache. She and Austin had tentative plans of him coming over, but they hadn't finalized them because of her workload.

Then her migraine had hit, and she'd lain in bed moaning before finally falling asleep.

That was when she'd missed Austin's call and odd message.

Now it was morning. While Jasinda and Becky handled the store, she was going to get some coffee from Hailey and bring it over to her man. Not only did she want to see him, she wanted to make sure he was okay.

Not speaking to him for almost a full day made her a little uneasy, and that, in turn, made her freak out a little. They'd gotten serious extremely quickly, but she couldn't say she regretted it. Austin made her feel whole again. Not that she needed him to feel human. It was more that she'd been missing something in her life. He looked at her scars and saw strength and beauty, and she believed him. He got angry for her past and then helped her breathe through the steps she needed to take in order to overcome it.

He was there for her, and now she wanted to be there for him. She just prayed that whatever was going on with Austin wasn't something serious. God, what if it was about his father? She knew the older Montgomery had his first full treatment the day before, and she prayed that there hadn't been any complications.

Sierra let out a breath. That had to be it on some level. Maybe Austin was just freaking out over his father being sick. Damn it, and she hadn't been there. She'd been in bed with a migraine and not by his side like she should have been.

Well, that wouldn't be happening again. No, next time she'd help him through it, even if she had to rest her head on a cool compress the entire time.

He'd helped her through her pain, and she'd be damned if she let him go through this on his own.

Shoulders rolled back, she said goodbye to her girls then walked across the street to Hailey's. She glanced over at Montgomery Ink, saw a young boy sitting on the front steps in the corner, and thought it must have been one of their clients' kids. It was still early, but the cool air from the morning dew still stung a bit. She hoped the kid kept warm because she wouldn't want to stay outside long. It didn't matter if it was in the dead of summer in Colorado, once you were in the shade and before the sun really hit, the mountain drafts went to work on the air.

She'd just ask Austin who the boy was as soon as she made her way over. Maybe she'd go the long way around, rather than through the connecting doors between Taboo and Montgomery Ink like she'd grown accustomed to. That way she could see if the kid needed anything. Honestly, she didn't know why she cared so much about this kid who probably had two parents inside waiting for him or watching out for him, but she couldn't help it.

As soon as she stepped into Taboo, she smiled at Hailey, who was doing some sort of wiggle behind the counter, dancing to the beat of the music as she filled coffee orders.

There wasn't too much of a line thankfully, so Sierra didn't have to wait long. Normally she might have gone to the coffee shop next to Eden in the mornings because of the rush, but she'd wanted to see her friend, and the line was worth it.

"Hey, girlie, good morning," Hailey said as she continued to wiggle.

Sierra couldn't help but snort. "You're in a chipper mood."

Hailey shook her head then made the two lattes for Sierra and Austin. "Not really. I just happened to be highly caffeinated. I tried a new bean for our espresso, and it has a punch."

Sierra's eyes lit up. "Oh really? Are you keeping it then?"

Hailey nodded. "Yep. It'll be good for the early morning drag-ins. Plus, it doesn't taste like burnt tar like *some* of the coffee houses."

Sierra had the grace to blush. "You know when I go to the other place, I only think of you. It's just faster."

Hailey rolled her eyes. "That's what they all say, champ. Two lattes to go. Say hi to Austin for me."

"How did you know I was seeing Austin?" Sierra asked, her best ice-princess face on. "I just ordered two drinks. One could have been for Jasinda or Becky."

Hailey snorted. "It could have been, but you came here during your morning to work on inventory, books, and other admin things, so it must have been important. There's only one person right now that comes to mind. So tell him I said hi." Hailey stopped dancing and gave Sierra a look she couldn't quite understand.

"What's wrong?" Damn it. Something was up, and she couldn't shake that feeling.

"I don't know, hon. Something's up over there. They closed up shop yesterday before closing hours, and Sloane looked even more solemn than usual." Hailey's cheeks pinked at the mention of Sloane, but Sierra couldn't think about that right then.

"They closed up shop?" she asked, her heart racing. "They *never* do that, do they?"

Hailey shook her head and started making the customer sitting at the counter a cup of coffee. "No, they don't. Maybe if they had a family emergency, but I don't know." Hailey blinked back tears and shook her head. "Go over there and make sure everything is okay with Harry, will you? I'm worried. I know I was dancing earlier, but I'm trying to keep my mind off it, you know? Since I'm stuck here."

Sierra nodded, swallowing hard. She cleared her throat then picked up her lattes. "I'll find out. I'm sure they're all fine."

Hailey gave her a sad smile. "Yeah. I'm sure we're just freaking out over nothing. Now go see those Montgomerys."

Sierra gave one last goodbye then walked toward the connecting door before stopping and turning back to the front door. Even if her mind whirled at whatever could be wrong with Austin, she hadn't forgotten about that boy completely. She wanted to make sure he was okay as well. She would have ordered him a hot chocolate or something, but since he wasn't her kid, she didn't want to encroach. Plus the kid could be allergic to sugar or something. That was a thing. Right?

Damn it. How could getting two cups of coffee make her mind go as crazy as it had? Now she had a boy she didn't know to worry about—who she probably didn't need to worry about anyway—and a man she cared for in need. Well, at least that's what she thought. For all she knew, she was blowing everything out of proportion and he'd just laugh and call her Crazy Legs when she asked him.

Yes, that was what was going to happen.

But they'd closed the store...

Nope. Not going to dwell on that. Not yet.

The boy still sat on the front step when she got there. His brown hair looked tousled, like he hadn't brushed it in awhile, and he had on a thin jacket and holey jeans. For all she knew, that was the style of boys his age, but the utter sadness on his face wasn't.

He had his arms wrapped around his legs, and his chin rested on his knees. Now that she got a good look at him, she saw that he wasn't exactly sitting on the front step. He was more off to the side and under the full windows so whoever was in Montgomery Ink couldn't see him.

While she hoped that his family was inside, she had a feeling this boy had slept out here or near here the night before. She couldn't see evidence of a nest nearby or any other evidence, but it was a feeling she couldn't shake off.

What was she supposed to do?

Well, calmly talking to him would be the first step. Though she was a stranger, and he probably shouldn't talk to her in the first place, she couldn't just walk past him.

She put on a smile and tried to not look like a murderer or whatever a little boy would think some woman on the street might look like.

"Good morning," she said brightly.

The kid, who had been staring off into space, jolted then turned to her, his eyes wide. "Good...good morning," he mumbled then shut his mouth quickly, as if scared to say anything else.

Oh, this poor boy. Something was surely up with him. Or she just scared the crap out of him. Either way, she had to fix it.

Sierra bit her lip then said to hell with it. Careful not to spill her lattes, she took a deep breath then sat on the stoop next to him. The boy looked startled for a moment then shrugged his shoulders like he didn't care.

"So, what are you doing outside Montgomery Ink this morning?" Too pushy? God, she didn't know how to deal with kids. The fact that this child looked to be the same age as the one she'd lost would have been...well she wasn't going to think about that. She couldn't think about that.

The boy sighed. "I came to see my dad."

Came? As if he hadn't come *with* his parents? Was he a runaway? Oh damn. This was so far out of her scope. She needed Austin and maybe the police.

"Oh?"

"Yeah." He looked over his shoulder then the other way as if he were hiding. And damn it, he *was* hiding. "I don't know if he'll like me being here though, you know?"

No, she didn't know, but she wasn't about to leave this kid out on the stoop to find out. "Is...is he in the shop?" That had to be the only answer considering where the boy hid. An odd prickling sensation went up her spine as the boy thought over his answer.

No. Surely not. There had to be a customer in there. Or maybe even Sloane. Right?

"He's in there. I think. That's what the paper said."

She'd ask about the paper later. Right then, he was at least talking. She didn't want to spook him.

"Do you want to go in?" she asked, her throat closing.

He met her gaze and she swallowed hard. Blue eyes. She *knew* those eyes but she had to be wrong. A lot of people had blue eyes and dark hair. Tons of them in fact. It was just a coincidence.

"I guess I want to," the boy mumbled. "It's why I'm here."

Sierra nodded, her mind going blank. "What...what's your name?"

The boy licked his lips then ran a hand through his hair on a shrug. "Leif. Leif Montgomery."

Montgomery.

Oh shit. She was going to be sick.

Austin had a son. That had to be the answer. Holy fuck. He wouldn't have kept a secret from her, not something like this, she *knew* that. Meaning he either hadn't known about his kid or she was wrong about this whole thing.

Yesterday.

Oh, God. He *knew* now.

337

He knew and he hadn't told her.

At least not that night. That had to be why he'd left the odd message. Why he'd closed the shop the day before. Dear God. What was she supposed to do? How as she supposed to deal with this turn of events? What was *Austin* going to do?

He hadn't talked to her, but honestly, if she was acting this out of sorts, he had to be doing the same. He'd called her right away if she was correct on the timeline, meaning he'd tried. That had to be something.

She took a deep breath. Freaking out over something she wasn't a hundred percent sure about wasn't helping anything. She'd find out what was really happening and then take the next step. Hadn't she just thought that she needed to be by Austin's side no matter what? This was a true test of what she felt for him, and running away or being angry at something out of her control wouldn't help anyone.

It *clearly* wouldn't help the boy who started at her with sadness in his eyes.

Questions like how he'd gotten there, where was his mother, *who* was his mother filled her brain, but she set them to the side. First she needed confirmation. Then she'd deal with the outcome.

"Oh. Well." What the hell could she say? "You're in front of Montgomery Ink, so you must be in the right place." Unless it was all a mistake. A very large one.

The boy, Leif, nodded. "I'm in the right place. That's what the paper said. My dad works here so now I'm here to see him."

Sierra swallowed hard. "Okay then. Let's go inside and see him. It's a bit cold out this morning to sit on the stoop for too much longer, don't you think?" It was true, but as a good as an excuse as any.

Leif shrugged. "I've been out here and in the alley all night, so it's actually warmer. But sure, let's go in. I've been trying to figure out what to say, but I told you, so that's good. Right?"

"Right." All night? An alley in the city of Denver? Leif was lucky to be there right then. Denver wasn't one of the most dangerous cities, but it was still a metro area and Leif was still a young boy.

She held back a shudder at the thought of what could have happened to him. She'd ask the proper questions and get down to the heart of everything once they got inside. She just had to see Austin and everything would be fine.

Or everything would shatter around them but she wouldn't know which until she stepped inside.

She stood on shaky legs, her cooling lattes in her hand. "Okay then. Let's go inside."

Leif nodded then stood beside her. His hands fisted at his side before he looked at her and the lattes. He scrambled to the door and opened it for her. Well, he had manners, that had to mean something.

Right?

Oh, God.

She stepped in first since he held the door open for her and looked around the shop, desperate to see Austin. Only he wasn't in the front. Maya was in the corner, working on something on paper while Sloane had just walked out from behind the counter.

He froze at the sight of her...or maybe it was Leif behind her.

His eyes widened and Maya mumbled something under her breath.

It seemed Sierra's guesses had been correct.

At least that's what it looked like.

"Sierra," Austin said from behind Sloane as he walked up from the back.

Her arms shook yet she couldn't move. Sloane quickly came up to her and took the coffee from her hands, setting them down on the counter. She gave him a grateful smile. Well, at least she thought she did. From the look on his face, it had probably come out as more of a grimace.

"Austin," she said after she cleared her throat. "Good morning."

He frowned then looked behind her, his face draining of color. He saw it, too. He couldn't miss it. What on earth were they going to do about this? What *could* be done about this?

"Who...who is your friend?" he asked, his voice level.

She turned around then did what was instinctual. She held out her hand and Leif took it quickly, surprising them both from the look on his face. He leaned closer, as if she could help him.

Oh, buddy, if that were only true.

She met Austin's gaze. The only people in the building other than her and Leif, were Austin, Maya and Sloane—they were his family, both by blood and by choice. From the look on the latter two's faces, they had an inkling of what was going on.

She didn't let that hurt her—or she tried not to as a little slice went across her heart. They must have been there when he'd found out or something. After all, he'd *tried* to call. Once. No, she wasn't going to be petty. She would help. There was no other choice.

Sierra looked down at Leif who had his gaze on Austin, his eyes wide, his lips pressed together tightly in a thin line.

"This is Leif," she said softly, her eyes on Austin. "He says he's here to see his Dad."

Tears prickled at the corner of her eyes, but she didn't cry. Not then. There would be time to wrestle her emotions later.

"Leif," Austin grunted out, seeming to come out of whatever trance that he'd been in. "Leif."

Sierra squeezed Leif's shoulder. Time for her to buck up and be strong. "I think we all need to sit down and talk about what is going on here. I don't know anything at all, but I think I can guess. What do you say?"

Leif pressed into her harder, his whole body shaking.

She quickly knelt so she was at eye level. "Tell me what's happening, honey. I can't help if you don't help me." She'd said it to Leif, but it was for Austin as well.

Leif met her gaze and nodded, speaking to her alone. "I ran away from the group home. They were mean there. I don't want to live there anymore. I know Mom is...dead...but that doesn't mean I have to live there. Right? I mean, my dad is right there." He didn't look at Austin, but his words were a punch to the gut.

"You ran away?" Austin asked, suddenly closer than he'd been before.

Sierra looked over only to find Austin kneeling beside the two of them.

Thank God.

Leif looked over hesitantly. "Yeah. So?"

Austin shook his head. They would have to deal with this. Deal with all of it. "You're Maggie's son?"

Maggie. He'd mentioned that name before when they'd talked about ex's. He hadn't said they'd been too serious. Apparently they'd been serious enough.

"You shouldn't have run away, Leif," Austin said softly.

Leif's eyes filled and Sierra held back a curse, glaring at Austin.

"Wait. I mean people would be looking for you. They're probably worried. Not that I didn't want to meet you, because I do kid. Damn it." His eyes widened. "I guess I probably shouldn't curse."

"No, you shouldn't," Sierra mumbled, and held back a sign as Austin ran a hand down her back.

That was something at least.

"So...you're Leif," Austin said, sounding like he had no idea what to say.

That made two of them.

Leif turned toward Austin and Sierra held back a breath. "I don't want to live there anymore. Mom said you were my Dad because I had your name. If you don't want me. Fine. But I don't want to go back. I'll live in the alley like I did last night."

Tears filled Sierra's eyes and she looked into Austin's who had the same look on his face as she was sure she had.

Alley? he mouthed over Leif's head.

She shook her head. They'd deal with that later.

Maya walked toward them, the phone in her hand. "We need to call the lawyer and then his social worker. They need to know he's safe."

"I'm not going with them!" Leif wrapped his arms around Sierra and hung on tight.

341

She gasped, not ready for his weight, but Austin steadied her. She wrapped her arms around his slight frame, soothing him as his body racked with sobs.

"Oh honey," she murmured. Austin ran his hand down her back, but didn't touch Leif. She didn't blame him. She didn't even know the full story.

Austin came closer, kissing her temple before whispering, "I'll tell you everything soon. Trust me?"

She pulled away to meet his gaze and said the only thing she could say. "Yes. Always."

Austin's shoulders relaxed marginally. "Don't leave me, okay?" he whispered again.

"Never," she whispered then squeezed Leif tight. "Okay, honey. We need to call them like your Aunt Maya said." Leif froze then looked over his shoulder.

Fuck. She hadn't meant to say that, it just seemed natural. Well, hell, she was going about this all wrong but there wasn't a guidebook for when your boyfriend's secret love child came out of nowhere.

At least she didn't think so.

"Then we'll figure it all out," she continued as if she hadn't made the mistake.

"Okay," Leif mumbled and Sierra let out a breath.

Austin couldn't keep his eyes off Leif and Sierra felt for him. She had no idea what he was thinking or planning, but she knew she wouldn't leave his side.

She couldn't.

Not when she loved him.

Leif squeezed tighter and her heart lurched.

This had come out of nowhere but she wasn't going to run away. Not again. She was done with running.

CHAPTER EIGHTEEN

Two weeks.

Two weeks and everything in Austin's life had changed. He had a little boy under his roof, a woman he loved but hadn't confessed the latter to, and a whirlwind of emotions that he didn't think he'd ever untangle.

As soon as Sierra took charge the morning Leif had shown up, things had been rolling. Leif wouldn't let her go, but that hadn't stopped her. Austin had stayed by her side, trying to get ahold of his own thoughts and emotions but failing miserably. He was always the one in control, the one who knew what to do, but the last two crises in his life had shown him he hadn't been as steady as he thought.

That scared him more than he thought it would.

Way fucking more.

Maya had called the lawyer, but Sierra had been the one to talk with him. His woman hadn't even heard the whole story from Austin's lips but took control when he wasn't sure what to do.

He didn't know what he'd have done without her.

While Leif had clung to Sierra's side, refusing to let her go, she talked to the lawyer about what to do then handed Austin the phone when things turned to his choices.

The phone call had changed his life.

"Austin, I can push through and find a solution that will allow Leif to live with you now if that's what the both of you want. But you have to tell me what you want."

Austin had looked into Leif's and Sierra's eyes and realized there was only one thing to say.

"Push it though. He's not going back there if we can help it." Maggie had put Austin's name on the birth certificate, meaning that Austin had the legal right to his son.

Leif had let out a breath while Sierra hiccupped a sob. Austin felt the sort of numbness that came over him when he had too much going on within himself. He had no idea if he'd made the best choice or even the choice that would be good for both of them, but he made the only choice he could.

Things moved quickly and slowly at the same time after that call. Sierra had to go back to the store, only to pick up her things. She'd left Becky and Jasinda alone at Eden, and that alone told Austin how much she'd do for him. Sure, she'd left them alone before, but they were about to open and she was on call. Eden was her rock, her baby, and she'd left it to take care of him and his son.

When the results from the DNA test came back positive four days after Leif had moved in, Austin's world rocked once more.

This was his son.

His kid.

It wouldn't be a foster care or adoption but a son returning to his father. And yet he didn't know him.

His *son.*

Holy fuck, that still rocked him, and it had been two weeks of him saying it over and over to himself for him to actually understand what had happened.

The group home hadn't been bad to Leif, despite the worst-case scenarios that had been running through Austin's head. They'd just been, like most places that were state funded, understaffed and over capacity. Leif hadn't been abused, truly neglected, starved, or beaten.

But he hadn't been home either.

The kid refused to talk about his mom more than to say she was gone, and Austin understood that. Considering he was going through the pain of the possibility of losing his father, Austin didn't begrudge the kid a bit.

He also had no idea what to do with a ten-year-old boy. His family and Sierra had stepped up to the plate and helped him though. He'd forced his mother and father to stay home and keep healthy while the rest of the family worked on setting up the house. Leif wouldn't leave without Sierra, so Austin stayed home with the two of them, clearing out a guest room and letting Leif pick what he wanted. At the time, Austin wasn't sure if this would be temporary or permanent, but it didn't matter. Leif needed a home, and if looks said anything, Austin had been almost certain Leif was his son. The DNA results were a formality, confirmation for the lawyers and courts. He would find a way to make this work—for all of them. Sierra had been on her way to changing how he was thinking anyway.

His sister Meghan had pitched in first. She had two kids of her own and immediately brought them over. Leif was four years older than Cliff and even older than Sasha, but the kids kept him distracted enough that Sierra and Austin could breathe. It was awkward as hell at first, but Cliff had brought over his toys, which might have been too young for Leif, but the kids played together and got to know one another.

It didn't surprise him that his sister hadn't thought twice about introducing her children to their cousin.

Cousin.

Shit.

Miranda, Wes, and Storm had gone shopping for things a ten-year-old boy would need. Leif had a few things in storage, but until the judge ruled that Leif could stay permanently, he needed clothes and other things. Alex was off on assignment and couldn't be there to help. Plus, Alex had his own issues, so Austin didn't blame him for not dropping everything. Maya was running the shop and dealing with that other part of Austin's life. Griffin had been the one to help with the lawyer and legal issues.

Sierra coordinated it all while Austin stood by her and tried to help where he could—even if it was just agreeing or putting his two cents in.

Austin didn't know what he'd do without his family. Without Sierra.

She hadn't said a word about what had happened in his past, merely nodded, rolled her shoulders back, and dug in. They had discussed the probability that Leif was his son, but Sierra just shook her head.

"Wait until you're ready to tell me the whole story. If you're not ready and just trying to make me feel better, then it's not helping anyone."

"It's not much of a story," he said softly. He'd kissed her hard then relaxed.

She slept over each night, practically moving in. They hadn't made love, but they'd spooned, holding each other deep into the night.

Sierra worked during the day and helped him at night.

Austin worked at getting Leif in school, dealt with lawyers during the day, and was learning how to be a father at night.

Taking care of the details and practicalities had taken over their lives, and now that those were somewhat under control, the emotional punch was taking its toll.

Now here he was, a father, a single one at that. Yes, Sierra was his in every way, but they hadn't had the discussion they'd needed to. That would have to come soon because he wasn't sure he could put any more of his own issues on her shoulders. He already felt like a heel for doing as much as he had so far.

Sierra was at work when Austin came home to find Leif sitting on the porch, staring out at the mountain range, his body language closed off. While Austin had been worrying out his own life, Sierra's life, and that of his family, Leif was always in the forefront.

He'd always known that one day he'd become a father.

He just hadn't expected to skip the first ten years of the child's life. Now he had a ten-year-old on his hands and no idea what to do with him. How did one get to know one's son when neither of them seemed to be very good at communication?

He saw his own eyes in that little face. Saw his chin, his hair, his cheekbones. Leif had Maggie's nose, but that was it.

Leif was a Montgomery, and yet Austin didn't know what the next step was.

"Go out there, son," his mother said from his side. She'd taken the afternoon to watch Leif when he got out of school so Austin could try to catch up at work. Harry was doing okay considering and hadn't wanted Marie around hovering. A new grandchild had been just the ticket for the both of him.

Funny how things happened.

"I don't know what to say to him, Mom," Austin said softly. He'd never felt the need to lie to his mother as an adult. Sure, he'd been a dumb kid when he was growing up, but now that he was older, he wanted advice and comfort. He didn't hide things.

Other than what he felt for Sierra, but that was something he needed to process on his own.

Eventually.

"Go find out what his hobbies are. Find out his favorite color. Ask about his day. He finished his homework, but you can ask about it." Marie cupped his face, and Austin sighed. "He's a very bright boy, Austin. He smiles when he thinks no one is looking."

"I know. I've seen that." Hadn't he been watching? Hadn't he been trying to figure out what to do?

"I know, baby. You're trying. This has thrown us all for a loop. I liked Maggie when you were dating her, though I didn't know her well. It's really sad that she's gone."

Austin nodded. "I know. I don't know how Leif is dealing with that."

Marie shook her head. "Well, thankfully, Sierra set up time with a counselor."

Austin sighed. "She said hers helped her, and frankly, though I don't like telling strangers my feelings, if it helps him, then sure."

"Good for you, son. This is a blessing. I know it. The fact that we have a chance with him now is something we can't take for granted. I'm just upset we lost ten years with him."

His mother's mouth thinned, and Austin pinched his nose. They'd been over this before. No one, including Austin and Sierra, was pleased that Maggie had hidden him. In fact, Austin was fucking livid. But right then, yelling and storming around wasn't going to help Leif.

There had been no secret letter or notes to Austin in the case of Maggie's death. There had been nothing but Leif's last name and Austin's on his birth certificate. The lack of answers raged in Austin to no end, but at this point, there was nothing he could do but move on and find a future with the son he'd just met.

"I know you're upset, Mom."

Marie let out a breath. "I'm sorry for bringing it up again. I'll try to stop it, but I can't right now. Go out on the porch with your son and get to know him. He's not that scary, and I'm pretty sure he doesn't bite."

Austin cracked a grin then kissed his mom on the cheek. "I love you. Thank you for everything."

Marie smiled softly. "I love you too. Will Sierra be home soon?"

Home. Sierra technically didn't live there, but he'd gotten accustomed to her being there. God, he didn't find it fair that he was throwing all of his on her shoulders. She'd lost a child of her own, and now she was essentially raising his with him—one that was the same age as her child would have been.

It wasn't fucking fair, and Austin wasn't sure what he was going to do about it.

"Should be," he said absently.

His mom studied his face, frowning. "See you soon, honey."

"Thanks, Mom," he said again as he walked her out.

He found himself watching Leif on the porch, his hands in his pockets just like his son's.

His son.

He wasn't sure he'd ever get used to saying that.

"What are you doing out here?"

Leif turned around, his eyes wide. "Just thinking."

Like pulling teeth, Austin thought, though he wasn't much different. Like father, like son.

Fuck.

"About what?"

Leif shrugged again and sank down into one of the deck chairs. "Things. How was work, Austin?"

The kid called him Austin, not Dad, something they both probably weren't ready for—not by a long shot.

Austin shrugged much like Leif had. "Good, I guess." The kid blinked and looked away. Ah, yeah, maybe he should share a bit more to get Leif to do the same. The kid was a human being, and Austin had interacted with plenty of those. Why was this so hard?

"I had two consults today. That's where I talk with clients about what they want."

Leif perked up and turned. "Really? Do you tattoo them right then?"

Austin relaxed at Leif's interest. Tattoos were something he could talk about. He might not look like the perfect dad with his sleeves, beard, and build, but tattoos weren't taboo to him. Maybe he'd show Leif that too.

"Sometimes. It depends on the design and timeframe. A huge design might take more than one sitting. Plus, I like for the people I work with to go home with something like that and think about it just in case. I don't want to ink them and have them freak out that they made the wrong choice."

"Because tattoos are permanent."

Austin nodded, holding out his arm. "Yep. I can do cover-ups, and there's tattoo removal if they really need it, but that hurts like a bit— It hurts a lot. Plus, you're just scarring the tissue then, so it's not really the same."

Leif studded Austin's arm intently. "So you have it all tattooed?"

"Yeah. Both arms. I did some of it. Maya did the rest. They're called sleeves."

Leif looked up, his eyes wide. "You tattooed *yourself*."

Austin grinned. "Yeah. I can't do big ones on my own because the pain gets to me in a way that I get a little tired, and most angles are too hard, but I like to know I have my own artwork on my body."

"That's cool." Leif held out a hesitant hand. "What's this one? It's the same thing on your sign."

Austin sucked in a breath. "It's the Montgomery Iris. Wes and Storm's company has the same logo. It's our family logo or crest. All of us Montgomerys have the same tattoo, just in different places and in different colors sometimes."

"Really? Even Marie and Harry?"

Austin grinned. "Even Marie and Harry."

"So what do you have to do to get one?" Leif asked, his gaze on Austin's ink rather than his face.

Austin swallowed hard. "Be family. And eighteen."

Leif looked up and grinned. "Do you think..."

Austin sucked in a breath. "I think when you're eighteen and if you want one, then sure. But not in a place that shows if you want to work in a place that doesn't like tattoos. We might like them and have no problem with them, but some people judge, and I'd rather you not have to deal with that when you're eighteen."

Leif blinked, his eyes wet. Austin knew his were the same. Must be allergies. "Only eight years then."

Holy shit. Only eight years. He'd lost so fucking much. Yeah, it sucked, and he shouldn't blame the dead, but he did. Maggie had taken something precious from him for one reason or another. She'd put his name on the birth certificate so yeah, he could be traced eventually like he had been, but she'd kept his son from him. Maybe deep down she wanted him to know about Leif, but he didn't know if that was the case. She'd hidden him. Most likely because she thought he was a freak, but right then, he didn't care about the reason. He just cared about the fact he'd missed Leif's birth, missed his first words, his first steps, his first day of school.

He'd missed so much, and now he was missing more because they had a long road to figure out how the two of them would work together as a unit.

Life was short, and Austin didn't want to lose any more time with his son.

"Hey, you two, I brought dinner," Sierra said from the doorway, a box of chicken in her hand.

Austin stood and took the box out of her hands, leaning down to kiss her. "Thank you, Legs."

She grinned up at him then looked under his arm at Leif. "You hungry, Leif?"

"Uh huh. Did you get the beans and rice? That's my favorite." He ducked his head and blushed.

Hell, he was falling for his own kid.

Austin looked into Sierra's eyes, and he knew she was falling too.

They needed to talk.

Soon.

"Yeah," she said after clearing her throat. "I got the beans and rice. It's my favorite part too."

"Mine three," he added, noting how they were acting like a family.

The three of them.

He wasn't sure how he felt about that, but he would take it one day at a time. It was all he could do.

"Is he asleep?" Sierra asked, running her hands over her hair.

Austin walked into the bedroom, closing the door behind him. Leif had taken the room upstairs and across the hall, meaning it was the farthest from Austin's first-floor master bedroom. It worked for now, and knowing what Austin wanted to do that night, he was grateful.

"Yeah. He went right out. Apparently, he had a field day during gym so he was tired."

Sierra cocked her head to the side. "Did we know he had a field day?"

Austin shook his head. "No, at least you and I didn't. I don't think Mom did either, or she would have mentioned it. Leif said it was a small one though, just during gym and not a whole-day thing like we used to have when we were kids."

She frowned. "If you're sure then. That sounds like something we should have known, right?"

Austin ran a hand over his face. "I honestly have no idea, but we know now, and I think he's opening up enough that if he has one in the future, we'll know." At least he hoped so. At this point it was a gamble if he got Leif to open up about what was going on in his life. Their talk about tattoos and family on the porch, though, had been decent, better than most of the talks they usually had.

Sierra stood next to the bed wearing one of his shirts and a pair of volleyball shorts. Shorts that made her legs look even sexier. His cock perked up at the sight, and he swallowed back a groan. It had been a long while since they'd made love. They'd been too afraid to do anything in the house with Leif around. Sure, it wasn't a problem for most couples with kids in the house, but this was a first for him, and he didn't want to fuck it up.

As it was, he and Decker had quietly taken down the dungeon in the basement. It had been pretty easy considering Austin hadn't had that much of a setup, but it was a little like saying goodbye to a part of him in the process. He couldn't risk having a place Leif could easily find. What he and Sierra did in private wasn't any of his business, but it was still irresponsible not to find a way to shield him from things he didn't understand. In addition, nothing had been formally finalized when it came to Leif staying there. Yes, the kid was his blood, but the courts had to put their rubber stamp on it. People feared what they didn't understand, and considering the reasons Maggie had left him, he wasn't about to do anything that could disrupt Leif's life yet again.

"What's going on in that mind of yours?" Sierra asked, walking to him slowly.

He opened his arms, and she sank into him, her head resting on his chest. "I've missed you," he whispered.

Sierra pulled back, her brow furrowed. "I've been here the whole time, Austin. How could you miss me?"

He let his hand fall through her hair. "You *have* been with me this whole time. I don't know how to thank you." He frowned. "Have I thanked you at all? Or have I just taken your help, guidance, and generally kick-ass attitude for granted?"

She smiled softly then cupped his cheek. He turned into her palm, kissing it gently. "You've said thank you. You've also worked your butt off in an impossible situation. You have a *son*, Austin. That is so freaking scary, and yet you raised your chin and said, 'okay, let's do this.' "

He shook his head. "I was only able to say that because you were there every step of the way. Sure, there was no other answer when it came to Leif. I wasn't about to leave him in a group home when I had plenty of room here, but you did the same, Sierra. You put everything on hold and then changed your life for him. And for me. You accepted him without argument. I don't know how I'll ever repay you."

She sighed. "You had room in your heart for him too, Austin. I believe that even if you can't see it yet."

Austin swallowed hard. He didn't know what to do with his feelings when it came to Leif. It was all a little too surreal to contemplate.

"I can see you're not ready for that yet, and I get it. As for repaying me? You don't have to. I get to watch you two work together and figure out what it means for him to be here. I'm getting everything I need."

God, she was perfect. She was giving up so much for him. They had started out just trying to have fun and see where their relationship went, and now she was practically living with him and playing house with Leif. She hadn't asked for any of it, and Austin felt like he kept waiting for her to say it was enough and leave.

He couldn't think about that right then though.

At the moment, he wanted to think about something else.

He leaned down and brushed his lips against her. "Are you sure you're getting *everything* you need?"

Sierra blushed, the heat of her skin scorching his. "Austin..."

"It's been two weeks, baby. He's across the house, and we can be quiet." He raised a brow. "Well, I can at least be quiet.

We might need to find a way to gag you to make sure you don't scream too loudly."

"Oh really? Gagging me now?"

He wasn't a huge fan of ball gags because he liked to hear her say his name, but...no, not then.

"I want to slide into your heat while my body covers you. I want to go slow and quiet, and make sure you feel every inch of me. What do you say, Legs?"

Her eyes widened, her pupils dilating at his words alone.

"Are you sure you can keep me quiet?"

Austin groaned then pulled her closer. "We can try our hardest. I'm not about to stop making love to you because Leif is here. We'll find a way."

"Then make love to me."

He slanted his mouth of hers, letting her sweet taste dance over his tongue. He walked her backward toward the bed, his hands in her hair, on her face, his mouth on hers. She moaned into his mouth, and he nipped her lip.

"Quiet," he whispered.

Her eyes brightened. "You taste so good though." Her hand cupped his dick, and he groaned.

"Quiet," she whispered.

He snorted then stood back before stripping her quickly. She gasped, apparently surprised he could move so fast.

"Get on the bed and stay on your back."

She did so, her gaze on his. Her pink-tipped nipples hardened, and he palmed his erection through his jeans.

"Spread your legs."

When she did, he held back another groan. "You're wet for me, baby," he whispered. "So fucking wet. You want me to eat you out before I sink my cock into you? Will that help the ache?"

She nodded, biting her lip.

Austin quickly shucked his clothes then got on the bed. He wrapped her legs around his neck and licked her pussy in one long swipe.

When he heard a muffled scream, he looked up to see a pillow over her face. Well, that was one way to be quiet. He went back to his feast, nibbling and sucking on her lower lips and clit. She rocked into his face, moaning softly as he increased pressure on her clit. When he hummed against her at the same time he rimmed her ass with his finger, she came.

Hard.

"My Sierra likes it when I play with her ass?" he asked, licking her taste off his lips.

She moved the pillow from her face and nodded. "Yes. I like anal sex. Sue me. We can do that later though. Please put that cock in me."

He raised a brow at her orders. Tonight was different with them, and they both knew it. They weren't a Dom and a sub. They were Austin and Sierra making love. That was their kink, and Austin counted himself lucky he'd found someone who felt the same.

"I'm going to fuck that ass later then, Legs. Now let me get a condom first so I can make love to you."

She gripped his wrist and shook her head. "No condom. Not ever again. I'm on birth control, and we both got tested. I want you in me."

He held back a groan and crushed his lips to hers. "I can't wait to be bare in you again, baby. I know we did it without one before, but this time it's for keeps. Got me?"

"Then be in me."

He positioned himself at her entrance, keeping his gaze on hers. As he pushed in, her mouth opened on a silent gasp. He slowly rocked into her, inch by inch until his balls rested against her ass and he could feel every sweet inch of her around his dick.

Austin swallowed hard, his arms shaking. "You feel so fucking good, baby," he whispered.

"I...I..." She blinked up at him then ran her hands up his back. "Move. I want to feel all of you."

He nodded then pulled out before slowly thrusting back in. They kept their gazes on one another as he made slow love to his woman, the one he loved. When they came together, they whispered each other's names, their bodies shaking.

He'd known what she was about to say before she'd told him to move. Just as he'd almost said it as well. There was a reason he wasn't saying it yet, but he couldn't get a hold on it. He loved Sierra Elder, but now that things had changed, he wasn't sure it would last.

His heart did a funny lurch thing, and he kissed Sierra softly, trying to get the sting to go away. He needed her more than anything, but Austin wasn't sure she needed him as much.

That scared him more than the thought of forever.

Way more.

CHAPTER NINETEEN

"I still can't get over the fact that you're a daddy," Shep said as he sat on his aunt and uncle's porch, enjoying a beer.

Austin snorted from his chair beside him. "I'm still not over it yet."

Shep shook his head then took another sip of his beer. "What do you think, Grandpa, you believe it?"

Harry, who sat on the other side of Austin, took a sip of his water. "I do, only because I can see Austin in every little motion Leif makes. It's funny that kid is so much like you when he had a full decade without you."

Shep held back an angry response to that. He'd met Maggie once right when he'd left Denver for good so he could move to New Orleans. She'd been spoiled, selfish, and not at all like what Austin had now. He'd had to hold back a few responses when it came to Leif's mom. It wasn't fair to speak ill of the dead, but she'd deprived his cousin and the rest of the Montgomerys memories and experiences they'd never get back. And Leif had been forced to stay in a group home, not knowing what his own future would hold because she kept him a secret. That was a fucking huge sin in Shep's book, and although she was gone, he wasn't sure he'd ever forgive her for the look on Austin's face.

His cousin might say he was over it and moving on, but Shep knew better. Austin had no idea how to act around his son, and that was a shame. Sure, the kid was starting to open up, but he hadn't been around the whole Montgomery clan all at once yet. That was enough to scare anyone, let alone a kid who'd had only his mother for most of his life.

"Leif doing good in school?" Harry asked, his hands shaking.

Shep held back the stinging at the back of his eyes. The radiation was hard on the man, they could all see that, but Harry was strong. Plus with Marie by his side, he was stronger. The prognosis was good according to Harry, and though they were all worried, Shep knew that if they stayed positive, they could make it though.

It didn't make it any less hard to watch Harry deal with the pain.

Shep met Austin's eyes and saw his cousin was dealing with the same thing as Shep. It was awful to feel so helpless for those you loved.

"He's doing good. He's got a test today that we studied for last night."

Shep smiled softly at that. The man sounded like such a dad—even though he knew Austin didn't feel it.

They talked about Leif some more, and Shep soaked it all up. He wanted to know more about the kid's life and how he was taking it all in.

"You think he's ready for the barbecue tomorrow?" Shep asked when Harry fell asleep.

Austin stood, throwing a blanket over his father. "Leif? Yeah. I think he'll be fine. If not, then we can leave. He's met most of you guys individually, but never as a group."

"We're a bit crazy to people who know us, let alone newcomers."

Austin snorted. "Sierra is coming too, and it's her first barbecue with the Montgomerys."

Shep let out a whistle. "Same for Shea actually. At least they'll have each other when we throw them to the wolves."

"True. Speaking of Shea, how is she? It's been a month, and she still seems, I don't know, off somehow."

Shep let out a breath. "I don't know, man. I've noticed it too and commented on it. All she says is that she's fine. Fine.

I hate that fucking word. It doesn't mean fine. It's a landmine of doom and tears."

"Damn. You think it's her mom?"

Shep sighed. Her mom was a first-class bitch and had tried to take everything from Shea more than once.

"I hope not, but the thought's crossed my mind."

"I don't know what to say, Shep. I'm not much help if we can't figure it out."

"You have enough on your plate right now that doesn't have to do with me. Worry about that, and I'll figure it out. It's got to be something because she isn't fine. We both know that. Hopefully she'll open up to me because it's killing me that she doesn't trust me enough to do so."

Austin looked over sharply. "Trust? You think that's it?"

Shep ran a hand over his face. "What else could it be? I thought we were open and honest about everything. I guess not."

"Shep."

"Whatever. I'm going to head out and back to Griffin's. Shea is there working on something, and, well, I want to be there." He met Austin's gaze then looked over at a sleeping Harry. "We'll probably head back to New Orleans soon. We've been here for a month, and though Shea can do everything from her computer and I've been working at Montgomery Ink, we need to get back."

Austin nodded. "I know. I figured. You just let me know when, and I'll help if you need me."

He hugged his cousin, ran a hand over his uncle's head, and then went back into the house so he could leave. Something was up with Shea. She wasn't happy, and he could only think it was something he'd done.

He swallowed hard. There was no way he could let her get away with not telling him. He loved her more than anything on this earth, and he needed to know how to help.

Even if it broke him.

CHAPTER TWENTY

"How many Montgomerys are there going to be again?"

Austin didn't answer her, and Sierra had to turn, narrowing her eyes. Her man grinned, his hands in his pockets.

"You sure look sexy in that dress, Legs."

She held back her smile at his words. She *did* look good in her sundress, but he wouldn't be let off the hook with nice words. Wait. Was she *too* sexy? She turned on her heel and looked in Austin's full-length mirror on the back of his closet door.

"Is it too sexy?" Damn it. She wanted to make a good impression and couldn't do it if she looked like some trollop on the hunt. Yes, she said trollop. It happens.

Strong hands wrapped around her waist as Austin came up from behind her. He tilted her head to the side and ran soft kisses up her neck. Shivers racked her body, and her knees went weak. Damn man and his prowess.

"You look amazing, Legs. Not too sexy," he added as she narrowed her eyes again. "Your legs look hot, but that's because they always do. In fact, the only way they could look hotter is if they were wrapped around my waist...or my neck." He kissed behind her temple. Seriously. Damn man. "In fact, I might have you change into pants or a nun's habit so my brothers don't get a look at those legs. Those are mine, baby."

She rolled her eyes. Territorial much? "They can look all they want, but I'm still coming home to you." Oh, boy. That sounded more like a wife's statement than a girlfriend's. She didn't meet Austin's eyes just in case he took it wrong. She didn't want to ruin their day before it even got started. "Now, you didn't answer my first question. How many Montgomerys are going to be there?"

Austin moved back and patted her ass. "Just the siblings and their spouses. Oh, and Shep, Shea, and Decker. Some might bring a girlfriend or, in Maya's case, Jake since he's always around, but other than that, Mom and Dad didn't want to overwhelm you, Shea, and Leif with all the extras right out the gate."

"You do realize that since there are eight of you in that one family it's *always* going to be overwhelming? There's no taking you in small doses."

He patted her ass again, and she rolled her eyes. "What can we say? We like the noise. It's comforting. Now finish getting ready since I know you want to make sure you're perfect—something that's already done in my eyes by the way—while I go get Leif ready. He's freaking out a bit."

She warmed at his compliment even as she worried for the little boy who had come into their lives so unexpectedly. "Do you want my help with Leif?"

Something odd came in his eyes, but he shook it away. Weird. "I've got it. I need to get to know him better anyway, right?"

Huh. That reaction was...different. He kissed her on the corner of her mouth then left the room. What had she done? Said? Maybe she was just looking into everything too hard. It *had* been a rough few weeks.

She finished putting on her mascara and called it good enough for meeting the family. The whole family. All at once. No pressure or anything. Thank God Shea would be there in similar shoes.

Her phone rang from her purse sitting on the bed, and she stepped over to answer it. Her shoe got caught on shirt

Austin had left on the floor, so she answered the phone without looking at the screen. "Hello?"

"Sierra, it's Rodney."

Her heart sped up, and she sat shakily on the edge of the bed. She'd heard from her lawyer and friend a few times since that horrible phone call from her in-laws, but not often. Thankfully, she hadn't heard from Todd and Marsha again. Actually, the more she thought about it, the more that worried her. If they had nothing up their sleeves, they'd call and harass her like they used to when they were out of options. Now they'd left her alone. That could mean they'd given up, but Sierra knew better. They were up to something, and she had no idea what it was.

That ball of worry turned into stone in her belly, and she had to take a deep breath before answering. "Yes, Rodney. What is it?"

"Well, I have good news and bad news."

She swallowed hard. "Okay."

"The good news is that we haven't received any court documents about their suit. The bad news is they are still trying to make waves."

Her body shook. "What does that mean?"

"It means we're not out of the dark yet and they're looking for ways to sue you. I'm sorry, Sierra."

"Thank you for letting me know. I have to go now."

She hung up before he could say anything back and tried to find her composure. Marsha and Todd wanted to sue her and take Eden. They wouldn't be able to. There was no way unless they found a way to pay their way into that outcome. The fact they'd almost done that before worried her, but she had to breathe. She had a family barbecue to attend and a little boy who needed her.

A little boy who wasn't her own, but she was damn sure acting like he was.

She put her phone back in her purse, straightened her dress, and then walked out of the bedroom, putting away her fears and what-ifs. She'd tell Austin about the call and what she was thinking *after* the barbecue. She didn't want to ruin the party and Leif's introduction with her own problems.

They had enough on their own without adding hers into the mix.

Austin and Leif sat in the living room, both silent, not looking at each other. Well, they looked, but only when they thought the other wasn't. She knew Austin was trying to get to know his son, but it was hard. They honestly didn't know how to go about it and were failing in some respects. Yes, Austin had gone full steam into being a father and hadn't pushed Leif away, and Leif had come to Austin in the first place, but it wasn't enough. They were two strangers in an impossible situation.

"Ready to head out?" she said, startling them both.

Austin stood quickly, running his hand over his hair. She held back a smile as Leif did the same thing. The two of them were so cute she just wanted to hold them and never let them go.

"Ready," Austin said gruffly.

"Ready," Leif said as the same time.

Too. Cute.

The number of Montgomerys in one place was a little startling—no, overwhelming and "of the oh-my-God variety.

"It's like they multiply when they're together," Shea whispered from her side.

"Exponentially," Sierra whispered back, grateful for the other woman's presence, though she did seem a bit pale. "You feeling okay, hon?"

Shea met her gaze, her eyes wide. "I'm fine."

Huh, Austin was right. Shea kept saying fine, and no one believed it. Poor Shep must be out of his mind.

"If you're sure."

"I am. I'm going to go find Shep. You okay right here?"

Sierra nodded and watched Shea walk away toward her husband. Whatever was going on with that woman, she hoped she'd be better than fine soon.

A small body leaned into her, and she looked down at Leif, wrapping her arm around his shoulders.

"What's up, honey?"

"Just looking," he mumbled, and she rubbed his back.

Poor guy. There *were* a lot of Montgomerys congregated in Marie and Harry's backyard. Thankfully, no one had brought any significant others that they weren't married to, other than Maya who brought Jake. Sierra still didn't understand that relationship other than the fact that the two were best friends who didn't sleep with each other. If that worked for them, good; however, Sierra still didn't understand the odd undercurrents. Not that it was her place to judge in the first place.

Well, that wasn't quite right, Austin had brought Sierra. Since when had she thought of him as her husband? Must have been a slip of the tongue.

They stood together silently, watching the others talk and joke around. Leif had already made the rounds with Austin at first. She'd held back so she wouldn't interfere. She'd make her own introductions later. It wasn't like she hadn't met them all before—Leif as well. This was just the first full family event for the both of them.

There was that word again.

Family.

She shook it off. Today was about Leif's future, not hers. Her gaze landed on Harry, who sat in an outdoor chair, a smile on his pale face. God, the man had to be in pain, but he looked like he was just resting. Apparently, he was doing better than what they'd all thought, so that was good. However, she knew prostate cancer didn't go away overnight. He was fighting, so that was all that mattered then.

Austin prowled toward her then, his gaze on hers, his shoulders wide, his stride strong. God, she loved him. If only she could actually buck up the nerve and say that. She didn't know what was holding her back, but it was something.

His gaze left hers to Leif at her side, and a cold glint washed over his eyes before he blinked it away.

Yes. That. That was part of why she held back from telling him she loved him. Leif went to her first. Always. He trusted her and leaned into her hold more than he did with Austin...if he ever leaned at all.

God. Was Austin *jealous* of her? No, that couldn't be it. She must just be imagining things.

"Hey you," she said softly, shrugging off her feelings. She was blowing things out of proportion. That had to be it.

"Hey." He leaned down, brushing his lips over hers. He pulled away, reaching out for Leif, then put his hand down as Leif burrowed into her side more.

The shattered look on Austin's face broke her heart.

"Having fun?" Austin asked after an odd moment of silence.

Leif shrugged.

A clatter of feet on the deck and Cliff ran up to them, Sasha right on his heels, even at such a young age. That little girl wasn't about to be left out of whatever her big brother got into. Sierra couldn't help but smile.

"Hey, Leif. Want to go play?" Cliff held a rubber ball like the one she'd used in gym for dodge ball or even kick ball.

"Play!" Sasha said as she clapped her hands.

Sierra's ovaries—the ones she'd thought long dead—perked up.

Well, that complicated things.

"Can I?" Leif asked. Her. Not Austin.

She met Austin's gaze, helpless. Leif wasn't hers, no matter how hard she tried. She was only Austin's girlfriend, not a replacement for Maggie.

Austin gave her a slight nod, his mouth drawn tight.

"Sure, honey. Have fun and make sure you let Sasha play without hurting her."

Leif rolled his eyes and hugged her hard before running off with Cliff, Sasha trailing behind. There went those damn ovaries again.

"Be careful with Sasha, Cliff! And let her play," Meghan called out as she and her husband, Richard, walked toward Austin and Sierra.

Austin turned, holding out his arm so Sierra nestled under it, resting against his side. Honestly, there were only a few other places better than where she was right then.

"Hey, little sister," Austin said as the other couple came closer.

Meghan smiled and leaned into her brother, kissing his chin before coming over to hug Sierra too. This family sure loved hugging.

Well, most of them. Richard hadn't even looked her way or bothered to say hello. She hadn't liked him the first time she'd seen him, and that attitude hadn't changed.

Nor did she think it would any time soon.

"Richard," Austin said, his tone cooler.

The other man raised a brow. "I believe we already did introductions when you brought over that child about twenty minutes ago. Is there a reason we are doing this again?"

"Richard," Meghan whispered.

Yep. He was an asshole.

"We like to say hello to people when we walk up to them," Austin said casually, his body strung tight against Sierra. "You know, being polite and all that crap."

"Whatever you say," Richard said dully then turned to Meghan. "This is the second one we've come to in a row. I think we can call it a day."

Meghan's eyes pleaded for Austin to not say anything, and Sierra felt for the woman. There was clearly something going on here that Sierra wasn't privy to, and Austin didn't like it one bit.

"I see Griffin and Alex over there. Let's go talk to them since I really haven't seen them today," Sierra said, blinking up at Austin.

Austin growled softly then sighed. "I need to go ask Mom a question, so you head on over. I'll be there in a bit." He glared at Richard. "Let me know if you need anything, Meghan. Anything."

"I believe my *wife* is just fine," Richard bit out.

"I'm fine, Austin," Meghan said, her voice tired. "I just need to say goodbye to Richard and then I'll mingle. Promise."

"Excuse me?" Richard asked, his cheeks going red.

"You're right, honey. If you're busy, then head on home. I'll take care of the kids, and since we came in separate cars, we're fine."

Sierra pulled Austin away as the couple fought. Meghan stood up for herself, saying she and the kids were staying at the barbecue at least, but Sierra had a feeling things weren't about to end there.

"I'm going to kill that bastard for putting that look on her face," Austin ground out.

Sierra stopped him then stood in front of him. "Don't do anything here. Not in front of their kids. Not in front of Leif. Okay?" She stood on her toes and kissed the bottom of his chin along his beard.

Austin growled again then kissed her hard. Right there in front of the entire Montgomery clan. "For them and for you. If it wasn't for that, I'd beat the shit out of him."

"I don't think that's what Meghan wants."

"Screw what Meghan wants. That guy is an asshole."

Sierra snorted. "He is, but you not doing what Meghan wants puts you in the same lump with that jerk, so respect her wishes."

He narrowed his eyes then nodded. "Fine. I need to go talk to Mom like I said I was going to. You gonna be okay with Griffin and Alex?"

She patted his chest and smiled. "Of course I will. They're your brothers."

"That's what scares me."

He left her laughing before she walked over to where Griffin and Alex sat on two lawn chairs. A third one sat next to them, empty.

"You mind if I join you?" she asked.

Griffin grinned at her and waved her to sit. "Of course. We're just talking about random crap."

Alex gave her a nod then took a sip of his drink.

"What Alex means to say with that nod is, hello there, Sierra, are you enjoying yourself?"

Sierra searched Alex's face and held back a frown at the glassy look in his eyes. It was only the afternoon. Surely he couldn't have drunk that much already?

It wasn't her business, but from the worried look in Griffin's eyes, it was going to be a family problem soon.

"Are you enjoying yourself?" Griffin asked after yet another awkward Montgomery moment passed.

Sierra smiled. "Yes, you have a lovely family."

Alex snorted but didn't say anything, merely took another drink.

Griffin sighed then leaned forward. Since he was on the other side of Alex, he had to talk over his quiet brother in order to speak to her. "Have you heard any good Austin stories yet?"

Sierra perked up. "Austin stories?"

"Oh yeah. We have tons of them. Wes and Storm have more since they're closer in age, but we have enough for blackmail."

Sierra laughed and shook her head. "Are you sure Austin wants you dishing these out if they're blackmail material?"

"Hell no. That's why we're going to tell you."

Sierra leaned back in the chair and listened to Griffin tell her stories of Austin's youth that included a trip or two to the ER. The kid might have wanted to take care of all his younger siblings, but he got in a lot of trouble with a younger Shep. God, she really loved this family. Even the grumpy people opened their arms for her. Well, maybe not Alex, but he didn't spit at her at least. They were just getting to the really juicy stuff—Austin's teenage years—when Wes and Storm joined them, bringing over their own chairs.

"There was this one time we caught him and what's her name down in his truck near the train tracks," Wes said. "Damn, what was her name?"

Storm smiled. "Susan. Susan Lady."

"Lady? Hell, I forgot that," Wes said on a laugh.

"What are we laughing at?" Maya asked as she strolled over with Jake by her side. The man didn't talk much, but, damn, Maya had one sexy friend. Not that Sierra was really looking.

Much.

"They're telling me Austin stories," Sierra answered.

"I have a few of those," Jake said, his voice low and deep.

Maya rolled his eyes. "We all do. You don't get much privacy in this family. So, what do you want to know? I'm pretty sure we all know the night he lost his virginity since Mom freaked out."

Sierra raised a brow, holding back a grin. "I'm good without knowing that."

Maya shrugged. "Your loss. Hmm, there was the night he turned twenty-one and got really, really drunk. That was fun."

"If you are all done making fun of the man who can't stand up for himself, I'm here to rescue Sierra," Decker said as he came over.

Sierra cocked her head. "I need to be rescued?"

Decker snorted. "No, but Austin does. Griffin, buddy, I expected better of you. What would you do if you brought a woman over and they told her all your stories?"

Griffin smiled. "I did. Once. Never again. Oh, the humanity." He shuddered even as he laughed, and Sierra rolled her eyes and stood.

"I wouldn't want Austin to feel bad, so lead the way."

Decker held out his arm, and she linked hers with his. "Thanks for all the stories, guys. I'm glad I came."

They waved her off then started back on Austin stories. Apparently when they had one, there were three more to be told. What a family.

"Are you really having fun?" Decker asked as he led her to Austin.

Sierra nodded. "Totally. Your family is a hoot." She held back a wince.

"It's okay, Sierra. They're my family if not by blood."

She relaxed, keeping her eye on where Meghan watched over the children. Leif was having a blast it looked like, so at least that was one less thing to worry about.

"I'm glad to hear that," she said then held back a reaction at the look on Miranda's face. The woman stood by her parents but watched Decker move, never letting her eyes leave him.

Interesting.

Seriously, she loved this family.

"Hey, Legs, having fun?" Austin asked as he met them halfway, drinks in his hand. "Thanks for rescuing her, Decker."

Decker smiled and shook his head. "No problem. Now I'm going to go back and tell them that story about you and the turkey baster."

Sierra coughed up her drink. "Turkey baster?"

Austin blushed. "It's not what you think."

"I'm not sure what to think."

Decker just laughed and left them alone.

"No really, what did you do with the turkey baster?"

"There was alcohol involved, but it wasn't a sex thing. I promise. Let's just leave it at that."

Sierra's mind went in so many different directions she shuddered at what else could have happened. "Nope. I don't want to know."

Austin wrapped his free arm around her then leaned down, kissing her softly. "Thanks for coming."

She sighed, closing her eyes as she leaned into him. "I love this."

He froze before relaxing as if he'd figured out exactly what she'd said. She swallowed her disappointment and let it go. Something was going on with him, and she couldn't tell what it was. But whatever happened, it scared her more than threatening phone calls and the unknown.

Much more.

CHAPTER TWENTY-ONE

Austin guided the needle across his client's skin, paying extra attention to detail. He did *not* want to fuck up this tattoo. The man in the chair, Saint, was one big-ass motherfucker.

Scary too.

Austin knew he was part of the local Hell's Legion MC, but that was about it. He didn't know what else the guy did, nor did he particularly want to know.

While Austin was big, Saint was bigger. He didn't have as much ink as Austin did, but it was cutting it close. Over the years, he'd worked on a few pieces on the man, but unlike what he normally did, he never asked what they meant.

He valued his life too much.

Not that he thought Saint was going to kill him or anything.

Maybe.

He finished up the shading of Anubis on Saint's side, wiping it clean for the last time. The scary-ass dude hadn't moved an inch during the entire five-hour session. The man hadn't even groaned or twitched.

Austin even winced sometimes during his sessions.

Not Saint.

He went through the aftercare instructions as Saint stood, that bored yet I-will-cut-you look on his face telling Austin everything he needed to know.

Do not mess with this guy.

Saint left a roll of hundreds on the front desk then walked out, throwing his colors—his leather vest that told what MC he was part of—back on without wincing at the contact with his tattoo.

As soon as the man left, Austin let out a breath. Jesus, he didn't know what it was about that guy, but Austin was never fully calm around him. In fact, when Saint made an appointment—or showed up randomly as he was prone to do—Austin made sure he cleared out the place as much as possible. The man seemed to want privacy, and Austin didn't want to step on his toes.

"Is he gone?" Maya asked as she walked out from the back, her eyes on the door.

"Yep. He paid up front, though I didn't quote him. Let me go see how much he put down."

Maya sighed. "That man sure is built, and I wouldn't mind taking a ride, but he scares me a bit too much, you know?"

Austin repressed a shudder. "Never say anything about riding Saint or any other man again. We may be friends, but you're also my sister. Oh, and if you touch Saint, or think about touching Saint, I'm sending you to a convent."

His sister snorted. "Yes, I can totally see me in a nun's habit with my eyebrow piercing and ink. And anyway, I'm allowed to think of Saint in naughty ways without actually touching him. He's hot in a serial-killer kinda way. You see those blue eyes? Ice cold...but I'd sure like to warm them up. He looks like a buffer, hotter Spike."

"Spike?" Where the hell did his sister come up with this crap?

She rolled her eyes before she turned away to get back to her station. "You know, Spike? From Buffy? All hot and spiky blond."

"So he's Spike because of his hair?" He was so confused.

"No, it's more because of a thing with railroad spikes and blood I think. Anyway, Saint is hot, but I would never get involved with an MC. We're a crazy enough family without that."

"Thank God," he mumbled as he put the three grand Saint had left in the till. He'd paid way too much as usual, but Austin took it anyway. He'd tried to give some back last time and had almost wept at Saint's look. He wasn't less of a man to cry because of Saint.

"So, what's on the rest of the schedule today? Saint came in early this morning so we have the rest of the late afternoon and evening, right?"

Austin nodded, fumbling with the computer yet again. "Yeah. I have another session this evening that should only take an hour. Saint's ink took a long time this morning, and I don't want to hurt my back by doing any more."

"Good to hear it," Callie said as she walked in with a spring in her step.

"What's up with you?" Austin asked.

"I just saw the hottest man ever outside. He looked just like Spike!"

"No!" Austin and Maya yelled at the same time.

Callie's eyes widened, and she took a step back. The action forced a laugh out of Austin. "Sorry, honey. Don't look at Spike again, okay? He's not for you."

Callie raised a brow. "Really? Because he's hot, and telling me I can't have someone just makes me want him more. Or at least to try since, once I get to know someone, it's all about what I want and not what others don't want. Make sense?"

"No," Austin said, rubbing his temples. Jesus, Callie was just alike Miranda with a little Meghan and Maya thrown in. Whoever had the luck of having Callie as their woman in the future had a lot to handle.

"Honey, don't taunt Austin. Saint is bad news. He might be hot, but he scares even me. Okay?"

Callie shrugged. "That's fine. I wasn't really going to chase after him and beg for a ride...on his bike." She snorted as Austin clenched his jaw. "I like a man in a suit more than leather anyway."

"Really? You?" Maya asked, and Austin had to agree.

"Sure. They can have ink, piercings, and other fun and tasty things under the suit. But there's nothing like a man in a suit to rev my engines."

Austin closed his eyes and said a silent prayer. "Please stop talking about revving anything. And for the love of God, Maya, don't encourage her. And don't talk about riding. Please. I can't take anymore. You two are killing me."

"Aww, poor Austin can't handle his little sister having sex," Callie said, teasing.

"I swear I'm going to fire your ass, Callie."

"I'd like to see you try. You can't get on without me." With that, she pranced off to the back, humming a tune Austin didn't recognize.

"Why didn't I get a nice apprentice who happens to have a dick and doesn't bug the shit out of me?"

Maya grinned. "Because Callie fucking rocks at ink, and she needed your help."

"True, but I don't think I can take any more sex talk for the day."

"So I guess I shouldn't ask how you and Sierra are doing?"

Austin sighed then went to his station, pulling out his notepad. He still hadn't finished Sierra's sketch. She also hadn't asked about it. Had she forgotten? Or maybe had second thoughts?

For some reason he felt like if he finished this sketch, then a part of what he and Sierra had would be over. It didn't make any sense, but Austin couldn't quite place what was wrong there. It sucked to think that the initial burst of heat and attraction would be over and, in its place, a comfort he'd never had would remain.

No, that wouldn't be right. He still got hard and wanted to fuck her up against any wall or surface he could when he saw her. Maybe this was what a real serious relationship felt like. Something different, something comfortable.

It didn't make any sense then that he was still so fucking twitchy.

"Uh, earth to Austin, you okay?"

Austin shook his head, clearing out the thoughts that wouldn't go away at Maya's words. "I'm good. Just thinking too much."

Maya came up to him. "About what? I mentioned Sierra, and you got all serious. Is there something going on there you need to talk about? I might joke and tease with you, but you're my big brother, and I love you. If you need to talk, I'm here."

Austin set the unfinished sketch on his pad down and sighed. "I don't know, Maya. I just have an odd feeling, I guess."

She sat down on the bench next to his chair, her teeth nibbling at her lip. "You guys really work well together. I mean it's like you guys fit, you know?"

He nodded, knowing she was right. "I know that. It's just..."

"This all happened really fast?"

He let out a breath, glad that Maya got the situation and him. "I feel like one minute we're sniping at each other over Shannon and the next minute Sierra's living with me and my kid."

"Insta-family."

"Fuck. Yeah. I guess. It's not that I don't *want* this to happen. I just didn't think that it would happen within two months of actually knowing her."

"And having Leif show up out of the blue doesn't help either."

"I don't know what to do with him," he whispered.

Maya punched him in the shoulder. "You're not thinking of trying to get rid of him or anything? Because if you do, I'll not only kick your ass, I'll take that kid from you so fast you won't even have time to blink."

"What? No! That's not what I meant. There's not another alternative. There's never been one. I'm not letting him go. I just don't know what to do with him now that he's here."

"Be his dad, Austin."

He growled, throwing his sketchpad across the room. "I fucking know that. I know I'm his dad, not that he actually says the words. No, he barely talks to me. Sure, he'll talk to

Mom and Sierra, but me? Nothing. I tried to talk to him, and it even worked a bit when we talked about tattoos, but that's it. He just mumbles and looks like he's ready to bolt at any moment. I don't know what to fucking do."

Maya sighed as Callie came out of the back room. She bent over and picked up the sketchbook, holding it to her chest.

"I don't want to lose him, but do I really have him? I feel like I'm just standing here and making a home for him so he's safe, but I'm only the landlord. He doesn't need me."

"Oh, Austin, of course he needs you," Callie said.

"Really? Because it sure doesn't seem like it. He needs Sierra for sure, but he doesn't need me." As soon as he said it, he felt like an ass.

"You can't be jealous of your girlfriend, honey," Maya said softly. The fact that she spoke softly and didn't hit him spoke volumes.

"God, I'm so fucking jealous, and I hate myself even more for it."

"He had Maggie before," Callie added in, still clutching the sketchbook. "He had a mom and not a dad. Yeah, it sucks that he didn't have it before, but he's not used to men in his life. At least as far as I can tell. And, honey, there are a lot of male Montgomerys in the world. You all are a bit overwhelming."

"You need to talk to Sierra about this," Maya added. "She's not going to judge you, but if you keep it bottled up inside, you're going to end up resenting her for being an awesome woman, who not only deals with your surly ass but opened her arms to a little boy she didn't know without even blinking. Don't just talk to me and Callie. Talk to your girlfriend. I know you love her."

"Who said anything about love?" he bit out.

"Oh shut up," Maya snapped. "You love her, and she loves you. Just because you might not have said the words to each other doesn't make it any less true. Maybe if you actually said it, you'd get over whatever is blocking you from feeling settled with her."

God, he loved Sierra. He loved her more than he ever thought he could love someone else, but it all happened so fast. He thought he'd be ready for the emotion and all it meant when it finally came to him, but he didn't know it would feel like getting hit in the head with a two-by-four. He'd wanted to settle down and find a wife and have a baby. Now he had a girlfriend who felt like she was already a permanent part of his life and a ten-year-old who wanted nothing to do with him.

What the hell was he supposed to do with that?

"I don't know what to do, girls," he finally said after he sat there silently.

"Talk to her," Callie said.

The door opened, and Austin looked up to see a pale Sierra walk in with Leif in front of her. He opened his mouth to ask what was wrong then got a look at his son's face.

"What the hell happened?" Austin roared. "How the fuck did he get a black eye?"

"Austin, please," Sierra whispered, shaking her head.

Austin stormed over to the pair, only to freeze, and Leif shrunk into Sierra. It was like a punch in the gut, and he wanted to scream. He swallowed hard, forcing his fists to relax.

"What happened?" he asked, softer this time. He knelt before Leif and held out a hand. When Leif didn't flinch, he took his son's chin and tilted his head. "Ouch."

"Tell him, honey," Sierra whispered.

Leif shuffled his feet then sighed. "Some kid called me a bastard, so I hit him. I broke his nose, so his friend punched me in the eye." He sniffed. "But the first kid bled a lot."

Pride and anger warred within him. If it had been only the two of them, he'd have said good job for hitting a kid who called him names, but he knew that wasn't the right reaction.

"Hell," he whispered. "You get ice on that?" he asked, not knowing what else to day.

"I did in the nurse's office."

"Hey, buddy, let's go get you an ice pack next door," Maya said from behind him. He heard the edge to her voice, the one that spoke of punching people for hurting their blood, but he wasn't sure if anyone else heard it.

"Okay," Leif said then turned to hug Sierra before walking away.

He didn't even bother telling Austin goodbye.

Great.

Just fucking great.

Austin stood, running a hand over his beard. "What the fuck, Sierra? Why didn't I get a call?"

Sierra narrowed her eyes. "We tried. Your cell is off, and your work number keeps getting a busy signal. Don't snap at me for being there when you couldn't. That's why we put my name and number on the emergency list."

He cursed and looked down at his phone. "Fuck. It must have accidently turned off."

"And someone knocked the phone off the cradle," Callie said as she hung the work phone back up. "That really sucks."

"No shit." It wasn't lost on him that he hadn't said thank you or even kissed Sierra, but he couldn't. The fact that Leif had been hurt and he hadn't been available made him sick. What kind of father was he? Maybe the kid was right for choosing Sierra over him.

"If you're done. I need to go back to work. I was at my accountant's so that's why I didn't stop by here on my way over to the school if you were wondering. Oh, and your son has in-school suspension for two weeks, and you need to meet with the other boys' families with the vice principal. I wrote it all down." She took out a piece of paper from her purse and threw it at him. "I'm sorry you feel like I hid it from you but don't yell at me for helping. Leif was scared, Austin, and I didn't know what else to do."

Damn it. He felt like a heel. "Sierra..."

"No, don't. I need to go back to work, and then I'm heading to my place tonight. I need a breather, and frankly, it's been so long since I slept in my own bed I don't know if it's even still there."

Panic hit him hard, and he took a step toward her. She held up a hand, stopping him. "Just one night, Austin," she said, her voice shaky. "Tell Leif I will see him tomorrow."

She walked away, and Austin staggered back.

"Go after her, you idiot," Callie barked.

"I can't. She'll just turn me away. I'll make it up to her in the morning. I know I'm an idiot. I'm not going to lose her."

"You might have already done that," Callie said sadly then walked away.

Austin thought the same but pushed that away. He wasn't going to lose her, but he knew he'd fucked up.

Badly.

With that thought, he turned back to Hailey's to go see the son that didn't want him. He wasn't giving up on either of them.

That didn't mean it would be easy.

CHAPTER TWENTY-TWO

Sierra's stomach lurched again, and she forced herself not to freak out. She hadn't exactly walked out on Austin the day before, but it was close enough to the truth that her palms went damp at the thought. Work waited for her, and the strained smile on her face hadn't gotten past Becky, though her customers didn't seem to notice she was breaking inside.

That was something at least.

Just a few more hours of work and she could go home—which home, well, she hadn't decided yet.

When she'd gotten the phone call from Leif's school, she dropped everything, leaving her accountant with an understanding look on his face. Luckily, Sierra had almost been done with everything so she hadn't missed out on much, but she'd still put Leif before her other responsibilities and dreams.

Or at least the money side of her dreams.

And she'd do it again too.

The fact that Leif meant so much to her so quickly made things worse for her and Austin. She knew that, but now she'd just have to deal. The look on that little boy's face when she'd walked into the office would be forever cemented on her mind.

At first he'd looked so...*disappointed*. That hadn't hurt her, not in the sense that she felt she wasn't the one he'd wanted. Leif, despite the fact that he didn't know how to communicate it, wanted his father to be there. Because of a set of circumstances that seemed to be out against them, Austin hadn't been there.

Leif had only looked that way for a moment before the relief had clearly hit him. At least he was happy to see her. The black eye had jolted her, but she'd pushed through, demanding to know what had happened and what would be done with the other boys. Bullying was not to be tolerated. Violence was not to be tolerated.

Leif had learned a lesson, and she'd be damned if those other boys didn't learn one as well. The school had been on her side, but they needed Austin as well. He'd be there for the next meeting; she was certain of it. No amount of dead phones and odd occurrences would keep him away from Leif.

From her, however? Well, that was another matter altogether.

The look in his eyes when she'd told him how she'd gone instead...

God, she wasn't sure she'd ever get that out of her brain.

It wasn't rational for him to be jealous of her for how Leif connected with her so quickly, but that didn't make it any less of a valid response. She knew something was bothering him, yet she hadn't been able to fix it.

Just as he'd been angry at her and the situation, she'd also been just as angry. So she lashed out and walked away, determined not to let Austin dig into her like he had before. He might have had second thoughts and regretted the way he treated her, but she was right in that she needed a night apart.

Damn it, though, it had been tough.

She hadn't slept without him in a month, and his side of the bed had been so cold. Her apartment felt barren and small, empty without his presence. Empty without the heat and care that came from Austin being who he was.

Although she'd told him it was only for a night, she was afraid it might be more. They hadn't parted on good terms, and she wasn't sure how he'd react to seeing her again.

Frankly, she wasn't sure how *she* would react at seeing *him* again.

They'd fought before, sure. Both of them were strongly opinionated, and it was only a matter of time before they clashed, but this one...this one was big. This wasn't something that could be brushed under the rug and forgotten. In fact, she wasn't even sure how to talk about it. Throwing a secret love child into a situation would never end up on an easy road. The rough and tumble paths to find a way to live with Leif and find out how Austin and Sierra could have a future seemed almost overwhelming to her.

They'd taken Leif in without a second thought, and now they were going to have to learn to find a way to cope with it. Letting the state have him had never been an option to Austin, and it sure hadn't been to her, but having him blend into Austin's family at the same time Sierra was trying to find a way to do the same wasn't making things easy.

She and Austin needed to talk.

Well, that was the understatement of the year right there.

"Miss? Miss? Does this come in purple?"

Sierra blinked then shook her head, trying to clear it. Her customer took the movement as a no to the question and pinched her lips.

"Well, if you don't have the color I desire, I guess I will go to another store. You have every other color here but the one I want."

"Oh, I'm sorry, yes, we have purple in the back I believe. Someone must have bought the other one I had laid out this morning."

"Then why did you shake your head?" the woman demanded. Sierra's temple started to pulse loudly.

"I was clearing my thoughts, I'm sorry. Let me go get that for you."

"She tells me you're the owner," the customer said, pointing over at Becky. "If you're going to sit and daydream all day, I think you might need another job."

Apparently this woman had no problem in voicing her opinions and kicking her while she was down.

"I'm so sorry. Let me get that scarf for you. I will be right back."

The woman pursed her lips even harder. "Do so. Then we'll see if I even want it. I have important things to do today, dear, so be quick about it."

Dear Lord, that woman reminded her of Marsha in so many ways it was a bit jarring. Sierra had never been good enough, pretty enough, fast enough, and classy enough for Marsha's precious, precious baby boy.

Now Sierra couldn't be punished enough for it.

Wow. Where had that come from? She'd done her best not to think about her ex's parents too hard, knowing there was nothing she could do about them until the next step was taken legally. However, they were always in the back of her mind, haunting her like the ghost of their son. If experience told her anything, it was to get that woman what she wanted and send her on her way as quickly as possible. It was impossible to please everyone, and pursed lips would never unclench unless people went a bit crazy.

Sierra quickly got the scarf and gave it to the woman, who sniffed then made her way to Becky, purchase in hand. Apparently she wanted the scarf more than she wanted to belittle the owner. Well, that was good for her bank account anyway.

As soon as the woman left, Becky hurried to Sierra's side. "Dear God, that woman was something."

Sierra shook her head, making sure no one was in the shop. They were in a lull since it was right before they were closing, but they could never be too careful.

"Something is a decent word for it," she said finally as she went behind the counter to start the closing-out process.

"I would have said something worse, but I was afraid she'd be able to hear me through the glass across the street. You never know with those types."

Sierra nodded, her mind on the task in front of her so she wouldn't have to think too hard on what her next step was that night: Austin or being alone.

Walking out and not calling for a day wasn't the most mature response, she knew that, but it had been the only thing she could do then. The look on Austin's face when he'd heard the whole story was enough to break her all over again. She didn't want to see it again. Having him apologize and say he would do better wouldn't be enough. Things would have to change, but it wasn't as if they hadn't been trying to make things better in the first place. It was just a hard and awkward situation that needed time to settle. However, that didn't mean Sierra wanted to be the emotional punching bag when things went wrong.

That would have to change.

She was already the outlet for pain, grief, and rage for Marsha and Todd. She couldn't be for Austin when he had issues communicating with his son.

"Hey, what's wrong, honey?" Becky asked as she switched the sign to closed.

"Nothing, I'm just a bit tired."

"Well, yeah, you opened today and refused to leave. So go now. I can finish up closing the store and doing everything that needs to be done. You should have left hours ago, but you seemed to need to stay busy."

To her horror, tears fill her eyes, and Sierra blinked quickly.

"Honey, tell me what's wrong."

She shook her head. "Nothing."

"You're lying, but if you don't want to talk about it yet, I understand. Just know I'm here for you. Go see Hailey if you need to talk to someone and I'm not the right one. I would have said Austin, but from that look on your face and the fact that you didn't do lunch with him today, he might be the center of whatever issues you have going on."

Sierra wiped her eyes and nodded. "Thanks, Becky. I'll go home and get some rest. I think I'm just tired."

"I can handle Eden, Sierra. It's what you pay me to do. I won't let your baby fall to ruin. I might throw a large rave here tonight, but that's another story altogether."

She laughed, just as Becky must have intended, and then went to get her purse. She'd been on her feet for over twelve hours, and she could feel it in every step now that she let herself feel in the first place.

"Good night, love," Becky called, and Sierra waved, making her way to her car behind Montgomery Ink. She refused to look inside just in case Austin was there. Or Maya. Or Sloane. Or Callie. Anyone that had seen her walk out of the shop the day before or could know about it.

By the time she got to her car and started up the highway, she knew what she needed to do. Austin's home was farther away, but it was where she needed to be. The night before she hadn't been able to sleep without his presence, and she didn't want to do that again. Running away from her problems was not the answer, and she would face them with her chin held high, darn it.

She pulled into Austin's driveway and got out of the car, her hands shaking. Austin had given her a key as soon as Leif moved in, the significance of that action paling in comparison to her taking care of his son.

She set her purse down on the bookshelf that stood in the foyer and took a deep breath. No one was home, the silence of the house deafening. Nothing had changed since she'd been there last. In fact, it was as if she'd never left, but something was...off. She didn't feel like she quite fit in anymore. Leif's shoes were by the fireplace, haphazardly thrown off and near a pile of books he must have been reading. Austin's leather bracelet that he switched out for his metal one every once in a while was on the coffee table next to his tablet, sketchpad, and pencils. There were dirty breakfast dishes in the kitchen sink and crumbs on the counter.

That morning had been the first one where Austin had to get Leif ready for school on his own. She hated herself for not being there to see Leif off the day after he'd gotten in a fight. With all her own personal issues, she'd let him down. She *knew* that. She hadn't even bothered to say goodbye to him because if she'd waited around long enough to do so, she wouldn't have been able to leave his father even for the night.

She was weak, and she knew it.

"Sierra?"

She turned on her heel, her hand going over her racing heart. "Austin," she gasped.

He stood in the foyer by the door to the garage, his keys in his hand, his eyes full of pain. After staring at her for what seemed like an eternity, he cleared his throat. "Hey, Legs," he said, his voice falsely calm, "I was just coming home to grab a bag and head to your place."

She licked her lips. "My place?"

Austin set his keys on the shelf then took two powerful steps toward her. His hand tangled in her hair, pulling her head back so she met his eyes.

"I'm so fucking sorry, Sierra. I shouldn't have reacted like that. I shouldn't have taken out my frustrations on you."

"No, you shouldn't have." He might look sexy with that beard of his and the intensity in his eyes, but she couldn't walk away from what had happened. Not fully. It wouldn't do either of them any good.

"I can't believe I got jealous of you and Leif. Because that's what it was. It was petty jealousy because my son would rather go to you."

She shook her head. "You didn't see his face when I walked in, Austin. He wanted you there. He doesn't pick me over you. He just doesn't know how to tell you he wants you. Just like you don't know how to do the same to him."

He looked like he'd been struck at her words, but he nodded. "I...I don't know what to do, but I do know that I want you by my side when I do it."

Her heart lurched.

"You're mine. You get that? I was an asshole and scared about Leif, and I fucked us up. You had every right to leave me in the shop alone with my own troubles yesterday, but sleeping without you last night? Baby, that was horrible. I don't want to do that again. You get me?"

"I get you," she whispered. "But that's not the end of it. Do you get *me*?"

Austin sighed, moving close to rest his lips on her forehead. "I know. I know, baby."

Something inside her relaxed, and she leaned into his touch. They might not have fixed everything, nor had they said everything they needed to say, but she was in his arms, and that was a step forward.

"Where's Leif?" she asked after they stood there a few minutes in silence.

"At Meghan's. He wanted to stay with his cousins...and I wanted to be with you. To talk with you. To just be."

She pulled back slightly so she could look into his eyes. "I'm glad you're here. I...I just need you."

She couldn't say her true feelings out loud, not right then. Not when she might have trusted him with her body, but her heart was fearful of what was going on inside his head.

He collared her throat, and she sucked in a breath, her body shaking in anticipation. "I want you in my bed, but tonight isn't about sex. It's about you and me talking and just being ourselves."

She nodded, even though the disappointment of not having him inside her crashed into her. She wanted to hear his voice, feel his beard on her neck as he hugged her hard. He held her then, picking her up and cradling her to his chest. They laid in bed fully dressed, their legs entwined as they spoke of their days, starting with the small things and just listening to one another.

The major decisions would come and the challenges of being with a man who had a son he'd never met before would find their paths. Right then, though, her worries were voiced, and she could breathe again. It wouldn't be easy, but she had Austin's voice, his touch, and his body.

She just needed his heart.

CHAPTER TWENTY-THREE

Shea paced Griffin's living room, running her hands through her hair as she did so. They were leaving Denver in three days to head back home, and yet she didn't feel like she was ready. In fact, she felt like everything had taken a turn for the worse in her heart, rather than the actual reason they had come north in the first place.

Shep's uncle was doing okay, but not great and nowhere near out of the woods yet, but alive and breathing. That counted for something when cancer was involved. She'd met Shep's family and friends and had been welcomed with open arms.

If anything, that made what was going on within her even worse.

She had a clear example now of what a family was *supposed* to be rather than the farce she'd lived with. Her mother had attacked and emotionally abused her for her entire life while her father had cheated on his family and had ignored Shea since she was a baby.

Baby.

Damn it. She couldn't think about that. She couldn't think about what was going on within her while there were more important things. She was being stupid and silly, and yet she couldn't stop it. Shep was pulling away day by day because she wasn't telling him what was going on inside her head and body, yet she couldn't find the courage to actually tell him.

Maybe once they got back to New Orleans, everything would be okay and she'd be back to normal. That had to be the answer because, right then, she couldn't think about what was going on. She couldn't make decisions, and that was so unlike her. She'd spent her life doing what was expected her and following the path that others laid for her before she ventured out on her own. First with her job, then with leaving her ex—the same man her mother had chosen for her. Then Shea wanted a tattoo and found Shep.

Her happily ever after was supposed to be all roses and rainbows now.

Not pain, heartache, and nervousness.

"Shea?"

She turned on her heel quickly, almost falling in her haste. Shep put out a hand and held her steady, that ever-present worry in his gaze.

"You startled me." And she couldn't bear to look at him and keep this secret any longer.

"I can see that. Tell me what's wrong, Shea. You're killing me here. What did I do wrong? How can I fix it? I love you so fucking much, and you're pulling away from me. Please. Please tell me what's wrong."

Oh God, she was doing this all wrong. She was ruining something perfect because she was scared. Scared that she'd ruin it all.

"I...I..."

He cupped her face, kissing her softly. She leaned into him, letting his taste settle on her tongue. He anchored her. He was her first love, her only love, and she needed to be honest and open. She shouldn't be afraid of him; she wasn't.

No, she was afraid of herself.

"Tell me, Shea."

"We're having a baby," she blurted out, her body shaking. The relief that should have come from telling him what she'd kept secret for far too long never came. Instead, she wanted to throw up, and she didn't think that came from morning sickness.

Shep opened his mouth two or three times like a fish out of water then grinned. "A baby?" He picked her up, twirling her around the room. She clung to his shoulders, wanting to run away rather than search inside herself.

"We're having a baby! Oh god, Shea. I'm so fucking happy about this. All this time you were worried we were having a baby? That's it?" His eyes widened. "Is something wrong? Do we need to go to the doctor? Let me get my keys." He set her down like she was fine china then patted his chest and pockets looking for his keys. "Shouldn't you be sitting down? Do you want water? Or how about crackers? How are you feeling?"

The way he acted should have been cute. Instead, she could hear only her mother in her head. Her mother who had told her that she'd never amount to anything. Who had belittled her for her entire life, making her want to run away or find another more permanent end to the way things had been.

Shep had saved her life right then, and she couldn't think of how to stop the pattern.

To stop the torment that had plagued her for decades.

Shep cupped her face again, and she blinked back tears. "What's wrong, Shea? You're not speaking, and you look scared. You're pale, baby. Tell me what's wrong so I can fix it."

She hiccupped a sob then pulled away. "You can't fix it, Shep. I'm having a child. A baby."

Shep frowned. "I know, Shea. You just said it." His face went carefully blank. "Do you not want this child?"

The idea of not having this baby made her body turn to ice. The implication of his words forced her to say what she was thinking, rather than going around it.

"I...I want this baby. I've always wanted *our* baby, Shep. But...but you don't understand."

"I won't understand until you tell me, Shea. I don't know why you hid it from me, why you were so scared to tell me."

"If I told you, then it would be real," she whispered.

"And what is so wrong with it being real? We love each other, and we had said we wanted children."

She remembered them talking, but when they'd brought it up, it had seemed like a dream. Now it was a reality. A reality she wasn't prepared for. She didn't have the life experiences needed to be a good mother. She saw the way Shep's cousin Meghan cared for her babies, how Marie cared for her grown children.

Shea had never had that before.

How was she sure she wouldn't end up like her mother?

"We did this so fast, Shep."

Her husband's face set to stone. "Yes. We did. We *both* decided to marry quickly without a wedding. We *both* decided to have me go bare within you and deal with what happened if the Pill alone didn't work. Now tell me why you're so scared because you need to be clear."

"I don't want to turn into my mother."

Shep's face softened, and he took a step toward her. She pulled back, but he didn't let her stay away. Instead, he tugged her close, crushing her to his chest. He cupped her face, kissing her hard.

"You silly, thoughtful woman. I fucking love you."

Irritation warred with anger in her veins. "Don't call my fears silly, Shep. You don't understand. You have this perfect family. What do I have?"

"Me."

Her heart thudded, and she sighed. "Shep..."

"No. You'll listen to me now. You're scared you'll end up like you're mother? Bullshit. You stood up for yourself long before I came along and grew a backbone. You've seen what damage your mother did and know that's not how to raise a family. Fuck, you have my family to show you how to do it. Not saying we're perfect because God knows we're crazy assholes some days, but we aren't cruel. You are going to be a wonderful mother."

Tears poured down her cheeks, and she sank into him. She might know his words were right in her mind, but her heart was another matter.

"You have me by your side. I'm not going to turn into your father. I'm going to be by your side every step of the way. I'm going to watch you grow round with our child then change diapers and help our baby take his or her first steps. I'm going to let our child know that, no matter their choices, we will be by their side. They don't need to conform to our expectations but, rather, find out who they are on their own. Now kiss me, Shea. Kiss me then tell me you love me."

She kissed him softly, her eyes closed as her body finally relaxed. "I love you," she whispered. "I'm an idiot."

"Well, yes, but you're adorable when you're an idiot."

She punched him in the shoulder. Hard. "Patronizing much?"

"You love me. Now, I know we're in the middle of something else right now travel- and life-wise, but I need to tell you I'm so fucking happy we're having this kid. If she's a girl, we might need to lock her away from all boys until she's sixty, but that's just because I know boys. If he's a boy, well, we might need to lock him up as well since I know my brothers."

She snorted, hugging him around his middle. She'd kept the idea of the baby from him for a month because she'd been scared about her own reaction, not his. That had been selfish and horrible, but she couldn't go back and fix it.

She had another seven months to prove to him that she could do this. Prove to herself. With Shep by her side, she could do it. There was no other option.

"You're thinking hard again," he said as he rubbed her back, his hand dipping lower until she gasped into him.

"I'm sorry for not telling you."

"I'm sorry you felt you needed to deal with everything on your own. But that's not the important thing anymore."

"What is then?" she asked on a gasp as he kissed the side of her neck.

"The important thing is we're going to have a baby...and Griffin won't be home for hours."

She rocked into him, closing her eyes, and he cupped her face with his magic hands. "Whatever shall we do?"

Shep pulled back, grinning. "Oh, I think we can come up with something."

Shea stood on her tiptoes and kissed his chin. "Show me."

"Always, Shea. Always."

CHAPTER TWENTY-FOUR

"**I**f you keep staring at the nail rather than pounding it in, you'll be here for hours, man," Austin said from Decker's side, chuckling under his breath.

Decker growled then cursed as he slammed his thumb with the damn hammer. "Seriously, dude? You're going to distract me while I'm fixing the freaking hole in your wall?"

"You talk to me while I'm doing a tattoo, so I don't know what your problem is," Austin said casually as he meandered back to his stool. Griffin sat in the chair, a grin on his face.

"Let's keep the distracting of Austin on the low side, shall we?" Griffin teased. "He does have a needle in my skin after all."

"You wouldn't have this problem if I was doing it," Maya said as she walked toward them.

Decker laughed at the familiar complaint. Maya and Austin were proprietary when it came to the Montgomery family ink. Come to think of it, they acted the same way about his ink as well.

Kind of nice.

"You have one side, Maya," Griffin said, his voice calm even as Austin worked on his sleeve, doing the shading that sometimes hurt like a bitch. "Austin gets the other. Stop complaining that it's his turn."

Maya rolled her eyes even as she smiled. "Shut up."

"You first."

Ah, siblings. He was an only child and thankful for it. Though he'd been raised with the Montgomerys off and on during his childhood, when he went back to his birthplace, he was alone.

That was the way it had always been, and now that he was older, that was the way it would be. He wasn't a Montgomery, and no amount of ink or wishing would make that true.

He cleared his throat, shaking his head before he got back to work. He needed to keep his mind on task instead of thinking about what was coming, what would never change. The churning in his gut didn't make it easy, but he'd deal with it.

He had to.

Decker went back to work, trying to finish up so he could get back to his place and just be alone. He had come back to Denver, but he honestly didn't know if he could handle all the Montgomerys all at once *again*.

The door opened, and he sighed. Hopefully it would be a customer, rather than another Montgomery. He didn't know if he could deal with more family right then.

"Hey, family," Miranda Montgomery said as she walked in. He turned quickly, caught by her smile and the way she winked at her brother.

Decker froze, his body tight like a spring, and he held back a curse. His dick pressed against the zipper of his jeans, and he wanted to run the fuck away.

He couldn't get a hard-on for Griffin's little sister.

No fucking way.

She was Miranda. Little Miranda who used to chase him around the backyard.

She wasn't supposed to get his dick hard.

The object of his arousal and mortification turned to him and smiled. His dick perked up even more.

Traitor.

"Hey you. I didn't know you'd be here."

He blinked then cleared his throat. "I'm not. Here I mean."

Brilliant, Decker. Fucking brilliant.

She snorted as the rest of her family laughed. "Um, Decker, honey. You're here."

He shook his head, clearing his thoughts. Or at least trying to. "I just meant I'm leaving."

Austin stood up and frowned. "You're not done yet. What's up, Deck?"

Decker quickly gathered up his things. "I'll come back tomorrow and finish up. It needs to dry, and I didn't bring the last of the tools I need."

Austin's look told him he clearly didn't believe him, but Decker needed to get out of there. Fast.

"Okay, whatever. Thanks for coming and doing at least half of it."

Decker nodded then took his tools and ran, lifting his chin at the others as he scurried out the door, his toolbox in front of his crotch. The last thing he needed was for Miranda's big brothers to see his hard-on. He'd seen the look of surprise on Miranda's face as he left, and he didn't want to think about it.

Fuck. She was his best friend's little sister.

So off limits.

He just needed to get laid. As he put his things in the truck, he got out his phone. When the person on the other line picked up, he tensed, trying to clear his thoughts of the Montgomery he shouldn't want and could never have.

"Colleen, hey, you free tonight?"

Colleen was safe. Pretty. And not Miranda Montgomery. The perfect combination.

****

Sierra locked up Eden and made her way to her car. It had been a long day of customers who hadn't known what they wanted, blaming her and the girls for it. During that time, the customers from hell made their opinions known. Often.

All she really wanted to do was to go home—Austin's place—and relax. She didn't know when she'd begun to think of Austin's place as home, rather than her small apartment in Edgewater, but she'd take it. Things were going well for them. Really well. She and Austin talked and worked with Leif together. They were happy, and she was ready to actually tell him her feelings.

She loved him more than anything, and she wanted a future.

A future she never thought she'd have again.

There was that tingling in the back of her mind that told her that her ex's parents would still be there, but she wouldn't be alone in facing them this time.

Her phone rang as she started on the highway, and she answered using her car's Bluetooth. "Hello?"

"Sierra, it's Rodney."

Speak of the devil.

Her hands clenched the steering wheel, and she swallowed hard. "Hi, Rodney. What's going on?" She took the next exit and pulled off to the side of the road. There was a field around her since she'd gone north to Austin's place, but it was safer than being at the wheel right then.

"They threw out the case, Sierra. It's over. For real this time. Marsha and Todd don't have a leg to stand on."

Sierra blinked, and she turned off the car but kept the battery on so her phone would still work. "What?" She couldn't believe it. She must have misheard.

"Sierra. It's over. The case was thrown out with prejudice, and this was their last chance. They can't come at you again. You're free to live your life the way you want to without having to look over your shoulder.

"Seriously?" she asked, her words raspy. After all these years, it was over?

"Seriously. Go home to Austin and celebrate. You won't have this shadow over you anymore."

Tears streaked her cheeks, and she bowed her head. "Thank you, thank you so much. God."

"You're welcome, Sierra. Live your life."

After saying goodbye, he hung up, and she sat there, her body shaking.

She was free. Jason's parents couldn't hurt her anymore. She could love Austin freely and not worry about lawsuits and the past that wouldn't take its claws out of her.

She was free.

Headlights blinded her from the driver's side, and she turned, only to see a car coming right at her. She held up her hands, her mouth opened in a scream before the sound of crushing metal filled her ears. The darkness came over her as she thought of Austin one last time.

****

Austin ran his hands through his hair and sighed. "I hate math sometimes," he mumbled, and Leif snickered at his side. "Don't laugh. This is your homework after all."

"Math sucks," his son agreed.

He winced. Sierra wouldn't like him teaching Leif to hate subjects in school. The fact that he thought of Sierra in a parenting position again scared him a bit, but he was working on it. Hell, the fact that *he* was a parent scared him.

"Math doesn't suck. It's just not the most entertaining thing most times."

Leif raised a brow in a gesture so like Austin's that he blinked. Damn, Leif looked just like what Austin had always pictured his son might look like. The DNA test might have been needed for the courts, but none of the Montgomerys had thought twice about accepting him into their fold.

He looked just like a Montgomery.

"Sure, Austin. Whatever you say."

Austin held back the hurt at Leif still calling him Austin rather than Dad, but beggars couldn't be choosers. They hadn't known each other that long after all.

His phone rang, and he picked up, seeing an unknown number on the readout. "Hello?"

"Austin Montgomery?"

A chill ran down his spine, and he gripped the table. "Yes? This is Austin Montgomery."

"This is Denver Medical. We have a Sierra Elder here."

The floor fell out from under him, and he sank back into his chair. He felt small hands on his arm and looked over to see Leif standing, his eyes wide.

"What happened? Is she okay? Where are you located? I'm coming there."

"Mr. Montgomery, take a breath. I can't tell you her condition or the circumstances over the phone as you aren't family, but she requested we call you so you can come here." She rattled off the location, and Austin wrote it down on the top of Leif's homework, the only piece of paper near him.

"I'm coming. Tell her..." *I love her.* "Tell her I'll be right there."

He hung up and stood on shaky legs.

"What's going on?" Leif asked, his eyes filling with tears.

Shit. What was he going to do about the kid? Could he call his family and have them watch him?

"Sierra's in the hospital." There. He was honest.

Leif's lower lip wobbled. "What happened?"

"I don't know. They wouldn't tell me. I'm heading there now to see her." He picked up his phone. "I'll call Meghan to come and pick you up or I'll drop you off."

"No. I want to see Sierra too. Don't leave me."

Austin sucked in a breath then awkwardly patted Leif's shoulder. "Okay then. We'll go." There was no way he could deal with even hands-free calling with Leif in the back seat. He was too shaky as it was. "Grab what you need and let's go."

Leif scrambled off the chair and ran to the back of the house while Austin ran a hand over his hair. The doctor or nurse or whatever had refused to tell him what was going on. He got the legalities of that, but shit, couldn't they have given him a clue?

Austin grabbed his wallet and phone, texting Wes quickly and telling him to meet him with the family at the hospital. It seemed like a better deal than calling and having to talk to people. He ended the text with "don't call" since he would be driving.

Wes texted back right away saying he'd be there with the crew.

That was the Montgomerys. There, no matter what.

Leif ran back out with a Kindle in his hands and his shoes on his feet.

"What's with the Kindle?" Austin asked as he went into the garage, Leif on his trail.

"It's Sierra's. She was reading it and left it here last night."

Austin swallowed hard, nodding. That kid loved Sierra so much; that much was clear. God, she had to be okay. She had to.

He drove as fast as he could without endangering his precious cargo and made it to the hospital, parking in the lot and running toward the emergency room, gripping Leif's hand so he wouldn't lose him. Jesus, his life had changed so much since Sierra had first walked into the shop. He couldn't lose it all in one fell swoop.

When he got to the front desk, he was shaking alongside Leif. "I'm looking for Sierra Elder."

The woman nodded then raised a brow. "Are you family?"

"She's my family," he said instantly. It was true, just not legal. "I'm Austin Montgomery. You guys called me."

She nodded again then started clicking on the computer. "You're clear to come in." She looked down at Leif. "I'm afraid he isn't."

He knew the woman was just doing her job, but holy hell, he wanted to push past her. "This is my son. He's coming with me. Tell me where Sierra is."

"Don't get a nasty tone with me, young man. I'm only following the law."

"Judy, I can handle this," a man in a white coat said as he walked toward them. Judy huffed then went back to her computer.

"Where's Sierra?"

"I'm Dr. Michaels, Sierra's doctor." He held out a hand, and Austin impatiently shook it. "Sierra gave us permission to tell you her condition in person, and since he is your son, you're both welcome to come on back."

Austin glared at Judy then walked beside Dr. Michaels. Leif gripped his hand hard, and he pulled him closer.

"What happened?" he asked.

"She was involved in a hit and run accident. The other car hit the driver's side, but in the back rather than the front. The impact jarred her, and she had a few cuts and bruises and a mild concussion. However, since she wasn't moving, and the other car wasn't going that fast, the airbags were enough to keep her from serious harm."

Austin froze, clenching his free fist. "But she's going to be okay?"

The doctor nodded. "Yes. She's very lucky."

"And you said it was a hit and run? Did they find the bastard that did this?"

He nodded. "Yes. It was a woman. Apparently, she is the mother of Sierra's late fiancé. That's all I know, but you'll be able to talk to Sierra right away. She's a little tired, but other than that, she should be fine."

Fuck. Marsha had done this? And just where was Todd? Holy fuck, that family was insane.

"She's right in there, Mr. Montgomery."

Austin nodded absently as Dr. Michaels walked away.

"She's really okay?" Leif asked, his voice small.

Austin took a deep breath then looked down at his son.

"That's what the doctor says. Let's go see." His entire world was on his arm and in that room. He knew that. It was like a shock to the system. He didn't know what he'd do without her. God, he loved her so fucking much, and it scared him. He wasn't supposed to love someone this much. He didn't know if he could bear to lose her. He had his mind on his son and his father, two major life changes recently, and now he had the love of his life in a hospital bed.

It was just too goddamn much.

He took a step into the room and froze. Sierra lay on the bed, her hair tangled around her. Her eyes were open but turned the other way. She had cuts and bruises on her face and arms and he was sure in other places that were hidden by the hospital gown.

"Sierra," Leif said through tears then ran to her side. He stopped right at the edge of the bed, his hand out but not moving closer, as if afraid to touch her.

She turned toward him, a small smile on her face. "Hey, big guy."

"Are you okay?" Leif asked softly.

"Yeah, just a little banged up. I get to go home tomorrow. Don't be scared, okay, honey?"

Leif cried then, lowering his head to the side of her bed. "Okay," he whispered through tears.

Austin choked back his own tears. He hadn't moved from his spot near the door, not knowing if he could walk closer. The love of his life was helpless in that bed, and yet he couldn't stop thinking about what could have happened if the car had been moving faster or if it had hit her at another angle.

He'd almost lost one of the most precious things in the world, and he hadn't been there.

What kind of man was he?

Sierra ran a hand over Leif's back, murmuring to him. She met Austin's gaze, and what he found there scared him.

There wasn't love in those eyes.

No, they were blank.

Nothing.

"Austin."

He turned on his heel to see Maya and Jake in the doorway, Maya's eyes wide. "I'm here. It took sneaking in, but we're here." Her gaze moved to Sierra. "Hey you. How are you?"

Sierra looked stricken, and he didn't know what to do.

"I'm fine," the love of his life croaked. "Do you think you can take Leif out of the room for a moment? I need to talk to Austin."

Maya gave him a look then took a sniffling Leif toward the door. Before he walked away completely, he ran a hand over his son's hair then sighed as he was left alone in the room with Sierra.

"Baby, I'm so sorry this happened."

Sierra raised her chin, tears filling her eyes. "Me too. Marsha can't hurt me anymore though."

"That's not the point. You almost died, and I wasn't there."

"No, you weren't. But you weren't supposed to be."

Something slashed across his heart, and he moved toward her, needing her touch.

She held out a hand. "You and Leif could have easily been in that car. My past could have killed you. I can't let that happen. Marsha might be in jail, but Todd is still out there. I can't put you in danger. It's all too much, and I can't do this anymore. I shouldn't have taken a chance because it hurts. It hurts so much, Austin. Just get out. Please. Just please go. I don't know what to do and having you here...it messes me up. I love you, Austin, but I can't do it."

The first time she said she loved him and she was pushing him away. Pushing him away, and yet he wasn't fighting back.

Why wasn't he fighting back?

"Sierra..."

"Go, Austin. Please."

"I'm not leaving."

"Yes. Yes you are. We aren't a good fit, and you know it. You need to be with your father and son, and I can't deal with it all. It's not safe, and it's not enough. Just leave me alone."

He nodded then turned away, leaving her broken and bruised in her room. Why wasn't he staying? Why wasn't he saying anything? He knew he'd fallen for her too hard, too fast, but fuck, why was he leaving?

He was a fucking coward, but he was letting her push him away. He made his way toward the waiting room where Maya and Jake sat with Leif. His sister raised a brow, and he shook his head. He couldn't deal with the questions right then. His world was falling down around him, and he let it.

403

He needed to take a step back and think. He couldn't do that with people crowding him.

"We're heading home. Sierra needs rest." The words were hollow, and the questions in Maya's eyes made him want to scream.

"Why can't we stay?" Leif asked.

"Because we need to go," Austin said as he ran a hand over his face.

"Can we come tomorrow?"

"I don't think so, buddy."

Maya gasped, and Austin held back a curse.

"Why not?"

"We just need to go, okay?" He would have raised his voice, but he couldn't come up with the energy.

"Austin," Maya whispered.

"Not now, okay?"

He took Leif's hand and left his woman in the hospital. She'd begged him, but he hadn't fought hard enough.

Why?

That's all Austin could say.

Why?

CHAPTER TWENTY-FIVE

Austin needed a drink. It had been less than two days since he'd made the biggest mistake of his life and walked out of Sierra's hospital room. She'd told him to go, and he'd listened. Since when did he do exactly what she told him to?

It was the other way. At least in the bedroom. He was her Dominant. Her support. And yet he'd failed her. Holy *fuck* how he'd failed her.

He'd let her set the rules and hadn't taken care of her like he should have. What kind of man did that make him?

She'd been scared. Terrified. Just as he was. And he'd walked away. There was no amount of groveling that could make up for that, but he had to find a way.

"Dad?"

Austin froze then turned around to see Leif standing behind him, a frown on his face. He wanted to jump up and throw his arms around his son at the sound of Dad from the little boy's lips, but he refrained. He wouldn't make a big deal out of it; he'd let Leif think this was normal and okay, rather than shouting to the rooftops like he wanted to.

"Yeah, Leif?"

"When are we going to go get Sierra?"

Austin crouched down so he was at Leif's eye level. "You want me to get Sierra?"

Leif rolled his eyes. "Of course I do. She's our family. I know my mom isn't coming back, but you're my dad. You're family. And since you both love each other, you should be together. I don't know if I'll ever call her mom, but she takes care of me. You know? She loves me, and I love her. I don't want her to leave. I want to make sure she's okay. Can you do that? Can you make sure she knows she can come home? Just fix it. Okay?"

Out of the mouth of babes.

Austin cupped his son's head. "I'll bring her home, Leif. Do you want her to stay here forever? Is that what you have in mind?" He and Leif were a unit now. He couldn't make a decision that big without him.

"Just marry her, already. Okay? I like her a lot. She's pretty, and she smells nice."

"That's true." Marriage? Yeah. He was ready for that. He'd been ready but hadn't been able to think past his own worries to actually see it. "I just hope she takes me back."

Leif put his hand on Austin's beard. "She will. She loves you. Old people are just scared sometimes about saying it. It's okay. I'll help."

Austin let the old people comment pass and swallowed hard. "I love you, Leif. You're my son, and I'm so happy you're in my life."

Leif smiled. "I love you too, Dad. Now go get Sierra."

Austin crushed Leif to him, inhaling that little boy scent. Only he wasn't so little anymore. "I'll drop you off at Maya's. She and Jake are having an Xbox tournament."

"Sounds good to me. I'm packed already." He blushed, and Austin raised a brow. "Aunt Maya is ready for me. She said some curse words about you getting your butt in gear."

He chuckled then messed up Leif's hair. "Your Aunt Maya needs to watch her language around you."

"That's what she said about you."

"True. Okay, let's get going."

"So you can bring Sierra back."

"I hope."

By the time he left Leif at Maya's house, darkness had settled over the mountains, and he sat in his car in front of Sierra's apartment. He never should have let her get her way. He should have fought harder.

Fuck. He didn't know what to say, but staying out in his car while people walking by stared at him wasn't the way to go about it. He got out of his car, made his way to her door, and knocked softly. He heard her shuffle to the door, and then she opened it.

She stood there, her hair in a ponytail, her eyes full of sadness. Bruises marred her arms and legs, and he sucked in a breath.

"Oh, baby, I'm so sorry you're hurt."

Sierra took a step back, and he walked in. She closed the door behind him, and he put his hands in his pockets. He wanted to hold her close and never let her go. Right then he didn't think that was the best thing for either of them. They needed to talk first.

"Why are you here, Austin?" Sierra asked, her voice weary.

"I love you, Sierra. I love you more than my next breath. I need you in my life. I never should have let you push me away. I was so fucking scared that you got hurt, and then I was more worried about how my own life was changing rather than dealing with what was in front of me. I never should have left. You're my everything. I want you in my life, Sierra. I want you to grow old with me. Help me raise Leif. I want to marry you and have you take my name. I want to have babies with you and watch them grow up. I want to see you in my family and have you by my side as we deal with my father's illness. You are my future, and I should have seen that clearer. Don't leave me. Don't let me leave. Don't force me out. I love you. Please. Please let me stay."

Sierra's cheeks were wet with tears even as she shook her head. His body felt like he'd been slammed into a wall, and he took two steps toward her. He cupped her face, brushing her lips with his own.

"I love you Sierra. Whatever happens with Todd in the future will happen with me by your side. You don't need to fear for me. You don't need to fear for Leif. We're not letting you go."

Sierra hiccupped a sob. "They found Todd. He'd killed himself, Austin. It's over."

Stunned, Austin blinked. "You're safe?"

She nodded, sobbing into him. "Safe, but not whole. I shouldn't have pushed you away, but I was so scared."

"I was scared too. So scared, I *let* you push me away. We don't get to do that again, Sierra. We're in it for the rest of our lives. I want you to marry me. I want you in my life, and I want you to be mine in the bedroom. I want you to trust me with your heart, your body, and your soul. I never want to ask you again to kneel for me because I want you to do it on your own. I want you to trust me with every fiber of your being to care for you and nurture what we have until it grows into what I know it promises to be."

"Oh, Austin."

"Marry me, Sierra."

"Yes. Yes, I'll marry you."

He crushed his mouth to hers, knowing this was the first taste of their forever. His hand went to her hair, and she winced.

"Fuck. You're too hurt for what I want to do to you, baby." He narrowed his eyes. "I want to kill them for hurting you, Legs."

She cupped his face, and he leaned into her touch. "It's over, Austin. And while tonight we might not be able to go fully into some things, we can make love. We can do it softly."

His cock pressed against her belly, and he groaned. "Softly," he whispered.

She led him to the bedroom, and he slowly stripped her down, kissing each bruise and cut as he did so. He sucked her nipples, letting the peaks harden on his tongue, before kissing down her belly to her cunt. When he laid her down on the bed, she tangled her fingers in his hair so he could taste her.

Her sweet taste burst on his tongue as he licked her pussy, lapping up her juices. She moaned, rocking herself onto his face.

"Stay still," he ordered, and she froze. The fact she did so without complaint made him want to push into her right then, filling her with his cock.

Not until she came.

"Austin." She gasped as he pumped two fingers into her. Her channel clamped around them, and he flicked her clit. Her head hit the bed as she came, and he kept licking until she came down from her peak.

He pulled away, stripping quickly, before hovering over her body. "You ready for me, Legs?"

"Of course," she said, her voice thick like honey. "I'm always ready for you."

"Good," he answered as he entered her slowly, his gaze never leaving her eyes. He made love to her slowly, not wanting to hurt her. The sweet ache of her body wrapped around him as he thrust in and out of her made him want to scream her name to the heavens. After they came together, their bodies slick with sweat, he rolled to the side, keeping her with him and his cock still deep within her.

"I love you, Sierra Elder."

"I love you too, Austin Montgomery."

Austin sighed happily. He'd found his future, his life, his woman. No matter what came next he knew he could handle it with Sierra by his side. He was one lucky bastard, and he'd count his lucky stars until the day he died.

Sierra Elder was his.

Finally.

****

Sierra winced as Austin wiped down the area on her side again, the slow buzz of the needle grating. Apparently it was only when the needle was tattooing others that she thought it was sexy. The daisies Austin was inking on her side freaking hurt. Well, not the daisies, but the freaking needle piercing into her skin.

Not that she'd tell him that though. If she looked like she wanted to cry, he might stop, and then she'd have to sit in the chair again.

Okay, so it didn't hurt that bad, but since he had to keep moving her scarred skin around to fully outline the area with daises, it wasn't the most pleasant experience.

"All done, Legs," Austin said, squeezing her thigh. "You did good."

Sierra gave him a strained smile then tried to sit up.

"Wait, baby. Let me show you your ink and let you rest a bit. I know that hurt like a bitch." He leaned closer so only she could hear. "I know you like pain, but only from my palm or a flogger. It's okay."

She winced then closed her eyes, and she kissed him. "It wasn't that bad. Plus I have one more tattoo to get."

Austin raised a brow then smiled broadly. "You're getting the Montgomery Iris?"

"I'm going to be a Montgomery, aren't I? It's tradition."

Austin patted her ass and smiled even wider. "Fuck yeah you're going to be a Montgomery. I can't wait."

"I can't either."

He finished cleaning the area then went over after-care instructions. Luckily she was going home with her artist so he'd be there to help her. She had to admit, the daisies that cascaded around her scars were amazing. They hurt, but she'd wanted to go big for her tattoo, so she couldn't really blame anyone.

Austin cupped her face then sighed. "I'm so glad you came into the shop that morning."

"You were an asshole, but I love you anyway."

"Legs, I'm still an asshole, but I love you too."

"Dear Lord, stop with the mush already," Maya sneered from her corner, though she was smiling.

"Aww, we love you too, Maya!" Sierra joked. Austin chuckled by her side, and she licked her lips.

"So, uh, how long until we can properly test out my flexibility with that tattoo?" she whispered.

Austin's eyes darkened. "Soon, Legs. Soon." He groaned. "You do realize I have a client in, like, thirty minutes, right? I can't ink a dude while I have a hard-on."

She patted his face. "Oh, poor baby. I'm going to Eden and will let you get to it. Leif should be getting out of school in a couple hours, so we can all eat dinner together."

They sounded so normal. Like a family.

The idea made Sierra feel like she'd made the right choice, that she was the luckiest girl in the world.

In fact, she was.

She'd walked into Montgomery Ink all those months ago for a tattoo and had walked out not only with fresh ink, but a son, a future, and a man she was going to spend the rest of her life with.

Talk about lucky.

THE END

A Note from Carrie Ann

Thank you so much for reading **Ink Inspired, Ink Reunited, and Delicate Ink**. I do hope if you liked this story, that you would please leave a review. Not only does a review spread the word to other readers, they let us authors know if you'd like to see more stories like this from us. I love hearing from readers and talking to them when I can. If you want to make sure you know what's coming next from me, you can sign up for my newsletter at www.CarrieAnnRyan.com; follow me on twitter at @CarrieAnnRyan, or like my Facebook page. I also have a Facebook Fan Club where we have trivia, chats, and other goodies. You guys are the reason I get to do what I do and I thank you.

Make sure you're signed up for my MAILING LIST so you can know when the next releases are available as well as find giveaways and FREE READS.

The Montgomery Ink series is an on going series. I hope you get a chance to catch up!

Montgomery Ink:
Book 0.5: Ink Inspired
Book 0.6: Ink Reunited
Book 1: Delicate Ink
The Montgomery Ink Box Set #1: (Contains Books 0.5, 0.6, 1)
Book 1.5 Forever Ink
Book 2: Tempting Boundaries
Book 3: Harder than Words
Book 4: Written in Ink
Book 4.5: Hidden Ink (Coming Jan 2016)
Book 5: Ink Enduring (Coming June 2016)

Want to keep up to date with the next Carrie Ann Ryan Release? Receive Text Alerts easily!
Text CARRIE to 24587

About Carrie Ann and her Books

New York Times and USA Today Bestselling Author Carrie Ann Ryan never thought she'd be a writer. Not really. No, she loved math and science and even went on to graduate school in chemistry. Yes, she read as a kid and devoured teen fiction and Harry Potter, but it wasn't until someone handed her a romance book in her late teens that she realized that there was something out there just for her. When another author suggested she use the voices in her head for good and not evil, The Redwood Pack and all her other stories were born.

Carrie Ann is a bestselling author of over twenty novels and novellas and has so much more on her mind (and on her spreadsheets *grins*) that she isn't planning on giving up her dream anytime soon.

www.CarrieAnnRyan.com

Redwood Pack Series:
Book 1: An Alpha's Path
Book 2: A Taste for a Mate
Book 3: Trinity Bound
Book 3.5: A Night Away
Book 4: Enforcer's Redemption
Book 4.5: Blurred Expectations
Book 4.7: Forgiveness
Book 5: Shattered Emotions
Book 6: Hidden Destiny
Book 6.5: A Beta's Haven
Book 7: Fighting Fate
Book 7.5 Loving the Omega
Book 7.7: The Hunted Heart
Book 8: Wicked Wolf

The Talon Pack (Following the Redwood Pack Series):
Book 1: Tattered Loyalties
Book 2: An Alpha's Choice
Book 3: Mated in Mist (Coming Feb 2016)

The Redwood Pack Volumes:
Redwood Pack Vol 1
Redwood Pack Vol 2
Redwood Pack Vol 3
Redwood Pack Vol 4
Redwood Pack Vol 5
Redwood Pack Vol 6

Montgomery Ink:
Book 0.5: Ink Inspired
Book 0.6: Ink Reunited
Book 1: Delicate Ink
The Montgomery Ink Box Set #1: (Contains Books 0.5, 0.6, 1)
Book 1.5 Forever Ink
Book 2: Tempting Boundaries
Book 3: Harder than Words
Book 4: Written in Ink
Book 4.5: Hidden Ink (Coming Jan 2016)
Book 5: Ink Enduring (Coming Jun 2016)

Dante's Circle Series:
Book 1: Dust of My Wings
Book 2: Her Warriors' Three Wishes
Book 3: An Unlucky Moon
The Dante's Circle Box Set (Contains Books 1-3)
Book 3.5: His Choice
Book 4: Tangled Innocence
Book 5: Fierce Enchantment
Book 6: An Immortal's Song (Coming April 2016)
Book 7: Prowled Darkness (Coming May 2016)

The Branded Pack Series:
(Written with Alexandra Ivy)
Book 1: Stolen and Forgiven
Book 2: Abandoned and Unseen
Book 3: Buried and Shadowed (Coming July 2016)

Holiday, Montana Series:
Book 1: Charmed Spirits
Book 2: Santa's Executive
Book 3: Finding Abigail
The Holiday Montana Box Set (Contains Books 1-3)
Book 4: Her Lucky Love
Book 5: Dreams of Ivory

A Stand Alone Contemporary Romance
Finally Found You

Excerpt: Tempting Boundaries

Next From New York Times Bestselling Author Carrie Ann Ryan's Montgomery Ink Series

There was just something about the scent of a grill, the feel of a cold beer in his hand, and the company of a family that truly loved him that made Decker Kendrick want to relax after a long day's work. If he added in the fact that he could go home and have the woman at his side under him, over him, and all around him, it would be a pretty fantastic way to end the day.

Colleen, his date to the Montgomery family barbeque and engagement party, leaned into him and batted her false eyelashes. He had no idea why she wore them. He thought she looked decent without them. But whatever—it was her body to fake up any way she wanted to. He'd been seeing Colleen off and on for a few months, more often in the past month since he'd called her up, hoping to get his mind off a certain long-legged brunette he shouldn't be thinking about in the first place.

The woman in question hadn't shown up to the party yet, and Decker was grateful. Hard to ignore her and keep her off his mind if she kept popping up everywhere he went. Though that wasn't really fair considering she was part of his family.

More like *he* was part of hers.

He was an honorary Montgomery, and she was the little sister.

Totally not for him.

"Decker? Baby?"

He blinked and looked down at Colleen. Not the woman who haunted his dreams and kept him up late at night. Jesus, he was a bad man. A very, very bad man. Sure, he was keeping it casual with Colleen—something she'd put on the table to begin with—but he shouldn't be thinking about a woman with long legs he couldn't have when he was here with someone else.

That wasn't the kind of guy he wanted to be.

"Colleen?" he answered back, keeping his voice low. He didn't normally bring dates to the Montgomery family gatherings, and as such, he didn't want everyone to hear everything he said. They were all nosy in the we-are-family-and-we-can-be-nosy-if-want-to sort of way, and he'd learned to deal with it. He hadn't planned on bringing her at all, but when she'd called to ask him to dinner, he'd mentioned he had plans, and she'd sort of invited herself along. It hadn't bothered him too much then, but now he felt kind of like an awkward ass about it. Since this was the first time he'd brought Colleen to any type of function with the Montgomerys, he'd been prepared to have the family question the two of them until they pecked them to death.

So far, that hadn't happened, and frankly, that was more telling about what the others in his life thought of the relationship. Their politeness and lack of prodding meant they didn't see a future. Considering Colleen hadn't wanted a future to begin with when it came to her and Decker, that was just fine with him. He didn't see himself marrying the woman anyway. They were friends. Sort of.

"You're thinking too hard." She rubbed the little spot between his eyebrows, and he frowned. She wasn't usually so touchy-feely or attentive. Weird.

He pulled back, uncomfortable with the display of affection—or whatever it was—in front of the family that had taken him in so long ago.

"Just tired. Hauling a total of a half-ton of porcelain up and down stairs all day makes for a long workday. We also punched out our other project the day before. So I'm ready for a nap. Or another beer."

She wrinkled her nose, probably at the mention of his work. Another reason he'd never get too serious with her. She hated the fact he was a blue-collar worker and not some suit-wearing businessman who could keep her in diamonds and silks. She worked her butt off at her job and wore the expensive clothes that came with her world. That wasn't something he wanted in the long run. He worked for Montgomery Inc., the construction arm of the family businesses. He was the project manager right under Wes and Storm, the Montgomery twins who had taken over the family business when their parents, Harry and Marie, retired.

Wes was the OCD planner of the company and got his hands dirty daily with the bump and grind that came with being one of the top privately owned construction companies in Denver. Storm was the lead architect and a genius when it came to finding the right flow for a refurbished building or how to start from scratch with a piece of land that could be used carefully.

Decker had started out as a teenager working under Harry doing every kind of grunt work he could get his hands on. He'd gone to college only because the Montgomery twins had, as had his best friend, Griffin—another Montgomery— and because the state had helped him out. He wouldn't have been able to afford it otherwise. He'd gone to the local university, busted his ass for his degree, then went right back to working for the family that had raised him when his own blood family had failed.

He ground his teeth.

Best not think about the others right then. Not if he wanted to stay civil—he looked down at the beer in his hand—and sober.

"Must you talk about those matters with me?" Colleen asked, breaking through his thoughts.

He shrugged. He honestly didn't know why he'd brought her that evening other than because he was in a rut, and he hadn't thought to say no. They liked each other well enough, but they weren't in love. He hadn't slept with her in months either. Despite the fact that his balls were so blue from lack of sex—his right hand could only do so much—he hadn't wanted to sleep with one woman when his mind was on the other. Sure, he'd been trying to date to get those thoughts out of his head, but he wasn't about to use another woman fully like that.

"I work with everything that goes in a house or building," Decker said, his voice low. He had a deep, growly voice according to the-woman-who-shall-not-be-named, and when he got annoyed or emotional, his voice just got deeper.

Colleen didn't care for it.

"Yes, dear, but you don't have to talk about it." She raised her chin and looked out at the yard. He'd helped with the initial landscaping years ago when he was trying to find his place within the business. He'd been better at digging the holes and lifting bags of mulch, rather than doing the actual planning. Marie was the brains behind that. She'd told them what to do, and he and her boys had hopped to it.

In the end, the place looked great with tons of vegetation that looked as though it was natural, rather than lines and perfectly square things that made no sense.

"Did you hear me, Decker? What is going on with you? I said don't talk about things like that, not to stop talking at all."

He barely resisted the urge to roll his eyes. "Sorry to bother you," he mumbled, not sorry in the least. "Why don't you go talk to, uh, the girls over there while I get another drink?" He couldn't remember the two girls who worked with Sierra, the newly engaged woman and star of the party, but they seemed to get along with anyone. Hopefully, they'd make friends with Coleen so this evening wouldn't be a total waste.

She raised a brow and looked pointedly at his hand. Seriously? Jesus Christ. He shouldn't have brought her here. Or rather, he shouldn't have let her invite herself in the first place. She didn't belong, and he didn't know why he was kidding himself by trying to make it work when neither of them truly wanted it.

"I've had one beer, and I'll have one more since we have a couple hours left. I won't drink more than that." He wouldn't have had to explain himself to the Montgomerys. They knew enough about where he'd come from that him getting behind the wheel, even slightly buzzed, wasn't an option.

"If you say so," she clipped then strutted off to the girls on the other side of the backyard.

His shoulders relaxed marginally, and he cursed himself for it. He *liked* Colleen. He really did. She wasn't a bad person. She just didn't understand him.

Whose fault is that?

It wasn't like he'd told her all that much about himself, and he'd never once mentioned his past.

"Shit, bro, you look like you ate something rotten," Wes said as he walked toward him. He had the Montgomery blue eyes and chestnut hair, only his was neatly clipped and worked with his OCD persona.

Storm, Wes's twin, walked beside him. While Wes was a bit lanky, Storm had more of a build on him. He was also a bit more rugged with his shaggy hair, light beard, and flannel shirt over another light shirt, while Wes had his button-up shirt over nice jeans. It never made any sense to Decker that the twin who worked with his hands more often than not as the other general contractor preferred dressier clothes on his day off while the twin who sat behind his desk drawing when he wasn't in the field wore more rugged clothes. Well, considering each of them worked side by side with Decker and sweated their asses off regularly, it didn't matter what they wore now, as long as they worked hard during the day.

Which they did.

"Bro?" Decker asked, a smile on his face. "You working with the kids at Austin's shop now?" Austin was the oldest Montgomery and owned half of Montgomery Ink, the tattoo shop side of the family business, with their sister, Maya. It was also Austin and Sierra's engagement party and the reason they were all at the barbecue that evening.

Storm snorted. "We say bro sometimes. Doesn't make us some college kids who want bad ink."

"I don't do bad ink, asshole," Maya snapped as she came up to them. She wrapped her arm around Decker's middle, and he hugged her back. Why couldn't he be this comfortable around *all* the Montgomery women?

She pulled back before he could squeeze her tighter. Maya liked her space, and Decker liked her all the more for it. Her dark brown bangs were severe across her forehead, and she'd done a weird eyeliner thing that made her look like some fifties rocker pin-up. The red lipstick just made her look like she'd smile at you—then kick you in the ass.

"I meant that he wants bad ink because he doesn't know what good ink is," Storm said, backtracking. Wes and Storm might be the second oldest in the family, but no one messed with Maya and walked away without a limp. "Not that you give bad ink."

Wes laughed then shut up as Maya glared.

Decker, being the smart one of the group, kept his face neutral.

Maya narrowed her eyes at the three of them then nodded. "Okay, so tell me what's going on. Jake couldn't make it today, and I'm bored."

"When are you just going to admit that Jake is your boyfriend?" Wes asked.

Decker closed his eyes. It was like the twins *wanted* to die by her hand tonight.

"He's not my fucking boyfriend," Maya growled then lifted her chin, speaking softer this time. "He's my friend. I don't know why a guy and a girl can't just be friends without the rest of the world wondering if they're fucking."

Decker raised a brow then looked at the space between them.

Maya waved him off. "You're a brother, not a friend. So the world wouldn't ever think you'd be fucking a Montgomery girl. That'd be all kinds of wrong."

He swallowed hard and tried to keep the frown off his face. Shit. She was right. No one would think he'd ever be with a Montgomery girl. Maya was like his sister, as was Meghan, the eldest girl. Meghan was even married to an asshole, but married just the same.

Miranda though...Miranda was his best friend's little sister and had welcomed him into her family to boot.

There was no way he could ever think of her as more.

Or rather, he should *stop* thinking about her as possibly more.

"Anyway," Wes continued, "we came over here to ask what's up with Decker. He looked like he stepped in shit or something."

Decker rolled his eyes. Wes really liked making things sound worse than they were. "I'm fine. Just a long day." He rolled his shoulders, and the twins did the same. They'd hauled right by his side, and he knew they ached just as much.

"Tell me about it," Storm grumbled. "I never want to look at another toilet again."

"Charming," Maya said dryly.

"So, have you found a new receptionist yet?" Decker asked Maya, changing the subject from toilets to the running joke of the family. The shop had been through four or five receptionists this year alone. They had fantastic artists and had even just promoted their apprentice, Callie, to full time. However, they couldn't keep a receptionist to save their lives. The college kids always left for greener pastures, and the other ones thought it was fun to come in high around pointy needles. It might be legal to smoke, but that didn't mean they wanted their staff lit up while working.

"You can't have Tabby," Wes put it. "She's ours." Tabby was the Montgomery Inc. receptionist and a goddess with organization. She and Wes were a team in OCD heaven.

Maya cursed under her breath. "I don't want Tabby. She'd color code my ink in a weird way, and then I wouldn't want to move anything around. And no, we haven't found a receptionist. I don't know what it is. This latest guy just wanted free ink. Free. I pay for my own tattoos, you know. I won't let Austin do it for free because his work is *worth* my money. Wanting it free in our place just shows disrespect."

Decker snorted. "At least you get the family discount." Maya looked over her shoulder and discreetly flipped him off.

Decker frowned since she tried to hide it then smiled as Meghan's kids, Cliff and Sasha, ran into the backyard, barreling toward their uncles on the other side of the yard. They'd be over here soon for sure to see the rest of them. He loved those damn kids.

"You get the discount too, brother mine," Maya said. "But the discount isn't all that much in the scheme of things. This idiot wanted it all for free. So he huffed away and found another shop most likely." She shrugged. "Not as good a shop as ours, but whatever."

"There's no shop as good as yours." He rubbed between his shoulder blades. "Speaking of, I need to make an appointment for the ink on my back." Maya's eyes brightened, and he cursed. "With Austin, hon. It's his turn." All of the Montgomerys took turns with the other siblings when it came to their ink. Both of them were talented, and picking one over the other was nearly impossible.

Besides, they both had nasty tempers if they didn't get to be part of the siblings' and parents' art.

"Fine. I see how it is. You like him better." She sniffed and wiped a non-existent tear at the edge of her eye. Not that she actually touched her makeup in the process, but the move worked for her.

Decker rolled his eyes then punched her softly in the shoulder. "Shut up. You *just* did work on my arm, and you get my leg next. It's Austin's turn now."

She smiled, and he wasn't sure if it was a good one or a *you'll be sorry* one, but he rolled with it.

He looked over his shoulder to see Colleen in a conversation with one of Sierra's girls so he let her be then looked at the empty beer bottle in his hand. "I'm going to get a refill. Any of you want something?"

They shook their heads, and he said his goodbyes before walking over to the cooler. Alex, another Montgomery—seriously, there were eight siblings and countless cousins so he was always walking over a Montgomery or two—stood by the cooler, a tumbler of amber liquid in his hand.

Decker looked over his shoulder at the crowd and frowned. "Where's Jessica?" Jessica was Alex's high school sweetheart and wife. When they'd first gotten married a few years ago, she'd always come to the family events, though she never exactly fit in. It wasn't like she tried, either. The Montgomerys had tried on their part to welcome her into their midst, but for some reason, it never really took. Now, come to think of it, Decker hadn't seen her at one of these events in awhile.

Alex snorted then took another drink. From the glassy look in his eyes, this wasn't his first drink.

Well fuck. This wasn't good.

"Like she'd come to one of these," Alex drawled. He didn't sound drunk, but Decker could never tell with Alex. The fact that he knew something was off at all was because of experience. He'd dealt with enough drunks and near-drunks to last a lifetime. "She's off with her girls at the spa or something. She didn't feel like celebrating Sierra and Austin's engagement since she's never actually met Sierra."

Decker's eyebrows lifted toward his hairline. "She hasn't met Sierra yet? How is that possible?" Jessica was already a Montgomery, and it wasn't like Sierra was new to the family. She already lived with Austin and was helping raise his son.

"It's possible when you're Jessica." Alex took another drink and looked the other way.

Okay then. Conversation over.

Decker shifted from foot to foot. Alex had always been the one to joke and make people laugh. That wasn't what Decker saw now, and it scared him a bit. The man in front of him looked angry...and drunk. Decker knew drunks. He'd lived with one off and on until he'd finally been able to break free.

He didn't want to see it again.

"You want a water, Alex?" he asked calmly. Tiptoeing around it wouldn't help, but coming right out and asking if the man he called his brother was an alcoholic wouldn't either.

Alex gave him a small smile instead of getting angry, which surprised Decker. "I'm good." The man didn't leave to refill his drink, but that didn't mean he wouldn't do it once Decker was out of sight. He didn't know what to do, but as long as Alex knew he was there, maybe that could help.

"Okay. Just...you know I'm here, right?" he asked softly.

Alex's face closed up, and he lifted his chin. Damn. "I'm good," he repeated.

Decker searched his face and couldn't find a way past the barriers. He'd keep an eye on him though. This man was his brother, blood or no.

He got a soda instead of a beer, his stomach not quite ready for booze after that, and walked over to his best friend, Griffin. The man held the same look as the rest of the Montgomerys, dark hair and blue eyes, but with the same slender build as Wes, rather than the brick-house look of Austin or even Storm. Griffin was the easiest going of the family, the writer who spent most of his time in his own head, rather than in the real world. His mess of a house reflected that, but Decker loved him anyway. They were the same age, so they'd grown up like twins after a while. Decker might have more in common with Austin on some levels and work closely with Wes and Storm, but Griffin was the one he knew best.

"Glad to see you finally found your way over to me," Griffin joked. He sat in one of the outdoor chairs and waved at the empty one. "Take a seat. I'm people watching."

Decker laughed then did as he was told. "First, you could have come over to me. It wasn't like I was blocking you. Second, this is your family. Why are you watching them?"

Griffin took a sip of his beer then shook his head. "You were with Colleen, and as I can't stand that giggle of hers, I didn't want to join in."

"Giggle?" Decker asked, a little annoyed that Grif would judge his date. It wasn't like he and Colleen were married, but still. Pointing out something like that didn't seem right.

"Giggle," Griffin repeated. "You know it. Whenever she giggles, your shoulders tense, and you get that little twitch at the corner of your mouth."

Huh, now that he mentioned it... Nope, not going to think about it. He still had the rest of the night and probably more nights with the woman. It wouldn't do to nitpick and then zoom in on those quirks for too long. He wouldn't be able to get over it.

"You noticed all that?" he asked, draining some of his soda.

"Yep. I told you. I people watch. In fact, I'm watching that asshole and my sister right now. I really want to beat the shit out of him, but I'm not sure she'd appreciate that. She doesn't like when the rest of us threaten to maim or murder her husband."

Decker frowned then looked over at Meghan and her husband, Richard. Meghan was three years older than him and had always struck him as warm, friendly, and not to be messed with. She was like the mother hen of the clan and stood up for herself.

But not now.

Now she had her shoulders slouched and her head down. Richard was snapping about something, and each time he spoke, Meghan turned in on herself just that much more. Nope. This wasn't going to do.

Decker stood up, set his soda down, and then rolled his shoulders. "You ready?" he growled at Griffin, who had stood with him. Like there was any other way to react when he saw someone he cared about being beaten down emotionally.

"Yep. Let's not beat the shit out of him since their kids are here, and it's Austin and Sierra's time, but yeah, I'm ready."

They stalked toward the couple, and Richard puffed out his chest as he noticed them. The man had once had a decent build and hair on his head. Now it looked like he was balding a bit, but he brushed it in just the right way that you couldn't tell unless you'd seen him before. He also had a little bit of a gut that came with lack of activity. Though he wore suits that shouted their worth, the effect was lost at the straining button on his stomach.

"What?" the bastard snapped.

Decker smiled, but it wasn't a nice one. He put his arm around Meghan, who stiffened. He let that pass and kept his arm on her. The more people who cared about her, the better.

"Just wanted to say hi to my sister, that's all," he said smoothly.

Richard scoffed. "She's not your sister. You're just the trash. Get your hands off my wife."

He didn't even wince at the word trash. He'd heard worse and usually from people who should have meant more to him than this sack of shit.

"Richard," Meghan admonished, her voice gaining strength. *Atta girl.* "Decker is family."

Decker squeezed her shoulders, but she didn't relax. Damn.

"She's right about that," Griffin said easily.

"Well then, wife, you're not a Montgomery anymore," Richard said, baring his teeth. "You'd do best to remember that. Go get the brats. We're leaving. We said our hellos to the happy couple—they won't be happy for long knowing the way that brute is—so it's time to go."

Why the fuck was Meghan still with this man? He treated her like shit and beat down on her emotionally. Decker didn't think Richard touched her with his fists, but one could never tell. Decker should know.

Flashes of meaty fists and breath tainted with cheap booze filled his mind, and he shook it off.

"Once a Montgomery, always a Montgomery," Griffin said from his side.

"Pretty much," Decker said smoothly. "If you're in a hurry, you can head out and we'll get Meghan and the kids home when they're ready to leave."

"She's *my* wife. Not yours."

"Decker. Griffin. Let it go," she whispered.

Decker shook his head. "Sorry, hon, Austin and Sierra's party just started, and we haven't done the toasts yet. You should stay. If Richard needs to go, he can go." He looked into her eyes and prayed she understood he meant more than for that one night.

"Fine. Keep the brats here."

"I need the boosters," Meghan whispered.

"Then you should come with me," Richard snapped.

Meghan glared. Good. There was still some fire in her. "I'm not risking my children's lives because you want to leave early."

"Our children, Meghan. You best remember that." He smiled coolly, and Decker froze.

So that's why she stayed. For the kids. That motherfucker.

"We got boosters in the house," Griffin said. "Mom and Dad keep them in case they have the kids." He didn't mention that Decker had bought them when Richard had left Meghan alone with the kids and taken her car one time.

She didn't need to remember that. On second thought, maybe she did.

"Fine." Richard didn't even say goodbye to Cliff and Sasha before stomping away. Meghan visibly relaxed when the man left.

"Meghan..." Decker started, but she held up a hand.

"No. Not here. I need to take care of my children."

He nodded, knowing she was stronger than his own mother. At least he hoped. "I'm here if you need me."

"Me too," Griffin added. "We all are."

She cupped both their cheeks and smiled sadly. "I know. I love you both. Now go and talk to Austin or Sierra or something. I need a moment."

Decker nodded before leaving her alone with Griffin. His friend would take care of her until she pushed him away because she thought she was too strong to lean on someone. He wouldn't let her situation grow to be what his past had been, but he also knew there was only so much a person could do without physically pulling them away.

That wouldn't help anyone.

"That prick gone?" Austin growled when Decker reached him. Sierra punched her fiancé in the stomach, and he winced before wrapping his arm around her.

"Watch your mouth," she whispered and looked over his shoulder.

Austin and Decker looked as well. Austin's son, Leif, stood near, his attention on whatever Storm was saying and not on Austin's words thankfully. Leif had come to the family after his mother had passed and Austin had found out he was a daddy. Strange as hell to think of it all, but Decker loved the boy like he'd been raised with them from birth. He fit right in.

"Yep. That prick is gone. I'm worried about her. Alex too." He might as well let it all out. Austin was his big brother, and Sierra was going to be a new sister. They were family.

Sierra shook her head. "We all are. They know we're here, and if there's anything we can do, we'll figure it out."

Decker pulled her from Austin's arms and gave her a tight hug before pressing his lips to hers in a hard kiss.

"Hey, get your mouth off my woman."

Decker pulled back and smiled at a flushed Sierra. "But she's such a pretty woman." He tucked her into his side. "See? She fits just right."

Austin growled then pulled a laughing Sierra to him. "No, she fits against my side. You're an ass."

Decker grinned. "A hot ass. And you know it."

"You two are idiots, but I love you." Sierra laughed at her words, but Austin growled. "I mean I love Decker in a brotherly sort of way. I love you in a sexy, sweaty way. Okay?"

Decker raised his hands in mock surrender. "I so do not need to think about that. I'm going to go see how Harry's doing. Let me know when you want help with your toast or something."

Austin nodded, but his eyes were all for Sierra.

Fuck, what would it be like to have a love like that? A person who was by your side no matter what.

Decker didn't think he'd ever have that. Not with the way his mind and body wanted the one person he couldn't have. In his experience, love didn't last, and marriages were only shackles he knew some people could never be rid of.

Of course, that wasn't quite true since the couple he'd just left seemed to be on the right path, but he wasn't sure yet. Then of course, the couple he was in front of had been together for over four decades and still looked like they were more in love every day.

But love hurt when one person was sick.

Harry Montgomery had always been larger than life. He was a big man with an even bigger heart. Yet the man in the chair in front of him didn't look like that now. The extracorporeal radiation therapy—Decker had been reading up—that targeted Harry's prostate cancer had taken a toll.

The man looked so much smaller, weaker, and paler than Decker had ever seen.

The doctors told him they'd caught the cancer early and things were looking good, but the treatment looked like it hurt worse than the cancer. And now, in Decker's eyes, Marie was forced by love, duty and circumstance to stand by her husband's side as he grew weaker and weaker. How was that reward for love? How could that be worth it? The pain and loss that could come with growing close to someone didn't make sense to him, and he wasn't sure he deserved it in the first place.

"Come here, boy," Harry growled out, a sparkle in his eye.

Thank God.

Decker crouched near him, his hands shaking. He didn't know what to do. Did he hug him? It looked like, with just one hug, Decker would break the man he thought of as his father.

"How you feeling?" he asked. And damn if his voice hadn't choked up.

Harry patted his arm as Marie came to Decker's side, kneeling so she could hug him. He put his arm around her, inhaling that sweet Mom scent that had worked so well to calm him as a kid.

"I'm doing better," Harry said softly. "It doesn't look like it, but I'm not dying. Not yet."

Decker felt like he'd been stabbed in the heart with those words. Jesus. He couldn't lose Harry. He couldn't.

"Hey, don't look at me like that," Harry said. "I told you all I'd be honest with you about my recovery. We caught it early. The radiation hurts like a bitch, but we're pushing through. Now I wanted you to come over here because, one, you're my son and I wanted to see you, and two, because you helped with that prick of a husband my daughter chose. I couldn't get up to fix it, so thank you." The slight helplessness in Harry's eyes was too much.

Decker swallowed hard and willed his eyes not to fill with tears. Fuck.

"I'd have kicked his ass..." He shot a look at Marie. "I mean his butt, but the kids were there."

"You can say ass when it comes to Richard," Marie put in. "He *is* an ass."

Decker threw his head back and laughed. "I love you both. I just wanted to make sure you knew that."

Marie's eyes filled with tears. "Oh, that's the sweetest thing. The sweetest thing. We love you too, baby."

Harry nodded, and Decker leaned into the strong woman's arms.

The hairs on the back of his neck rose, and he stood up slowly. He turned to see Miranda walking into the backyard, her long legs bare under her sundress.

Holy fuck, she looked amazing.

He willed his cock not to fill, considering he was standing between her parents. Griffin came up to his side, and Decker knew there was a special place in hell for a man who lusted after his best friend's little sister.

Harry and Marie gave him a knowing look, and he held back a groan. Yep. He was going to hell. He was going to burn, and he'd deserve every moment of it.

Miranda turned to them and smiled brightly, her eyes twinkling.

He fought to keep his gaze on her face and not on her breasts or her legs that never quit.

He could do this.

This was Miranda Montgomery. The woman who was a girl no longer, and she was not for him.

He wouldn't drool over her. He wouldn't make an ass out of himself.

Griffin gave him a weird look, and Decker groaned inwardly.

Yep.

Going to hell.

Tattered Loyalties

From New York Times Bestselling Author Carrie Ann Ryan's Redwood Pack Series

When the great war between the Redwoods and the Centrals occurred three decades ago, the Talon Pack risked their lives for the side of good. After tragedy struck, Gideon Brentwood became the Alpha of the Talons. But the Pack's stability is threatened, and he's forced to take mate—only the one fate puts in his path is the woman he shouldn't want.

Though the daughter of the Redwood Pack's Beta, Brie Jamenson has known peace for most of her life. When she finds the man who could be her mate, she's shocked to discover Gideon is the Alpha wolf of the Talon Pack. As a submissive, her strength lies in her heart, not her claws. But if her new Pack disagrees or disapproves of fate's choice, the consequences could be fatal.

As the worlds Brie and Gideon have always known begin to shift, they must face their challenges together in order to help their Pack and seal their bond. But when the Pack is threatened from the inside, Gideon doesn't know who he can trust and Brie's life could be forfeit in the crossfire. It will take the strength of an Alpha and the courage of his mate to realize where true loyalties lie.

Dust of My Wings

From New York Times Bestselling Author Carrie Ann Ryan's Dante's Circle Series

Humans aren't as alone as they choose to believe. Every human possesses a trait of supernatural that lays dormant within their genetic make-up. Centuries of diluting and breeding have allowed humans to think they are alone and untouched by magic. But what happens when something changes?

Neat freak lab tech, Lily Banner lives her life as any ordinary human. She's dedicated to her work and loves to hang out with her friends at Dante's Circle, their local bar. When she discovers a strange blue dust at work she meets a handsome stranger holding secrets – and maybe her heart. But after a close call with a thunderstorm, she may not be as ordinary as she thinks.

Shade Griffin is a warrior angel sent to Earth to protect the supernaturals' secrets. One problem, he can't stop leaving dust in odd places around town. Now he has to find every ounce of his dust and keep the presence of the supernatural a secret. But after a close encounter with a sexy lab tech and a lightning quick connection, his millennia old loyalties may shift and he could lose more than just his wings in the chaos.

Warning: Contains a sexy angel with a choice to make and a green-eyed lab tech who dreams of a dark-winged stranger. Oh yeah, and a shocking spark that's sure to leave them begging for more.

Charmed Spirits

From New York Times Bestselling Author Carrie Ann Ryan's Holiday Montana Series

Jordan Cross has returned to Holiday, Montana after eleven long years to clear out her late aunt's house, put it on the market, and figure out what she wants to do with the rest of her life. Soon, she finds herself facing the town that turned its back on her because she was different. Because being labeled a witch in a small town didn't earn her many friends...especially when it wasn't a lie.

Matt Cooper has lived in Holiday his whole life. He's perfectly content being a bachelor alongside his four single brothers in a very small town. After all, the only woman he'd ever loved ran out on him without a goodbye. But now Jordan's back and just as bewitching as ever. Can they rekindle their romance with a town set against them?

Warning: Contains an intelligent, sexy witch with an attitude and drop-dead gorgeous man who likes to work with his hands, holds a secret that might scare someone, and really, *really*, likes table tops for certain activities. Enough said.

CPSIA information can be obtained
at www.ICGtesting.com
Printed in the USA
LVHW011059280420
654654LV00002B/557